Praise for
Sara Paretsky
and the V. I. Warshawski Novels

"No one, male or female, writes better P.I. books
than Paretsky."—*The Denver Post*

"V. I. is undoubtedly one of the best-written characters
in mystery fiction."—*The Baltimore Sun*

"Who is America's most convincing and engaging
professional female private eye?
V. I. Warshawski . . ."
—*Entertainment Weekly*

"Paretsky's books are beautifully paced and plotted,
and the dialogue is fresh and smart."—*Newsweek*

"Paretsky is still the best . . . she doesn't pull
punches."—*The Washington Post Book World*

"Sara Paretsky has hit the big time . . . she gets better
and better."—*Los Angeles Times Book Review*

Also by Sara Paretsky

A V. I. WARSHAWSKI NOVEL

SARA PARETSKY

TOTAL RECALL

A DELL BOOK

Published by
Dell Publishing
a division of
Random House, Inc.
1540 Broadway
New York, New York 10036

The notebook entries on pages 209, 213, 390, and 391 are set in Sütterlin, a font created by Waldenfonts.com that replicates the handwriting script taught in German schools at that time.

Library of Congress Catalog Card Number: 2001028801
ISBN: 0-440-29595-5

Reprinted by arrangement with Delacorte Press

Manufactured in the United States of America

March 2002

OPM 10 9 8 7 6 5 4 3 2 1

For Sara Krupnik and Hannah Paretsky,
whose names I bear

May the One who establishes
peace in the high places
grant us all peace

Thanks

Thanks to Wolfson College, Oxford, where I was a Visiting Scholar in 1997, which enabled me to pursue archival research. Thanks to Dr. Jeremy Black of Wolfson for making my time there possible.

The archives of letters and audiotapes in the Imperial War Museum, London, are an important source about the Kindertransport, England's generous acceptance of ten thousand Jewish children from central Europe in the years immediately before the Second World War. As is true of librarians everywhere, those at the Imperial War Museum were extremely helpful—even allowing me into the archives on a day they were closed when I confused an appointment date.

The Royal Free Hospital, London, gave me access to their archives, allowed me to send Lotty Herschel to school there, and were in general most helpful.

Dr. Dulcie Reed, Dr. Lettice Bowen, Dr. Peter Scheuer, and Dr. Judith Levy, all of whom trained in medicine in Great Britain around the same time as

Lotty Herschel, were generous in giving me time and information about that period in their lives.

In the case of all archival material, as well as the reminiscences of these four doctors, I have avoided turning people's real-life experiences into fiction—with the exception of Lotty and her roommates making lingerie out of parachute silk: Dr. Bowen and her friends did this—an amazing feat, as anyone who has ever tried to construct lingerie from scratch will appreciate.

Professor Colin Divall of the Institute of Railway Studies, York, was helpful with information about train routes and timetables in the 1940's.

Because of the constraints of a novel focusing on Chicago, contemporary crime, and V I Warshawski, I was not able to make as deep a use of any of my English research as I would have wished; perhaps it will find a home in a different story on another day.

In Chicago, Kimball Wright advised me on the guns used in the book. Forensic pathologist Dr. Robert Kirschner was helpful in making accurate the deaths and near deaths of various unfortunate characters; the events described in Chapters 38 and 43 do happen. Sandy Weiss was helpful as always on forensic engineering arcana.

Jolynn Parker did invaluable research on a number of topics, including finding street maps of Jewish neighborhoods of Vienna in the 1930's. More important, her astuteness as a reader helped me pick my way through some thorny problems as I developed the story line. Jonathan Paretsky helped with German, Yiddish—and star gazing.

Special thanks to Kate Jones for her insightful discussion of this novel, both at its end and at its beginnings.

As always, the first C-dog was there with advice, encouragement—and renewable kneecaps.

This is a work of fiction. No resemblance is intended between any character in this novel and any real person, living or dead, whether in public office, in corporate boardrooms, on the streets, or in any other walk of life. Similarly, all the institutions involved, including Ajax Insurance, Edelweiss Re, Gargette et Cie, are phantasms of the author's fevered brain and are not intended to resemble any actual existing body. The issues of slave reparations and Holocaust asset recovery are very real; the positions taken on them by characters in the novel do not necessarily reflect the author's own, nor should they be taken to reflect the positions taken by people in public life who are debating them.

Note: Anna Freud's "An Experiment in Group Upbringing" is in Volume IV of her collected works. The adult lives of the children she describes are explored in Sarah Moskovitz's *Love Despite Hate*.

Contents

TOTAL
RECALL

Lotty Herschel's Story:

Work Ethic

The cold that winter ate into our bones. You can't imagine, living where you turn a dial and as much heat as you want glows from the radiator, but everything in England then was fueled by coal and there were terrible shortages the second winter after the war. Like everyone I had little piles of six-penny bits for the electric fire in my room, but even if I'd been able to afford to run it all night it didn't provide much warmth.

One of the women in my lodgings got a length of parachute silk from her brother, who'd been in the RAF. We all made camisoles and knickers out of it. We all knew how to knit back then; I unraveled old sweaters to make scarves and vests—new wool cost a fortune.

We saw newsreels of American ships and planes bringing the Germans whatever they needed. While we swathed ourselves in blankets and sweaters and ate grey bread with butter substitutes, we joked bitterly that we'd done the wrong thing, bringing the Americans in to win the war—they'd treat us better if we'd lost, the same woman who'd gotten the parachute silk said.

Of course, I had started my medical training, so I couldn't spend much time wrapped up in bed. Anyway, I was glad to have the hospital to go to—although the wards weren't warm, either: patients and sisters would huddle around the big stove in the center of the ward, drinking tea and telling stories—we students used to envy their camaraderie. The sisters expected us medical students to behave professionally—frankly, they enjoyed ordering us about. We'd do rounds with two pairs of tights on, hoping the consultants wouldn't notice we wore gloves as we trailed after them from bed to bed, listening to symptoms that came from deprivation as much as anything.

Working sixteen or eighteen hours a day without proper food took a toll on all of us. Many of my fellow students succumbed to tuberculosis and were granted leave—the only reason the hospital would let you interrupt your training and come back, as a matter of fact, even though some took more than a year to recover. The new antibiotics were starting to come in, but they cost the earth and weren't yet widely available. When my turn came and I went to the Registrar, explaining that a family friend had a cottage in Somerset where I could recuperate, she nodded bleakly: we were already down five in my class, but she signed the forms for me and told me to write monthly. She stressed that she would hope to see me in under a year.

In fact, I was gone eight months. I'd wanted to return sooner, but Claire—Claire Tallmadge, who was a senior houseman by then, with a consultancy all but certain—persuaded me I wasn't strong enough, although I was aching to get back.

When I returned to the Royal Free it felt—oh, so good. The hospital routine, my studies, they were like a balm, healing me. The Registrar actually called me into her office to warn me to slow down; they didn't want me to suffer a relapse.

She didn't understand that work was my only salvation. I suppose it had already become my second skin. It's a narcotic, the oblivion overwork can bring you. *Arbeit macht frei*—that was an obscene parody the Nazis thought up, but it is possible *Arbeit macht betäubt*—what? Oh, sorry, I forgot you don't speak German. They had *1984*-type slogans over the entrance to all their camps, and that was what they put over Auschwitz: *work will make you free.* That slogan was a bestial parody, but work can numb you. If you stop working even for a moment, everything inside you starts evaporating; soon you are so shapeless you can't move at all. At least, that was my fear.

When I first heard about my family, I became utterly without any grounding at all. I was supposed to be preparing for my higher-school certificate—the diploma we took in those days when we finished high school—the results determined your university entrance—but the exams lost the meaning they'd had for me all during the war. Every time I sat down to read I felt as though my insides were being sucked away by a giant vacuum cleaner.

In a perverse way, cousin Minna came to my rescue. Ever since I arrived on her doorstep she had been unsparing in her criticisms of my mother. The news of my mother's death brought not even a respectful silence but a greater barrage. I can see now, through the prism of experience, that guilt drove her as much as anything: she had hated my mother, been jealous of her for so many years, she couldn't admit now that she'd been unfeeling, even cruel. She was probably grief-stricken as well, because her own mother had also perished, all that family that used to spend summers talking and swimming at Kleinsee; well, never mind that. It's old news now.

I would come home from walking the streets, walking until I was too exhausted to feel anything, to Minna: you think you're suffering? That you're the only person who was ever orphaned, left alone in a strange country? And weren't you supposed to give Victor his tea? He says he waited for over an hour for you and finally had to make it himself because you're too much a lady—"*die gnädige Frau*"—Minna only ever spoke German at home—she had never really mastered English, which made her furious with shame—and she curtsied to me—to get your hands dirty doing work, housework or a real job. You're just like Lingerl. I wonder how a princess like her lived as long as she did in such a setting, with no one to pamper her. Did she tilt her head and bat her eyes so that the guards or other inmates gave up their bread to her? Madame Butterfly is dead. It's time you learned what real work is.

A fury rose up in me greater than any I remember since. I smacked her in the mouth and screamed, if people took care of my mother it's because she repaid them with love. And if they don't care for you it's because you're utterly loathsome.

She stared at me for a moment, her mouth slack with shock. She recovered quickly, though, and hit me back so hard she split my lip with her big ring. And then hissed, the only reason I let a mongrel like you accept that scholarship to the comprehensive was on the understanding that you would repay my generosity by taking care of Victor. Which I might point out you have failed utterly to do. Instead of giving him tea you've been flaunting yourself at the pubs and dance halls just like your mother. Max or Carl or one of those other immigrant boys is likely to give you the same present that Martin, as he liked to call himself, gave Madame Butterfly. Tomorrow morning I'm off to that precious headmistress, that Miss Skeffing you're so fond of, to tell her you can't continue your education. It's time you started pulling your weight around here.

Blood pouring down my face, I ran pell-mell across London to the youth hostel where my friends lived—you know, Max and Carl and the rest of them: when they turned sixteen the year before they hadn't been able to stay in their foster homes. I begged them to find me a bed for the night. In the morning, when I knew Minna would be with her great love, the glove factory, I sneaked back for my books and my clothes—it was only two changes of underwear and a second dress. Victor was dozing in the living room, but he didn't wake up enough to try to stop me.

Miss Skeffing found a family in North London who gave me a room in exchange for doing their cooking. And I began to study as if my mother's life could be redeemed by my work. As soon as I finished the supper dishes I would solve chemistry and math problems, sometimes sleeping only four hours until it was time to make the family's morning tea. And after that, I never stopped working, really.

That was where the story ended, sitting on a hillside on a dull October day overlooking a desolate landscape, listening to Lotty until she could talk no more. It's harder for me to figure out where it began.

Looking back now, now that I'm calm, now that I can think, it's still hard to say, Oh, it was because of this, or because of that. It was a time when I had a million other things on my mind. Morrell was getting ready to leave for Afghanistan. I was worrying most about that, but of course I was trying to run my business, and juggle the nonprofit work I do, and pay my bills. I suppose my own involvement began with Isaiah Sommers, or maybe the Birnbaum Foundation conference—they happened on the same day.

Baby-Sitters' Club

They wouldn't even start the funeral service. The church was full, ladies were crying. My uncle was a deacon and he was a righteous man, he'd been a member of that church for forty-seven years when he passed. My aunt was in a state of total collapse, as you can imagine. And for them to have the nerve to say the policy had already been cashed in. When! That's what I want to know, Ms. Warashki, when was it ever cashed in, with my uncle paying his five dollars a week for fifteen years like he did, and my aunt never hearing word one of him borrowing against the policy or converting it."

Isaiah Sommers was a short, square man who spoke in slow cadences as if he were himself a deacon. It was an effort to keep from drowsing off during the pauses in his delivery. We were in the living room of his South Side bungalow, at a few minutes after six on a day that had stretched on far too long already.

I'd been in my office at 8:30, starting a round of the routine searches that make up the bulk of my business, when Lotty Herschel called with an SOS. "You know Max's son brought Calia and Agnes with him from

London, don't you? Agnes suddenly has a chance to show her slides at a Huron Street gallery, but she needs a minder for Calia."

"I'm not a baby-sitter, Lotty," I'd said impatiently; Calia was Max Loewenthal's five-year-old granddaughter.

Lotty swept imperiously past that protest. "Max called me when they couldn't find anyone—it's his housekeeper's day off. He's going to that conference at the Hotel Pleiades, although I've told him many times that all he's doing is exposing—but that's neither here nor there. At any rate, he's on a panel at ten—otherwise he'd stay home himself. I tried Mrs. Coltrain at my clinic, but everyone's tied up. Michael is rehearsing all afternoon with the symphony and this could be an important chance for Agnes. Vic—I realize it's an imposition, but it would be only for a few hours."

"Why not Carl Tisov?" I asked. "Isn't he staying at Max's, too?"

"Carl as a baby-sitter? Once he picks up his clarinet the roof of the house can blow off without his noticing. I saw it happen once, during the V-1 raids. Can you tell me yes or no? I'm in the middle of surgical rounds, and I have a full schedule at the clinic." Lotty is the chief perinatologist at Beth Israel.

I tried a few of my own connections, including my part-time assistant who has three foster children, but no one could help out. I finally agreed with a surly lack of grace. "I have a client meeting at six on the far South Side, so someone had better be able to step in before five."

When I drove up to Max's Evanston home to collect Calia, Agnes Loewenthal was breathlessly grateful. "I can't even find my slides. Calia was playing with them and stuck them in Michael's cello, which got him terribly cross, and now the wretched beast can't imagine where he's flung them."

Michael appeared in a T-shirt with his cello bow in one hand. "Darling, I'm sorry, but they have to be in the drawing room—that's where I was practicing. Vic, I can't thank you enough—can we take you and Morrell to dinner after our Sunday afternoon concert?"

"We can't do that, Michael!" Agnes snapped. "That's Max's dinner party for Carl and you."

Michael played cello with the Cellini Chamber Ensemble, the London group started back in the forties by Max and Lotty's friend Carl Tisov. The Cellini was in Chicago to kick off their biannual international tour. Michael was also scheduled to play some concerts with the Chicago Symphony.

Agnes gave Calia a quick hug. "Victoria, thank you a million times. Please, though, no television. She only gets an hour a week and I don't think American shows are suitable for her." She darted back into the drawing room, where we could hear her furiously tossing cushions from the couch. Calia grimaced and clutched my hand.

It was Max who actually got Calia into her jacket and saw that her dog, her doll, and her "favoritest story" were in her day pack. "So much chaos," he grunted. "You'd think they were trying to launch the space shuttle, wouldn't you. Lotty tells me you have an evening appointment on the South Side. Perhaps you could meet me in the Pleiades lobby at four-thirty. I should be able to finish up by then so I can collect this whirling dervish from you. If you have a crisis, my secretary will be able to reach me. Victoria, we are grateful." He walked outside with us, kissing Calia lightly on the head and me on the hand.

"I hope your panel isn't too painful an outing," I said.

He smiled. "Lotty's fears? She's allergic to the past. I don't like wallowing in it, but I think it can be healthy for people to understand it."

I strapped Calia into the backseat of the Mustang. The Birnbaum Foundation, which often underwrites communications issues, had decided to hold a conference on "Christians and Jews: a New Millennium, a New Dialogue." They came up with the program after Southern Baptists announced plans to send a hundred thousand missionaries to Chicago this past summer to convert the Jews. The Baptist drive fizzled out; only about a thousand stalwart evangelizers showed up. It cost the Baptists something in cancelation fees at the hotels, too, but by then the planning for the Birnbaum conference was well under way.

Max was taking part in the bank-account panel, which infuriated Lotty: he was going to describe his postwar experiences in trying to track down his relatives and their assets. Lotty said he was going to expose his misery for the world at large to stare at. She said it only reinforced a stereotype of Jews as victims. Besides, she would add, dwelling on missing assets only gave people fuel for the second popular stereotype, that all Jews cared about was money. To which Max invariably replied, Who cares about money here, really? The Jews? Or the Swiss who refuse to return it to the people who earned it and deposited it? And the fight went on from there. It had been an exhausting summer, being around them.

In the seat behind me, Calia was chattering happily. The private eye as baby-sitter: it wasn't the first image you got from pulp fiction. I don't think Race Williams or Philip Marlowe ever did baby-sitting, but by the end of the morning I decided that was because they were too weak to take on a five-year-old.

I started at the zoo, thinking trudging around for an hour would make Calia eager to rest while I did some work in my office, but that proved to be an optimism born of ignorance. She colored for ten minutes, needed to go to the bathroom, wanted to call Grandpapa, thought we should play tag in the hall that runs the length of the warehouse where I lease space, was "terrifically" hungry despite the sandwiches we'd eaten at the zoo, and finally jammed one of my picklocks into the back of the photocopier.

At that point I gave up and took her to my apartment, where the dogs and my downstairs neighbor gave me a merciful respite. Mr. Contreras, a retired machinist, was delighted to let her ride horseback on him in the garden. The dogs joined in. I left them to it while I went up to the third floor to make some calls. I sat at the kitchen table with the back door open so I could keep an ear cocked for when Mr. Contreras's patience waned, but I did manage to get an hour of work in. After that Calia consented to sit in my living room with Peppy and Mitch while I read her "favoritest" story, *The Faithful Dog and the Princess.*

"I have a dog, too, Aunt Vicory," she announced, pulling a blue stuffed one from her day pack. "His name is Ninshubur, like in the book. See, it says, *Ninshubur means 'faithful friend' in the language of the princess's people.*"

"Vicory" was the closest Calia could get to Victoria when we met almost three years ago. We'd both been stuck with it ever since.

Calia couldn't read yet, but she knew the story by heart, chanting "For far rather would I die than lose my liberty" when the princess flung herself into a waterfall to escape an evil enchantress. "Then Ninshubur, the faithful hound, leapt from rock to rock, heedless of any danger." He jumped into the river and carried the princess to safety.

Calia pushed her blue plush dog deep into the book, then threw him on the floor to demonstrate his leap into the waterfall. Peppy, well-bred golden retriever that she was, sat on the alert, waiting for a command to fetch, but her son immediately bounded after the toy.

Calia screamed, running after Mitch. Both dogs began to bark. By the time I rescued Ninshubur, all of us were on the brink of tears. "I hate Mitch, he is a bad dog, I am most annoyed at his behavior," Calia announced.

I was thankful to see that it was three-thirty. Despite Agnes's prohibition, I plunked Calia in front of the television while I went down the hall to shower and change. Even in the era of casual dress, new clients respond better to professionalism: I put on a sage rayon suit with a rose silk sweater.

When I got back to the living room, Calia was lying with her head on Mitch's back, blue Ninshubur between his paws. She bitterly resisted restoring Mitch and Peppy to Mr. Contreras.

"Mitch will miss me, he will cry," she wailed, so tired herself that nothing made sense to her.

"Tell you what, baby: we'll get Mitch to give Ninshubur one of his dog tags. That way Ninshubur will remember Mitch when he can't see him." I went into my storage closet, where I found one of the small collars we'd used when Mitch had been a puppy. Calia stopped crying long enough to help buckle it in place around Ninshubur. I attached a set of Peppy's old tags, which looked absurdly big on the small blue neck but brought Calia enormous satisfaction.

I stuffed her day pack and Ninshubur into my own briefcase and scooped her up to carry her to my car. "I'm not a baby, I don't get carried," she sobbed, clinging to me. In the car she fell asleep almost at once.

My plan had been to leave my car with the Pleiades Hotel valet for fifteen minutes while I took Calia in to find Max, but when I pulled off Lake Shore Drive at Wacker, I saw this wasn't going to be possible. A major crowd was blocking the entrance to the Pleiades driveway. I craned my head, trying to see. A demonstration, apparently, with pickets and bullhorns. Television crews added to the chaos. Cops were furiously whistling cars away, but the traffic was so snarled I had to sit for some minutes in mounting frustration, wondering where I would find Max and what to do with Calia, heavily asleep behind me.

I pulled my cell phone out of my briefcase, but the battery was dead. And I couldn't find the in-car charger. Of course not: I'd left it in Morrell's car when he and I went to the country for a day last week. I pounded the steering wheel in useless frustration.

As I sat fuming, I watched the picketers, who belonged to conflicting causes. One group, all white, was carrying signs demanding passage of the Illinois Holocaust Asset Recovery Act. "No deals with thieves," they were chanting, and "Banks, insurers, where is our money?"

The man with the bullhorn was Joseph Posner. He'd been on the news so many times lately I could have picked him out in a bigger crowd than this. He was dressed in the long coat and bowler hat of the ultra-Orthodox. The son of a Holocaust survivor, he had become ostentatiously religious in a way that made Lotty grind her teeth. He could be seen picketing everything from X-rated movies, with the support of Christian fundamentalists, to Jewish-owned stores like Neiman Marcus that were open on Saturday. His followers, who seemed to be a cross between a yeshiva and the Jewish Defense League, accompanied him everywhere. They called themselves the Maccabees and seemed to think their protests should be modeled on the original Maccabees' military prowess. Like a growing number of fanatics in America, they were proud of their arrest records.

Posner's most recent cause was an effort to get Illinois to pass the Illinois Holocaust Asset Recovery Act. The IHARA, suggested by legislation in Florida and California, would bar insurance companies from doing business in the state unless they proved that they weren't sitting on any life or property claims from Holocaust victims. It also had clauses dealing with banks and with firms that benefited from use of forced labor during the Second World War. Posner had been able to generate enough publicity that the bill was being debated in committee.

The second group outside the Pleiades, mostly black, was carrying signs with a large red slash through *Pass the IHARA*. NO DEALS WITH SLAVE OWNERS and ECONOMIC JUSTICE FOR ALL, their signs proclaimed. The guy leading this group was also easy to recognize: Alderman Louis "Bull" Durham. Durham had been looking for a long time for a cause that would turn him into a high-profile opponent to the mayor, but opposition to the IHARA didn't strike me as a citywide issue.

If Posner had his Maccabees, Durham had his own militant followers. He'd set up Empower Youth Energy teams, first in his own ward and then around town, as a way of getting young men off the streets and into job-training programs. But some of the EYE teams, as they were called, had a shadier side. There were whispers on the street of extortion and beatings for store owners who didn't contribute to the alderman's political campaigns. And Durham himself always had his own group of EYE-team bodyguards, who surrounded him in their signature navy blazers whenever he appeared in public. If the Maccabees and the EYE team were going head to head, I was glad I was a private detective trying to make my way through traffic, not one of the policemen hoping to keep them apart.

The traffic finally inched me past the hotel entrance. I turned east onto Randolph Street, where it perches over Grant Park. All the meters there were taken, but I figured the cops were too busy at the Pleiades to spare time for ticketing.

I locked my briefcase in the trunk and pulled Calia from the backseat. She woke briefly, then slumped against my shoulder. She wasn't going to manage the walk to the hotel. I gritted my teeth. Making the best load I could of her forty-pound deadweight, I staggered down the stairs leading to the lower level of Columbus Drive, where the hotel's service entrance lay. It was already almost five: I hoped I'd find Max without too much trouble.

As I'd hoped, no one was blocking the lower entrance. I walked past the attendants with Calia and rode the elevator up to the lobby level. The crowd here was as thick as the mob outside, if quieter. Hotel guests and Birnbaum conference participants were wedged around the doors, anxiously wondering what was going on and what to do about it.

I was despairing of finding Max in this mob when I spotted a face I knew: Al Judson, the Pleiades security chief, was near the revolving doors, talking on a two-way radio.

I elbowed my way to him. "What's up, Al?"

Judson was a small black man, unobtrusive in crowds, an ex-cop who'd learned how to keep an eye on volatile groups from patrolling Grant Park with my dad forty years ago. When he saw me he gave a smile of genuine pleasure. "Vic! Which side of the door are you here for?"

I laughed, but with some embarrassment: my dad and I had argued about my joining antiwar protesters in Grant Park when he was assigned to riot control duty. I'd been a teenager with a dying mother and emotions so tangled I hadn't known what I wanted. So I'd run wild with the Yippies for a night.

"I need to find this small person's grandfather. Should I take to the streets instead?"

"Then you'd have to choose between Durham and Posner."

"I know about Posner's crusade on the life-insurance payments, but what's Durham's?"

Judson hunched a shoulder. "He wants the state to make it illegal for a company to do business here if they profited from slavery in the U.S. Unless they pay restitution to the descendants of slaves, that is. So he says, Don't pass the IHARA unless you add that clause to it."

I gave a little whistle of respect: the Chicago City Council had passed a resolution demanding reparations for descendants of slaves. Resolutions are a nice gesture—nods to constituencies without costing businesses anything. The mayor might be in an awkward spot if he fought Durham publicly over turning the resolution into a law with teeth in it.

It was an interesting political problem, but not as immediate a one for me as Calia, who was making my arms feel as though they were on fire. One of Judson's subordinates was hovering, ready to snatch his attention. I quickly explained my need to find Max. Judson spoke into his lapel radio. Within a few minutes, a young woman from hotel security appeared with Max, who took Calia from me. She stirred and began to cry. He and I had time for a few flustered words, about his panel, the melee outside, Calia's day, before I left him the unenviable task of soothing Calia and getting her to his car.

As I sat in the thicket of traffic waiting to move back past the protest site toward Lake Shore Drive, I nodded off several times. By the time I reached Isaiah Sommers's house in Avalon Park, I was thick with sleepiness. I was almost twenty minutes late, though. He swallowed his annoyance as best he could, but it wouldn't do for me to fall asleep in front of him.

Cash on the Coffin

When did your aunt give the policy to the funeral home?" I shifted on the couch, the heavy plastic covering the upholstery crinkling as I moved.

"On the Wednesday. My uncle passed on the Tuesday. They came for the body in the morning, but before they would collect it, they wanted proof that she could pay for the funeral. Which was scheduled for the Saturday. My mother had gone over to be with my aunt, and she found the policy in Uncle Aaron's papers just like we knew it would be. He was methodical in everything he did, great and small, and he was methodical in his documents, as well."

Sommers massaged his neck with his square hands. He was a lathe operator for the Docherty Engineering Works; his neck and shoulder muscles were bunched from leaning over a machine every day. "Then, like I said, when my aunt got to the church on Saturday they told her they weren't starting the funeral until she came up with the money."

"So after they took your uncle's body on Wednesday, the funeral parlor must have called the policy number in to the company, who told them that the policy had already been cashed. What a horrible experience for all of you. Did the funeral director know who the money had been paid to?"

"That's just my point." Sommers pounded his fist on his knee. "They said it was to my aunt. And that they wouldn't do the funeral—well, I told you all that."

"So how did you manage to get your uncle buried? Or did you?" I had an uneasy vision of Aaron Sommers lying in cold storage until the family shelled out three thousand dollars.

"I came up with the money." Isaiah Sommers looked reflexively toward the hall: his wife, who had let me in, had made clear her disapproval of his exerting himself for his uncle's widow. "And believe me, it wasn't so easy. If you're worried about your fee, don't be: I can take care of that. And if you can find out who took the money, maybe we can get it back. We'd even give you a finder's fee. The policy was worth ten thousand dollars."

"I don't need a finder's fee, but I will need to see the policy."

He lifted a presentation copy of *Roots* from the coffee table. The policy was folded carefully underneath.

"Do you have a photocopy of it?" I asked. "No? I'll mail you one tomorrow. You know that my fee is a hundred dollars an hour, with a minimum of five hours' work, right? I charge for all non-overhead expenses, as well."

When he nodded that he understood, I pulled two copies of my standard contract from my case. His wife, who had obviously been lurking outside the door, came in to read it with him. While they slowly went through each clause, I looked at the life-insurance policy. It had been sold to Aaron Sommers by the Midway Agency, and it dated back, as Isaiah said, some thirty years. It was drawn on the Ajax Life Insurance company. That was a help: I had once dated the guy who now headed claims operations at Ajax. I hadn't seen him for a number of years, but I thought he would probably talk to me.

"This clause here," Margaret Sommers said, "it says you don't refund money if we don't get the results we're looking for. Is that right?"

"Yes. But you can halt the investigation at any point. Also, I will report to you after my initial inquiries, and if it doesn't seem as though they're going anywhere, I'll tell you that frankly. But that's why I ask for a five-hundred-dollar earnest payment up front: if I start to look and don't find anything, people are tempted not to pay."

"Hmmph," she said. "It doesn't seem right to me, you taking money and not delivering."

"I'm successful most of the time." I tried not to let fatigue make me cranky—she wasn't the first person to raise this point. "But it wouldn't be fair to say I always am able to find out what someone wants to know. After my first inquiry, I can estimate the amount of time it will take to complete the investigation: sometimes people see that as more than they're willing to invest. You may decide that, too."

"And you'd still keep Isaiah's five hundred dollars."

"Yes. He's hiring my professional expertise. I get paid for providing that. Just as a doctor does, even when she can't cure you." It's taken years in the business to become hard-hearted—or maybe headed—about asking for money without embarrassment.

I told them if they wanted to talk it over some more they could call me when they'd made a decision, but that I wouldn't take the uncle's policy or make any phone calls until they'd signed a contract. Isaiah Sommers said he didn't need more time, that his cousin's neighbor Camilla Rawlings had vouched for me and that was good enough for him.

Margaret Sommers folded her arms across her chest and announced that as long as Isaiah understood he was paying for it, he was free to do as he pleased; she wasn't keeping books for that mean old Jew Rubloff to throw her money away on Isaiah's useless family.

Isaiah gave her a hard look, but he signed both contracts and pulled a roll from his trousers. He counted out five hundred dollars in twenties, watching me closely while I wrote out a receipt. I signed the contracts in turn, giving one back to Isaiah, putting the other with the policy in my case. I jotted down his aunt's address and phone number, took the details for the funeral parlor, and got up to leave.

Isaiah Sommers escorted me to the door, but before he could close it I heard Margaret Sommers say, "I just hope you don't come to me when you've found yourself throwing good money after bad."

I turned down the walk on his angry response. I'd had my fill of bitterness lately, what with Lotty's arguing with Max, and now the Sommerses taking each other on. Their snarling seemed endemic to the relationship; it would be difficult to be around them often. I wondered if they had friends and what the friends did when faced with this sniping. If Max and Lotty's quarrel hardened into the same kind of misery I would find it intolerable.

Ms. Sommers's gratuitous remark about the mean old Jew she worked for also hit me hard. I don't like mean-spirited remarks of any kind, but this one jarred me, especially after listening to Max and Lotty go ten rounds on whether he should speak at today's conference. What would Margaret Sommers say if she heard Max detail his life when the Nazis came to power—forced to leave school, seeing his father compelled to kneel naked in the street? Was Lotty right, was his speaking a demeaning exposure that would do no good? Would it teach the Margaret Sommerses of the world to curb their careless prejudices?

I'd grown up a few blocks south of here, among people who would have used worse epithets than Margaret Sommers's if she'd moved next door. If she sat on a stage rehearsing the racial slurs that she probably grew up hearing, I doubted that my old neighbors would change their thinking much.

I stood on the curb, trying to stretch out the knife points in my trapezius before starting the long drive north. The curtains in the Sommerses' front window twitched. I got into my car. The September nights were drawing in; only the faintest wisp of light still stained the horizon as I turned north onto Route 41.

Why did people stay together to be unhappy? My own parents hadn't shown me a Harlequin picture of true love, but at least my mother struggled to create domestic harmony. She had married my father out of gratitude, and out of fear, an immigrant alone on the streets of the city, not knowing English. He'd been a beat cop when he rescued her in a Milwaukee Avenue bar where she'd thought she could use her grand opera training to get a job as a singer. He'd fallen in love and never, to the best of my knowledge, fallen out of it. She was affectionate toward him, but it seemed to me her true passion was reserved for me. Of course, I wasn't quite sixteen when she died: what does one know of one's parents at that age?

And what about my client's uncle? Isaiah Sommers was certain that if his uncle had cashed in his life-insurance policy, he would have told his aunt. But people have many needs for money, some of them so embarrassing that they can't bring themselves to tell their families.

My melancholy reflections had carried me unnoticing past the landmarks of my childhood, to where Route 41 became the gleaming eight-lane drive skirting the lake shore. The last color had faded from the sky, turning the lake to a spill of black ink.

At least I had a lover to turn to, even if only for a few more days: Morrell, whom I've been seeing for the past year, was leaving on Tuesday for Afghanistan. A journalist who often covers human-rights issues, he's been longing to see the Taliban up close and personal since they consolidated their power several years back.

The thought of unwinding in the comfort of his arms made me accelerate through the long dark stretch of South Lake Shore Drive, up past the bright lights of the Loop to Evanston.

III

What *Is* in a Name?

Morrell greeted me at the door with a kiss and a glass of wine. "How'd it go, Mary Poppins?"

"Mary Poppins?" I echoed blankly, then remembered Calia. "Oh, that. It was great. People think day-care workers are underpaid but that's because they don't know how much fun the job is."

I followed him into the apartment and tried not to groan out loud when I saw his editor on the couch. Not that I dislike Don Strzepek, but I'd badly wanted an evening where my conversation could be limited to an occasional snore.

"Don!" I said as he got up to shake hands. "Morrell didn't tell me to expect this pleasure. I thought you were in Spain."

"I was." He patted his shirt for cigarettes, remembered he was in a no-smoking zone, and ran his fingers through his hair instead. "I got back to New York two days ago and learned that the boy reporter was leaving for the front. So I wangled a deal with *Maverick* magazine to do a story on this Birnbaum conference and came out. Of course now I have to work for the pleasure of bidding Morrell adieu. Which I won't let you forget, amigo."

Morrell and Don had met in Guatemala when they were both covering the dirty little war there a number of years back. Don had gone on to an editorial job at Envision Press in New York, but he still undertook some reporting assignments. *Maverick* magazine, a kind of edgier version of *Harper's,* published most of his work.

"Did you get here in time for the Maccabees–EYE-team standoff?" I asked.

"I was just telling Morrell. I picked up literature from both Posner and Durham." He waved at a pile of pamphlets on the coffee table. "I'll try to talk to both of them, but of course that's breaking news; what I need is background. Morrell says you might be able to supply me with some."

When I looked a question, he added, "I'd like a chance to meet Max Loewenthal, since he's on the national committee dealing with missing assets for Holocaust survivors. His Kindertransport story alone would make a good sidebar, and Morrell tells me that you know two of his friends who also came to England as children in the thirties."

I frowned, thinking of Lotty's furies with Max over exposing the past. "Maybe. I can introduce you to Max, but I don't know whether Dr. Herschel would want to talk to you. And Carl Tisov, Max's other friend, he's here from London on a concert tour, so whether he'd have the time, let alone the interest—"

I broke off with a shrug and picked up the pamphlets Don had brought back from the demonstrations. These included a flyer from Louis Durham, printed expensively in three colors on glossy stock. The document proclaimed opposition to the proposed Illinois Holocaust Asset Recovery Act, unless it also covered descendants of African slaves in America. Why should Illinois ban German companies who profited from the backs of Jewish and Gypsy workers but accept American companies who grew rich on the backs of African slaves?

I thought it was a good point, but I found some of the rhetoric disturbing: *It's not surprising Illinois is considering the IHARA. Jews have always known how to organize around the issue of money, and this is no exception.* Margaret Sommers's casual comment about "the mean old Jew Rubloff" echoed uncomfortably in my head.

I put the flyer back on the table and rifled through Posner's screed, which was irritating in its own way: *The day of the Jew as victim is over. We will not sit idly by while German and Swiss firms pay their shareholders with our parents' blood.*

"Ugh. Good luck in talking to these two specimens." I flipped through the rest of the literature and was surprised to see the company history Ajax Insurance had recently printed: "One Hundred Fifty Years of Life and Still Going Strong," by Amy Blount, Ph.D.

"You want to borrow it?" Don grinned.

"Thanks, I have my own copy—they held a gala a couple of weeks ago to celebrate. My most important client sits on their board, so I got chapter and verse close up. I even met the author." She'd been a thin, severe-looking young woman, dreadlocks tied back from her face with grosgrain ribbons, sipping mineral water on the fringes of a black-tie crowd. I tapped her booklet. "How'd you get this? Bull Durham going after Ajax? Or is Posner?"

Don patted his cigarette pocket again. "Both, as far as I can tell. Now that Edelweiss Re owns Ajax, Posner wants a printout of all their policies from 1933 on. And Durham is quite as insistent that Ajax open their books so he can see whom they insured from 1850 to 1865. Naturally Ajax is fighting like crazy to keep the

IHARA, with or without Durham's amendment, from getting passed here or anywhere. Although the Florida and California legislation that inspired the Illinois act doesn't seem to have hurt insurers any. I guess they've figured they can stall until the last beneficiary dies. . . . Morrell, I'm going to kill in a minute if I don't get some nicotine. You cuddle Vic. I'll give my great hacking smoker's cough to warn you I'm coming back in."

"Poor guy." Morrell followed me as I went into the bedroom to change. "Mmph. I don't remember that bra."

It was a rose and silver number I rather liked myself. Morrell nuzzled my shoulder and fiddled with the hooks. After a few minutes I pulled away. "That smoker's cough is going to hack in our ears in a minute. When did you find out he was coming to town?"

"He called from the airport this morning. I tried to let you know, but your mobile phone wasn't on."

Morrell took my skirt and sweater and hung them in the closet. His extreme tidiness is a big reason I can't imagine our ever living together.

He perched on the edge of the tub when I went into the bathroom to take off my makeup. "As much as anything, I think Don wanted an excuse to get away from New York. You know, since Envision's parent company was bought by that big French firm, Gargette, he hasn't been having much fun in publishing. So many of his authors are being axed that he's afraid his job will be cut. He wants to scope out the issues surrounding the Birnbaum conference—see if there's enough in them for a book of his own."

We went back into the bedroom, where I pulled on jeans and a sweatshirt. "What about you?" I leaned against him, closing my eyes and letting the wall of fatigue I'd been battling crash over me. "Is there any risk of your contract for the Taliban book being canceled?"

"No such luck, babe." Morrell ruffled my hair. "Don't sound so hopeful."

I blushed. "I didn't mean to be so obvious. But— Kabul. An American passport is as big a liability there as a woman's exposed arms."

Morrell held me more tightly. "You're more likely to get into trouble here in Chicago than I am in Afghanistan. I've never been in love before with a woman who was beaten up and left to die on the Kennedy."

"But you could visit me every day while I was recuperating," I objected.

"I promise you, Victoria Iphigenia, that if I am left to die in the Khyber Pass, I will get Humane Medicine to fly you over so you can see me every day."

Humane Medicine was a human-rights group Morrell had traveled with in the past. They were based in Rome and were hoping to set up an inoculation program for Afghan children before the Himalayan winter set in in earnest. Morrell was going to roam around talking to anyone he could, observe the state-sanctioned boys' schools, see if he could find any of the underground girls' schools, and generally try to get some understanding of the Taliban. He'd even been taking a course on the Koran in a mosque on Devon Avenue.

"I'm going to fall asleep if I don't start moving," I murmured into his chest. "Let's get some dinner for Don. We've got that fettuccine I bought on the weekend. Put some tomatoes and olives and garlic in it; that'll do the job."

We went back into the living room, where Don was flipping through a copy of the *Kansas City Review*— Morrell had a critique of some recent books on Guatemala in it. "Good job, Morrell—it's a tough question, what to do about old juntas in new clothes, isn't it? Tough question to know what to do about our own government's involvement with some of these groups, too."

I drifted for a bit while they talked about South

American politics. When Don announced a need for another cigarette, Morrell followed me to the kitchen to pull supper together. We ate at the island countertop in the kitchen, perched on barstools, while Don talked with a certain gloomy humor about the changes in publishing. "While I was in Barcelona, my corporate masters announced to the *Journal* that writers are just content providers. Then they sent out a protocol on how to type manuscripts, demoting the content providers to clerk-typists."

A few minutes before ten he pushed his chair away from the counter. "There should be some coverage of the Birnbaum conference on the ten o'clock news. I'd like to watch, although the cameras probably concentrated on the action out front."

He helped Morrell scrape the plates into the garbage, then went to the back porch for another cigarette. While Morrell loaded the dishwasher, wiped down the counters, and wrapped leftovers in airtight containers, I went into the living room to turn on Channel 13, Global Entertainment's Chicago station. The evening anchor, Dennis Logan, was just finishing his summary of the upcoming news.

"Events turned stormy at times at the conference on Jews in America being held today at the Hotel Pleiades, but the real surprise came at the end of the afternoon from someone who wasn't even on the program. Beth Blacksin will have the whole story later in our broadcast."

I curled up in the corner of Morrell's couch. I started to nod off, but when the phone rang, I woke up to see two young women on-screen raving about a drug for yeast infections. Morrell, who'd come into the room behind me, muted the set and answered the phone.

"For you, sweet. Max." He stretched the receiver out to me.

"Victoria, I'm sorry to phone so late." Max's tone

was apologetic. "We have a crisis here that I'm hoping you can solve. Ninshubur—that blue stuffed dog Calia takes everywhere—do you have it by any chance?"

I could hear Calia howling in the background, Michael shouting something, Agnes's voice raised to yell something else. I rubbed my eyes, trying to remember far enough back in the day to Calia's dog. I had stuffed Calia's day pack into my case, then forgotten about it in the harassment of getting her to Max. I put the phone down and looked around. I finally asked Morrell if he knew where my briefcase was.

"Yes, V I," he said in a voice of long-suffering. "You dropped it on the couch when you came in. I put it in my study."

I set the receiver on the couch and went down the hall to his study. My briefcase was the only thing on his desk, except for his copy of the Koran, with a long green string marking his place. Ninshubur was buried in the bottom, with some raisins, Calia's day pack, and the tale of the princess and her faithful hound. I picked up the study extension and apologized to Max, promising to run right over with the animal.

"No, no, don't disturb yourself. It's only a few blocks and I'll be glad to get out of this upheaval."

When I returned to the living room, Don said the suspense was mounting: we were on the second commercial break with the promise of fireworks to come. Max rang the bell just as Dennis Logan began speaking again.

When I let Max into the little entryway, I saw he had Carl Tisov with him. I handed the toy dog to Max, but he and Carl lingered long enough that Morrell came over to invite them in for a drink.

"Something strong, like absinthe," Carl said. "I had always wished for a large family, but after this evening's waterworks, I think I didn't miss so much. How can one small diaphragm generate more sound than an entire brass section?"

"It's the jet lag," Max said. "It always hits small ones hard."

Don called out to us to hush. "They're finally getting to the conference."

Max and Carl moved into the living room and stood behind the couch. Don turned up the volume as Beth Blacksin's pixieish face filled the screen.

"When the Southern Baptists announced their plan to send a hundred thousand missionaries to Chicago this past summer as part of their plan to convert Jews to Christianity, a lot of people were troubled, but the Birnbaum Foundation took action. Working with the Illinois Holocaust Commission, the Chicago Roman Catholic archdiocese, and Dialogue, an interfaith group here in Chicago, the foundation decided to hold a conference on issues that affect not just Illinois's substantial Jewish population but the Jewish community in America as a whole. Hence today's conference, 'Christians and Jews: a New Millennium, a New Dialogue.'

"At times, it seemed as though dialogue was the last thing on anyone's mind." The screen shifted to footage of the demonstrations out front. Blacksin gave both Posner and Durham equal sound bites, then shifted back to the hotel ballroom.

"Sessions inside the building also grew heated. The liveliest one covered the topic which sparked the demonstrations outside: the proposed Illinois Holocaust Asset Recovery Act. A panel of banking and insurance executives, arguing that the act would be so costly that all consumers would suffer, drew a lot of criticism, and a lot of anguish."

Here the screen showed furious people yelling into the mikes set up in the aisles for questions. One man shouted the insult that Margaret Sommers and Alderman Durham had both made earlier, that the reparations debate proved that all Jews ever thought about was money.

Another man yelled back that he didn't understand why Jews were considered greedy for wanting bank deposits their families had made: "Why aren't the banks called greedy? They held on to the money for sixty years and now they want to hang on to it forever." A woman stomped up to a mike to say that since the Swiss reinsurer Edelweiss had bought Ajax, she assumed Edelweiss had their own reasons to oppose the legislation.

Channel 13 let us watch the melee for about twenty seconds before Blacksin's voice cut in again. "The most startling event of the day didn't take place in the insurance session, but during one on forcible conversion, when a small man with a shy manner made the most extraordinary revelation."

We watched as a man in a suit that seemed a size too big for him spoke into one of the aisle mikes. He was closer to sixty than fifty, with greying curls that had thinned considerably at his temples.

"I want to say that it is only recently I even knew I was Jewish."

A voice from the stage asked him to identify himself.

"Oh. My name is Paul—Paul Radbuka. I was brought here after the war when I was four years old by a man who called himself my father."

Max sucked in his breath, while Carl exclaimed, "What! Who is this?"

Don and Morrell both turned to stare.

"You know him?" I asked.

Max clamped my wrist to hush me while the little figure in front of us continued to speak. "He took everything away from me, most especially my memories. Only recently have I come to know that I spent the war in Terezin, the so-called model concentration camp that the Germans named Theresienstadt. I thought I was a German, a Lutheran, like this man Ulrich who called himself my father. Only after he died, when I went through his papers, did I find out the truth. And I say it is wrong, it is criminally wrong, to take away from people the identity which is rightfully theirs."

The station let a few seconds' silence develop, then Dennis Logan, the anchor, appeared in a split screen with Beth Blacksin. "It's a most extraordinary story, Beth. You caught up with Mr. Radbuka after the session, didn't you? We'll be showing your exclusive interview with Paul Radbuka at the end of our regular newscast. Coming up, for fans who thought the Cubs couldn't sink lower, a surprising come-from-ahead loss today at Wrigley."

IV

Memory Plant

D o you know him?" Don asked Max, muting the sound as yet another round of ads came up.

Max shook his head. "I know the name, but not this man. It's just—it's a most unusual name." He turned to Morrell. "If I can impose on you—I'd like to stay for the interview."

Like Max, Carl was a short man, not quite as tall as I am, but where Max smiled good-naturedly on the world around him—often amused by the human predicament—Carl held himself on alert—a bantam rooster, ready to take on all comers. Right now, he seemed edgier than usual. I looked at him but decided not to quiz him in front of Don and Morrell.

Morrell brought Max herbal tea and poured brandy for Carl. Finally the station finished its lengthy dissection of the weather and turned to Beth Blacksin. She was talking to Paul Radbuka in a small meeting room at the Pleiades. Another woman, with wings of black hair framing her oval face, was with them.

Beth Blacksin introduced herself and Paul Radbuka, then let the camera focus on the other woman. "Also here this evening is Rhea Wiell, the therapist who has treated Mr. Radbuka and helped him recover his hidden memories. Ms. Wiell has agreed to talk to me later tonight in a special edition of 'Exploring Chicago.'"

Blacksin turned to the small man. "Mr. Radbuka, how did you come to discover your true identity? You said in the meeting that it was in going through your father's papers. What did you find there?"

"The man who called himself my father," Radbuka corrected her. "It was a set of documents in code. At first I paid no attention to them. Somehow after he died I lost my own will to live. I don't understand why, because I didn't like him; he was always very brutal to me. But I became so depressed that I lost my job, I even stopped getting out of bed on many days. And then I met Rhea Wiell."

He turned to the dark-haired woman with a look of adoration. "It sounds melodramatic, but I believe I owe my life to her. And she helped me make sense of the documents, to use them to find my missing identity."

"Rhea Wiell is the therapist you found," Beth prodded him.

"Yes. She specializes in recovering memories of events that people like me block because the trauma around them is so intense."

He continued to look at Wiell, who nodded reassuringly at him. Blacksin stepped him through some of his highlights, the tormenting nightmares that he had been ashamed to speak of for fifty years, and his dawning realization that the man who called himself his father might really be someone completely unrelated to him.

"We had come to America as DP's—displaced persons—after the Second World War. I was only four, and when I was growing up, this man said we were from Germany." He gasped for air between sentences, like an asthmatic fighting to breathe. "But what I've finally learned from my work with Rhea is that his story was only half true. *He* was from Germany. But I was a—a camp child, camp survivor. I was from some other place, some country under Nazi control. This man attached himself to me in the confused aftermath of the war to get a visa to America." He looked at his hands as if he were terribly ashamed of this.

"And do you feel up to telling us about those dreams—those nightmares—that led you to Rhea Wiell?" Beth prompted him.

Wiell stroked Radbuka's hand in a reassuring fashion. He looked up again and spoke to the camera with an almost childish lack of self-consciousness.

"The nightmares were things that haunted me, things I couldn't speak out loud and could experience only in sleep. Terrible things, beatings, children falling dead in the snow, bloodstains like flowers around them. Now, thanks to Rhea, I can remember being four years old. We were moving, this strange angry man and I, we were first on a ship and then on a train. I was crying, 'My Miriam, where is my Miriam? I want my Miriam,' but the man who kept saying he was '*Vati*,' my father, would hit me and finally I learned to keep all those cries to myself."

"And who was Miriam, Mr. Radbuka?" Blacksin leaned toward him, her eyes wide with empathy.

"Miriam was my little playmate, we had been together since—since I was twelve months old." Radbuka began to cry.

"When she arrived at the camp with you, isn't that right?" Beth said.

"We spent two years in Terezin together. There were six of us, the six musketeers I think of us now, but my Miriam, she was my special—I want to know she is still alive someplace, still healthy. And maybe she remembers her Paul as well." He cupped his face in his hands; his shoulders shook.

Rhea Wiell's face loomed suddenly between him and

the camera. "Let's finish here, Beth. That's all Paul can handle today."

As the camera pulled back from them, Dennis Logan, the station anchor, spoke over the scene. "This sad, sad story continues to haunt not only Paul Radbuka but thousands of other Holocaust survivors. If any of you think you know Paul's Miriam, call the number on our screen, or go to our Web site, www.Globe-All.com. We'll make sure Paul Radbuka gets your message."

"How disgusting," Carl burst out when Morrell muted the set again. "How can anyone expose himself like that?"

"You sound like Lotty," Max murmured. "I suppose his hurt is so great that he isn't aware that he's exposing himself."

"People like to talk about themselves," Don put in. "That's what makes a journalist's job easy. Does his name mean something to you, Mr. Loewenthal?"

Max looked at him quizzically, wondering how Don knew his name. Morrell stepped in to perform introductions. Don explained that he had come out to cover the conference and recognized Max from today's program.

"Did you recognize the guy—Radbuka, wasn't it? The name or the person?" he added.

"You're a journalist who would like me to talk about myself to you?" Max said sharply. "I have no idea who he is."

"He was like a child," Carl said. "Utterly unself-conscious about what he was saying, even though he was recounting the most appalling events."

The phone rang again. It was Michael Loewenthal, saying that if his father had Calia's dog to please come home with it.

Max gave a guilty start. "Victoria, may I call you in the morning?"

"Of course." I went into the back to get a card from my case so that Max would have my cell-phone number, then I walked out to the car with him and Carl. "Did you two recognize the guy?"

Under the street lamp I saw Max look at Carl. "The name. I thought I recognized the name—but it doesn't seem possible. I'll call you in the morning."

When I went back inside, Don was in purdah again with a cigarette. I joined Morrell in the kitchen, where he was washing Carl's brandy glass. "Did they tell all away from the prying ears of journalism?"

I shook my head. "I'm beat, but I'm curious, too, about the therapist. Are you guys going to stay up for the special segment with her?"

"Don is panting for it. He thinks she may be his career-saving book."

"You'd better believe it," Don called through the screen door. "Although the guy would be hard to work with—his emotions seem awfully volatile."

We all returned to the living room just as the "Exploring Chicago" logo came up on the screen. The show's regular announcer said they had a special program for us tonight and turned the stage over to Beth Blacksin.

"Thank you, Dennis. In this special edition of 'Exploring Chicago,' we have the opportunity to follow up on the exciting revelations we heard earlier today, exclusively on Global Television, when a man who came here as a boy from war-torn Europe told us how therapist Rhea Wiell helped him recover memories he had buried alive for fifty years."

She ran a few segments from Radbuka's speech to the convention, followed by excerpts from her own interview with him.

"We're going to follow up on today's extraordinary story by talking to the therapist who worked with Paul Radbuka. Rhea Wiell has been having remarkable success—and started remarkable controversy, I might add—with her work in helping people get access to forgotten memories. Memories they've usually forgotten because the pain of remembering them is too great. We don't bury happy memories so deep, do we, Rhea?"

The therapist had changed into a soft green outfit that suggested an Indian mystic. She nodded with a slight smile. "We don't usually suppress memories of ice-cream sodas or romps on the beach with our friends. The memories we push away are the ones that threaten us in our core as individuals."

"Also with us is Professor Arnold Praeger, the director of the Planted Memory Foundation."

The professor was given due face time to say that we lived in an era that celebrated victims, which meant people needed to prove they had suffered more terribly than anyone else. "Such people seek out therapists who can validate their victimization. A small number of therapists have helped a large number of would-be victims remember the most shocking events: they begin recalling satanic rituals, sacrificing pets that never even existed, and so on. Many families have been terribly damaged by these planted memories."

Rhea Wiell laughed softly. "I hope you are not going to suggest that any of my patients have recovered memories of satanic sacrifices, Arnold."

"You've certainly encouraged some of them to demonize their parents, Rhea. They've ruined their parents' lives by accusing them of the most heinous brutality—accusations which can't be proved true in a court of law because the only witnesses to them are your patients' imaginations."

"You mean the only witness besides the parent who thought he was safe from ever being found out," Wiell said, keeping her voice gentle as a contrast to Praeger's sharp speech.

Praeger cut her off. "In the case of this man whose

tape we just watched, the father is dead and can't even be summoned to speak on his own behalf. We're told about documents in code, but I wonder what key you used to break the code? And whether someone like me would get the same result if I looked at the documents."

Wiell shook her head, smiling gently. "My patients' privacy is sacrosanct, Arnold, you know that. These are Paul Radbuka's documents. Whether anyone else can see them is his decision alone."

Blacksin stepped in here to draw the conversation back to what recovered memories actually were. Wiell talked a little about post-traumatic stress disorder, explaining that there are a number of symptoms that people share after trauma, whether it's from battle—as soldiers or civilians—or experiencing other fragmenting events, like sexual assault.

"Children who've been sexually abused, adults who've been tortured, soldiers who've endured battle, all share some common problems: depression, inability to sleep, inability to trust people around them or form close connections."

"But people can be depressed and have sleep disorders without having been abused," Praeger snapped. "When someone comes into my office complaining of those symptoms, I am very careful about forming an opinion of the root cause: I don't immediately suggest he's been tortured by Hutu terrorists. People are at their most dependent and vulnerable with psychotherapists. It is all too easy to suggest things to them which they come ardently to believe. We like to think that our memories are objective and accurate, but unfortunately, it's very easy to create memories of events that never took place."

He went on to summarize research on planted, or created, memories that showed how people were persuaded they had taken part in marches or demonstrations when there was objective evidence that they'd never been in the city where the demonstration was held.

A little before eleven, Blacksin cut the argument short. "Until we truly understand the workings of the human mind, this debate will continue between people of goodwill. Why don't each of you take thirty seconds to summarize your positions, before we say good night. Ms. Wiell?"

Rhea Wiell looked at the camera with a wide, serious gaze. "We often like to dismiss other people's horrible memories, not because we're not compassionate. And not because we don't want to be victims. But because we're afraid to look inside ourselves. We're afraid to find out what lies hidden—what we've done to other people, or what has happened to us. It takes a lot of courage to take a journey to the past. I would never start someone on that journey who wasn't strong enough to make it to the end. I certainly never let them travel that dangerous road alone."

After that, Professor Praeger's rebuttal sounded cruel and unfeeling. If the rest of the viewing audience was like me, they wanted Wiell back, wanted her to say they were strong enough to travel to the past, and good or interesting enough that she would guide them on the way.

When the camera faded to commercials, Morrell switched off the set. Don rubbed his hands.

"This woman has book, six figures, written all over her. I'll be a hero in Paris and New York if I get her before Bertelsmann or Rupert Murdoch does. If she's legitimate. What do you two think?"

"Remember the shaman we met in Escuintla?" Morrell said to Don. "He had the same expression in his eyes. As if he saw into the most secret thoughts of your mind."

"Yes." Don shuddered. "What a horrible trip. We spent eighteen hours underneath a pigsty outwaiting the army. That was when I decided I'd be happier working full-time at Envision Press and letting people like you hog the glory, Morrell. So to speak. You think she's a charlatan?"

Morrell spread his hands. "I don't know anything about her. But she certainly believes in herself, doesn't she?"

A yawn split my face. "I'm too tired to have an opinion. But it should be easy enough to check her credentials in the morning."

I pushed myself upright on leaden legs. Morrell said he'd join me in a minute. "Before Don gets too carried away with this new book, I want to go over a few things about my own."

"In that case, Morrell, we're doing it outside. I'm not dueling with you over contracts without nicotine."

I don't know how late the two of them sat up: I was asleep almost before the door out to the porch closed behind them.

V
—

Sniffing for a Scent

When I got back from my run the next morning, Don was where I'd left him the night before: on the back porch with a cigarette. He was even wearing the same jeans and rumpled green shirt.

"You look horribly healthy. It makes me want to smoke more in self-defense." He sucked in a final mouthful of smoke, then ground the butt tidily on a broken piece of pottery Morrell had given him. "Morrell said you'd operate the coffee thingy for me; I suppose you know he's gone into town to see someone or other at the State Department."

I knew: Morrell had gotten up when I did, at six-thirty. As his departure date loomed, he'd stopped sleeping well—several times in the night I'd woken to find him staring rigidly at the ceiling. In the morning, I slid out of bed as quietly as possible, going to the guest bathroom in the hall to wash, then using his study to leave a message for Ralph Devereux, head of claims at Ajax Insurance, asking for a meeting at his earliest convenience. By the time I finished that, Morrell was up. While I did my stretches and drank a glass of juice, he answered his mail. When I left for my run, he was deep in an on-line chat with Humane Medicine in Rome.

My return route took me past Max's lakefront home. His Buick was still in the driveway, as were two other cars, presumably Carl's and Michael's rentals. There didn't seem to be any signs of life: musicians go to bed late and get up late. Max, who usually is at work by eight, must be following his son's and Carl's rhythms.

I stared at the house, as if the windows would lead me to the secret thoughts of the men inside. What had the man on television last night meant to Max and Carl? They had at least recognized the name, I was pretty sure of that. Had one of their London friends been part of the Radbuka family? But Max had made it clear last night that he wasn't ready to talk about that. I shouldn't try to trespass. I shook out my legs and finished my run.

Morrell had a semicommercial espresso machine. Back in his apartment, I made cappuccinos for Don and myself before showering. While I dressed, I checked my own messages. Ralph had called from Ajax and would be delighted to squeeze me in at a quarter of twelve. I put on the rose silk sweater and sage skirt I'd worn yesterday. It gets complicated spending part of my life at Morrell's—the clothes I want are always in my own apartment when I'm with him, or in his place when I'm home.

Don had moved to the kitchen eating island with the *Herald-Star* when I came in. "If they took you for a ride on a Russian mountain in Paris, where would you be?"

"Russian mountain?" I mixed yogurt and granola with orange slices. "Is this helping you get ready to ask searching comments of Posner and Durham?"

He grinned. "I'm sharpening my wits. If you were going to do some fast checking on the therapist who was on television last night, where would you start?"

I leaned against the counter while I ate. "I'd search the accreditation databases for therapists to see if she was licensed and what her training was. I'd go to ProQuest—she and the guy from the memory foundation have been mixing it up—there might be some articles about her."

Don scribbled a note on the corner of the crossword-puzzle clues. "How long would it take you to do it for me? And how much would you charge?"

"Depends on how deep you wanted to go. The basics I could do pretty fast, but I charge a hundred dollars an hour with a five-hour initial minimum. How generous is Gargette's expenses policy?"

He tossed the pencil aside. "They have four hundred cost accountants in their head office at Rheims just to make sure editors like me don't eat more than a Big Mac on the road, so they're not too likely to spring for a private investigator. Still, this could be a really big book. If she is who she says she is—if the guy is who he says he is. Could you do some checking for me on spec?"

I was about to agree when I thought of Isaiah Sommers, carefully counting out his twenties. I shook my head unhappily. "I can't make exceptions for friends. It makes it hard for me to charge strangers."

He pulled out a cigarette and tapped it on the paper. "Okay. Can you do some checking and trust me for the money?"

I grimaced. "Yeah. I guess. I'll bring a contract back with me tonight."

He returned to the porch. I finished my breakfast and ran water over the bowl—Morrell would have a fit if he came home to find case-hardened yogurt on it— then followed Don out the back door: my car was parked in the alley behind the building. Don was reading the news but looked up to say good-bye. On my way down the back stairs the word came to me from nowhere. "Roller coaster. If it's the same in French as Italian, a Russian mountain is a roller coaster."

"You've already earned your fee." He picked up his pencil and turned back to the crossword page.

Before going to my office, I swung by Global Entertainment's studios on Huron Street. When the company moved into town a year ago, they bought a skyscraper in the hot corridor just northwest of the river. Their Midwest regional offices, where they control everything from a hundred seventy newspapers to a big chunk of the broadband DSL business, are on the upper levels, with their studios on the ground floor.

Global executives are not my biggest fans in Chicago, but I've worked with Beth Blacksin since before the company took over Channel 13. She was on the premises, editing a segment for the evening news. She ran out to the lobby in the sloppy jeans she can't wear on-air, greeting me like a long-lost friend—or, anyway, a valuable source.

"I was riveted by your interview yesterday with that guy Radbuka," I said. "How'd you find him?"

"Warshawski!" Her expressive face came alive with excitement. "Don't tell me he's been murdered. I'm getting to a live mike."

"Calm down, my little newshound. As far as I know he's still on the planet. What can you tell me about him?"

"You've found out who the mysterious Miriam is, then."

I took her by the shoulders. "Blacksin, calm down— if you're able. I'm purely on a fishing expedition right now. Do you have an address you'd be willing to give out? For him, or for the therapist?"

She took me with her past the security station to a warren of cubicles where the news staff had desks. She went through a stack of papers next to her computer and found the standard waiver sheet people sign when they give interviews. Radbuka had listed a suite number at an address on North Michigan, which I copied down. His signature was large and untidy, kind of the way he'd looked in his too-big suit. Rhea Wiell, by contrast, wrote in a square, almost printlike hand. I copied out the spelling of her name. And then noticed that Radbuka's address was the same as hers. Her office at Water Tower.

"Could you get me a copy of the tape? Your interview, and the discussion between the therapist and the guy from the antihypnosis place? That was good work, pulling them together at the last minute."

She grinned. "My agent's happy—my contract's coming up in six weeks. Praeger has a real bee in his bonnet about Wiell. They've been adversaries on a bunch of cases, not just in Chicago but all around the country. He thinks she's the devil incarnate and she thinks he's the next thing to a child molester himself. They've both had media training—they looked civilized on camera, but you should have heard them when the camera wasn't rolling."

"What did you think of Radbuka?" I asked. "Up close and personal, did you believe his story?"

"Do you have proof he's a fraud? Is that what this is really about?"

I groaned. "I don't know anything about him. Zippo. Niente. Nada. I can't say it in any more languages. What was your take on him?"

Her eyes opened wide. "Oh, Vic, I believed him completely. It was one of the most harrowing interviews I've ever done—and I talked to people after Lockerbie. Can you imagine growing up the way he did and then finding the man who claimed to be your father was like your worst enemy?"

"What was his father—foster father's name?"

She scrolled through the text on her screen. "Ulrich.

Whenever Paul referred to him, he always used the man's German name, instead of 'Daddy' or 'Father' or something."

"Do you know what he found in Ulrich's papers that made him realize his lost identity? In the interview he said they were in code."

She shook her head, still looking at the screen. "He talked about working it through with Rhea and getting the correct interpretation. He said they proved to him that Ulrich had really been a Nazi collaborator. He talked a lot about how brutal Ulrich had been to him, beating him for acting like a sissy, locking him in a closet when he was away at work, sending him to bed without food."

"There wasn't a woman on the scene? Or was she a participant in the abuse?" I asked.

"Paul says Ulrich told him that his mother—or Mrs. Ulrich, anyway—had died in the bombing of Vienna as the war was ending. I don't think Mr. Ulrich ever married here, or even had women to the house. Ulrich and Paul seemed to have been a real pair of loners. Papa went to work, came home, beat Paul. Paul was supposed to be a doctor, but he couldn't handle pressure, so he ended up as an X-ray technician, which earned more ridicule. He never moved out of his father's house. Isn't that creepy? Staying with him even when he was big enough to earn his own living?"

That was all she could, or at least all she would, tell me. She promised to messenger over a tape of the various segments with Radbuka, as well as the meeting between the therapists, to my office later in the day.

I still had time before my appointment at Ajax to do some work in my office. It was only a few miles north and west of Global—but a light-year away in ambience. No glass towers for me. Three years ago a sculptor friend had invited me to share a seven-year lease with her for a converted warehouse on Leavitt. Since the building was a fifteen-minute drive from the financial district where most of my business lies and the rent was half what you pay in those gleaming high-rises, I'd signed on eagerly.

When we moved in, the area was still a grimy no-man's-land between the Latino neighborhood farther west and a slick Yuppie area nearer the lake. At that time, bodegas and palm readers vied with music stores for the few retail spaces in what had been an industrial zone. Parking abounded. Even though the Yuppies are starting to move in, building espresso bars and boutiques, we still have plenty of collapsing buildings and drunks. I was against further gentrification—I didn't want to see my rent skyrocket when the current lease expired.

Tessa's truck was already in our little lot when I pulled in. She'd received a major commission last month and was putting in long hours to build a model of both the piece and the plaza it would occupy. When I passed her studio door she was perched at her outsize drafting table, sketching. She's testy if interrupted, so I went down the hall to my own office without speaking.

I made a couple of copies of Isaiah Sommers's uncle's policy and locked the original in my office safe, where I keep all client documents during an active investigation. It's really a strongroom, with fireproof walls and a good sturdy door.

Midway Insurance's address was listed on the policy: they had sold the policy to Aaron Sommers all those years back. If I couldn't get satisfaction from the company, I'd have to go back to the agent—and hope he remembered what he'd done thirty years ago. I checked the phone book. The agency was still on Fifty-third Street, down in Hyde Park.

I had two queries to complete for bread-and-butter

clients. While I sat on hold with the Board of Health, I logged on to Lexis and ProQuest and submitted a search on Rhea Wiell, as well as Paul Radbuka.

My Board of Health connection came on the phone and for once answered all my questions without a lot of hedging. When I'd wrapped up my report I checked back with Lexis. There was nothing on the Radbuka name. I checked my disks of phone numbers and addresses for the U.S.—more up-to-date than Web search engines—and found nothing. When I looked up his father's name, Ulrich, I got forty-seven matches in the Chicago area. Maybe Paul hadn't changed his name legally when he became Radbuka.

Rhea Wiell, on the other hand, gave me a lot of hits. She had apparently appeared as an expert witness in a number of trials, but tracking them down so I could get transcripts would be a tedious business. However, I did find she was a clinical social worker, fully accredited by the State of Illinois: at least she had started from an authentic position. I logged off and swept my papers together into my case so I could be on time for my meeting with the head of the Ajax claims department.

VI

Staking a Claim

I originally met Ralph Devereux early in my life as an investigator. It hasn't been so many years, but at the time I was the first woman in Chicago, maybe even the country, with a PI license. It was a struggle to get clients or witnesses to treat me seriously. When Ralph took a bullet in his shoulder because he couldn't believe his boss was a crook, our relationship fractured as abruptly as his scapula.

I hadn't seen him since; I admit I felt a little nervous anticipation as I rode the L down to Ajax's headquarters on Adams Street. When I got off the elevator at the sixty-third floor, I even stopped in the ladies' room to make sure my hair was combed and my lipstick tidily confined to my mouth.

The executive-floor attendant escorted me down a mile of parquet to Ralph's corner; his secretary pronounced my name perfectly and buzzed the inner sanctum. Ralph emerged smiling, both arms held out in greeting.

I took his hands in my own, smiling back, trying to hide a twinge of sadness. When I'd met him, Ralph had been a slim-hipped, ardent young man with a shock of black hair falling in his eyes and an engaging grin. His hair was still thick, although liberally tinged with grey, but he had jowls now, and while he wasn't exactly fat, those slim hips had disappeared into the same past as our brief affair.

I exchanged conventional greetings, congratulating him on his promotion to head of the claims department. "It looks as though you recovered full use of your arm," I added.

"Just about. It still bothers me when the weather's damp. I got so depressed after that injury—waiting for it to heal, feeling like a moron for letting it happen at all—that I took to cheeseburgers. The big shake-ups here the last few years haven't helped any, either. You look great, though. You still running five miles every morning? Maybe I should hire you to coach me."

I laughed. "You're already in your first meeting before I get out of bed. You'd have to take a lower-pressure job. The shake-ups you mentioned—those from Edelweiss acquiring Ajax?"

"That came at the end, really. We took a lot of hits in the market at the same time that Hurricane Andrew overwhelmed us. While we were dealing with that, and laying off a fifth of our workforce worldwide, Edelweiss snapped up a chunk of our depressed stock. They were a hostile suitor—I'm sure you followed that in the financial pages—but they certainly haven't been a hostile master. They seem quite eager to learn how we do things here, rather than wanting to interfere. In fact, the managing director from Zurich who's looking after Ajax wanted to sit in on my meeting with you."

His hand in the small of my back, he ushered me into his office, where a man with tortoiseshell glasses, dressed in a pale wool suit and a bold tie, stood when I entered. He was around forty, with a round merry face that seemed to match the tie more than the suit.

"Vic Warshawski, Bertrand Rossy from Edelweiss

Re in Zurich. You two should get along well—Vic speaks Italian."

"Oh, really?" Rossy shook hands. "With the name Warshawski I would have assumed Polish."

"My mother was from Pitigliano—*vicino* Orvieto," I said. "I can only stumble through a few stock phrases of Polish."

Rossy and I sat in chrome tube chairs next to a glass-topped table. Ralph himself, who had always had an incongruous-seeming taste for modernism, leaned against the edge of the aluminum tabletop he used as a desk.

I asked Rossy the usual things, about where he had acquired his perfect English (he had gone to school in England) and how he liked Chicago (very much). His wife, who was Italian, had found the summer weather oppressive and had taken their two children to her family's estate in the hills above Bologna.

"She just returned this week with Paolo and Marguerita for the start of the school year here and already I'm better dressed than I was all summer, isn't that right, Devereux? I could barely persuade her to let me out the front door in this tie this morning." He laughed loudly, showing dimples at the corners of his mouth. "Now I make a campaign to persuade her to try the Chicago opera: her family have been in the same box at La Scala since it opened in 1778 and she can't believe a raw young city like this can really produce opera."

I told him I went to a production once a year in tribute to my mother, who had taken me every fall, but of course I couldn't compare it to a European opera company. "Nor do I have a family box: it's the upper gallery for me, what we call the nosebleed section."

He laughed again. "Nosebleed section. My colloquial American is going to improve for talking to you. We shall all go together one evening, if you can condescend to climb down from the nosebleed section. But I see Devereux looking at his watch—oh, very discreetly, don't be embarrassed, Devereux. A beautiful woman is an inducement to waste precious business minutes, but Miss Warshawski must have come here for some other purpose than to discuss opera."

I pulled out the photocopy of the Aaron Sommers policy and explained the events around his aborted funeral. "I thought if I came straight to you with the situation, you could get me an answer fast."

When Ralph took the photocopy out to his secretary, I asked Rossy if he'd attended yesterday's Birnbaum conference. "Friends of mine were involved. I'm wondering if Edelweiss is concerned about the proposed Holocaust Asset Recovery Act."

Rossy put his fingertips together. "Our position is in line with the industry, that however legitimate the grief and the grievances—of both the Jewish and the African-American communities—the expense of a policy search shall be most costly for all policyholders. For our own company, we don't worry about the exposure. Edelweiss was only a small regional insurer during the war, so the likelihood of involvement with large numbers of Jewish claimants is small.

"Of course, now I'm learning that we do have this fifteen-year history of slavery still taking place in America while Ajax was in its early days. And I am just now suggesting to Ralph that we get Ms. Blount, the woman who wrote our little history, to look in the archives so we know who our customers were in those very old days. Assuming she has not already decided to send our archives to this Alderman Durham. But how expensive it is to go back to the past. How very costly, indeed."

"Your history? Oh, that booklet on 'One Hundred Fifty Years of Life.' I have a copy—which I confess I've yet to read. Does it cover Ajax's pre-Emancipation years? Do you really think Ms. Blount would hand your documents to an outsider?"

"Is this the true reason for your visit here? Ralph says you are a detective. Are you doing something very subtle, very Humphrey Bogart, pretending to care about the Sommers claim and trying to trick me with questions about the Holocaust and slavery claims? I did think this little policy was small, small potatoes for you to bring to the director of claims." He smiled widely, inviting me to treat this as a joke if I wanted to.

"I'm sure in Switzerland as well as here people call on those they know," I said. "Ralph and I worked together a number of years ago, before he became so exalted, so I'm taking advantage of our relationship in the hopes of a fast answer for my client."

"*Exalted*'s the word for me," Ralph came back in. "And Vic has such a depressing habit of being right about financial crime that it's easier to go along with her from the start than fight her."

"What crime surrounds this claim, then—what are you correct about today?" Rossy asked.

"So far, nothing, but I haven't had time to consult a psychic yet."

"Psychic?" he repeated doubtfully.

"*Indovina*," I grinned. "They abound in the area where I have my office."

"Ah, psychic," Rossy exclaimed. "I have been pronouncing it wrong all these years. I must remember to tell my wife about this. She is keenly interested in unusual events in my business day. Psychics and nosebleeds. She will enjoy them so much."

I was saved from trying to respond by Ralph's secretary, who ushered in a young woman clutching a thick file. She was wearing khaki jeans and a sweater that had shrunk from too many washings.

"This is Connie Ingram, Mr. Devereux," the secretary said. "She has the information you wanted."

Ralph didn't introduce Rossy or me to Ms. Ingram. She blinked at us unhappily but showed her packet to Ralph.

"This here is all the documents on L-146938-72. I'm sorry about being in my jeans and all, but my supervisor is away, so they told me to bring the file up myself. I printed the financials from off the microfiche, so they aren't as clear as they could be, but I did the best I could."

Bertrand Rossy joined me when I got up to look over her shoulder at the papers. Connie Ingram flipped through the pages until she came to the payment documents.

Ralph pulled them out of the file and studied them. He looked at them for a long moment, then turned to me sternly. "It seems that your client's family was trying to collect twice on the same policy, Vic. We frown on that here."

I took the pages from him. The policy had been paid up in 1986. In 1991, someone had submitted a death certificate. A photocopy of the canceled check was attached. It had been paid to Gertrude Sommers, care of the Midway Insurance Agency, and duly endorsed by them.

For a moment, I was too dumbfounded to speak. The grieving widow must be quite a con artist to convince the nephew into shelling out for his uncle's funeral when she'd collected on the policy a decade ago. But how on earth had she gotten a death certificate back then? My first coherent thought was mean-spirited: I was glad I'd insisted on earnest money up front. I doubted Isaiah Sommers would have paid to learn this bit of news.

"This isn't your idea of a joke, is it, Vic?" Ralph demanded.

He was angry because he thought he looked fool-

ishly incompetent in front of his new master: I wasn't
going to ride him. "Scout's honor, Ralph. The story I
told you is the identical one I got from my client. Have
you ever seen something like this before? A fraudulent
death certificate?"

"It happens." He flicked a glance at Rossy. "Usually
it's someone faking his own death to get away from
creditors. And then the circumstances of the policy—
the size—the timing between when it was sold and
when it was cashed—make us investigate before we
pay. For something like this"—he snapped the canceled
check with his middle finger—"we wouldn't investigate
such a small face value—and one where we'd collected
all the premium years before."

"So the possibility exists? The possibility that people
are submitting claims that aren't rightfully theirs?"
Rossy took the whole file from Ralph and started going
through it one page at a time.

"But the company would only pay once," Ralph
said. "As you can see, we had all the information available when the funeral home submitted the policy, so
we didn't pay the claim twice. I don't suppose anyone
from the agency would have bothered to check
whether the purchaser"—he looked at the tab on the
file—"whether Sommers was really dead when his wife
filed the claim."

Connie Ingram asked doubtfully if she should talk to
her supervisor about calling the agency or the funeral
home. Ralph turned to me. "Are you going to talk to
them anyway, Vic? Will you let Connie know what you
find out? The truth, I mean, not some version that you
want Ajax to learn?"

"If Miss Warshawski is in the habit of hiding her
findings from the company, Ralph, perhaps we
shouldn't trust her with these delicate questions." Rossy
gave me a little bow. "I'm sure you would ask your

questions so skillfully that our agent might be startled into telling you—what he ought to keep between himself and the company."

Ralph started to say that he was only trying to bait me, then sighed and told Connie by all means to ask any questions she needed to reclose the file.

"Ralph, what if someone else filed the claim, someone pretending to be Gertrude Sommers," I said. "Would the company make her whole?"

Ralph rubbed the deepening crease between his eyes. "Don't ask me to make moral decisions without the facts. What if it was her husband—or her kid? He's listed as a secondary beneficiary after her. Or her minister? I'm not going to commit the company to anything until I know the truth."

He was talking to me but looking at Rossy, who was looking at his watch, not at all discreetly. Ralph muttered something about their next appointment. This made me more uneasy even than the fraud over the claim: I don't like my lovers, even long-former lovers, to feel the need to be obsequious.

As I left the office, I asked Ralph for a photocopy of the canceled check and the death certificate. Rossy answered for him. "These are company documents, Devereux."

"But if you don't let me show them to my client, then he has no way of knowing whether I'm lying to him," I said. "You remember the case this last spring, where various life-insurance companies admitted to charging black customers as much as four times the amount they did whites? I assure you, that will leap into my client's mind. And then, instead of me coming around asking for documents in a nice way, you might have a federal lawsuit with a subpoena attached."

Rossy stared at me, suddenly frosty. "If the threat of a lawsuit seems to your mind to be 'asking in a nice way,' then I have to ask myself questions about your business practices."

With the dimples in abeyance, he showed he could be a formidable corporate presence. I smiled and took his hand, turning it to look at the palm. He was startled into standing motionless.

"Signor Rossy, I wasn't threatening you with a lawsuit: I was an *indovina,* reading your fortune, foreseeing an inevitable future."

The frost melted abruptly. "What other things do you divine?"

I put his hand down. "My powers are limited. But you seem to have a long lifeline. Now, with your permission may I copy the canceled check and the death certificate?"

"Forgive my Swiss habits of being unwilling to part with official documents. By all means, make copies of these two papers. But the file as a whole I think I'll keep with me. Just in case your charm makes you more persuasive with this young lady than her normal loyalties would allow you to be."

He gestured at Connie Ingram, who blushed. "Sir, I'm really sorry, sir, but can you fill out a slip for me? I can't let a claim file stay out of our area without a notice of the number and of who has it."

"Ah, so you have respect for documents as well. Excellent. You write down what you need, and I will sign it. Will that fulfill the requirements?"

Her color spreading to her collarbone, Connie Ingram went out to Ralph's secretary to type up what she needed. I followed with the documents I was allowed to have; Ralph's secretary copied them for me.

Ralph walked partway down the hall with me. "Stay in touch, Vic, okay? I would be grateful to hear from you if you learn anything about this business."

"You'll be the second to know," I promised. "You going to be equally forthcoming?"

"Naturally." He grinned, briefly showing a trace of the old Ralph. "And if I remember right, I'm likely to be much more forthcoming than you."

I laughed, but I still felt sad as I waited for the elevator. When the doors finally opened with a subdued *ding*, a young woman in a prim tweed suit stepped off, clutching a tan briefcase to her side. The dreadlocks tidily pulled away from her face made me blink in recognition.

"Ms. Blount—I'm V I Warshawski—we met at the Ajax gala a month ago."

She nodded and briefly touched my fingertips. "I need to be in a meeting."

"Ah, yes: with Bertrand Rossy." I thought of putting her on her guard against Rossy's accusation that she was siphoning off company documents for Bull Durham, but she whisked herself down the hall toward Ralph's office before I could make up my mind.

The elevator that brought her had left. Before another arrived, Connie Ingram joined me, her paperwork apparently finished.

"Mr. Rossy seems very protective of his documents," I commented.

"We can't afford to misplace any paper around here," she said primly. "People can sue us if we don't have our records in tiptop shape."

"Are you worried about a suit from the Sommers family?"

"Mr. Devereux said the agent was responsible for the claim. So it's not our problem here at the company, but of course he and Mr. Rossy—"

She stopped, red-faced, as if remembering Rossy's comment about my persuasive charms. The elevator arrived and she scurried into it. It was twelve-forty, heart of the lunch hour. The elevator stopped every two or three floors to take in people before making its express descent from forty to the ground. I wondered what indiscretion she had bitten back, but there wasn't any way I could pump her.

VII

Cold Call

Something there is that doesn't love a fence," I muttered as I boarded the northbound L. Lots of people on the train were muttering to themselves: I fit right in. "When someone is guarding documents, is it because his corporate culture is obsessive, as Rossy said? Or because there's something in them he doesn't want me to see?"

"Because he's in the pay of the U-nited Nations," the man next to me said. "They're bringing in tanks. Those U-nited Nations helie-copters landing in Dee-troit, I seen them on TV."

"You're right," I said to his beery face. "It's definitely a UN plot. So you think I should go down to Midway Insurance, talk to the agent, see if my charms are persuasive enough to wangle a look at the sales file?"

"Your charms plenty persuasive enough for me," he leered.

That was esteem-enhancing. When I got off the train at Western, I picked up my car and immediately headed south again. Down in Hyde Park, I found a meter with forty minutes on it on one of the side streets near the bank where Midway Insurance had their offices. The bank building itself was the neighborhood's venerable dowager, its ten stories towering over Hyde Park's main shopping street. The facade had recently been cleaned up, but once I got off the elevator onto the sixth floor, the dim lights and dingy walls betrayed a management indifference to tenant comfort.

Midway Insurance was wedged between a dentist and a gynecologist. The black letters on the door, telling me they insured life, home, and auto, had been there a long time: part of the *H* in *Home* had peeled away, so that it looked as though Midway insured *nome*.

The door was locked, but when I rang the bell someone buzzed me in. The office beyond was even drearier than the hall. The flickering fluorescent light was so dim that I didn't notice a peeling corner of linoleum until I'd tripped on it. I grabbed at a filing cabinet to keep from falling.

"Sorry—I keep meaning to fix that." I hadn't noticed the man until he spoke—he was sitting at a desk that took up most of the room, but the light was bad enough I hadn't seen him when I opened the door.

"I hope you buy premises insurance, because you're inviting a nasty suit if you don't glue that down," I snapped, coming all the way into the room.

He turned on a desk lamp, revealing a face with freckles so thick that they formed an orange carpet across his face. At my words the carpet turned a deeper red.

"I don't get much walk-in business," he explained. "Most of the time we're in the field."

I looked around, but there wasn't a desk for a second person. I moved a phone book from the only other chair and sat down. "You have partners? Subordinates?"

"I inherited the business from my dad. He died three years ago, but I keep forgetting that. I think the business is going to die, too. I never have been much good with cold calls, and now the Internet is killing independent agents."

Mentioning the Internet reminded him that his computer was on. He flicked a key to start the screensaver, but before the fish began cascading I saw he'd been playing some kind of solitaire.

The computer was the only newish item in the room. His desk was a heavy yellow wooden one, the kind popular fifty years ago, with two rows of drawers framing a kneehole for the user's legs. Black stains from decades of grime, coffee, ink, and who knows what scarred the yellow in the places I could see it—most of the surface was covered in a depressing mass of paper. My own office looked monastic by comparison.

Four large filing cabinets took up most of the remaining space. A curling poster of the Chinese national table-tennis team provided the only decoration. A large pot hung from a chain above the window, but the plant within had withered down to a few drying leaves.

He sat up and tried to put a semblance of energy into his tone. "What can I do for you?"

"I'm V I Warshawski." I handed him one of my cards. "And you are?"

"Fepple. Howard Fepple." He looked at my card. "Oh. The detective. They told me you'd be calling."

I looked at my watch. It had been just over an hour since I left Ajax. Someone in the company had moved fast.

"Who told you that? Bertrand Rossy?"

"I don't know the name. It was one of the girls in claims."

"Women," I corrected irritably.

"Whatever. Anyway, she told me you'd be asking about one of our old policies. Which I can't tell you anything about, because I was in high school when it was sold."

"So you looked it up? What did it tell you about who cashed it in?"

He leaned back in his chair, the man at ease. "I can't see why that's any of your business."

I grinned evilly, all ideas about charm and persuasion totally forgotten. "The Sommers family, whom I represent, have an interest in this matter that could be satisfied by a federal lawsuit. Involving subpoenas for the files and suing the agency for fraud. Maybe your father sold the policy to Aaron Sommers back in 1971, but you own the agency now. It wouldn't be the Internet that would finish you off."

His fleshy lips pursed together in a pout. "For your information it wasn't my father who sold the policy but Rick Hoffman, who worked for him here."

"So where can I find Mr. Hoffman?"

He smirked. "Wherever you look for the dead. But I don't imagine old Rick ended up in heaven. He was a mean SOB. How he did as well as he did . . ." He shrugged eloquently.

"You mean unlike you he wasn't afraid of the cold call?"

"He was a Friday man. You know, going into the poor neighborhoods on Friday afternoons collecting after people got paid. A lot of our business is life insurance like that, small face value, enough to get someone buried right and leave a little for the family. It's all someone like this Sommers could probably afford, ten thousand, although that was big by our standards, usually they're only three or four thousand."

"So Hoffman collected from Aaron Sommers. Had he paid up the policy?"

Fepple tapped a file on top of the mess of papers. "Oh, yes. Yes, it took him fifteen years, but it was paid in full. The beneficiaries were his wife, Gertrude, and his son, Marcus."

"So who cashed it in? And if they did, how come the family still had the policy?"

Looking at me resentfully, Fepple started through the file, page by page. He stopped at one point, staring at a document, his lips moving soundlessly. A little smile flickered at the corners of his mouth, an unpleasant, secretive smile, but after a moment he continued the search. Finally he pulled out the same documents I'd already seen at the company: a copy of the death certificate and a copy of the countersigned check.

"What else was in the file?" I asked.

"Nothing," he said quickly. "There was nothing unusual about it at all. Rick did a zillion of these little weekend sales. There's no surprise to them."

I didn't believe him, but I didn't have a way to call his bluff. "Not much of a way to make a living, three-and four-thousand-dollar sales."

"Rick did real well for himself. He knew how to work the angles, I'll tell you that much."

"And what you're not telling me?"

"I'm not telling you my private business. You've barged in here without an appointment, fishing around for dirt, but you don't have any grounds to ask questions. And don't go waving federal lawsuits at me. If there was any funny business about this, it was the company's responsibility, not mine."

"Did Hoffman have any family?"

"A son. I don't know what happened to him—he was a whole lot older than me, and he and old Rick didn't hit it off too great. I had to go to the funeral, with my old man, and we were the only damned people in the church. The son was long gone by then."

"So who inherited Hoffman's share of the business?"

Fepple shook his head. "He wasn't a partner. He

worked for my old man. Strictly commission, but—he did well."

"So why don't you pick up his client list and carry on for him?"

The nasty little smile reappeared. "I might just do that very thing. I didn't realize until the company called me what a little gold mine Rick's way of doing business represented."

I wanted to see that file badly, but short of grabbing it from the desk and running off down the stairs into the arms of the guard in the lobby, I couldn't think of any way to look at it. At least, not at the moment. As I left, I tripped again on the corner of the linoleum. If Fepple didn't fix it soon I'd be suing him myself.

Since I was already south, I went on another two miles to Sixty-seventh Street, where the Delaney Funeral Parlor stood. It was in an imposing white building, easily the grandest on the block, with four hearses parked in the lot behind it. I left my Mustang next to them and went in to see what I could learn.

Old Mr. Delaney talked to me himself, about how sorry they were to have had to inflict such grief on a sweet decent woman like Sister Sommers but that he couldn't afford to bury people for charity: if you did it once, every freeloader on the South Side would be coming around with some story or other about their insurance falling through. As to how he'd learned that Sommers's policy had already been cashed in, they had a simple procedure with the life-insurance companies. They had called, given the policy number, and been told that the policy had already been paid. I asked who he'd spoken to.

"I don't give anything away free, young lady," Mr. Delaney said austerely. "If you want to pursue your own inquiries at the company, I urge you to do so, but don't expect me to give you for nothing information I spent my hard-earned money finding out. All I will tell you is that it isn't the first time this has happened, that a bereaved family has discovered that their loved one had disposed of his resources without privileging them with the information. It isn't a regular occurrence, but families are often sadly surprised at the behavior of their loved ones. Human nature can be all too human."

"A lesson I'm sure Gertrude Sommers and her nephew learned at Aaron Sommers's funeral," I said, getting up to leave.

He bowed his head mournfully, as if unaware of the bite behind my words. He hadn't gotten to be one of the richest men in South Shore by apologizing for his rigorous business methods.

VIII

Tales of Hoffman

The score so far today seemed to be Warshawski zero, visitors three. I hadn't gotten any satisfaction from Ajax, or the Midway Agency, or the funeral director. While I was south, I might as well complete my sweep of frustrating meetings by visiting the widow.

She lived a few blocks from the Dan Ryan Expressway, in a rickety twelve-flat with a burnt-out building on one side and a lot with bits of masonry and rusted-out cars on the other. A couple of guys were leaning over the engine of an elderly Chevy when I pulled up. The only other person on the street was a fierce-looking woman muttering as she sucked from a brown paper bag.

The Sommerses' doorbell didn't seem to work, but the street door hung loosely on its hinges, so I went on into the building. The stairwell smelled of urine and stale grease. Dogs barked from behind several doors as I passed, briefly overwhelming the thin hopeless wail of a baby. I was so depressed by the time I reached Gertrude Sommers's door that I was hard put to knock instead of beating a craven retreat.

A few minutes passed. Finally I heard a slow step

and a deep voice calling to know who it was. I told her my name, that I was the detective her nephew had hired. She scraped back the three dead bolts holding the door and stood in the entrance for a moment, looking me over somberly before letting me in.

Gertrude Sommers was a tall woman. Even in old age she was a good two inches taller than my five-eight, and even in grief she held herself erect. She was wearing a dark dress that rustled when she walked. A black lace handkerchief, tucked in the cuff of her left sleeve, underscored her mourning. Looking at her made me feel grubby in my work-worn skirt and sweater.

I followed her into the apartment's main room, standing until she pointed regally at the sofa. The bright floral upholstery was shielded in heavy plastic, which crackled loudly when I sat down.

The building's squalor ended on her doorstep. Every surface that wasn't encased in plastic shone with polish, from the dining table against the far wall to the clock with its fake chimes over the television. The walls were hung with pictures, many of the same smiling child, and a formal shot of my client and his wife on their wedding day. To my surprise, Alderman Durham was on the wall—once in a solo shot, and again with his arms around two young teens in his blue Empower Youth Energy sweatshirts. One of the boys was leaning on metal crutches, but both were beaming proudly.

"I'm sorry for your loss, Ms. Sommers. And sorry for the terrible mix-up over your husband's life insurance."

She folded her lips tightly. She wasn't going to help.

I plowed ahead as best I could, laying the photocopies of the fraudulent death certificate and canceled insurance check in front of her. "I'm bewildered by this situation. I'm wondering if you have any suggestions about how it could have occurred."

She refused to look at the documents. "How much did they pay you to come here and accuse me?"

"No one paid me to do that, and no one could pay me to do that, Ms. Sommers."

"Easy words, easy words for you to say, young woman."

"True enough." I paused, trying to feel my way into her point of view. "My mother died when I was fifteen. If some stranger had cashed in her burial policy and then accused my dad of doing it, well, I can imagine what he would have done, and he was an easygoing guy. But if I can't ask you any questions about this, how am I ever going to find out who cashed this policy all those years ago?"

She clamped her lips together, thinking it over, then said, "Have you talked to the insurance man, that Mr. Hoffman who came around every Friday afternoon before Mr. Sommers could spend his pay on drink, or whatever he imagined a poor black man would do instead of putting food on his family's table?"

"Mr. Hoffman is dead. The agency is in the hands of the previous owner's son, who doesn't seem to know too much about the business. Did Mr. Hoffman treat your husband with disrespect?"

She sniffed. "We weren't people to him. We were ticks in that book he carried around with him. Driving up in that big Mercedes like he did, we knew just where our hard-saved nickels went. And no way to question whether he was honest or not."

"You think now he cheated you?"

"How else do you explain this?" She slapped the papers on the table, still without looking at them. "You think I am deaf, dumb, and blind? I know what goes on in this country with black folk and insurance. I read how that company in the south got caught charging black folk more than their policies were worth."

"Did that happen to you?"

"No. But we paid. We paid and we paid and we paid. All to have it go up in smoke."

"If you didn't file the claim in 1991, and you don't think your husband did, who would have?" I asked.

She shook her head, but her gaze inadvertently went to the wall of photographs.

I drew a breath. "This isn't easy to ask, but your son was listed on the policy."

Her look scorched me. "My son, my son died. It was because of him we went after a bigger policy, thinking to leave him a little something besides our funerals, Mr. Sommers's and mine. Muscular dystrophy, our boy had. And in case you're thinking, Oh, well, they cashed the policy to pay his medical bills, let me tell you, miss, Mr. Sommers worked two shifts for four years, paying those bills. I had to quit my job to take care of my son when he got too sick to move anymore. After he passed, I worked two shifts, too, to get rid of the bills. At the nursing home where I was an aide. If you're going to pry into all my private details you can have that one without charging my nephew a nickel for it: the Grand Crossing Elder Care Home. But you can go snooping through my life. Maybe I have a secret *drinking* vice— you'll go ask them at the church where I became a Christian and where my husband was a deacon for forty-five years. Maybe Mr. Sommers *gambled* and used all my housekeeping money. That's the way you plan on ruining my reputation, isn't it."

I looked at her steadily. "So you won't let me ask you any questions about the policy. And you can't think of anyone who might have cashed it in. You don't have other nephews or nieces besides Mr. Isaiah Sommers who might have?"

Again her gaze turned to the wall. On an impulse, I asked her who the other boy was in the picture of Alderman Durham with her son.

"That's my nephew Colby. And no, you're not getting a shot along with the cops to pin something on him, nor yet on the alderman's Empower Youth Energy organization. Alderman Durham has been a good friend, to my family and to this neighborhood. And his group gives boys something to do with their time and energy."

It didn't seem like the right time or place to ask about the rumors that EYE members hustled campaign contributions with a judicious use of muscle. I turned back to the papers in front of us and asked about Rick Hoffman.

"What was he like? Can you imagine him stealing the policy from you?"

"Oh, what do I know about him? Except, like I said, his leather book that he ticked off our names in. He could have been Adolf Hitler for all I know."

"Did he sell insurance to a lot of people in this building?" I persisted.

"And why do you want to know that?"

"I'd like to find out if other people who bought from him had the same experience you did."

At that she finally looked at me, instead of through me. "In this building, no. At where Aaron—Mr. Sommers—worked, yes. My husband was at South Branch Scrap Metal. Mr. Hoffman knew people want to be buried decent, so he came around to places like that on the South Side, must have had ten or twenty businesses he'd hit on Friday afternoon. Sometimes he'd collect at the shop yard, sometimes he'd come here, it all depended on his schedule. And Aaron, Mr. Sommers, he paid his five dollars a week for fifteen years, until he was paid up."

"Would you have any way of knowing the names of some of the other people who bought from Hoffman?"

She studied me again, trying to assess whether this was a soft sell, and deciding finally to take a chance that I was being genuine. "I could give you four names, the men my husband worked with. They all bought from Hoffman because he made it easy, coming around like he did. Does this mean you understand I'm telling the truth about this?" She swept a hand toward my documents, still without looking at them.

I grimaced. "I have to consider all the possibilities, Ms. Sommers."

She eyed me bitterly. "I know my nephew meant it for the best, hiring you, but if he'd known how little respect you'd have—"

"I'm not disrespecting you, Ms. Sommers. You told your nephew you'd talk to me. You know the kinds of questions this must raise: there's a death certificate with your husband's name on it, with your name on it as the presenter, dated almost ten years ago, with a check made out to you through the Midway Insurance Agency. Someone cashed it. If I'm going to find out who, I have to start somewhere. It would help me believe you if I could find other people this same thing happened to."

Her face pinched up with anger, but after sitting in silence while the clock ticked off thirty seconds, she pulled a lined notepad from under the telephone. Wetting her index finger, she turned the pages of a weather-beaten address book and finally wrote down a series of names. Still without speaking, she handed the list to me.

The interview was over. I picked my way back along the unlit hall and down the stairs. The baby was still wailing. Outside, the men were still huddled over the Chevy.

When I unlocked the Mustang the men shouted over a jovial offer to trade. I grinned and waved. Oh, the kindness of strangers. It was only when people talked to me they got so hostile. There was a lesson in there for me, but not one I particularly wished to pursue.

It was almost three: I hadn't eaten since my yogurt at eight this morning. Maybe the situation would seem less depressing if I had some food. I passed a strip mall on my way to the expressway and bought a slice of cheese pizza. The crust was gooey, the surface glistened with oil, but I ate every bite with gusto. When I got out of my car at the office I realized I'd dripped oil down the front of my rose silk sweater. Warshawski zero, visitors five, at this point. At least I didn't have any business meetings this afternoon.

My part-time assistant, Mary Louise Neely, was at her desk. She handed me a packet with the video of the Radbuka interviews, which Beth Blacksin had messengered over. I stuffed it in my briefcase and brought Mary Louise up to date with the Sommers case, so she could check on the other men who had bought insurance from Rick Hoffman, then told her about Don's interest in Paul Radbuka.

"I couldn't find anyone named Radbuka in the system," I finished, "so either—"

"Vic—if he changed his name, he had to do so in front of a judge. There will be a court order." Mary Louise looked at me as though I were the village idiot.

I gaped at her like a dying pike and meekly went to turn on my computer. It was small comfort that if Radbuka or Ulrich or whatever his name was had taken any legal action, it wasn't in the system yet: I should have thought of that myself.

Mary Louise, not wanting to go stomping far and wide through the city, didn't believe Radbuka wasn't somewhere in the system. She did her own search and then said she would stop at the courts in the morning to double-check the paper record.

"Although maybe the therapist will tell you where to find him. What's her name?"

When I told her, her eyes opened wide. "Rhea Wiell? *The* Rhea Wiell?"

"You know her?" I spun around in my chair to face her.

"Not personally." Mary Louise's skin turned the same orangy pink as her hair. "But because, you know, because of my own story, I followed her career. I sat in on some of the trials where she testified."

Mary Louise had run away from an abusive home when she was a teenager. After a tumultuous ride through sex and drugs, she'd pulled herself together and become a police officer. In fact, the three children she was fostering had been rescued from an abusive home. So it wasn't surprising she paid special attention to a therapist who worked with molested children.

"Wiell used to be with the State Department of Children and Family Services. She was one of the staff therapists, she worked with kids, but she also was an expert witness in court cases that hinged on abuse. Remember the MacLean trial?"

As Mary Louise described it, the details began coming back to me. The guy was a law professor who'd started life as a Du Page County criminal prosecutor. When his name was put forward for a federal judgeship, his daughter, by then a grown woman, came forward to denounce him as having raped her when she was a child. She was insistent enough that she forced the state to bring charges.

Various right-wing family foundations had ridden to MacLean's rescue, claiming the daughter was the mouthpiece of a liberal smear campaign, since the father was a conservative Republican. In the end, the jury in the criminal sexual-assault trial found for the father, but his name was dropped from consideration for the judgeship.

"And Wiell testified?" I asked Mary Louise.

"More than that. She was the daughter's therapist. It was working with Rhea Wiell that made the woman recover the memories of abuse, when she'd blocked them for twenty years. The defense brought in Arnold Praeger from the Planted Memory Foundation. He tried all kinds of cheap shots to make her look bad, but he couldn't shake her." Mary Louise glowed with admiration.

"So Praeger and Wiell go back a ways together."

"I don't know about that, but they definitely have been adversaries in court for quite a few years."

"I put in a search to ProQuest before I left this morning. If their fights have been in the news, I should have the stories." I brought up my ProQuest search. Mary Louise came to read over my shoulder. The case she had mentioned had generated a lot of ink at the time. I skimmed a couple of pieces in the *Herald-Star,* which praised Wiell's unflappable testimony.

Mary Louise bristled with anger over an op-ed piece Arnold Praeger had run in *The Wall Street Journal,* criticizing both Wiell and the law, which would allow the testimony of young children who had clearly been coached in what they remembered. Wiell wasn't even a reputable therapist, Praeger concluded. If she was, why had the State of Illinois dropped her from its payroll?

"Dropped her?" I said to Mary Louise, sending the piece to the printer with several of the others. "Do you know about that?"

"No. I assumed she decided private practice was a better place to be. Sooner or later, just about everyone gets burned out working for DCFS." Mary Louise's pale eyes were troubled. "I thought she was a really good, really genuine therapist. I can't believe the state would fire her, or at least not for any good reason. Maybe out of spite. She was the best they had, but there's always a lot of jealousy in offices like that. When I saw her in court, I used to imagine she was my mother. In fact, I was incredibly jealous of a woman I met who saw her professionally."

She laughed in embarrassment. "I've got to go, time

for me to pick up the kids before class. I'll do those Sommers queries first thing tomorrow. You filling in your time sheets?"

"Yes, ma'am," I saluted her smartly.

"It's not a joke, Vic," she said sternly. "It's the only way—"

"I know, I know." Mary Louise doesn't like to be teased, which can be boring—but probably also is why she's such a good office manager.

When Mary Louise had left, promising to stop by the courts to check for Radbuka's change-of-name filing, I called a lawyer I knew in the State Department of Children and Family Services. We'd met at a seminar on women and law in the public sector and kept in touch in a desultory way.

She referred me to a supervisor in the DCFS office who would speak if it was far off the record. The supervisor wanted to call me back from a pay phone, in case her desk line was being monitored. I had to wait until five, when the woman stopped at a public phone in the basement of the Illinois Center on her way home. Before she'd tell me anything, my informant made me swear I wasn't calling on behalf of the Planted Memory Foundation.

"Not everyone at DCFS believes in hypnotherapy, but nobody here wants to see our clients hurt by one of those Planted Memory lawsuits."

When I assured her, by running through a list of possible references until I hit on a name she knew and trusted, she was amazingly frank. "Rhea was the most empathic therapist we ever used. She got incredible results from kids who would hardly even give their names to other therapists. I still miss her when we have certain kinds of trauma cases. The trouble was, she began to see herself as the priestess of DCFS. You couldn't question her results or her judgment.

"I don't remember exactly when she started her private practice, maybe six years ago, doing it part-time. But it was three years ago when we decided to sever her contract with the state. The press release said it was her decision, that she wanted to concentrate on her practice, but the feeling here was that she wouldn't take direction. She was always right; we—or the state attorney general, or anyone who disagreed with her—were wrong. And you can't have a staff person, someone you rely on with kids and in court, who always wants to be Joan of Arc."

"Did you think she might misrepresent a situation for her own glory?" I asked.

"Oh, no. Nothing like that. She wasn't out for glory—she was on a mission. I'm telling you, some of the younger women started calling her Mother Teresa, and not always out of admiration. Actually, that was part of the problem; she split the office straight in half between Rhea worshipers and Rhea doubters. And then she wouldn't let you question how she came to a conclusion. Like in that one case where the guy she was accusing of molestation was a former prosecutor who'd been nominated for a federal judgeship. Rhea wouldn't let us see her case notes before she testified. If the case had backfired, we could have been facing a ton of damages."

I thumbed through my stack of printouts. "Wasn't the daughter who brought the charges part of Wiell's private practice?"

"Yes, but Rhea was still on the state payroll, so the guy could have claimed she was using state office space or facilities for photocopying or whatnot—anything like that would have brought us into a lawsuit. We couldn't afford that kind of exposure. We had to let her go. Now you tell me, since I've been so frank with you, what's Rhea done that means a PI is interested in her?"

I'd known I'd have to cough up something. Tit for tat, it's how you keep information coming to you. "One of her clients was in the news this week. I don't know if you saw the guy with the recovered memories from the Holocaust? Someone wants to write a book about him and about how Rhea works. I've been asked to do some background checking."

"One thing Rhea knows better than any other therapist who ever worked for this office, and that's how to attract attention." My informant hung up smartly.

IX

Princess of Austria

So she is a legitimate therapist. Controversial but legitimate," I said to the glowing tip of Don's cigarette. "If you did a book with her, you wouldn't be signing on with a fraud."

"Actually, they're excited enough in New York that I went ahead and scheduled an appointment with the lady. Tomorrow at eleven. If you're free, want to sit in on it? Maybe she'll allow you to bring back a report to Dr. Herschel that will help you allay her concerns."

"Under the circumstances I can't imagine that happening. But I would like to meet Rhea Wiell."

We were sitting on Morrell's back porch. It was close to ten, but Morrell was still downtown at a meeting with some State Department officials—I had an uneasy feeling they were trying to persuade him to do some spying while he was in Kabul. I was wrapped in one of Morrell's old sweaters, drawing some small comfort from it—which made me feel like Mitch and Peppy— the dogs like to have my old socks to play with when I'm out of town. Lotty had brought my day to such a ragged end that I needed what comfort I could find.

I'd been running since I kissed Morrell good-bye this

morning. Even though I still had a dozen urgent tasks, I was too tired to keep going. Before dictating my case notes, before calling Isaiah Sommers, before going home to run the dogs, before heading back to Morrell's place with a contract for Don Strzepek to cover my queries about Rhea Wiell, I needed to rest. Just half an hour on the portable bed in my back room, I'd thought. Half an hour would make me fit enough to cram another day's work into the evening. It was almost ninety minutes later that my client roused me.

"What made you go down to my aunt with all those accusations?" he demanded when the phone dragged me awake. "Couldn't you respect her widowhood?"

"What accusations?" My mouth and eyes felt as though they'd been stuffed with cotton.

"Going to her home and saying she stole money from the insurance company."

If I hadn't been bleary from my nap I might have answered more coolly. But maybe not.

"I will make every allowance for your aunt's grief, but that is not what I said. And before you call to accuse me of such abominable behavior, why don't you ask me what I said."

"All right. I'm asking you." His voice was leaden with suppressed anger.

"I showed your aunt the canceled check the company issued when a death claim was submitted nine years ago. I asked her what she knew about it. That is not an accusation. A check for her had been made out in care of the Midway Insurance Agency. I couldn't pretend her name wasn't on the check. I couldn't pretend Ajax hadn't issued it based on a bona fide death certificate. I had to ask her about it."

"You should have talked to me first. I'm the person who paid you."

"I cannot consult with clients about every step I take in an investigation. I'd never get anything done."

"You took my money. You spent it on accusing my aunt. Your contract says I can terminate our arrangement at any time. I am terminating it now."

"Fine," I snapped. "Terminate away. Someone committed fraud with your uncle's policy. If you want them to get away with it, so be it."

"Of course I don't want that, but I'll look into the matter on my own, in a way that will respect my aunt. I should have known a white detective would act just like the police. I should have listened to my wife." He hung up.

It wasn't the first time an angry client had fired me, but I've never learned to take it with equanimity. I could have done things differently. I should have called him, called him before I went to see his aunt, gotten him on my side. Or at least called him before I went to sleep. I could have kept my temper—my besetting sin.

I tried to remember exactly what I'd said to his aunt. Damn it, I should do as Mary Louise said, dictate my notes as soon as I finished a meeting. Better late than never: I could start with my phone conversation with the client. Ex-client. I dialed up the word-processing service I use and dictated a summary of the call, adding a letter to Sommers confirming that he'd canceled my services; I'd enclose his uncle's policy with the letter. When I'd finished with Isaiah Sommers, I dictated notes from my other conversations of the day, working backward from my informant at Family Services to my meeting with Ralph at Ajax.

Lotty called on the other line when I was halfway through reconstructing my encounter with the insurance agent Howard Fepple. "Max told me about the program he saw with you at Morrell's last night," she said, without preamble. "It sounded very disturbing."

"It was."

"He didn't know whether to believe the man's story or not. Did Morrell make a tape of the interview?"

"Not that I know of. I got a copy of the tape today, which I can—"

"I want to see it. Will you bring it to my apartment this evening, please." It came out as a command, not a request.

"Lotty, this isn't your operating room. I don't have time to stop at your place tonight, but in the morning I—"

"This is a very simple favor, Victoria, which has nothing to do with my operating room. You don't need to leave the tape with me, but I want to see it. You can stand over me while I watch it."

"Lotty, I don't have the time. I will get copies made tomorrow and let you have one of your very own. But this one is for a client who hired me to investigate the situation."

"A client?" She was outraged. "Did Max hire you without either of you talking to me?"

My forehead felt as though it were squeezed inside a vise. "If he did, that's between him and me, not you and me. What difference does it make to you?"

"What difference? That he violated a trust, that's what matters. When he told me about this person at the conference, this man calling himself Radbuka, I said we shouldn't act hastily and that I would give him my opinion after I had seen the interview."

I took a deep breath and tried to bring my brain into focus. "So the Radbuka name means something to you."

"And to Max. And to Carl. From our days in London. Max thought we should hire you to find out about this man. I wanted to wait. I thought Max respected my opinion."

She was almost spitting mad, but her explanation made me say gently, "Take it easy, Lotty. Max didn't hire me. This is a separate matter."

I told her about Don Strzepek's interest in doing a book about Rhea Wiell, showcasing Paul Radbuka's recovered memory. "I'm sure he wouldn't object to sharing the tape with you, but I really don't have time to do it tonight. I still need to finish some work here, go to my own place to look after the dogs, and then I'm going up to Evanston. Do you want me to tell Morrell that you'll be coming up to view the tape at his place?"

"I want the dead past to bury the dead," she burst out. "Why are you letting this Don go digging around in it?"

"I'm not letting him, and I'm not stopping him. All I'm doing is checking to see whether Rhea Wiell is a genuine therapist."

"Then you're letting, not stopping."

She sounded close to tears. I picked my words carefully. "I can only begin to imagine how painful it must be to you to be reminded of the war years, but not everyone feels that way."

"Yes, to many people it is a game. Something to romanticize or kitschify or use for titillation. And a book about a ghoul feasting on the remains of the dead only helps make that happen."

"If Paul Radbuka is not a ghoul but has a genuine past in the concentration camp he mentioned, then he has a right to claim his heritage. What does the person in your group who's connected to the Radbukas say about this? Did you talk to him? Or her?"

"That person no longer exists," she said harshly. "This is between Max and Carl and me. And now you. And now this journalist, Don whoever he is. And the therapist. And every jackal in New York and Hollywood who will pick over the bones and salivate with pleasure at another shocking tale. Publishers and movie studios make fortunes from titillating the comfortable well-fed middle class of Europe and America with tales of torture."

I had never heard Lotty speak in such a bitter way. It hurt, as if my fingers were being run through a grater. I didn't know what to say, except to repeat my offer to bring her a copy of the tape the next day. She hung up on me.

I sat at my desk a long time, blinking back tears of my own. My arms ached. I lacked the will to move or act in any meaningful way, but in the end, I picked up the phone and continued dictating my notes to the word-processing center. When I had finished that, I got up slowly, like an invalid, and printed out a copy of my contract for Don Strzepek.

"Maybe if I talked to Dr. Herschel myself," Don said now, as we sat on Morrell's porch. "She's imagining me as a TV reporter sticking a mike in front of her face after her family's been destroyed. She's right in a way, about how we comfortable Americans and Europeans like to titillate ourselves with tales of torture. I shall have to keep that thought in mind as a corrective when I'm working on this book. All the same, maybe I can persuade her that I also have some capacity for empathy."

"Maybe. Max will probably let me bring you to his dinner party on Sunday; at least you could meet Lotty in an informal way."

I didn't really see it, though. Usually, when Lotty got on her high horse, Max would snort and say she was in her "Princess of Austria" mode. That would spark another flare from her, but she'd back away from her more extreme demands. Tonight's outburst had been rawer than that—not the disdain of a Hapsburg princess, but a ragged fury born of grief.

Lotty Herschel's Story:
Four Gold Coins

My mother was seven months pregnant and weak from hunger, so my father took Hugo and me to the train. It was early in the morning, still dark, in fact: we Jews were trying not to attract any more attention than necessary. Although we had permits to leave, all our documents, the tickets, we could still be stopped at any second. I wasn't yet ten and Hugo only five, but we knew the danger so well we didn't need Papa's command to be silent in the streets.

Saying good-bye to my mother and Oma had frightened me. My mother used to spend weeks away from us with Papa, but I had never left Oma before. By then of course everyone was living together in a little flat in the Leopoldsgasse—I can't remember how many aunts and cousins now, besides my grandparents—but at least twenty.

In London, lying in the cold room at the top of the house, on the narrow iron bed Minna considered appropriate for a child, I wouldn't think about the cramped space on the Leopoldsgasse. I concentrated on remembering Oma and Opa's beautiful flat where I had my own white lacy bed, the curtains at the window dotted

with rosebuds. My school, where my friend Klara and I
were always one and two in the class. How hurt I was—I
couldn't understand why she stopped playing with me and
then why I had to leave the school altogether.

I had whined at first over sharing a room with six other
cousins in a place with peeling paint, but Papa took me for
a walk early one morning so he could talk to me alone
about our changed circumstances. He was never cruel, not
like Uncle Arthur, Mama's brother who actually beat Aunt
Freia, besides hitting his own children.

We walked along the canal as the sun was rising and
Papa explained how hard things were for everyone, for
Oma and Opa, forced out of the family flat after all these
years, and for Mama, with all her pretty jewels stolen by
the Nazis and worrying about how her children would be
fed and clothed, let alone educated. "Lottchen, you are the
big girl in the family now. Your cheerful spirit is Mama's
most precious gift. Show her you are the brave one, the
cheerful one, and now that she's sick with the new baby
coming, show her you can help her by not complaining
and by taking care of Hugo."

What shocks me now is knowing that my father's
parents were also in that flat and how little I remember of
them. In fact, I'm pretty sure that it was their flat. They
were foreign, you see, from Belarus: they were part of the
vast throng of Eastern European Jews who had flocked into
Vienna around the time of the First World War.

Oma and Opa looked down on them. It confuses me,
that realization, because I loved my mother's parents so
much. They doted on me, too: I was their precious
Lingerl's beloved child. But I think Oma and Opa despised
Papa's parents, for speaking only Yiddish, not German, and
for their odd clothes and religious practices.

It was a terrible humiliation for Oma and Opa, when
they were forced to leave the Renngasse to live in that
immigrant Jewish quarter. People used to call it the
Matzoinsel, the matzo island, a term of contempt. Even

Oma and Opa, when they didn't think Papa was around, would talk about his family on the Insel. Oma would laugh her ladylike laugh at the fact that Papa's mother wore a wig, and I felt guilty, because I was the one who had revealed this primitive practice to Oma. She liked to interrogate me about the "customs on the Insel" after I had been there, and then she would remind me that I was a Herschel, I was to stand up straight and make something of my life. And not to use the Yiddish I picked up on the Insel; that was vulgar and Herschels were never vulgar.

Papa would take me to visit his parents once a month or so. I was supposed to call them Zeyde and Bobe, Grandpa and Grandma in Yiddish, as Opa and Oma are in German. When I think about them now I grow hot with shame, for withholding from them the affection and respect they desired: Papa was their only son, I was the oldest grandchild. But even to call them Zeyde and Bobe, as they requested, seemed disgusting to me. And Bobe's blond wig over her close-cropped black hair, that seemed disgusting as well.

I hated that I looked like Papa's side of the family. My mother was so lovely, very fair, with beautiful curls and a mischievous smile. And as you can see, I am dark, and not at all beautiful. *Mischlinge*, cousin Minna called me, half-breed, although never in front of my grandparents: to Opa and Oma I was always beautiful, because I was their darling Lingerl's daughter. It wasn't until I came to live with Minna in England that I ever felt ugly.

What torments me is that I can't recall my father's sisters or their children at all. I shared a bed with five or maybe six cousins, and I can't remember them, only that I hated not being in my own lovely white bedroom by myself. I remember kissing Oma and weeping, but I didn't even say good-bye to Bobe.

You think I should remember I was only a child? No. Even a child has the capacity for human and humane behavior.

Each child was allowed one small suitcase for the train. Oma wanted us to take leather valises from her own luggage—those had not been of interest to the Nazis when they stole her silver and her jewels. But Opa was more practical and understood Hugo and I mustn't attract attention by looking as though we came from a rich home. He found us cheap cardboard cases, which anyway were easier for young children to carry.

By the day the train left, Hugo and I had packed and repacked our few possessions many times, trying to decide what we couldn't bear to live without. The night before we left, Opa took the dress I was going to wear on the train out to Oma. Everyone was asleep, except me: I was lying rigid with nervousness in the bed I shared with the other cousins. When Opa came in I watched him through slits in my closed eyes. When he tiptoed out with the dress, I slid out of bed and followed him to my grandmother's side. Oma put a finger on her lips when she saw me and silently picked apart the waistband. She took four gold coins from the hem of her own skirt and stitched them into the waist, underneath the buttons.

"These are your security," Opa said. "Tell no one, not Hugo, not Papa, not anyone. You won't know when you will need them." He and Oma didn't want to cause friction in the family by letting them know they had a small emergency hoard. If the aunts and uncles knew Lingerl's children were getting four precious gold coins—well, when people are frightened and living too close together, anything can happen.

The next thing I knew Papa was shaking me awake, giving me a cup of the weak tea we all drank for breakfast. Some adult had found enough canned milk for each child to get a tablespoon in it most mornings.

If I had realized I wouldn't see any of them again—but it was hard enough to leave, to go to a strange country where we knew only cousin Minna, and only that she was a bitter woman who made all the children uncomfortable

when she came to Kleinsee for her three-week holiday in
the summers—if I'd known it was the last good-bye I
wouldn't have been able to bear—the leaving, or the next
several years.

When the train left it was a cold April day, rain pouring
in sheets across the Leopoldsgasse as we walked—not to
the central station but a small suburban one that wouldn't
attract attention. Papa wore a long red scarf, which he put
on so Hugo and I could spot him easily from the train. He
was a café violinist, or had been, anyway, and when he saw
us leaning out a window, he whipped out his violin and
tried to play one of the Gypsy tunes he had taught us to
dance to. Even Hugo could tell misery was making his
hand quaver, and he howled at Papa to stop making such
a noise.

"I will see you very soon," Papa assured us. "Lottchen,
you will find someone who needs a willing worker. I can
do anything, remember that—wait tables, haul wood or
coal, play in a hotel orchestra."

As the train pulled away I held the back of Hugo's
jacket and the two of us leaned out the window with all
the other children, waving until Papa's red scarf had
turned to an invisible speck in our own eyes.

We had the usual fears all Kindertransport children
report as we traveled through Austria and Germany, of the
guards who tried to frighten us, of the searches through
our luggage, standing very still while they looked for any
valuables: we were allowed a single ten-mark piece each. I
thought my heart would be visible through my dress, it
was beating so hard, but they didn't feel my clothes, and
the gold coins traveled with me safely. And then we passed
out of Germany into Holland, and for the first time since
the Anschluss we were suddenly surrounded by warm and
welcoming adults, who showered us with bread and meat
and chocolates.

I don't remember much of the crossing. We had a calm
sea, I think, but I was so nervous that my stomach was

twisted in knots even without any serious waves. When we landed we looked around anxiously for Minna in the crowd of adults who had come to meet the boat, but all the children were claimed and we were left standing on the dock. Finally a woman from the refugee committee showed up: Minna had left instructions for us to be sent on to London by train, but she had delayed getting word to the refugee committee until that morning. We spent the night in the camp at Harwich with the other children who had no sponsors, and went on to London in the morning. When we got to the station, to Liverpool Street—it was massive, we clung to each other while engines belched and loudspeakers bellowed incomprehensible syllables and people brushed past us on important missions. I clutched Hugo's hand tightly.

Cousin Minna had sent a workman to fetch us, giving him a photograph against which he anxiously studied our faces. He spoke English, which we didn't understand at all, or Yiddish, which we didn't understand well, but he was pleasant, bustling us into a cab, pointing out the Houses of Parliament and Big Ben, giving us each a bit of queer paste-filled sandwich in case we were hungry after our long trip.

It was only when we got to that narrow old house in the north of London that we found out Minna would take me and not Hugo. The man from the factory settled us in a forbidding front room, where we sat without moving, so fearful we were of making a noise or being a nuisance. After some very long time, Minna swept in from work, full of anger, and announced that Hugo was to go on, that the foreman from the glove factory would be coming for him in an hour.

"One child and one child only. I told her highness Madame Butterfly that when she wrote begging for my charity. She may choose to roll around in the hay with a Gypsy but that doesn't mean the rest of us have to look after her children."

I tried to protest, but she said she could throw me out on the street. "Better be grateful to me, you little mongrels. I spent all day persuading the foreman to take Hugo instead of sending him to the child welfare authorities."

The foreman, Mr. Nussbaum his name was, actually turned out to be a good foster father to Hugo; he even set him up in business many years later. But you can only guess how the two of us felt that day when he arrived to take Hugo away with him: the last sight either of us had then of any familiar face of our childhood.

Like the Nazi guards, Minna searched my clothes for valuables: she refused to believe the penury to which the family was reduced. Fortunately, my Oma had been clever enough to evade both Nazis and Minna. Those gold coins helped pay my fees in medical school, but that was a long way ahead, in a future I didn't imagine as I sobbed for my parents and my brother.

X

In the Mind Reader's Lair

When I finally woke the next morning, my head was heavy with the detritus of dreams and difficult sleep. I once read that a year or eighteen months after losing them, you dream of your dead as they were in their prime. I suppose I must sometimes dream of my mother as she was in my childhood, vivid and intense, but last night she was dying, eyes heavy with morphine, face unrecognizable as disease had leached flesh from bone. Lotty and my mother are such intertwined strands in my mind that it was almost inevitable that her distress would overlay my sleep.

Morrell looked at me questioningly when I sat up. He had come in after I went to bed, but I was tossing, not sleeping. His impending departure made him feverishly nervous; we made love with a kind of frantic unsatisfying energy but fell asleep without talking. In the morning light he traced my cheekbones with his finger and asked if it was his leaving that had disturbed my sleep.

I gave a twisted smile. "My own stuff this time." I gave him a brief synopsis of the previous day.

"Why don't we go to Michigan for the weekend?" he

said. "We both need a breather. You can't do anything on a Saturday, anyway, and we can give each other better comfort away from all these people. I love Don like a brother, but having him here right now is a bit much. We'll come back in time for Michael and Carl's concert on Sunday."

My muscles unknotted at the thought, and it sent me into the day with better energy than my tormented night warranted. After stopping at home to take the dogs for a swim, I drove into the West Loop to the Unblinking Eye, the camera and video place I use when only the best will do. I explained what I wanted to Maurice Redken, the technician I usually work with.

We ran my copy of the Channel 13 video through one of their machines, watching Radbuka's naked face as he went through the torments of his life. When he said, "My Miriam, where is my Miriam? I want my Miriam," the camera was right in his face. I froze the image there and asked Maurice to make prints of that and a couple of other close-ups for me. I was hoping Rhea Wiell would introduce me to Radbuka, but if she didn't, the stills would help Mary Louise and me track him down.

Maurice promised to have both the stills and three copies of the tape ready for me by the day's end. It wasn't quite ten-thirty when we finished. There wasn't time for me to go to my office before Don's appointment with Rhea Wiell, but I could walk the two miles from the Eye to Water Tower if I didn't dawdle—I hate paying Gold Coast parking fees.

Water Tower Place is a shopping mecca on North Michigan, a favorite drop-off place for tour buses from small Midwestern towns as well as an oasis for local teens. Threading my way through girls whose pierced navels showed below their cropped T-shirts and women pushing expensive baby buggies overflowing with packages, I found Don leaning against the back entrance. He was so engrossed in his book he didn't look up when I stopped next to him. I squinted to read the spine: *Hypnotic Induction and Suggestion: an Introductory Manual.*

"Does this tell you how Ms. Wiell does it?" I asked.

He blinked and closed the book. "It tells me that blocked memories really can be accessed through hypnosis. Or at least the authors claim so. Fortunately I only have to see if Wiell has a sellable book in her, not sort out whether her therapy is legitimate. I'm going to introduce you as an investigator who may help collect background data if Wiell and the publisher come to terms. You can say anything you like."

He looked at his watch and fished a cigarette from his breast pocket. Although he'd changed clothes, into a pressed open-necked shirt and a tweed jacket, he still looked half-asleep. I took the book on hypnotic induction while Don lit his cigarette. Broadly speaking, hypnosis seemed to be used in two main ways: suggestive hypnosis helped people break bad habits, and insight or exploratory hypnosis helped them understand themselves better. Recovering memories was only one small part of using hypnosis in therapy.

Don pinched off the glowing end of his cigarette and put the stub back in his pocket. "Time to go, Ms. Warshawski."

I followed him into the building. "This book could help you end that expensive habit for good."

He stuck out his tongue at me. "I wouldn't know what to do with my hands if I quit."

We went behind a newsstand on the ground floor, in a dark alcove which held the elevators to the office floor. It wasn't exactly secret, just out of the way enough to keep the shopping hordes from straying there by mistake. I studied the tenant board. Plastic surgeons, endodontists, beauty salons, even a synagogue. What an odd combination.

"I called over to the Jane Addams School, as you suggested," Don said abruptly when we were alone on an elevator. "First I couldn't find anyone who knew Wiell—she did her degree fifteen years ago. But when I started talking about the hypnotherapy, the department secretary remembered. Wiell was married then, used her husband's name."

We got off the elevator and found ourselves at a point where four long corridors came together. "What did they think of her at UIC?" I asked.

He looked at his appointment book. "I think we go right here. There's some jealousy—a suggestion she was a charlatan, but when I pushed it seemed to stem from the fact that social work had made her rich—doesn't happen to too many people, I gather."

We stopped in front of a blond door with Wiell's name and professional initials painted on it. I felt a tingle from the idea that this woman might read my mind. She might know me better than I knew myself. Was that where hypnotic suggestibility got its start? The urgent desire to be understood so intimately?

Don pushed the door open. We were in a tiny vestibule with two shut doors and a third one that was open. This led to a waiting room, where a sign invited us to sit down and relax. It added that all cell phones and pagers should be turned off. Don and I obediently pulled out our phones. He switched his off, but mine had run down again without my noticing.

The waiting room was decorated with such attention to comfort that it even held a carafe of hot water and a selection of herbal teas. New Age music tinkled softly; padded chairs faced a four-foot-high fish tank built into the far wall. The fish seemed to rise and fall in time to the music.

"What do you think this setup costs?" Don was trying the other two doors. One turned out to be a bathroom; the other was locked.

"I don't know—installing it took a bundle, but looking after it wouldn't take too much. Except for the rent, of course. The nicotine in your system is keeping you awake. These fish are putting me to sleep."

He grinned. "You're going to sleep, Vic: when you wake up—"

"It isn't like that, although people are always nervous at first and imagine the television version." The locked door had opened and Rhea Wiell appeared behind us. "You're from the publishing company, aren't you?"

She seemed smaller in person than she had on television, but her face held the same serenity I'd noticed on screen. She was dressed as she had been on camera, in soft clothes that flowed like an Indian mystic's.

Don shook her hand, unembarrassed, and introduced both of us. "If you and I decide to work together, Vic may help with some of the background checking."

Wiell stood back to let us pass in front of her into her office. It, too, was designed to put us at ease, with a reclining chair, a couch, and her own office chair all covered in soft green. Her diplomas hung behind her desk: the MSW from the Jane Addams School of Social Work, a certificate from the American Institute of Clinical Hypnosis, and her Illinois license as a psychiatric social worker.

I perched on the edge of the recliner while Don took the couch. Wiell sat in her office chair, her hands loosely crossed in her lap. She looked like Jean Simmons in *Elmer Gantry*.

"When we saw you on Channel Thirteen the other night, I immediately realized you had a very powerful story to tell, you and Paul Radbuka," Don said. "You must have thought about putting it into a book before I called, hadn't you?"

Wiell smiled faintly. "Of course I've wanted to: if you saw the whole program, then you're aware that my work is—misunderstood—in a number of circles. A book validating the recovery of blocked trauma would be enormously useful. And Paul Radbuka's story would be unusual enough—powerful enough—to force people to pay serious attention to the issue."

Don leaned forward, chin on his clasped hands. "I'm new to the subject—my first exposure came two nights ago. I've been cramming hard, reading a manual on hypnotic suggestion, looking at articles about you, but I'm definitely not up to speed."

She nodded. "Hypnosis is only one part of a total therapeutic approach, and it's controversial because it isn't understood very well. The field of memory, what we remember, how we remember, and maybe most interestingly why we remember—none of that is really known right now. The research seems exciting to me, but I'm not a scientist and I don't pretend to have the time to follow experimental work in depth."

"Would your book focus exclusively on Paul Radbuka?" I asked.

"Since Don—I hope you don't mind my using your first name?—Don called yesterday, I've been thinking it over; I believe I should use some other case histories, as well, to show that my work with Paul isn't—well, the kind of fly-by-night treatment that Planted Memory therapists like to claim."

"What do you see as the book's central point?" Don patted his jacket pocket reflexively, then pulled out a pen in lieu of his half-smoked cigarette.

"To show that our memories are reliable. To show the difference between planted memories and genuine ones. I began going through my patient files last night after I finished work and found several people whose histories would make this point quite strongly. Three had complete amnesia about their childhoods when they started therapy. One had partial memories, and two had what they thought were continuous memories, although therapy unlocked new insights for them. In some ways it's most exciting to uncover memories for someone who has amnesia, but the harder work is verifying, filling in gaps for people who have some recall."

Don interrupted to ask if there was some way to verify memories that were uncovered in treatment. I expected Wiell to become defensive, but she responded quite calmly.

"That's why I earmarked these particular cases. For each of them there is at least one other person, a witness to their childhood, who can corroborate what came up in here. For some it's a brother or sister. In one case it's a social worker; for two, there are primary-school teachers."

"We'd have to get written permission." Don was making notes. "For the patients and for their verifiers. Witnesses."

She nodded again. "Of course their real identities would be carefully concealed, not just to protect themselves but to protect family members and colleagues who could be harmed by such narratives. But, yes, we'll get written permission."

"Are these other patients also Holocaust survivors?" I ventured.

"Helping Paul was an incredible privilege." A smile lit her face with a kind of ecstatic joy, so intense, so personal, that I instinctively shrank back on the recliner away from her. "Most of my clients are dealing with terrible traumas, to be sure, but within the context of this culture. To get Paul to that point, to the point of being a little boy speaking broken German with his helpless playmates in a concentration camp, was the most powerful experience of my life. I don't even know how we can do it justice in print." She looked at her hands, adding in a choked voice, "I think he's recently recovered a fragment of memory of witnessing his mother's death."

"I'll do my best for you," Don muttered. He, too, had shifted away from her.

"You said you'd be concealing people's real identities," I said. "So is Paul Radbuka not his real name?"

The ecstasy left Wiell's face, replaced again by her patina of professional calm. "He's the one person who doesn't seem to have any living family left to be upset by his revelations. Besides, he's so intensely proud of his newly recovered identity that it would be impossible to persuade him to use a cover name."

"So you've discussed it with him?" Don asked eagerly. "He's willing to take part?"

"I haven't had time to talk about it with any of my patients." She smiled faintly. "You only broached the idea yesterday, after all. But I know how intensely Paul feels: it's why he insisted on speaking up at the Birnbaum conference earlier this week. I think, too, he'd do anything he could to support my work, because it's changed his life so dramatically."

"How did he come to remember the name Radbuka?" I said. "If he was raised by this foster father from the age of four and wrenched from his birth family in infancy—have I got that chronology right?"

Wiell shook her head at me. "I hope your role isn't to try to set traps for me, Ms. Warshawski. If it is, I'll have to look for a different publisher than Envision Press. Paul found some papers in his father's desk—his foster father, I should say—and they pointed the way to his birth name for him."

"I wasn't trying to set a trap, Ms. Wiell. But it would certainly strengthen the book if we could get some outside corroboration of his Radbuka identity. And it's remotely possible that I am in a position to provide that. To be candid, I have friends who came to England from central Europe with the Kindertransport in the last months before the war began. Apparently one of their group of special friends in London was named

Radbuka. If it turns out your client is a relation, it might mean a great deal, both to him and to my friends who lost so many family members."

Again the rapturous smile swept across her face. "Ah, if you can introduce him to his relatives, that would be an indescribable gift to Paul. Who are these people? Do they live in England? How do you know them?"

"I know two of them who live here in Chicago; the third is a musician who's visiting from London for a few days. If I could talk to your client—"

"Not until I've consulted with him," she cut me off. "And I would have to have your—friends'—names before I could do so. I hate to have to be so suspicious, but I have had too many traps set for me by the Planted Memory Foundation."

My eyes narrowed as I tried to hear behind her words. Was this paranoia born of too much skirmishing with Arnold Praeger, or a legitimate prudence?

Before I could decide, Don said, "You don't think Max would mind your giving his name, do you, Vic?"

"Max?" Wiell cried. "Max Loewenthal?"

"How do you know him?" Don asked, again before I could respond.

"He spoke at the session on the efforts of survivors to track down the fates of their families and whether they had any assets tied up in Swiss or German banks. Paul and I sat in on that: we hoped we could learn some new ideas for ways of looking for his family. If Max is your friend, I'm sure Paul would be glad to talk to him—he seemed an extraordinary man, gentle, empathic, yet assured, authoritative."

"That's a good description of his personality," I said, "but he also has a strong sense of privacy. He would be most annoyed if Paul Radbuka approached him without my having a chance to speak to Mr. Radbuka first."

"You can rest assured that I understand the value of

privacy. My relations with my clients would not be possible if I didn't protect them." Wiell gave me the same sweet, steely smile she'd directed at Arnold Praeger on TV the other night.

"So can we arrange a meeting with your client, where I can talk to him before introducing him to my friends?" I tried to keep irritation out of my voice, but I knew I couldn't match her in sanctity.

"Before I do anything, I will have to talk to Paul. Surely you understand that any other course would violate my relationship with him." She wrote Max's name in her datebook next to Paul Radbuka's appointment: her square, printlike hand was easy to read upside down.

"Of course I understand that," I said with what patience I could muster. "But I can't let Paul Radbuka come to Mr. Loewenthal out of the blue in the belief that they're related. In fact, I don't think Mr. Loewenthal is himself a part of the Radbuka family. If I could ask Paul a few questions first, it might spare everyone some anxiety."

She shook her head with finality: she would not turn Paul over to someone like me, an unskilled outsider. "Whether it's Mr. Loewenthal or his musician friend who is part of the family, I assure you, I would approach them with the utmost empathy. And the first step is to talk to Paul, to get his permission for me to go to them. How long will your musician be in Chicago?"

At this point I didn't want to tell her anything about anyone I knew, but Don said, "I think he said that he's leaving for the West Coast on Monday."

While I fumed to myself, Don got Wiell to give a précis on how hypnosis worked and how she used it—sparingly, and only after her patients felt able to trust her—before he brought up the kind of controversy the book was likely to generate.

He grinned engagingly. "From our standpoint,

controversy is highly desirable, because it gives a book access to the kind of press coverage you can't buy. But from yours—you may not want that kind of spotlight on you and your practice."

She smiled back at him. "Like you, I would welcome the publicity—although for a different reason. I want as many people as possible to start understanding how we block memories, how we recover them, and how we can become liberated in the process. The Planted Memory Foundation has done a great deal of damage to people suffering from trauma. I haven't had the resources to make the truth clear to a wider audience. This book would help me greatly."

A silvery bell, like a Japanese temple bell, chimed on her desk. "We'll have to stop now—I have another patient coming and I need time to prepare for my session."

I handed her my card, reminding her that I wanted an early meeting with Paul Radbuka. She shook my hand in a cool, dry clasp, giving my hand a slight pressure intended to reassure me of her goodwill. To Don she added that she could help him stop smoking if he wanted.

"Most of my hypnotic work is in the arena of self-exploration, but I do work with habit management sometimes."

Don laughed. "I hope we'll be working closely together for the next year or so. If I decide I'm ready to quit we'll put the manuscript aside while I lie back on your couch here."

XI

Ramping Up

As we walked past the liposuckers to the elevator, Don congratulated himself on how well things had gone. "I'm a believer: it's going to be a great project. Those eyes of hers could convince me to do just about anything."

"They apparently did," I said dryly. "I wish you hadn't brought Max's name into the discussion."

"Chrissake, Vic, it was a pure fluke that she guessed it was Max Loewenthal." He stood back as the elevator doors opened to let out an elderly couple. "This is going to be a career-saving book for me. I bet I can get my agent to go to high six figures, not to mention the film rights—don't you see Dustin Hoffman as the broken-down Radbuka remembering his past?"

Lotty's bitter remark on ghouls profiting on the remains of the dead came back to me full force. "You said you wanted to prove to Lotty Herschel that you're not the mike-in-the-face kind of journalist. She's not going to be very persuaded if you're prancing around in glee about turning her friends' misery into commercial movies."

"Vic, get a grip," Don said. "Can't you let me have

my moment of triumph? Of course I won't violate Dr. Herschel's most sacred feelings. I started out feeling a bit doubtful of Rhea, but by the end of the hour she had me totally on her side—sorry if the excitement's gone to my head."

"She rubbed me the wrong way a bit," I said.

"That's because she wouldn't toss you her patient's home phone number. Which she absolutely should not give anyone. You know that."

"I know that," I had to agree. "I guess what bugs me is her wanting to mastermind the situation: she'll meet Max and Lotty and Carl, she'll decide what they're about, but she's resisting the idea that I might meet her client. Don't you think it's odd that he gave her office as his home address—as if his identity was wrapped up in her?"

"You're overreacting, Vic, because you like to be the one in control yourself. You read some of the articles you printed out for me on the attacks against her by Planted Memory, right? She's sensible to be cautious."

He paused while the elevator landed and we negotiated our way past the group waiting to get on. I scanned them, hoping I might see Paul Radbuka, wondering about the destination of the people boarding. Were they getting fat sucked out? Root canals? Which one was Rhea Wiell's next patient?

Don continued with the thought uppermost in his own mind. "Do you think it's Lotty, Max, or Carl who really is related to Radbuka? They sound pretty prickly for people who are only looking out for their friends' interests."

I stopped behind the newsstand to stare at him. "I don't think any of them is related to Radbuka. That's why I'm so annoyed that Ms. Wiell has Max's name now. I know, I know," I added, as he started to interrupt, "you didn't really give it to her. But she's so focused on her prize exhibit's well-being that she's not thinking outside that landscape now to anyone else's needs."

"But why should she?" he asked. "I mean, I understand that you want her to be as empathic to Max or Dr. Herschel as she is to Paul Radbuka, but how could she be that concerned about a group of strangers? Besides, she's got such an exciting event going on with what she's done with this guy that it's not surprising, really. But why are your friends so very defensive if it isn't their own family they're worrying about?"

"Good grief, Don—you're almost as experienced as Morrell in writing about war-scarred refugees. I'm sure you can imagine how it must have felt, to be in London with a group of children who all shared the same traumas—first of leaving their families behind to go to a strange country with a strange language, then the even bigger trauma of the horrific way in which their families died. I think you'd feel a sense of bonding that went beyond friendship—everyone's experiences would seem as though they had happened to you personally."

"I suppose you're right. Of course you are. I only want to get in with Rhea on the story of the decade." He grinned again, disarming me, and pulled the half-smoked cigarette out of his pocket again. "Until I decide to let Rhea cure me, I need to get this inside me. Can you come over to the Ritz with me? Share a glass of champagne and let me feel just a minute moment of euphoria about my project?"

I still wasn't in a very celebratory mood. "Let me check with my answering service while you go over to the hotel. Then a quick one, I guess."

I went back to the corner to use the pay phones, since my cell phone was dead. Why couldn't I let Don have his moment of triumph, as he had put it? Was he right, that I was only resentful because Rhea Wiell wouldn't give me Radbuka's phone number? But that sense of an ecstatic vision when she was talking about her triumph with Paul Radbuka had made me uncomfortable. It was the ecstasy of a votary, though, not the triumphant smirk of a charlatan, so why should I let it raise my hackles?

I fed change into the phone and dialed my answering service.

"Vic! Where have you been?" Christie Weddington, a day operator who'd been with the service for longer than me, jolted me back to my own affairs.

"What's up?"

"Beth Blacksin has phoned three times, wanting a comment; Murray Ryerson has called twice, besides messages from a whole bunch of other reporters." She read off a string of names and numbers. "Mary Louise, she called and said she was switching the office line over to us because she felt like she was under siege."

"But about what?"

"I don't know, Vic, I just take the messages. Murray said something about Alderman Durham, though, and—here it is." She read the message in a flat, uninflected voice. " 'Call me and tell me what's going on with Bull Durham. Since when have you started robbing the widow and orphan of their mite?' "

I was completely bewildered. "I guess just forward all those to my office computer. Are there any business messages, things that don't come from reporters?"

I could hear her clicking through her screen. "I don't think—oh, here is something from a Mr. Devereux at Ajax." She read me Ralph's number.

I tried Murray first. He's an investigative reporter with the *Herald-Star* who does occasional special reports for Channel 13. This was the first time he'd called me in some months—we'd had quite a falling out over a case that had involved the *Star*'s owners. In the end, we'd made a kind of fragile peace, but we've been avoiding involvement with each other's cases.

"Warshawski, what in hell did you do to yank Bull Durham's chain so hard?"

"Hi, Murray. Yes, I'm depressed about the Cubs and worried because Morrell is leaving for Kabul in a few days. But otherwise things go on same as always. How about you?"

He paused briefly, then snarled at me not to be a smart-mouthed pain in the ass.

"Why don't you start from the beginning?" I suggested. "I've been in meetings all morning and have no idea what our aldercreatures have been saying or doing."

"Bull Durham is leading a charge of pickets outside the Ajax company headquarters."

"Oh—on the slave-reparations issue?"

"Right. Ajax is his first target. His handouts name you as an agent of the company involved in the continuing suppression of black policyholders by depriving them of their settlements."

"I see." A recorded message interrupted us, telling me to deposit twenty-five cents if I wanted to continue the call. "Gotta go, Murray, I'm out of change."

I hung up on his squawk that that was hardly an answer—what had I *done*?! That must be why Ralph Devereux was calling. To find out what I'd done to provoke a full-scale picket. What a mess. When my client—ex-client—told me he was going to take steps, these must have been the ones he had in mind. I gritted my teeth and put another thirty-five cents into the phone.

I got Ralph's secretary, but by the time she put me through to him I'd been on hold so long I really had run out of quarters. "Ralph, I'm at a pay phone with no more money, so let's be brief: I just heard about Durham."

"Did you feed the Sommers file to him?" he asked, voice heavy with suspicion.

"So that he could denounce me as an Ajax stooge and have every reporter in the city hounding me? Thank you, no. My client's aunt reacted with indignation to my asking her about the previous death certificate and the check; my client fired me. I'm guessing he went to Durham, but I don't know that definitely. When I find out, I'll call you. Anything else? Rossy on your butt over this?"

"The whole sixty-third floor. Although Rossy is saying it shows he was right not to trust you."

"He's just flailing in fury, looking for a target. These are the snows of summer, they won't stick on Ajax, although they may freeze me some. I'm going to see Sommers to find out what he told Durham. What about your historian, Amy Blount, the young woman who wrote up the book on Ajax? Yesterday Rossy was saying he didn't trust her not to give Ajax data to Durham. Did he ask her that?"

"She denied showing our private papers to anyone, but how else could Durham have found out who we insured back in the 1850's? We mention Birnbaum in our history, bragging that they go back with us to 1852, but not the detail Durham has, about insuring plow shipments they made to slaveholders. Now the Birnbaum lawyers are threatening us with breach of fiduciary responsibility, although whether it extends back that far—"

"Do you have Blount's phone number? I could try asking her."

The metallic voice announced that I needed another twenty-five cents. Ralph quickly told me Blount had gotten her Ph.D. in economic history at the University of Chicago last June; I could reach her through the department. "Call me when you—" he started to add, but the phone company cut us off.

I dashed through the lobby to the cab rank, but the sight of a pair of smokers huddled along the wall made me remember Don, sitting in the Ritz bar. I hesitated, then remembered my phone charger was still in Morrell's car—I wouldn't be able to call Don from the road to explain why I'd stood him up.

I found him under a fern tree in the smoking section of the bar, with two glasses of champagne in front of him. When he saw me he put out his cigarette. I bent over to kiss his cheek.

"Don—I wish you every success. With this book and with your career." I picked up a glass to toast him. "But I can't stay to drink: there's a crisis involving the players you originally came here to interview."

When I told him about Durham's pickets outside Ajax and that I wanted to go see what they were up to, he relit his cigarette. "Did anyone ever tell you you have too much energy, Vic? It'll age Morrell before his time, trying to keep up with you. I am going to sit here with my champagne, having a happy conversation about Rhea Wiell's book with my literary agent. I will then drink your glass as well. If you learn anything as you bounce around Chicago like a pinball in the hands of a demented wizard, I will listen breathlessly to your every word."

"For which I will charge you a hundred dollars an hour." I swallowed a large gulp of champagne, then handed him the glass. I curbed my impulse to dart across the lobby to the elevators: the image of myself as a pinball careening around the city was embarrassing—although it kept recurring to me as the afternoon progressed.

XII

Pinball Wizard

I bounced first to the Ajax building on Adams. Durham only had a small band of pickets out—in the middle of a workday most people don't have time to demonstrate. Durham himself led the charge, surrounded by his cadre of Empower Youth Energy members, their eyes watching the passersby with the sullenness of men prepared to fight on a moment's notice. Behind them came a small group of ministers and community leaders from the South and West Sides, followed by the usual handful of earnest college students. They chanted "Justice now," "No high-rises on the bones of slaves," and "No reparations for slaveowners." I walked in step with one of the students, who welcomed me as a convert to the fold.

"I didn't realize Ajax had benefited so much from slavery," I said.

"It's not just that, but did you hear what happened yesterday? They sicced a detective on this poor old woman who had just lost her husband. They cashed his life-insurance check and then, like, pretended she had done it and sent this detective down to accuse her, right in the middle of the funeral."

"What?" I shouted.

"Really sucks, doesn't it. Here—you can read the details." He thrust a broadsheet at me. My name jumped out at me.

AJAX—HAVE YOU NO MERCY?
WARSHAWSKI—HAVE YOU NO SHAME?
BIRNBAUM—HAVE YOU NO COMPASSION?

Where is the widow's mite? Gertrude Sommers, a God-fearing woman, a churchgoing woman, a taxpaying woman, lost her son. Then she lost her husband. Must she lose her dignity, as well?

Ajax Insurance cashed her husband's life-insurance policy ten years ago. When he died last week, they sent their tame detective, V I Warshawski, to accuse Sister Sommers of stealing it. In the middle of the funeral, in front of her friends and loved ones, they shamed her.

Warshawski, we all have to make a living, but must you do it on the bodies of the poor? Ajax, make good the wrong. Pay the widow her mite. Repair the damage you have done to the grandchildren of slaves. Birnbaum, give back the money you made with Ajax on the backs of slaves. No Holocaust restitution until you make the African-American community whole.

I could feel the blood drumming in my head. No wonder Ralph was angry—but why should he take it out on me? It wasn't his name that was being slandered. I almost jumped out of the line to tackle Alderman Durham, but in the nick of time I imagined the scene on television—the EYE team wrestling with me as I screamed invective, the alderman shaking his head more in sorrow than anger and declaiming something sanctimonious to the camera.

I watched, fuming, as the circle of marchers brought Durham parallel to me. He was a big, broad-shouldered man in a black-and-tan houndstooth jacket which looked as though it had been made to measure, so carefully did the checks line up along the smooth-fitting seams. His face gleamed with excitement behind his muttonchop whiskers.

Since I couldn't punch him, I folded the broadsheet into my purse and ran down Adams toward my car. A cab would have been faster, but my rage needed a physical outlet. By the time I reached Canal Street, the soles of my feet throbbed from running in pumps on city pavement. I was lucky I hadn't sprained an ankle. I stood outside my car gulping in air, my throat dry.

As my pulse returned to normal, I wondered where Bull Durham had gotten the money for custom tailoring. Was someone paying him to harass Ajax and the Birnbaums—not to mention me? Of course, all alder-creatures have plenty of chances to stick their fingers in the till in perfectly legal ways—I was so furious with him I wanted to assume the worst.

I needed a phone, and I needed water. As I looked for a convenience store where I could buy a bottle, I passed a wireless shop. I bought another in-car charger: my life would be easier this afternoon if I was plugged in.

Before I got onto the expressway to track down my client—ex-client—I called Mary Louise on my private office line. She was understandably upset at my leaving her holding the bag. I explained how that had happened, then read her Bull Durham's broadsheet.

"Good grief, he's got a nerve! What do you want to do about it?"

"Start with a statement. Something like this:

"In his zeal to make political hay out of Gertrude Sommers's loss, Alderman Durham overlooked a few things, including the facts. When Gertrude Sommers's husband died last week, the Delaney Funeral Parlor humiliated her by halting the funeral just as she took her seat in the chapel. They did so because her husband's life-insurance policy had been cashed some years ago. The family briefly employed investigator V I Warshawski to get at the facts of what happened. Contrary to Alderman Durham's claims, Ajax Insurance did not hire Warshawski. Warshawski was not at Aaron Sommers's funeral and did not see or meet the unfortunate widow until the following week. It is inconceivable that Warshawski would ever interrupt a funeral in the fashion the alderman is claiming. If Alderman Durham was utterly mistaken about the facts of Warshawski's involvement in the case, are his other statements open to the same questions?"

Mary Louise read it back to me. We tweaked it a few times, then she agreed to phone or e-mail it to the reporters who had been calling. If Beth Blacksin or Murray wanted to talk to me in person, she should tell them to come to my office around six-thirty—although if they were like the rest of the Chicago media, they would probably be camped outside the doors of members of the Birnbaum family, hoping to accost them.

A cop tapped my parking meter and made an ugly comment. I put the car in gear and started down Madison toward the expressway.

"Do you know what the Birnbaum part of Durham's handout is about?" Mary Louise asked.

"Apparently Ajax insured the Birnbaums back in the 1850's. Part of the vast Birnbaum holdings came from something in the South. Ajax execs are steaming over how Durham got that information."

As I oozed onto the expressway I was glad I'd bought the water: traffic seems to run freely these days only between ten at night and six the next morning. At two-thirty, the trucks heading south on the Ryan formed a solid wall. I put Mary Louise on hold while I slid my Mustang in between an eighteen-wheel UPS truck and a long flatbed with what looked like a reactor coil strapped to it.

Before hanging up, I asked her to dig up Amy Blount's home phone number and address. "Phone them to me here in my car, but don't call her yourself. I don't know yet if I want to talk to her."

The flatbed behind me gave a loud hoot that made me jump: I had let three car lengths open up in front of me. I scooted forward.

Mary Louise said, "Before you go, I tracked down those men Aaron Sommers worked with at South Branch Scrap Metal. The ones who bought life insurance from Rick Hoffman along with Mr. Sommers."

The Durham attack on me personally had driven the earlier business from my mind. I'd forgotten to tell Mary Louise the client had fired me, so she'd gone ahead with the investigation and had found three of the four men still alive. Claiming to be doing an independent quality check for the company, she'd persuaded the policyholders to call the Midway Agency. The men said their policies were still intact; she'd double-checked with the carrier. The third man had died eight years ago. His funeral had been duly paid for by Ajax. So whatever fraud had been committed, it wasn't some wholesale looting by Midway or Hoffman of those particular burial policies. Not that it really mattered at this point, but I thanked her for the extra effort—she'd done a lot in a short morning—and turned my attention to the traffic.

When I reached the Stevenson cutoff, my motion slowed to something more like a turtle on Valium than a pinball—construction, now in its third year, cut off half the lanes. The Stevenson Expressway is the key to the industrial zone along the city's southwest corridor. Truck traffic along it is always heavy; with the construction and the afternoon rush building, we all bumped along at about ten miles an hour.

At Kedzie I was glad to leave the expressway for the maze of plants and scrap yards alongside it. Even though the day was clear, down here among the factories the air turned blue-grey from smoke. I passed yards full of rusting cars, yards making outboard motors, a rebar mill, and a mountain of yellowish salt, ominous portent of the winter ahead. The roads were deeply rutted. I drove cautiously, my car slung too low to the ground for the axle to survive a major hole. Trucks jumped past me with a happy disregard of any traffic signs.

Even with a good detail map I blundered a few times. It was a quarter past three, fifteen minutes after Isaiah Sommers's shift ended, before I jolted into the yard of the Docherty Engineering Works. A roughly graveled area, it was as scarred by heavy trucks as the surrounding streets. A fourteen-wheeler was snorting at a loading dock when I got out of the Mustang.

It was my lucky afternoon—it looked as though the seven-to-three shift was just leaving the shop. I leaned against my car, watching men straggle through a side door. Isaiah Sommers appeared about halfway through the exodus. He was talking to a couple of other men, laughing in an easy way that took me by surprise: when I'd met him he'd been hunched and surly. I waited until he'd clapped his coworkers on the shoulder and gone on to his own truck before straightening up to follow him.

"Mr. Sommers?"

The smile vanished, leaving his face in the guarded lines I'd seen the other night. "Oh. It's you. What do you want?"

I pulled the broadsheet from my purse and handed it to him. "I see the steps you took on your own led you straight to Alderman Durham. There are a few factual errors, but it's having quite a galvanizing effect on the city: you should be pleased."

He read the sheet with the same slow concentration he'd given my contract. "Well?"

"You know as well as I that I wasn't present at your uncle's funeral. Did you tell Mr. Durham that I was?"

"Maybe he put the two pieces of the story together wrong, but, yes, I did talk to him. Told him about you accusing my aunt." He stuck his jaw out pugnaciously.

"I'm not here to play he-said, she-said with you but to find out why you went out of your way to pillory me in this public way, instead of trying to work things out in private."

"My aunt—she doesn't have money or connections or a way to get even when someone like you comes along to accuse her unjustly."

Several men passed us, looking us over curiously. One of them called a greeting to Sommers. He flipped up a palm, but kept his angry gaze on me.

"Your aunt feels bereft. She needs someone to blame, so she's blaming me. Almost ten years ago, someone using your aunt's name cashed a check for the policy, with a death certificate claiming your uncle was dead to back up the claim. Either your aunt did it, or someone else. But her name was on the check. I had to ask her. You've fired me, so I won't be asking any more questions, but don't you wonder how it got there?"

"The company did it. The company did it and hired you to frame me, like it says here." He pointed at the broadsheet, but his voice lacked conviction.

"It's a possibility," I conceded. "It's a possibility the company did it. We'll never know, of course."

"Why not?"

I smiled. "I have no reason to look into it. You could hire someone else to do so, but it would cost you a fortune. Of course it's much easier to toss accusations around than it is to look for facts. It's the American way these days, isn't it: find a scapegoat instead of a fact."

His face was bunched in confusion. I took the broadsheet from him and turned back to my car. The phone, which I'd left attached to the charger, was ringing—Mary Louise, with Amy Blount's details. I scribbled them down and started the car.

"Wait," Isaiah Sommers yelled.

He shook off someone who'd stopped to talk to him and ran over to my car. I put it in park and looked up at him, my brows raised, my expression bland.

He fumbled for words, then blurted out, "What do you think?"

"About—"

"You said it's a possibility that the company cashed in the policy. Is that what you think?"

I turned off the engine. "To be honest, no. I won't say it's impossible: I uncovered claims fraud at that company once before, but it was under a different management team, which had to resign when the news got out. The thing is, it would mean collusion between someone in the company and the agent, since the agency deposited the check, but the claims manager made no demur about bringing the file up where I could see it." It's true Rossy had put me through a song and dance to keep me from examining the complete file—but Edelweiss had only been involved with Ajax for four months, so I didn't see how he could possibly be part of an Ajax life-insurance fraud.

"The agent is a more likely candidate. Although none of the other policies Hoffman sold at your uncle's workplace was fraudulently cashed, the check was paid through Midway. It's also possible your uncle did it, for reasons you might never know or you might find very painful to know. Or some other family member. And before you blow your stack and get on to Bull Durham from the nearest phone, I don't seriously think it was your aunt, not after talking to her. But your family or the agency would be the two places I would look. If I was looking."

He slammed the roof of my car in frustration. He was strong enough that the car bounced slightly.

"Look here, Ms. Warashki. I don't know who to believe, or who to listen to. My wife—she thought I should go talk to Alderman Durham. Camilla Rawlings, the lady who gave me your name to begin with, she already chewed me out for firing you: she thinks I should make my peace with you. But what can I believe? Mr. Durham, he said he had proof the insurance company profited from slavery, and this is one more cover-up, and no offense, but you being white, how can you understand?"

I got out of the car so he wouldn't have to bend over and I wouldn't get a crick in my neck looking up. "Mr. Sommers, I can't ever, completely, but I do try to listen empathically—and impartially—to whatever I hear. The situation with your aunt, I realize it's complicated by America's history. If I want to ask her how her name got to be on that check, then you and your wife and your aunt see me as a white woman, someone in league with the company to defraud you. But if I start screaming in chorus with you—company cover-up! fraud!— when I have no facts, then I'm useless as a detective. My only lodestar is sticking to the truth—as far as I can know it. It's a costly decision—I lose clients like you, I lost a wonderful man in Camilla's brother. I'm not always right, but I have to stick to the truth or be buffeted like a leaf by every wind that blows."

It took me a long time to get over my breakup with

Conrad Rawlings. I love Morrell, he's a great guy—but Conrad and I were attuned in a way that you only find once in a very blue moon.

Sommers's face contorted with strain. "Would you consider going back to work for me?"

"I'd consider it. I'd be a little wary, though."

He nodded in a kind of rueful understanding, then blurted out, "I'm sorry about Durham getting the facts mixed up. I do have cousins, one anyway, that could have gone and done it. But you see, it's painful, too painful, to expose my family like that. And if it was my cousin Colby, then, hell, I'll never see the money again. I'd be out the price of the funeral and the price of your fee, besides making my family ashamed in public."

"It's a serious problem. I can't advise you on it."

He shut his eyes tightly for a moment. "Is there—do you still owe me any more time from my five hundred dollars?"

He'd had an hour and a half coming to him before Mary Louise checked with the men at South Branch Scrap Metal. Any more work would be with the meter running again.

"About an hour," I said gruffly, cursing myself.

"Could you—is there anything you could find out about the agent in just an hour?"

"You going to call Mr. Durham and tell him he made a mistake? I have a press interview scheduled at six-thirty; I don't want to mention your name if I'm working for you."

He took a breath. "I'll call him. If you'll ask a few questions of the insurance agency."

XIII

Secret Agent

Family spokesman Andy Birnbaum, great-grandson of the patriarch who parlayed a scrap-metal pushcart into one of America's great fortunes, said the family is bewildered by Durham's accusations. The Birnbaum Foundation has supported inner-city education, arts, and economic development for four decades. Birnbaum added that relations of the African-American community with both the Birnbaum Corporation and its foundation have been mutually supportive, and he is sure that if Alderman Durham sits down to talk, the alderman will realize there has been a misunderstanding."

I got that sound bite on the radio as I was riding back into the city. The inbound traffic was heavy but moving fast, so I didn't pay close attention until my own name jumped out at me.

"Investigator V I Warshawski said in a written statement that Durham's accusations that she had interrupted Aaron Sommers's funeral with demands for money are a complete fabrication. Joseph Posner, who is lobbying hard for Illinois to pass the Holocaust Asset Recovery Act, said that Durham's charges against Ajax were a red herring to keep the legislature from considering the act. He said Durham's anti-Semitic comments were a disgrace to the memory of the dead, but that as the Sabbath started in a few hours he would not violate its peace by appearing in public to confront the alderman."

Thank heavens we were at least spared Joseph Posner joining the fray just now. I couldn't absorb any more news; I turned to music. One of the classical stations was soothing the commuter's savage breast with something very modern and spiky. The other was running a high-voltage ad for Internet access. I turned off the radio altogether and followed the lake south, back to Hyde Park.

Given Howard Fepple's lackadaisical attitude toward his business, there was only an outside chance that I'd find him still in his office at four-thirty on Friday. Still, when you're a pinball, you bounce off all the levers in the hopes of landing in the money. And this time I had a bit of luck—or whatever you'd call the chance to talk to Fepple again. He was not only in but he'd installed fresh lightbulbs, so that the torn linoleum, the grime, and his eager expression when I opened the door all showed up clearly.

"Mr. Fepple," I said heartily. "Glad to see you haven't given up on the business yet."

He turned away from me, his eager look replaced by a scowl. It obviously wasn't the hope of seeing me that had led him to put on a suit and tie.

"You know, an amazing thought occurred to me when I was driving back from seeing Isaiah Sommers this afternoon. Bull Durham knew about me. He knew about the Birnbaums. He knew about Ajax. But even though he went on for days about the injustice to the Sommers family, he didn't seem to know about you."

"You don't have an appointment," he muttered, still not looking at me. "You can leave now."

"Walk-in business," I chirped brightly. "You need to

cultivate it. So let's talk about that policy you sold Aaron Sommers."

"I told you, it wasn't me, it was Rick Hoffman."

"Same difference. Your agency. Your legal liability for any wrongdoing. My client isn't interested in dragging this out in court for years, although he could sue you for a bundle under ERISA—you had a fiduciary responsibility to his uncle, which you violated. He'd be happy if you'd cut him a check for the ten thousand that the policy was worth."

"He's not your—" he blurted, then stopped.

"My, my, Howard. Who has been talking to you? Was it Mr. Sommers himself? No, that can't be right, or you'd know he'd brought me back in to finish the investigation. So it must have been Alderman Durham. If that's the case, you are going to have so much publicity you'll be turning business away. I have an interview with Channel Thirteen in a little bit, and they will be salivating when they hear that your agency has been tipping off Bull Durham about your own customers' affairs."

"You're all wet," he said, curling his lip. "I couldn't talk to Durham—he's made it clear he doesn't have any use for whites."

"Now I'm really curious." I settled myself in the rickety chair in front of his desk. "I'm dying to see who you're all dolled up for."

"I have a date. I do have a social life that has nothing to do with insurance. I want you to leave so I can close up my office."

"In a little bit. As soon as you answer some questions. I want to see the file on Aaron Sommers."

His carpet of freckles turned a deeper orange. "You have a helluva nerve. Those are private papers, none of your damned business."

"They are my client's business. One way or another, either by you cooperating now or by my getting a court order, you're going to show me the file. So let's do it now."

"Go get your court order if you can. My father trusted me with his business; I am not going to let him down."

It was a strange and rather sad attempt at bravado. "Okay. I'll get a court order. One other thing. Rick Hoffman's notebook. That little black book he carried around with him, ticking off his clients' payments. I want to see it."

"Join the crowd," he snapped. "Everyone in Chicago wants to see his notebook, but I don't have it. He took it home with him every night like it was the secret of the atom bomb. And when he died it was at his home. If I knew where his son was, maybe I'd know where the damned notebook was. But that creep is probably in an insane asylum someplace. He's not in Chicago, at any rate."

His phone rang. He jumped on it so fast it might have been a hundred-dollar bill on the sidewalk.

"There's someone with me right now," he blurted into the mouthpiece. "Right, the woman detective." He listened for a minute, said, "Okay, okay," jotted what looked like numbers on a scrap of paper, and hung up.

He turned off his desk lamp and made a big show of locking his filing cabinets. When he came around to open the door, I had no choice but to get up, as well. We rode the elevator down to the lobby, where he surprised me by going up to the guard.

"See this lady, Collins? She's been coming around my office, making threats. Can you make sure she doesn't get into the building again tonight?"

The guard looked me up and down before saying, "Sure thing, Mr. Fepple," without much enthusiasm. Fepple went outside with me. When I congratulated him on a successful tactic, he smirked before striding off down the street. I watched him go into the pizza restaurant on the corner. They had a phone in the entryway, which he stopped to use.

I joined a couple of drunks outside a convenience store across the street. They were arguing about a man named Clive and what Clive's sister had said about one of them, but they broke off to try to cadge the price of a bottle from me. I moved away from them, still watching Fepple.

After about five minutes he came out, looked around cautiously, saw me, and darted toward a shopping center on the north side of the street. I started after him, but one of the drunks grabbed me, telling me not to be such a stuck-up bitch. I stuck a knee in his stomach and jerked my arm free. While he shouted obscenities I ran north, but I was still in my pumps. This time the left heel gave and I tumbled to the concrete. By the time I got myself collected, Fepple had disappeared.

I cursed myself, Fepple, and the drunks with equal ferocity. By a miracle, damage was limited to the shreds in my panty hose and a bloody scrape on my left leg and thigh. In the fading daylight I couldn't tell if I'd ruined my skirt, a silky black number that I was rather fond of. I limped back to my car, where I used part of my bottle of water to clean the blood from my leg. The skirt had some dirt ground into it, fraying the fabric surface. I picked at the gravel bits disconsolately. Maybe when it was cleaned the torn threads wouldn't show.

Leaning back in the front seat with my eyes shut, I wondered whether it was worthwhile trying to get back into the Hyde Park Bank building. Even if I could charm my way past the guard in my current disarray, if I took anything, Fepple would know it had been me. That project could wait until Monday.

I still had over an hour before I was due to meet Beth Blacksin—I should just go home and clean up properly for my interview. On the other hand, Amy Blount,

Ph.D., the young woman who'd written Ajax's history, lived only three blocks from the bank. I called the number Mary Louise had dug up for me.

Ms. Blount was home. In her polite, aloof way she acknowledged that we'd met. When I explained that I wanted to ask some questions about Ajax, she turned from aloof to frosty.

"Mr. Rossy's secretary has already asked me those questions. I find them offensive. I won't answer them from you any more than from him."

"Sorry, Ms. Blount, I wasn't very clear. Ajax didn't send me to you. I don't know what questions Rossy wants to ask you, but they're probably different from mine. Mine come from a client who's trying to find out what happened to a life-insurance policy. I don't think you know the answer, but I'd like to talk to you because—" Because of what? Because I was so frustrated at being stiffed by Fepple, defamed by Durham, that I was clutching at any straw? "Because I cannot figure out what's going on and I'd like to talk to someone who understands Ajax. I'm in the neighborhood; I could stop by now for ten minutes if you can spare the time."

After a pause, she said coldly she would hear what I had to say but couldn't promise she'd answer any questions.

She lived in a shabby courtyard building on Cornell, the kind of haphazardly maintained property that students can afford. Even so, as I knew from the plaint of an old friend whose son was starting medical school down here, Blount probably paid six or seven hundred a month for the broken glass on the sidewalk, her badly hung lobby door, and the hole in the stairwell wall.

Blount stood in the open door to her studio apartment, watching while I climbed the third flight of stairs. Here at home, her dreadlocks hung loosely about her face. Instead of the prim tweed suit she'd worn to Ajax, she had on jeans and a big shirt. She ushered me in politely but without cordiality, waving a hand at a hardwood chair while seating herself in the swivel desk chair at her work station.

Except for a futon with a bright kente cover and a print of a woman squatting behind a basket, the room was furnished with monastic severity. It was lined on all sides by white pasteboard bookshelves. Even the tiny eating alcove had shelves fitted around a clock.

"Ralph Devereux told me you had a degree in economic history. Is that how you came to be involved with writing the Ajax history?"

She nodded without speaking.

"What did you do your dissertation on?"

"Is this relevant to your client's story, Ms. Warshawski?"

I raised my brows. "Polite conversation, Ms. Blount. But that's right, you said you wouldn't answer any questions. You said you had already heard from Bertrand Rossy, so you know that Alderman Durham has had Ajax under—"

"His secretary," she corrected me. "Mr. Rossy is too important to call me himself."

Her voice was so toneless that I couldn't be sure whether her intent was ironic. "Still, he made the questions take place. So you know Durham's picketing the Ajax building, claiming that Ajax and the Birnbaums owe restitution to the African-American community for the money they both made from slavery. I suppose Rossy accused you of supplying Durham the information out of the Ajax archives."

She nodded fractionally, her eyes wary.

"The other piece of Durham's protest concerns me personally. Have you encountered the Midway Insurance Agency over in the bank building? Howard Fepple is the rather ineffectual present owner, but thirty years ago one of his father's agents sold a policy to a man named Sommers." I outlined the Sommers family problem. "Now Durham has hold of the story. Based on your work at Ajax, I'm wondering if you have any ideas on who might give the alderman such detailed inside information about both the company history and this current claim. Sommers complained to the alderman, but the Durham protest had one detail that I don't think Sommers would have known: the fact that Ajax insured the Birnbaum Corporation in the years before the Civil War. I'm assuming that information is accurate, or Rossy wouldn't have called you. Had his secretary call you."

When I paused, Blount said, "It is, sort of. That is, the original Birnbaum, the one who started the family fortune, was insured by Ajax in the 1850's."

"What do you mean, sort of?" I asked.

"In 1858, Mordecai Birnbaum lost a load of steel plows he was sending to Mississippi when the steamship blew up on the Illinois River. Ajax paid for it. I suppose that's what Alderman Durham is referring to." She spoke in a rapid monotone. I hoped when she lectured to students she had more animation, or they'd all be asleep.

"Steel plows?" I repeated, my attention diverted. "They existed before the Civil War?"

She smiled primly. "John Deere invented the steel plow in 1830. In 1847 he set up his first major plant and retail store here in Illinois."

"So the Birnbaums were already an economic power in 1858."

"I don't think so. I think it was the Civil War that made the family fortune, but the Ajax archives didn't include a lot of specifics—I was guessing from the list of assets being insured. The Birnbaum plows were only a small part of the ship's cargo."

"In your opinion, who could have told Durham about Birnbaum's plow shipment?"

"Is this a subtle way to get me to confess?"

She could have asked the question in a humorous vein—but she didn't. I made an effort not to lose my own temper in return. "I'm open to all possibilities, but I have to consider the available facts. You had access to the archives. Perhaps you shared the data with Durham. But if you didn't, perhaps you have some ideas on who did."

"So you did come here to accuse me." She set her jaw in an uncompromising line.

I sank my face into my hands, suddenly tired of the matter. "I came here hoping to get better information than I have. But let it be. I have an interview with Channel Thirteen to discuss the whole sorry business; I need to go home to change."

She tightened her lips. "Do you plan to accuse me on air?"

"I actually didn't come here to accuse you of anything at all, but you're so suspicious of me and my motives that I can't imagine you'd believe any assurances I gave you. I came here hoping that a trained observer like you would have seen something that would give me a new way to think about what's going on."

She looked at me uncertainly. "If I told you I didn't give Durham the files, would you believe me?"

I spread my hands. "Try me."

She took a breath, then spoke rapidly, looking at the books over her computer. "I happen not to support Mr. Durham's ideas. I am fully cognizant of the racial injustices that still exist in this country. I have researched and written about black economic and commercial history, so I am more familiar with the history of these injustices than most: they run deep, and they run wide. I took the job of writing that Ajax history, for instance, because I'm having a hard time getting academic history or economics programs to pay attention to me, outside of African-American studies, which are too often marginalized for me to find interesting. I need to earn something while I'm job-hunting. Also, the Ajax archives will make an interesting monograph. But I don't believe in focusing on African-Americans as victims: it makes us seem pitiable to white America, and as long as we are pitiable we will not be respected." She flushed, as if embarrassed to reveal her beliefs to a stranger.

I thought of Lotty's angry vehemence with Max on the subject of Jews as victims. I nodded slowly and told Blount that I could believe her.

"Besides," she added, her color still deepened, "it would seem immoral to me to make the Ajax files available to an outsider, when they had trusted me with their private documents."

"Since you didn't feed inside Ajax information to the alderman, can you think who might have?"

She shook her head. "It's such a big company. And the files aren't exactly secret, at least they weren't when I was doing my research. They keep all of the old material in their company library, in boxes. Hundreds of boxes, as a matter of fact. Recent material they guarded carefully, but the first hundred years—it was more a question of having the patience to wade through it than any particular difficulty gaining access to it. Although you do have to ask the librarian to see it—still, anyone who wanted to study those papers could probably get around that difficulty."

"So it might be an employee, someone with a grudge, or someone who could be bribed? Or perhaps a zealous member of Alderman Durham's organization?"

"Any or all of those could be reasonable possibilities, but I have no names to put forward. Still, thirty-seven hundred people of color hold low-level clerical or manual-laboring positions in the company. They are underpaid, underrepresented in supervisory positions, and often are treated to overt racial slurs. Any of them could become angry enough to undertake an act of passive sabotage."

I stood up, wondering if someone in the Sommers extended family was among the low-level clerks at Ajax. I thanked Amy Blount for being willing to talk to me and left her one of my cards, in case anything else occurred to her. As she walked me to the door I stopped to admire the picture of the squatting woman. Her head was bent over the basket in front of her; you didn't see her face.

"It's by Lois Mailou Jones," Ms. Blount said. "She also refused to be a victim."

XIV

Running the Tape

Late that night, I lay in the dark next to Morrell, fretting uselessly, endlessly, about the day. My mind bounced—like a pinball—from Rhea Wiell to Alderman Durham, my fury with him rising each time I thought of that flyer he was handing out in the Ajax plaza. When I tried to put that to rest I'd go back to Amy Blount, to Howard Fepple, and finally to my gnawing worries about Lotty.

When I'd gone to my office from Amy Blount's place, I'd found the copies of the Paul Radbuka video the Unblinking Eye had made for me, along with the stills of Radbuka.

My long afternoon dealing with Sommers and Fepple had pushed Radbuka out of my mind. At first I only stared at the packet, trying to remember what I'd wanted from the Eye. When I saw the stills of Radbuka's face, I recalled my promise to Lotty to get her a copy of the video today. Numb with fatigue, I was thinking I might hang on to it until I saw her on Sunday at Max's, when she phoned.

"Victoria, I'm trying to be civilized, but have you not had my messages this afternoon?"

I explained that I hadn't had a chance to check with my answering service. "In about fifteen minutes I'm talking to a reporter about the charges that Bull Durham's been flinging at me, so I was trying to organize my response into sincere, succinct nuggets."

"Bull Durham? The man who's been protesting the Holocaust Asset Recovery Act? Don't tell me he's involved now with Paul Radbuka!"

I blinked. "No. He's involved in a case I've been working on. Insurance fraud involving a South Side family."

"And that takes precedence over responding to messages from me?"

"Lotty!" I was outraged. "Alderman Durham handed out flyers today defaming me. He marched around a public space bellowing insults about me through a bullhorn. It doesn't seem extraordinary that I had to respond to that. I walked into my office five minutes ago. I haven't even seen my messages."

"Yes, I see," she said. "I—but I need some support, too. I want to see this man's video, Victoria. I want to know that you're trying to help me. That you won't aban—that you won't forget our—"

Her voice was panicky; she was flailing about for words in a way that made my insides twist. "Lotty, please, how could I forget our friendship? Or ever abandon you? As soon as I finish with this interview, I'll be right over. Say in an hour?"

When we hung up I checked my messages. She'd phoned three times. Beth Blacksin had phoned once, to say she'd love to talk to me but could I come to the Global building, since she was jammed up with editing all the interviews and demonstrations of the day. She'd seen Murray Ryerson—he'd join us at the studio. I thought wistfully of my cot in the back room but gathered up my things and drove back downtown.

Beth spent twenty minutes taping me while she and

Murray peppered me with questions. I was being careful not to implicate my client, but I freely tossed them
Howard Fepple's name—it was time someone besides
me started pushing on him. Beth was gleeful enough to
get this exclusive new source that she happily shared
what she had with me, but neither she nor Murray had
any idea who had given Durham the information on the
Birnbaums.

"I got thirty seconds with the alderman, who says it's
common knowledge," Murray said. "I talked to the
Birnbaum legal counsel, who said it's overblown
ancient history. I couldn't get to the woman who wrote
their history, Amy Blount—someone at Ajax suggested
it was her."

"I talked to her," I said smugly. "I'd bet hard against
her. It has to be another Ajax insider. Or maybe someone in the Birnbaum company with a grudge. You talk
to Bertrand Rossy? I gather he's fulminating—the Swiss
probably aren't used to street demonstrations. If
Durham hadn't libeled me, I'd be chortling over it."

"You know that piece we did on Wednesday on Paul
Radbuka?" Beth said, changing the subject to something she cared about personally. "We've had about a
hundred and thirty e-mails from people who say they
know his little friend Miriam. My assistant's tracking
them down. Most of them are unstable glory-seekers,
but it will be such a coup if one of them turns out to be
the real deal. Just think if we reunite them on-air!"

"I hope you're not building that up on-air," I said
sharply. "It may turn out to be just that: air."

"What?" Beth stared at me. "You think he made up
his friend? No, Vic, you're wrong about that."

Murray, whose six-eight frame had been curled
against a filing cabinet, suddenly stood up straight and
began pelting me with questions: what inside dope did
I have on Paul Radbuka? What did I know about his
playmate Miriam? What did I know about Rhea Wiell?

"Nothing on all of the above," I said. "I haven't talked to the guy. But I met Rhea Wiell this morning."

"She's not a fraud, Vic," Beth said sharply.

"I know she's not. She's not a fraud and she's not a con artist. But she believes in herself so intensely that— I don't know, I can't explain it," I finished helplessly, struggling to articulate why her look of ecstasy when she discussed Paul Radbuka had unnerved me so much. "I agree—it doesn't seem possible that someone as experienced as Wiell could be conned. But—well, I guess I won't have an opinion until I meet Radbuka," I finished lamely.

"When you do, you'll really believe in him," Beth promised.

She left a minute later to edit my remarks for the ten o'clock news. Murray tried to talk me into a drink. "You know, Warshawski, we work together so well, it'd be a shame not to get back in the habit."

"Oh, Murray, you sweet-talker, you, I can see how badly you need your own private angle on this stuff. I can't stay tonight—it's vital that I get to Lotty Herschel's place in the next half hour."

He followed me down the hall to the security station while I handed in my pass. "What's the real story for you here, Warshawski? Radbuka and Wiell? Or Durham and the Sommers family?"

I frowned up at him. "They both are. That's the problem. I can't quite focus on either of them."

"Durham is about the slickest politico in town these days next to the mayor. Be careful how you tangle with him. Say hey to the doc for me, okay?" He squeezed my shoulder affectionately and turned back up the hall.

I've known Lotty Herschel since I was an undergraduate at the University of Chicago. I was a blue-collar girl on an upscale campus, feeling rawly out of place, when I met her—she was providing medical advice to an abortion underground where I volunteered. She took me under her wing, giving me the kind of social skills I'd lost when I lost my mother, keeping me from losing my way in those days of drugs and violent protest, taking time from a dense-packed schedule to cheer my successes and condole over failures. She'd even gone to some college basketball games to see me play—true friendship, since sports of all kind bore her. But it was my athletic scholarship that made my education possible, so she supported my doing my best at it. If she was collapsing now, if something terrible was wrong with her—I couldn't even finish the thought, it was so frightening to me.

She'd recently moved to a high-rise on the lakefront, to one of the beautiful old buildings where you can watch the sun rise with nothing between you and water but Lake Shore Drive and a strip of park. She used to live in a two-flat a short walk from her storefront clinic, but her one concession to aging was to give up on being a landlady in a neighborhood full of drug-dealing housebreakers. Max and I had both been relieved to see her in a building with an indoor garage.

When I left my car with her doorman, it was only eight o'clock. The day seemed to have been spinning on so long I was sure we must have come round the other side of dark to begin a new one.

Lotty was waiting in the hall for me when I got off the elevator, making a valiant effort at composure. Even though I held the envelope of stills and video out to her, she didn't snatch it from me but invited me in to her living room, offering me a drink. When I said I only wanted water, she still ignored the envelope, trying to make a joke that I must be ill if I wanted water instead of whisky. I smiled, but the deep circles under her dark eyes disturbed me. I didn't comment on her appearance, just asking as she turned to go to the kitchen if she would bring me a piece of fruit or cheese.

She seemed to really look at me for the first time. "You haven't eaten? I can see from the lines on your face that you're exhausted. Stay in here; I'll fix you something."

This was more like her usual brisk manner. I was slightly reassured, slumping against her couch and dozing until she returned with a tray. Cold chicken, carrot sticks, a small salad, and slices of the thick bread a Ukrainian nurse at the hospital bakes for her. I tried not to spring on the food as if I were one of my own dogs.

While I ate, Lotty watched me, as if keeping her eyes from the envelope by an act of will. She kept up a flow of random chatter—had I decided to go away with Morrell for the weekend, would we make it back for Sunday afternoon's concert, Max was expecting forty or fifty people at his house for dinner afterward, but he—and especially Calia—would miss me if I didn't come.

I finally interrupted the flow. "Lotty, are you afraid to look at the pictures because of what you will see or because of what you may not see?"

She gave the ghost of a smile. "Acute of you, my dear. A little of both, I think. But—if you will run the tape for me, maybe I am ready to see it. Max warned me that the man was not prepossessing."

We went to the back bedroom she uses for television and loaded the tape into the VCR. I glanced at Lotty, but the fear in her face was so acute that I couldn't bear to watch her. As Paul Radbuka recounted his nightmares and his heartbreaking cries for his childhood friend, I kept my eyes glued to him. When we'd seen everything, including the "Exploring Chicago" segment with Rhea Wiell and Arnold Praeger, Lotty asked in a thread of a voice to return to Radbuka's interview.

I ran it through for her twice more, but when she wanted a third rerun I refused: her face was grey with strain. "You're torturing yourself with this, Lotty. Why?"

"I—the whole thing is hard." Even though I was sitting on the floor next to her armchair I could barely make out her words. "Something is familiar to me in what he's saying. Only I can't think, because—I can't think. I hate this. I hate seeing things that make my mind stop working. Do you believe his story?"

I made a helpless gesture. "I can't fathom it, but it's so remote from how I want to see life that my mind is rejecting it. I met the therapist yesterday—no, it was today, it just seems like a long time ago. She's a legitimate clinician, I think, but, well, fanatical. A zealot for her work in general and most particularly for this guy. I told her I wanted to interview Radbuka, to see if he could be related to these people you and Max know, but she's protecting him. He's not in the phone book, either as Paul Radbuka or Paul Ulrich, so I'm sending Mary Louise out to all the Ulrichs in Chicago. Maybe he's still living in his father's house, or maybe a neighbor will recognize his picture—we don't know his father's first name."

"How old would you say he is?" she asked unexpectedly.

"You mean, could he be the right age for the experiences he's claiming? You'd be a better judge of that than I, but again, it would be easier to answer if we saw him in person."

I took the stills out of the envelope, holding the three different shots so that the light shone full on them. Lotty looked at them a long time but finally shook her head helplessly.

"Why did I imagine something definite would jump out at me? It's what Max said to me. Resemblance is so often a trick of the expression, after all, and these are only photographs, photographs of a picture, really. I would have to see the man, and even then—after all, I'd be trying to match an adult face against a child's memory of someone who was much younger than this man is now."

I took her hand in both of mine. "Lotty, what is it you're afraid of? This is so painful for you it's breaking my heart. Is it—could he be part of your family? Do you think he's related to your mother?"

"If you knew anything of those matters, you would know better than to ask such a question," she said with a flash of her more imperious manner.

"But you do know the Radbuka family, don't you?"

She laid the pictures on the coffee table as if she were dealing cards and then proceeded to rearrange them, but she wasn't really looking at them. "I knew some members of the family many years ago. The circumstances—when I last saw them it was extremely painful. The way we parted, I mean, or anyway the whole situation. If this man is—I don't see how he could be what he says. But if he is, then I owe it to the family to try to befriend him."

"Do you want me to do some digging? Assuming I can get hold of any information to dig with?"

Her vivid, dark face was contorted with strain. "Oh, Victoria, I don't know what I want. I want the past never to have happened, or since it did and I can't change it, I want it to stay where it is, past, dead, gone. This man, I don't want to know him. But I see I will have to talk to him. Do I want you to investigate him? No, I don't want you near him. But find him for me, find him so I can talk to him, and you, you—what you can do is try to see what piece of paper convinced him his name was really Paul Radbuka."

Late that night, her unhappy, contradictory words kept tumbling through my mind. Sometime after two, I finally fell asleep, but in my dreams Bull Durham chased me until I found myself locked up with Paul Radbuka at Terezin, with Lotty on the far side of the barbed wire watching me with hurt, tormented eyes. "Keep him there among the dead," she cried.

Lotty Herschel's Story:

English Lessons

School still had three weeks to go when Hugo and I reached London, but Minna didn't think it worthwhile to register me, since my lack of English would keep me from understanding any lessons. She set me to doing chores in the house and then in the neighborhood: she would write a shopping list in her slow English script, spelling the words under her breath—incorrectly, as I saw when I learned to read and write in the new language. She would give me a pound and send me to the corner shop to buy a chop for dinner, a few potatoes, a loaf of bread. When she got home from work she would count the change twice to make sure I hadn't robbed her. Still, each week she gave me sixpence in pocket money.

Hugo, whom I saw on Sundays, was already chattering in English. I felt humiliated, the big sister not able to speak because Minna kept me barricaded behind a wall of German. She hoped day to day that I would be sent back to Vienna. "Why waste your time on English when you may leave in the morning?"

The first time she said it my heart skipped a beat. "*Mutti und Oma, haben sie dir geschrieben?* They wrote you? I can go home?"

"I haven't heard from Madame Butterfly," Minna spat. "In her own good time she will remember you."

Mutti had forgotten me. It hit my child's heart like a fist. A year later, when I could read English, I despised the children's books we were given in school, with their saccharine mothers and children. "My mother would never forget me. She loves me even though she is far away, and I pray every night to see her again, as I know she is praying for me and watching over me." That's what the girls in *Good Wives* or *English Orphans* would have said to Cousin Minna, boldly defiant in their trembling little-girl voices. But they didn't understand anything about life, those little girls.

Your own mother lies in bed, too worn to get up to kiss you good-bye when you get on a train, leave your city, your home, your Mutti and Oma, behind. Men in uniforms stop you, look in your suitcase, put big ugly hands on your underwear, your favorite doll, they can take these things if they want, and your mother is lying in bed, not stopping them.

Of course I knew the truth, knew that only Hugo and I could get visas and travel permits, that grown-ups weren't allowed to go to England unless someone in England gave them a job. I knew the truth, that the Nazis hated us because we were Jews, so they took away Opa's apartment with my bedroom: some strange woman was living there now with her blond child in my white-canopied bed—I had gone early one morning on foot to look at the building, with its little sign, *Juden verboten*. I knew these things, knew that my mama was hungry as we all were, but to a child, your parents are so powerful, I still half believed my parents, my Opa, would rise up and make everything go back the way it used to be.

When Minna said my mother would remember me in her own good time, she only voiced my deepest fear. I had been sent away because Mutti didn't want me. Until September, when the war started and no one could leave

Austria anymore, Minna would say that at regular intervals.

Even today I'm sure she did this because she so resented my mother, Lingerl, the little butterfly with her soft gold curls, her beautiful smile, her charming manners. The only way Minna could hurt Lingerl was to hurt me. Perhaps the fact that my mother never knew made Minna twist the knife harder: she was so furious that she couldn't stab Lingerl directly that she kept on at me. Maybe that's why she was so hateful when we got the news about their fate.

The one thing I knew for sure my first summer in London, the summer of '39, was what my papa told me, that he would come if I could find him a job. Armed with a German–English dictionary, which I found in Minna's sitting room, I spent that summer walking up and down the streets near Minna's house in Kentish Town. My cheeks stained with embarrassment, I would ring doorbells and struggle to say, "Mine vater, he need job, he do all job. Garden, he make garden. House, he clean house. Coal, he bring coal, make house warm."

Eventually I ended up at the house behind Minna's. I had been watching it from my attic window because it was so different from Minna's. Hers was a narrow frame structure whose neighbors almost touched on the east and west sides. The garden was a cold oblong, as narrow as the house and only holding a few scraggly raspberry bushes. To this day I won't eat raspberries. . . .

Anyway, the house behind was made of stone, with a large garden, roses, an apple tree, a little patch of vegetables, and Claire. I knew her name because her mother and her older sister would call to her. She sat on a swing-bench under their pergola, her fair hair pulled away from her ears to hang down her back, while she pored over her books.

"Claire," her mother would call. "Teatime, darling. You'll strain your eyes reading in the sun."

Of course, I didn't understand what she was saying at first, although I could make out Claire's name, but the words were repeated every summer, so my memory blurs all those summers; in my memory I understand Mrs. Tallmadge perfectly from the start.

Claire was studying because next year she would take her higher-school certificate; she wanted to read medicine—again, I only learned this later. The sister, Vanessa, was five years older than Claire. Vanessa had some refined little job, I don't remember what now. She was getting ready to be married that summer; that I understood clearly—all little girls understand brides and weddings, from peeping over railings at them. I would watch Vanessa come into the garden: she wanted Claire to try on a dress or a hat or admire a swatch of fabric, and finally, when she could get her sister's attention no other way, she would snatch Claire's book. Then the two would chase each other around the garden until they ended up in a laughing heap back under the pergola.

I wanted to be part of their life so desperately that at night I would lie in bed making up stories about them. Claire would be in some trouble from which I would rescue her. Claire would somehow know the details of my life with Cousin Minna and would boldly confront Minna, accuse her of all her crimes, and rescue me. I don't know why it was Claire who became my heroine, not the mother or the bride—maybe because Claire was closer to my age, so I could imagine being her. I only know that I would watch the sisters laughing together and burst into tears.

I put off their house until last because I didn't want Claire to pity me. I pictured my papa as a servant in her house; then she would never sit laughing with me on the swing. But in the letters that still passed between England and Vienna that summer, Papa kept reminding me that he needed me to get him a job. All these years later I am still bitter that Minna couldn't find a place for him at the glove

factory. It's true it wasn't her factory, but she was the
bookkeeper, she could talk to Herr Schatz. Every time I
brought it up she screamed that she wasn't going to have
people pointing a finger at her. During the war, the glove
factory was working treble shifts to supply the army. . . .

Finally, one hot August morning, when I had seen
Claire go into the garden with her books, I rang their
doorbell. I thought if Mrs. Tallmadge answered I could
manage to speak to her; if Claire was in the garden I was
safe from having to face my idol. Of course it was a maid
who came to the door—I should have expected that, since
all of the bigger houses in our neighborhood had maids.
And even the small, ugly ones like Minna's had at least a
charwoman to do the heavy cleaning.

The maid said something too fast for me to understand.
I only knew her tone was angry. Quickly, as she started to
shut the door in my face, I blurted out in broken English
that Claire wanted me.

"Claire ask, she say, you come."

The maid shut the door on me, but this time she told
me to wait, a word I had learned in my weeks of doorbell
ringing. By and by Claire came back with the maid.

"Oh, Susan, it's the funny little girl from over the way.
I'll talk to her—you go on." When Susan disappeared,
sniffing, Claire bent over and said, "I've seen you watching
me over the wall, you queer little monkey. What do you
want?"

I stammered out my story: father needed job. He could
do anything.

"But Mother looks after the garden, and Susan cleans
the house."

"Play violin. Sister—" I pantomimed Vanessa as a bride,
making Claire burst into gales of laughter. "He play. Very
pretty. Sister like."

Mrs. Tallmadge appeared behind her daughter,
demanding to know who I was and what I wanted. She
and Claire had a conversation that went on for some time,

which I couldn't follow at all, except to recognize Hitler's name, and the Jews, of course. I could see that Claire was trying to persuade Mrs. Tallmadge but that the mother was obdurate—there was no money. When my English became fluent, when I got to know the family, I learned that Mr. Tallmadge had died, leaving some money— enough to maintain the house and keep Mrs. Tallmadge and her daughters in respectable comfort—but not enough for extravagance. Sponsoring my father would have been extravagant.

At one point Claire turned to ask me about my mother. I said, Yes, she would come, too, but Claire wanted to know what kind of work my mother could perform. I stared blankly, unable to imagine such a thing. Not just because she had been sick with her pregnancy, but no one expected my mother to work. You wanted her around to make you gay, because she danced and talked and sang more beautifully than anyone. But even if my English had allowed me to express those ideas, I knew they would be a mistake.

"Sewing," I finally remembered. "Very good sewing, mother make. Makes."

"Maybe Ted?" Claire suggested.

"You can try," her mother snorted, going back into the house.

Ted was Edward Marmaduke. He was going to be Vanessa's husband. I had seen him in the garden, too, a pale Englishman with very blond hair who turned an unhealthy pinky-red under the summer sun. He would serve in Africa and Italy but come home in one piece in 1945, his face scorched to a deep brick that never really faded.

That summer of '39 he didn't want a poor immigrant couple to encumber the start of his married life with Vanessa: I heard that argument, crouched on the other side of the wall between Minna's yard and Claire's, knowing it was about me and my family but only understanding his loud "no" and from Vanessa's tone that she was trying to please both Claire and her fiancé.

Claire told me not to give up hope. "But, little monkey, you need to learn English. You have to go to school in a few weeks."

"In Vienna," I said. "I go home. I go on the school there."

Claire shook her head. "There may be war in Europe; you might not go home for a long time. No, we need to get you speaking English."

So my life changed overnight. Of course, I still lived with Minna, still ran her errands, endured her bitterness, but my heroine actually did take me to the pergola. Every afternoon she made me speak English with her. When school started, she took me to the local grammar school, introduced me to the headmistress, and helped me at odd intervals to learn my lessons.

I repaid her with lavish adoration. She was the most beautiful girl in London. She became my standard of English manners: Claire says one doesn't do that, I would say coldly to Minna. Claire says one always does this. I imitated her accent and her ways of doing things, from how she draped herself in the garden swing to how she wore her hats.

When I learned Claire was going to read medicine if she got a place at the Royal Free, that became my ambition, too.

XV

Gate Crasher

Morrell's and my brief vacation in Michigan helped drive Friday's worries to the back of my mind—thanks chiefly to Morrell's good sense. Since I was driving the outbound route I started to detour to Hyde Park, thinking I could make a quick trip in and out of Fepple's office to look for the Sommers family file. Morrell vetoed this sharply, reminding me that we'd agreed to forty-eight hours without business.

"I didn't bring my laptop, so that I wouldn't be tempted to e-mail Humane Medicine. You can stay away from an insurance agent who sounds like a disgusting specimen for that long, too, V I." Morrell took my picklocks out of my bag and stuck them in his jeans. "Anyway, I don't want to be a party to your extracurricular information-gathering techniques."

I had to laugh, despite a momentary annoyance. After all, why would I want to spoil my last few days with Morrell by bothering with a worm like Fepple? I decided not even to bother with the morning papers, which I'd stuck in my bag without reading: I didn't need to raise my blood pressure by seeing Bull Durham's attacks on me in print.

Less easy to put aside were my worries about Lotty, but our ban on business didn't include concerns about friends. I tried to describe her anguish to Morrell. He listened to me as I drove but couldn't offer much help in deciphering what lay behind her tormented speech.

"She lost her family in the war, didn't she?"

"Except for her younger brother Hugo, who went to England with her. He lives in Montreal—he runs a small chain of upscale women's boutiques in Montreal and Toronto. Her uncle Stefan, I guess he was one of her grandfather's brothers, he came to Chicago in the 1920's. And spent most of the war as a guest of the federal government in Fort Leavenworth. Forgery," I added in response to Morrell's startled question. "A master engraver who fell in love with Andrew Jackson's face but overlooked a few details. So he wasn't part of her childhood."

"She was nine or ten when she last saw her mother, then. No wonder those wartime memories are too painful for her. Didn't you say he was dead—the person named Radbuka?"

"Or she. Lotty revealed no details at all. But she did say it, said that the person no longer exists." I thought about it. "It's a peculiar construction: that person no longer exists. It could mean several things—the person died, the person changed identities, or maybe the person betrayed her in some way so that someone she loved or who she thought loved her never really existed."

"Then the pain could come from the reminder of a second loss. Don't go sleuthing after her, Vic. Let her bring the story to you when she's strong enough to."

I fixed my eyes on the road. "And if she never tells me?"

He leaned over to wipe a tear from my cheek. "It's not your failure as a friend. These are her demons, not your failures."

I didn't speak much for the rest of the ride. We were going about a hundred miles around the big U of Lake Michigan's southern end; I let the rhythm of car and road fill my mind.

Morrell had booked a room at a rambling stone inn overlooking Lake Michigan. After checking in we took a walk along the beach. It was hard to believe that this was the same lake that Chicago bordered—the long stretches of dunes, empty of everything but birds and prairie grasses, were a different world than the relentless noise and grime of the city.

Three weeks after Labor Day we had the lakefront to ourselves. Feeling the wind from the lake in my hair, making the crystalline sand along the shore sing by rubbing it with my bare heel, gave me a cocoon of peace. I felt the tension lines smooth out of my cheeks and forehead.

"Morrell—it will be very hard for me to live without you these next few months. I know this trip is exciting and that you're eager to go. I don't grudge it to you. But it will be hard—especially right now—not to have you here."

He pulled me to him. "It will be hard for me to be away from you, too, *pepaiola*. You keep me stirred up, sneezing, with your vigorous remarks."

I'd told Morrell once that my father used to call my mother and me that—one of the few Italian words he'd picked up from my mother. Pepper mill. My two *pepaiole*, he'd say, pretending to sneeze when we were haranguing him over something. You're making my nose red, okay, okay, we'll do it your way just to protect my nose. When I was a little girl he could make me burst out laughing with his fake sneezes.

"*Pepaiola*, huh—sneeze at this!" I tossed a little sand at Morrell and sprinted away from him down the beach. He chased after me, which he normally wouldn't do—he doesn't like to run, and anyway, I'm faster. I slowed so he could catch me. We spent the rest of the day avoiding all difficult topics, including his imminent departure. The air was chilly, but the lake was still warm: we swam naked in the dark, then huddled in a blanket on the beach, making love with Andromeda overhead and Orion the hunter, my talisman, rising in the east, his belt so close it seemed we might pluck it from the sky. Sunday at noon we changed reluctantly into our dress clothes and drove back into the city for the Cellini's final Chicago concert.

When we stopped for gas near the entrance to the tollway, the weekend felt officially over, so I bought the Sunday papers. Durham's protest led both the news and the op-ed sections in the *Herald-Star*. I was glad to see that my interview with Blacksin and Murray had made Durham cool his jets about me.

> Mr. Durham has dropped one of his complaints, that Chicago private investigator V I Warshawski confronted a bereaved woman in the middle of her husband's funeral. "My sources in the community were understandably devastated by the terrible inhumanity of an insurance company failing to keep its promise to pay to bury a loved one; in their agitation they may have misspoken Ms. Warshawski's role in the case."

"*May* have misspoken? Can't he come right out and say he was wrong?" I snarled at Morrell.

Murray had added a few sentences saying that my investigation was raising troubling questions about the role of both the Midway Insurance Agency and the Ajax Insurance company. Midway owner Howard Fepple had not returned phone calls. An Ajax spokesperson said the company had uncovered a fraudulent death claim submitted ten years ago; they were trying to see how that could have occurred.

The op-ed page had an article by the president of the Illinois Insurance Institute. I read it aloud to Morrell.

Imagine that you go into Berlin, the capital of Germany, and find a large museum dedicated to the horrors of three centuries of African slavery in the United States. Then imagine that Frankfurt, Munich, Cologne, Bonn all have smaller versions of American slavery museums. That's what it's like for America to put up Holocaust museums while completely ignoring atrocities committed here against Africans and Native Americans.

Now suppose Germany passed a law saying that any American company which benefited from slavery couldn't do business in Europe. That's what Illinois wants to do with German companies. The past is a tangled country. No one's hands are clean, but if we have to stop every ten minutes to wash them before we can sell cars, or chemicals, or even insurance, commerce will grind to a halt.

"And so on. Lotty isn't alone in wanting the past to stay good and buried. Pretty slick, in a superficial kind of way."

Morrell grimaced. "Yes. It makes him sound like a warmhearted liberal, worrying about African-Americans and Indians, when all he really wants to do is keep anyone from inspecting life-insurance records to see how many policies were sold which Illinois insurers don't want to pay out."

"Of course, the Sommers family also bought a policy they can't collect on. Although I don't think it was the company that defrauded them, but the agent. I wish I could see Fepple's file."

"Not today, Ms. Warshawski. I'm not giving back your picklocks until I board that 777 on Tuesday."

I laughed and subsided into the sports section. The

Cubs had gone so far into free fall that they'd have to send the space shuttle to haul them back to the National League. The Sox, on the other hand, were looking pretty, the best record in the majors going into the final week of the season. Even though the pundits were saying they'd be eliminated in the first round of the play-offs, it was still an amazing event in Chicago sports.

We reached Orchestra Hall seconds before the ushers closed the doors. Michael Loewenthal had left tickets for Morrell and me. We joined Agnes and Calia Loewenthal in a box, Calia looking angelic in white smocking with gold roses embroidered on it. Her doll and dog, festooned with ribbons in matching gold, were propped up in the chair next to hers.

"Where're Lotty and Max?" I whispered as the musicians took the stage.

"Max is getting ready for the party. Lotty came over to help him, then got into a huge row with both him and Carl. She doesn't look well; I don't know if she'll even stay for the party."

"Shh, Mommy, Aunt Vicory, you can't talk when Daddy is playing in public." Calia looked at us sternly.

She had been warned against this sin many times in her short life. Agnes and I obediently subsided, but my worries about Lotty rushed back to the front of my mind. Also, if she was having a major fight with Max, I wasn't looking forward to the evening.

As the musicians took the stage they looked remote in their formal wear, like strangers, not friends. For a moment I wished we'd skipped the concert, but once the music began, with the controlled lyricism that marked Carl's style, the knots inside me began to unwind. In a Schubert trio, the richness of Michael Loewenthal's playing, and the intimacy he seemed to feel—with his cello, with his fellow musicians—made me ache with longing. Morrell took my fingers and squeezed them gently: separation will not part us.

During intermission, I asked Agnes if she knew why Lotty and Max were fighting.

She shook her head. "Michael says they've been arguing off and on all summer over this conference on Jews where Max spoke on Wednesday. Now they seem to be fighting about a man Max met there, or heard speak, or something, but I was trying to get Calia to hold still while I braided the ribbons into her hair and didn't really pay attention."

After the concert Agnes asked if we would drive Calia up to Evanston with us. "She's been so good, sitting like a princess for three hours. The sooner she can run around and let off steam the better. I'd like to stay until Michael's ready to leave."

Calia's angelic mood vanished as soon as we walked out of Orchestra Hall. She ran shrieking down the street, shedding ribbons and even Ninshubur, the blue stuffed dog. Before she actually careened into the street, I caught up with her and scooped her up.

"I am not a baby, I do not get carried," she yelled at me.

"Of course not. No baby would be such a pain." I was panting with the exertion of carrying her down the stairs to the garage. Morrell was laughing at both of us, which made Calia at once assume an icy dignity.

"I am most annoyed at this behavior," she said, echoing her mother, her little arms crossed in front of her.

"Speaking for both of us," I murmured, setting her back on her feet.

Morrell handed her into the car and gravely offered Ninshubur back to her. Calia wouldn't allow me to fasten her seat belt but decided Morrell was her ally against me and stopped squirming when he leaned in to do the job. On the ride to Max's, she scolded me through the medium of lecturing her doll: "You are a very naughty girl, picking up Ninshubur and carrying him down the stairs when he was running. Ninshubur is not a baby. He needs to run and let off steam." She certainly took my mind off any other worries. Perhaps that would be a good reason to have a child: you wouldn't have energy left to fret about anything else.

A handful of cars were in Max's drive when we got there, including Lotty's dark-green Infiniti, its battered fenders an eloquent testimony to her imperious approach to the streets. She hadn't learned to drive until she arrived in Chicago at the age of thirty, when she apparently took lessons from a NASCAR crash dummy. She must have patched up her disagreement with Max if she was staying for the party.

A black-suited young man opened the door for us. Calia ran down the hall, shrieking for her grandfather. When we moved more slowly after her, we saw two other men in waiters' costumes folding napkins in the dining room. Max had set up a series of small tables there and in the adjacent parlor so that people could eat dinner sitting down.

Lotty, her back to the door, was counting forks into bundles and slapping them onto a sideboard. Judging from her rigid posture she was still angry. We slipped by without saying anything.

"Not the best mood for a party," I muttered.

"We can pay our respects to Carl and leave early," Morrell agreed.

We tracked Max down in the kitchen, where he was conferring with his housekeeper on how to manage the party. Calia ran to tug at his arm. He hoisted her up to the countertop but didn't let her stop his discussion with Mrs. Squires. Max has been an administrator for years—he knows you never finish anything if you keep accepting interruptions.

"What's going on with Lotty?" I asked when he and Mrs. Squires were done.

"Oh, she's having a temper tantrum. I wouldn't pay much attention to it," he said lightly.

"This isn't about the Radbuka business, is it?" I asked, frowning.

"Opa, Opa," Calia shouted, "I was quiet the whole time, but Aunt Vicory and Mommy talked and then Aunt Vicory was very bad, she hurted my tummy when she carried me down the stairs."

"Terrible, *puppchen*," Max murmured, stroking her hair, adding to me, "Lotty and I have agreed to keep our disagreements to one side for the evening. So I am not going to violate the concordat by giving my views."

One of the waiters brought a young woman in jeans into the kitchen. Max introduced her as Lindsey, a local student who was going to entertain the small ones at the party. When I told Calia I'd go upstairs to help her put on play clothes, she told me scornfully it was a *formal* party, so she had to keep her party dress on, but she consented to go with Lindsey to the garden.

Lotty swept into the kitchen, acknowledging Morrell and me with a regal nod, and said she was going up to change. Despite her daunting manner, it was a relief to see her imperious rather than anguished. She reappeared in a crimson silk jacket and long skirt about the time the other guests began to arrive.

Don Strzepek walked over from Morrell's, actually wearing an ironed shirt—Max had readily agreed to include Morrell's old friend in the invitation. The musicians showed up in a bunch. Three or four had children around Calia's age; the cheerful Lindsey scooped them all together and took them upstairs to watch videos and eat pizza.

Carl had changed from his tails into a soft sweater and trousers. His eyes were bright with pleasure in himself, his music, his friends; the tempo of the party began to accelerate with the force of his personality. Even Lotty was relaxing, laughing in one corner with the Cellini bass player.

I found myself discussing Chicago architecture with Michael Loewenthal's first cello instructor. Over wine and little squares of goat-cheese polenta, the Cellini's manager suggested today's anti-American sentiment in France resembled anti-Roman feelings in ancient Gaul. Near the piano Morrell was deep in the kind of political controversy he delights in. We forgot our idea of leaving early.

Around nine, when the rest of the guests had gone into the back of the house for dinner, the doorbell rang. I had lingered in the sunroom, listening to Rosa Ponselle sing *"L'amero, sarò costante."* It had been one of my mother's favorite arias and I wanted to hear the recording to the end. The bell rang again as I crossed the empty hall to join the rest of the party—the waiters were apparently too busy serving dinner to respond to it. I turned back to the heavy double doors.

When I saw the figure on the doorstep, I sucked in my breath. His curly hair was thinning at the temples, but despite the grey, and the lines around his mouth, his face had a kind of childlike quality. The pictures I'd been looking at showed him contorted with anguish, but even with his cheeks creased in a shy, eager smile, Paul Radbuka was unmistakable.

XVI

Contact Problems

He looked around the hall with a kind of nervous eagerness, as if he had arrived early for an audition. "Are you Mrs. Loewenthal, perhaps? Or a daughter?"

"Mr. Radbuka—or is it Mr. Ulrich—who invited you here?" I wondered wildly if that was what Lotty and Max had been fighting about—Max had found the guy's address and invited him to come while Carl was still in town; Lotty, with her intense fear of reawakening the past, strenuously objected.

"No, no, Ulrich was never my name; that was the man who called himself my father. I'm Paul Radbuka. Are you one of my new relatives?"

"Why are you here? Who invited you?" I repeated.

"No one. I came on my own, when Rhea told me that some of the people who knew my family, or perhaps are my family, were leaving Chicago tomorrow."

"When I talked to Rhea Wiell Friday afternoon, she said you didn't know there were any other Radbukas and that she'd see how you felt about meeting them."

"Oh. Oh—you were part of that meeting with Rhea. Are you the publisher who wants to write my story?"

"I'm V I Warshawski. I'm an investigator who spoke

to her about the possibility of meeting you." I knew I sounded chilly, but his unexpected arrival had me off-balance.

"I know—the detective who went to see her when she was talking to her publisher. Then you're the person who is friends with the survivors from my family."

"No," I said sharply, trying to slow him down. "I have friends who may know someone from the Radbuka family. Whether that person is related to you would depend on a lot of details that we can't really get into tonight. Why don't you—"

He interrupted me, his eager smile replaced by anger. "I want to meet anyone who could possibly be a relative. Not in some cautious way, going back to you, finding out who these other Radbukas are, checking to see whether they could really be related to me, whether they want to meet me. That might take months, even years—I can't wait for that kind of time to pass."

"So you prayed and the Lord directed you to Mr. Loewenthal's address?" I said.

Spots of color burned in his cheeks. "You're being sarcastic, but there's no need to be. I learned at Rhea's that Max Loewenthal was the man who was interested in finding me. That he had a musician friend who knew my family, and that the musician was here only until tomorrow. When she put it like that, that Max and his friend thought they might know someone of my family, I knew the truth: either Max or his musician friend must be my missing relation. They are hiding behind a cloak of pretending to have a friend—I know that—it's a common disguise, especially for people who are frightened of having their identities known. I saw I would have to take the initiative, come to them, over-come their fears of being found out. So I studied the newspapers, I saw the Cellini was visiting from England, with their last concert today, I saw the name

Loewenthal as the cellist and knew he must be Max's relation."

"Rhea told you Mr. Loewenthal's name?" I demanded, furious with her for breaching Max's privacy.

He gave a supercilious smile. "She made it clear she wanted me to learn it: she'd written Max's name next to mine in her appointment book. Which made me sure Max and I were linked."

I remembered reading her square hand upside down myself. I felt overwhelmed by his easy manipulation of facts to suit his wishes and demanded sharply how he'd found Max's house, since his home phone isn't listed.

"Oh, it was simple." He laughed with childish delight, his anger forgotten. "I told them at the symphony I was Michael Loewenthal's cousin and that I badly needed to see him while he was still in town."

"And the CSO gave you this address?" I was staggered: stalking is such a serious problem for performers that no symphony management worth its salt gives out home addresses.

"No, no." He laughed again. "If you're a detective, this will amuse you, maybe even be useful to you in your work. I did try to get the address from the symphony management, but they were very stuffy. So today I went to the concert. What a beautiful gift Michael has—how wonderfully he plays on that cello. I went backstage afterward to congratulate him, but that wasn't so easy, either—they make it hard to get in to see the performers."

He scowled in momentary resentment. "By the time I got backstage, my cousin Michael had left, but I heard the other performers talking about the party that Max was holding tonight. So I called the hospital where Max works and told them I was with the chamber players but I had lost Max's address. So they found someone in the administration—it took a while, because it's

Sunday, that's why I'm late—but they called me with the address."

"How did you know where Mr. Loewenthal works?" I was reeling so hard in the face of his narrative that I could only grasp at the corner points.

"It was in the program, the program for the Birnbaum conference." He beamed with pride. "Wasn't that clever, to say I was one of the musicians? Isn't that the kind of thing an investigator like you does to find people?"

It made me furious that he was right—it's exactly what I would have done. "Despite how clever it was, you're here under a false impression. Max Loewenthal is not your cousin."

He smiled indulgently. "Yes, yes, I'm sure you're protecting him—Rhea told me you were protecting him and that she respected you for it, but consider this: he wants to find out about me. What other possible reason could there be than that he knows we're related?"

We were still standing in the doorway. "You yourself know there's a party going on. Mr. Loewenthal can't possibly give you proper attention tonight. Why don't you give me your address and phone number—he will want to meet you when he can give you his total attention. You should go home before you find yourself in the embarrassing predicament of trying to explain yourself to a room full of strangers."

"You're not Max's daughter or his wife, you're only a guest here as I am myself," Radbuka snapped. "I want to meet him while his son and his friend are still here. Which one is his friend? There were three men of the right age playing in the concert."

Out of the corner of my eye, I saw a couple of people drifting back from the dining room toward the front of the house. I took Radbuka, or Ulrich, or whoever he was, by the elbow. "Why don't we go out to a coffee shop, where we can talk this over privately. Then we can figure out whether there's any chance you could be related to—anyone in Mr. Loewenthal's milieu. But this public forum isn't the best way to do it."

He wrenched himself away. "How do you spend your time? Looking for people's missing jewelry or their lost dogs? You're a property investigator. But I am not a piece of property, I am a man. After all these years— all these deaths and separations—to think I might have some family that survived the Shoah, I don't want to waste one more second before seeing them, let alone one more week or years, even, while you file information about me." His voice thickened with feeling.

"I thought—in your television interview last week, you said you'd only recently discovered your past?"

"But it's been weighing on me all this time, even though I didn't know it. You don't know what it was like, to grow up with a monster, a sadist, and never understand the reason for his hatred: he had attached himself to someone he despised in order to get a visa to America. If I had known what he really was—what he had done in Europe—I would have had him deported. Now, to have the chance to meet my true family—I will not let you put any barriers in my path." Tears started down his face.

"Even so, if you leave your details with me, I will see that Mr. Loewenthal gets them. He will arrange an appointment with you at an early date, but this—confronting him in a public gathering—what kind of welcome do you think he would give you?" I tried to hide my anxiety and dismay under a copy of Rhea Wiell's saintly smile.

"The same welcome I will give him—the heartfelt embrace of one survivor of the ashes to another. There is no way you can understand that."

"Understand what?" Max himself suddenly appeared

with the Cellini oboist on his arm. "Victoria, is this a guest whom I should know?"

"Are you Max?" Radbuka pushed past me to Max, grasping his hand, his face shining with pleasure. "Oh, that I had words to express how much this night means to me. To be able to greet my true cousin. Max. Max."

Max looked from Radbuka to me with the same confusion I was feeling. "I'm sorry, I don't know—oh—you—are you—Victoria—is this your doing?"

"No, it was all mine," Radbuka crowed in delight. "Victoria had mentioned your name to Rhea, and I knew you must be my cousin, either you or your friend. Why else would Victoria be trying so hard to protect you?"

Radbuka adapted himself quickly to the environment: he hadn't known my name when he arrived; now I was Victoria. He also made the childlike assumption that the people in his special world, like Rhea, must be familiar to anyone he spoke to.

"But why discuss me with this therapist at all?" Max said.

The crowd growing behind him included Don Strzepek, who stepped forward. "I'm afraid that was my doing, Mr. Loewenthal—I mentioned your first name, and Rhea Wiell immediately guessed it was you because you'd been on the program at the Birnbaum conference."

I made a helpless gesture. "I've tried to suggest to Mr.—Radbuka—that he come away with me to talk over his situation quietly."

"An excellent idea. Why don't you let Ms. Warshawski get you some supper, and go up to my study where I might be able to join you in an hour or so." Max was off-balance but trying to handle the situation gracefully.

Paul laughed, bobbing his head up and down. "I know, I know. Rhea suggested you might be reluctant to be public with our relationship. But truly, you have nothing to fear—I am not planning on asking for money, or anything of that nature—the man who called himself my father left me well off. Although since the money came from acts of monstrosity, perhaps I should not be taking it. But if he couldn't care for me emotionally, at least he tried to compensate with money."

"You came to my house under false pretenses. I assure you, Mr. Radbuka: I am not related to the Radbuka family."

"Are you ashamed?" Paul blurted. "But I'm not here to embarrass you, only to finally find my family, to see what I can learn about my past, my life before Terezin."

"What little I know I will tell you another time. When I'm at leisure to attend to you properly." Max took his elbow, trying futilely to propel him to the door. "And what you know about yourself you can tell me. Give your phone number to Ms. Warshawski and I will get in touch with you. Tomorrow, I promise you."

Radbuka's face crumpled, like a child about to cry. He reiterated his speech about not being able to wait one more minute. "And tomorrow your musician friend will be gone. What if he's the one who is my missing cousin—how will I ever find him again?"

"Don't you see," Max began helplessly. "All this flailing around with no information is only harder on you, harder on me. Please. Let Ms. Warshawski take you upstairs and talk to you in a quiet way. Or leave your number with her and go home now."

"But I came here by taxi. I can't drive. I don't have a way home," Radbuka cried out in a childlike bewilderment. "Why won't you make me welcome?"

As more people finished dinner, they began filling the hall on their way to the front room. An altercation at the foot of the stairs was a lightning rod for attention. The crowd began to grow, pressing against Max.

I took Paul's arm again. "You are welcome—but not

arguing in the hall in the middle of a party. Rhea wouldn't want you to be so distressed, would she? Let's sit down where we can be comfortable."

"Not until I meet Max's musician friend," he said stubbornly. "Not until he tells me to my face that he knows me, remembers the mother whom I saw pushed alive into a pit of lime."

Lotty had appeared at the door connecting the living room to the hall. She pushed her way through the group to my side. "What's going on, Victoria?"

"This is the guy calling himself Radbuka," I muttered to her. "He got here through some unfortunate fast footwork on his part."

Behind us, we heard a woman echo Lotty's question to someone else in the crowd. And we also heard the response: "I'm not sure; I think this man may be claiming Carl Tisov is his father or something."

Radbuka heard her as well. "Carl Tisov? Is that the name of the musician? Is he here now?"

Lotty's eyes widened in dismay. I whirled, determined to deny the rumor before it got started, but the crowd surged forward, the buzz catching like fire on straw and spreading through the room. Carl's appearance at the back of the hall caused a sudden silence.

"What is this?" he asked gaily. "Are you having a prayer vigil out here, Loewenthal?"

"Is that Carl?" Paul's face lit up again. "Is it you who is my cousin? Oh, Carl, I am here, your long-lost relation. Perhaps we are even brothers? Oh, will you people please move out of the way? I need to get to him!"

"This is horrifying," Lotty muttered in my ear. "How did he get here? How did he decide Carl was related to him?"

The crowd stood frozen with the embarrassment people get when confronted with an adult whose emotions are running wild. As Paul tried to push his way through the throng, Calia suddenly appeared at the top of the hall, shrieking loudly. The other small ones followed, yelling just as loudly, as she pelted down the stairs. Lindsey was running after them, trying to re-establish order—some game must have gotten out of hand.

Calia stopped on the lower landing when she realized the size of her audience. Then she gave a loud whoop of laughter and pointed at Paul. "Look, it's the big bad wolf, he's going to eat my grandpa. He'll catch us next."

All the children took up the chant, pointing at Paul and screeching, "It's a wolf, it's a wolf, it's the big bad wolf!"

When Paul realized he was the object of their taunting, he started to tremble. I thought he might cry again.

Agnes Loewenthal elbowed her way through the packed hall. She stomped up the short flight to the lower landing and scooped up her daughter.

"You're over the top just now, young lady. You littlies were supposed to stay in the playroom with Lindsey: I'm most annoyed at this behavior. It's long past time for your bath and bed—you've had enough excitement for the day."

Calia began to howl, but Agnes marched up to the upper landing with her. The other children became quiet at once. They tiptoed up the stairs in front of a red-faced Lindsey.

The lesser drama with the children had unfrozen the crowd. They let Michael Loewenthal divert them into the front room where coffee was set up. I saw Morrell, who had appeared in the hall when my attention was on Calia, talking to Max and Don.

Radbuka was covering his face in distress. "Why is everyone treating me this way? The wolf, the big bad wolf, that was my foster father. Ulrich, that's German for wolf, but it isn't my name. Who told the children to call me that?"

"No one," I said crisply, my sympathy worn completely thin. "The children were acting out, the way children will. No one here knows that Ulrich is German for big bad wolf."

"It isn't." I'd forgotten Lotty was standing behind me. "It's one of those medieval totemic names, wolflike ruler, something like that." She added something in German to Paul.

Paul started to answer her in German, then stuck out his lower lip, like Calia's when she was being stubborn. "I will not speak the language of my slavery. Are you German? Did you know the man who called himself my father?"

Lotty sighed. "I'm American. But I speak German."

Paul's mood shifted upward again; he beamed at Lotty. "But you are a friend of Max and Carl's. So I was right to come here. If you know my family, did you know Sofie Radbuka?"

At that question, Carl turned to stare at him. "Where the hell did you come up with that name? Lotty, what do you know about this? Did you bring this man here to taunt Max and me?"

"I?" Lotty said. "I—need to sit down."

Her face had gone completely white. I was just in time to catch her as her knees buckled.

XVII

Digging Up the Past

Morrell helped me support Lotty into the sunroom, where we laid her on a wicker settee. She hadn't fainted completely but was still pale and glad to lie down. Max, his face pinched with worry, covered Lotty with an afghan. Always calm in a crisis, he sent Don to the housekeeper for a bottle of ammonia. When I'd soaked a napkin with it and waved it under her nose, Lotty's color improved. She pushed herself to a sitting position, urging Max to return to his guests. After assuring himself that she was really better, he reluctantly went back to the party.

"Melodrama must be in the air this evening," Lotty said, trying unsuccessfully for her usual manner. "I've never done that before in my life. Who brought that extraordinary man here? Surely that wasn't you, Victoria?"

"He brought himself," I said. "He has an eel-like ability to wiggle into spaces. Including the hospital, where some moron in admin gave him Max's home address."

Morrell coughed warningly, jerking his head at the shadows on the far side of the room. Paul Radbuka was standing there, just beyond the edge of the circle of light cast by a floor lamp. Now he darted forward to stand over Lotty.

"Are you feeling better now? Do you feel like talking? I think you must know Sofie Radbuka. Who is she? How can I find her? She must be related to me in some way."

"Surely the person you are looking for was named Miriam." Despite her shaking hands, Lotty pulled herself together to use her "Princess of Austria" manner.

"My Miriam, yes, I long to find her again. But Sofie Radbuka, that is a name which was dangled in front of me like a carrot, making me believe one of my relations must still be alive somewhere. Only now the carrot has been withdrawn. But I'm sure you know her, why else did you faint when you heard the name?"

A question whose answer I would have liked to hear myself, but not in front of this guy.

Lotty raised haughty eyebrows at him. "What I do is no conceivable business of yours. It was my understanding from the uproar you caused in the hall that you came to see whether either Mr. Loewenthal or Mr. Tisov were related to you. Now that you've caused a great disturbance, perhaps you would be good enough to give your address to Ms. Warshawski and leave us in peace."

Radbuka's lower lip stuck out, but before he could dig his heels in, Morrell intervened. "I'm going to take Radbuka up to Max's study, as V I tried to do an hour ago. Max and Carl may join him there later, if they're able."

Don had been sitting quietly in the background, but he stood up now. "Right. Come on, big guy. Dr. Herschel needs to rest."

Don put an arm around him. With Morrell at his other elbow, they moved the unhappy Radbuka to the door, his neck hunched into his oversize jacket, his face so expressive of bewildered misery that he looked like a circus clown.

When they'd gone, I turned to Lotty. "Who was Sofie Radbuka?"

She turned her frosty stare to me. "No one that I know of."

"Then why did hearing her name make you faint?"

"It didn't. My foot caught on the edge of a rug and—"

"Lotty, if you don't want to tell me, keep it to yourself, but please don't make up stupid lies to me."

She bit her lip, turning her head away from me. "There's been far too much emotion in this house today. First Max and Carl furious with me, and now the man himself shows up. I don't need you angry with me as well."

I sat on the wicker table in front of her settee. "I'm not angry. But I happened to be alone in the hall when this guy came to the door, and after ten minutes with him my head was spinning like a hula hoop. If you faint, or start to faint, then claim nothing was wrong, it makes me even dizzier. I'm not here to criticize, but you were so upset on Friday you got me seriously worried. And your agony seems to have started with this guy's appearance at the Birnbaum conference."

She looked back at me, her hauteur suddenly changed to consternation. "Victoria, I'm sorry—I have been selfish, not thinking of the effect of my behavior on you. You do deserve some kind of explanation."

She sat frowning to herself, as if trying to decide what kind of explanation I deserved. "I don't know if I can make clear the relationships of that time in my life. How I came to be so close to Max, and even Carl.

"There was a group of nine of us refugee children who became good friends during the war. We met over music; a woman from Salzburg, a violist who was herself a refugee, came around London and gathered us up. She saw Carl's gift, got him lessons, got him into a good music program. There were various others. Teresz, who eventually married Max. Me. My father had been a violin player. Café music, not the stuff of the soirées Frau Herbst organized, but skillful—at least, I think he was skillful, but how can I know, when I only heard him as a child? Anyway, even though I had no gift myself, I loved hearing the music at Frau Herbst's."

"Was Radbuka the name of one of that group? Why does Carl care so much? Is it someone he was in love with?"

She smiled painfully. "You would have to ask him that. Radbuka was the name of—someone else. Max— he had great organizational skills, even as a young man. When the war ended, he went around London to the different societies that helped people find out about their families. Then he—went back to central Europe, looking. That was in—I think it was in '47, but after all this time I can't be sure of the exact year. That was when the Radbuka name came up—it wasn't anyone in the group's actual surname, you see. But that is why we could ask Max to look. Because we were all so close, not like a family, like something else, perhaps a combat team who fought together for years.

"For almost all of us, Max's reports came back with devastating completeness. No survivors. For the Herschels, the Tisovs, the Loewenthals—Max found his father and two cousins, and that was another terrible—" She cut herself off mid-sentence.

"I was starting my medical training. It consumed me to the exclusion of so much else. Carl always blamed me for—well, let's just say, something unpleasant came up around the person from the Radbuka family. Carl always thought my absorption with medicine made me behave in a fashion which he regarded as cruel . . . as if his own devotion to music had not been equally absolute."

This last sentence she muttered under her breath as an afterthought. She fell silent. She had never spoken to me of her losses in such a way, such an emotional way. I didn't understand what she was trying to say—or not to say—about the friend from the Radbuka family, but when it became clear she wouldn't expand on it, I couldn't press her.

"Do you know"—I hesitated, trying to think of the least painful way of asking the question—"do you know what Max learned about the Radbuka family?"

Her face twisted. "They—he didn't find any trace of them. Although traces were hard to find and he didn't have much money. We all gave him a bit, but we didn't have money, either."

"So hearing this man call himself Radbuka must have been quite a shock."

She shuddered and looked at me. "It was, believe me, it's been a shock all week. How I envy Carl, able to put the whole world to one side when he starts to play. Or maybe it's that he puts the whole world inside him and blows it out that tube." She repeated the question she'd asked when she saw Paul on video. "How old is he, do you think?"

"He says he came here after the war around the age of four, so he must have been born in '42 or '43."

"So he couldn't be—does he think he was born in Theresienstadt?"

I threw up my hands. "All I know about him is from Wednesday night's interview. Is Theresienstadt the same as what he calls Terezin?"

"Terezin is its Czech name; it's an old fortress outside Prague." She added with an unexpected gleam of humor, "That's Austrian snobbery, using the German name—a holdover from when Prague was part of the Hapsburg empire and everyone spoke German. This man tonight, he's insisting he's Czech, not German, by calling it Terezin."

We sat again in silence. Lotty was withdrawn into her own thoughts, but she seemed more relaxed, less tortured, than she had for the past few days. I told her I'd go up to see what I could learn from Radbuka.

Lotty nodded. "If I feel stronger I'll come up by and by. Right now—I think I'll just lie here."

I made sure she was well-covered in the afghan Max had provided before turning out the light. When I closed the French doors behind me, I could see across the hall into the front room, where a dozen or so people still lingered over brandy. Michael Loewenthal was on the piano bench, holding Agnes on his lap. Everyone was happy. I went on up the stairs.

Max's study was a large room overlooking the lake, filled with Ming vases and T'ang horses. It was at the far end of the second floor from where the children were watching videos; Max had picked the room when his own two children were small, because it was well-secluded from the body of the house. When I shut the door no outside sounds could disrupt the tension inside. Morrell and Don smiled at me, but Paul Ulrich-Radbuka looked away in disappointment when he saw it was me, not Max or Carl.

"I don't understand what's happening," he said pathetically. "Are people ashamed to be seen with me? I need to talk to Max and Carl. I need to find out how we're related. I'm sure Carl or Max will want to know he has a surviving family member."

I squeezed my eyes shut, as if that would block out his hyperemotional state. "Try to relax, Mr.—uh. Mr. Loewenthal will be with you as soon as he can leave his guests. Perhaps Mr. Tisov as well. Can I get you a glass of wine, or a soft drink?"

He looked longingly at the door but apparently realized he couldn't find Carl unaided. He subsided into an armchair and muttered that he supposed a glass of water would help settle his nerves. Don jumped up to fetch it.

I decided the only way to get any information out of him would be to act as though I believed in his identity. He was so unstable, leaping up the scale from misery to ecstasy by octaves, weaving straws in the conversation into clothes, that I wasn't sure anything he said would be reliable, but if I challenged him, he would only retreat into a defensive weeping.

"Do you have any clue about where you were born?" I asked. "I gather Radbuka is a Czech name."

"The birth certificate that was sent with me to Terezin said Berlin, which is one reason I'm so eager to meet my relatives. Maybe the Radbukas were Czechs hiding in Berlin: some Jews fled west instead of east, trying to get away from the *Einsatzgruppen*. Maybe they were Czechs who had emigrated there before the war ever started. Oh, how I wish I knew something." He knotted his hands in anguish.

I picked my next words with care. "It must have been quite a shock to you, to find that birth certificate when your—uh—foster father died. Telling you that you were Paul Radbuka from Berlin, instead of—where did Ulrich tell you you were born?"

"Vienna. But no, I've never seen my Terezin birth certificate, I only read about it elsewhere, once I realized who I was."

"How cruel of Ulrich, to write about it but not leave you with the document itself!" I exclaimed.

"No, no, I had to track it down in an outside report. It was—was just by chance I found out about it at all."

"What an extraordinary amount of research you've done!" I packed my voice with so much admiration that Morrell frowned at me in warning, but Paul brightened perceptibly. "I'd love to see the report that told you about your birth certificate."

At that he stiffened, so I hastily changed the subject. "You don't remember any Czech, I suppose, if you were separated from your mother at—what was it—twelve months?"

He relaxed again. "When I hear Czech I recognize it but don't really understand it. The first language I spoke is German, because that was the language of the guards. Also many of the women who worked in the nursery at Terezin spoke it."

I heard the door open behind me and held a hand out in a signal to be quiet. Don slid past me to put a glass of water next to Paul. Out of the corner of my eye I saw Max quietly follow Don into the room. Paul, caught up in the pleasure of my attending to his story, went on without paying attention to them.

"There were six of us small children who more or less banded together, and really, we formed a little brigade; even at the age of three we looked after one another because the adults were so overworked and so underfed they couldn't care for individual children. We clung to one another and hid together from the guards. When the war ended we were sent to England. At first we were scared when the adults started putting us on trains, because in Terezin we saw many children put on trains and everyone knew they went someplace to die. But after we got over our terror, we had a happy time in England. We were in a big house in the country, it had a name like that of an animal, a dog, which was scary at first because we were terrified of dogs. From having seen them used so evilly in the camps."

"And that's where you learned English?" I prompted.

"We learned English bit by bit, the way children do, and really, we forgot our German. After a time, maybe it was nine months or even a year, they started finding homes for us, people wanting to adopt us. They decided we were mentally recovered enough that we could stand the pain of losing one another, although how can you ever stand that pain? The loss of my special playmate, my Miriam, it haunts my dreams to this day."

His voice broke. He used the napkin Don had put under the water glass to blow his nose. "One day this man arrived. He was large and coarse-faced and said he was my father and I should go with him. He wouldn't even let me kiss my little Miriam good-bye. Kissing was *weibisch*—a sissy thing—and I must be a man now. He shouted to me in German and was furious that I didn't speak German anymore. Over and over as I was growing up he would beat me, telling me he was making a man out of me, beating the *Schwule und Weiblichkeit* out of me."

He was crying freely, in obvious distress. I handed him the glass of water.

"That must have been very horrible," Max said gravely. "When did your father die?"

He didn't seem to notice Max's sudden appearance in the conversation. "You mean, I presume, the man who is *not* my father. I don't know when my birth father died. That is what I am hoping you can tell me. Or perhaps Carl Tisov."

He blew his nose again and stared at us defiantly. "The man who stole me from my campmates died seven years ago. It was after that when I started having nightmares and became depressed and disoriented. I lost my job, I lost my bearings, my nightmares became more and more explicit. I tried various remedies, but— always I was being drawn to these unspeakable images of the past, images I have come to recognize as my experience of the Shoah. Not until I started working with Rhea did I understand them for what they were. I think I saw my mother being raped and pushed alive into a pit of lime, but of course it could have been some other woman, I was so little I can't even recall my mother's face."

"Did your foster father tell you what became of—well, his wife?" Morrell put in.

"He said the woman he called my mother had died when the Allies bombed Vienna. That we had lived in Vienna and lost everything because of the Jews, he was always very bitter about the Jews."

"Do you have any idea why he tracked you down in England? Or how he knew you were there?" I was struggling to make sense of his narrative.

He spread his hands in a gesture of bewilderment. "After the war—everything was so unsettled. Anything was possible. I think he wanted to come to America, and claiming he was a Jew, which he could do if he had a Jewish child in hand, that would put him at the head of the queue. Especially if he had a Nazi past he wanted to conceal."

"And you think he did?" Max asked.

"I know so. I know so from his papers, that he was a vile piece of *drek*. A leader of the *Einsatzgruppen*."

"What a horrible thing to uncover," Don murmured. "To be a Jew and find you've grown up with the worst of the murderers of your people. No wonder he treated you the way he did."

Paul looked at him eagerly. "Oh, you do understand! I'm sure that his bestial behavior—the way he would beat me, deprive me of food when he was angry, lock me in a closet for hours, sometimes overnight—all that came from his terrible anti-Semitism. You are a Jew, Mr. Loewenthal, you understand how ugly someone like that can be."

Max sidestepped the remark. "Ms. Warshawski says that you found a document in your—foster father's—papers that gave you the clue to your real name. I'm curious about that. Would you let me see it?"

Ulrich-Radbuka took his time to answer. "When you tell me which one of you is related to me, then perhaps I will let you see the papers. But since you will not help me, I see no reason why I should show you my private documents."

"Neither Mr. Tisov nor I is connected to the Radbuka family," Max said. "Please try to accept that. It is a different friend of ours who knew a family with your name, but I know as much as that person does about the Radbuka family—which I'm sorry to say isn't a great deal. If you could let me see these documents, it would help me decide if you are part of the same family."

When Radbuka refused in a panicky voice, I intervened to ask if he had any idea where his birth parents came from. Apparently taking the question as agreement to his Radbuka identity, Paul recounted what he knew with a return of his childlike eagerness.

"I know nothing whatsoever about my birth parents. Some of our six musketeers knew more, although that can be painful, too. My little Miriam, for instance, poor soul, she knew her mother had gone mad and died in the mental hospital at Terezin. But now—Max, you say you know the details of my family life. Who of the Radbukas would be in Berlin in 1942?"

"No one," Max said with finality. "No brothers, nor parents. I can assure you of that. This is a family which emigrated to Vienna in the years before the First World War. In 1941 they were sent to Lodz, in Poland. The ones who were still alive in 1943 were sent on to the camp where they all perished."

Paul Ulrich-Radbuka's face lit up. "But perhaps I was born in Lodz."

"I thought you knew you'd been born in Berlin," I blurted out.

"There are so few reliable documents from those times," he said. "Perhaps they gave me the paper of a boy who died in the camp. Anything like that is possible."

Talking to him was like walking in the marshes: just

when you thought you had a fact to stand on, the ground gave way.

Max looked at him gravely. "None of the Radbukas in Vienna had special standing: they weren't important socially or artistically, as was typically true of people who were sent to Theresien—to Terezin. Of course there were always exceptions, but I doubt you will find them in this case."

"So you're trying to tell me my family doesn't exist. But I can see it's just that you're hiding them from me. I demand to see them in person. I know they will claim me when they meet me."

"One easy solution to the problem is a DNA test," I suggested. "Max, Carl, and their English friend could give blood, we could agree on a lab in England or the U.S. and send a sample of Mr.—Mr. Radbuka's blood there, as well. That would resolve the question of whether he's related to any of you or to Max's English friend."

"I am not uncertain!" Paul exclaimed, his face pink. "You may be; you're a detective who makes a living by being suspicious. But I will not submit to being treated like a laboratory specimen, the way my people were in that medical laboratory at Auschwitz, the way my little Miriam's mother was treated. Looking at blood samples is what the Nazis cared about. Heredity, race, all those things, I won't take part in it."

"That brings us back to where we started," I said. "With a document that you alone know about and no way for suspicious detectives like me to verify your certainty. By the way, who is Sofie Radbuka?"

Paul turned sulky. "She was on the Web. Someone in a missing-persons chat room said they wanted information about a Sofie Radbuka who lived in England in the forties. So I wrote saying she must be my mother, and the person never wrote back."

"Right now we're all exhausted," Max said. "Mr.

Radbuka, why don't you write down everything you know about your family? I will get my friend to do the same. You can give me your document and I will give you the other one. Then we can meet again to compare notes."

Radbuka sat with his lower lip sticking out, not even looking up to acknowledge the suggestion. When Morrell, with a grimace at the clock, said he'd drive him home, Radbuka refused at first to get up.

Max looked at him sternly. "You must leave now, Mr. Radbuka, unless you wish to create a situation in which you would never be able to return here."

His clown face a tragic mask, Radbuka got to his feet. With Morrell and Don again at his elbows, like wardens in a high-class mental hospital, he shambled sullenly to the door.

XVIII

Old Lovers

Downstairs, the party was over. The waitstaff was cleaning up the remains, vacuuming food from the carpets and washing up the last of the dishes. In the living room, Carl and Michael were debating the tempo in a Brahms nonet, playing passages on the grand piano while Agnes Loewenthal watched from a couch with her legs curled under her.

She looked up when I glanced in the doorway, hurriedly untangling her feet to run over to me before I could follow Morrell and Don outside. "Vic! Who is that extraordinary man? Carl has been beside himself over this intrusion. He went into the sunroom and shouted at Lotty about it until Michael stopped him. What is going on?"

I shook my head. "I honestly don't know. This guy thinks he spent his childhood in the camps. He says he only recently discovered his birth name was Radbuka, so he came here hoping Max or Carl was related to him, because he thought that one of their friends in England had family of that name."

"But that doesn't make sense!" Agnes cried.

Max came down the stairs behind us, his gait heavy

with extreme weariness. "So he's gone, is he, Victoria? No, it doesn't make sense. Nothing tonight made much sense. Lotty fainting? I've watched her take bullets out of people without flinching. What did you think of this creature, Victoria? Do you believe his story? It's an extraordinary tale."

I was so tired myself that I was seeing sparks in front of my eyes. "I don't know what I think. He's so volatile, moving from tears to triumphal glee and back in thirty seconds. And every time he gets a new piece of information, he changes his story. Where was he born? In Lodz? Berlin? Vienna? I'm staggered that Rhea Wiell would hypnotize someone that unstable—I'd think it would demolish his fragile connection to reality. But— all these symptoms *could* be caused by exactly what he says happened to him. An infancy spent in Terezin—I don't know how you'd recover from that."

In the living room, Michael and Carl were playing the same passage on the piano over and over, with variations in tempo and tone that were too subtle for me. The repetition began grating on me.

The door to the sunroom opened and Lotty came into the hall, pale but composed. "Sorry, Max," she murmured. "Sorry to leave you alone to deal with him, but I couldn't face him. Nor could Carl, apparently— he came in to castigate me for refusing to join you upstairs. Now I gather Carl has returned to the world of music, leaving this one in our possession."

"Lotty." Max held up a hand. "If you and Carl want to keep fighting, take it someplace else. Neither of you had anything to contribute to what was going on upstairs. But one thing I would like to know—"

The doorbell interrupted him—Morrell, returning with Don.

"He must live close by," I said. "You were hardly gone a minute."

Morrell came over to me. "He asked to be dropped

at a place where he could get a cab. Which frankly I was happy to do. A little of the guy goes far with me, so I left him in front of the Orrington, where there's a taxi stand."

"Did you get his address?"

Morrell shook his head. "I asked when we got into the car, but he announced he would go home by cab."

"I tried asking for it, too," Don said, "because of course I want to interview him, but he'd decided we were an untrustworthy bunch."

"Ah, nuts," I said. "Now I'm back to square one with finding him. Unless I can track the cab."

"Did he say anything upstairs?" Lotty asked. "Anything about how he came to think his name was Radbuka?"

I leaned against Morrell, swaying with fatigue. "Just more mumbo jumbo about these mystery documents of his father. Foster father. And how they proved Ulrich was part of the *Einsatzgruppen*."

"What's that?" Agnes asked, her blue eyes troubled.

"Special forces that committed special atrocities in eastern Europe during the war," Max said tersely. "Lotty, since you're feeling better, I would like some information from you now: who is Sofie Radbuka? I think you might explain to me, and to Vic here, why it had such an effect on you."

"I told Vic," Lotty said. "I told her the Radbukas were one of the families that you inquired about for our group of friends in London."

I'd been about to suggest to Morrell that we go home, but I wanted to hear what Lotty would say to Max. "Could we sit down?" I asked Max. "I'm dead on my feet."

"Victoria, of course." Max ushered us into the living room, where Carl and Michael were still fiddling with their music.

Michael looked over at us. He told Carl they could

finish the discussion on the way to Los Angeles and came over to sit next to Agnes. I pictured Michael with his cello stuck between his legs in an airplane seat, bowing the same twelve measures over and over while Carl played them on his clarinet at a different pace.

"You haven't eaten, have you?" Morrell said to me. "Let me try to rustle you up a snack—you'll feel better."

"You didn't get dinner?" Max exclaimed. "All this upheaval is erasing ordinary courtesy from my mind."

He sent one of the waiters to the kitchen for a tray of leftovers and drinks. "Now, Lotty, it's your turn on the hot seat. I've respected your privacy all these years and I will continue to do so. But you need to explain to us why the name Sofie Radbuka rattled you so badly this evening. I know I looked for Radbukas for you in Vienna after the war. Who were they?"

"It wasn't the name," Lotty said. "It was the whole aspect of that—" She broke off, biting her lip like a schoolgirl, when she saw Max gravely shake his head.

"It—it was someone at the hospital," Lotty muttered, looking at the carpet. "At the Royal Free. Who didn't want their name public."

"So that was it," Carl said with a venom that startled all of us. "I knew it at the time. I knew it and you denied it."

Lotty flushed, a wave of crimson almost as dark as her jacket. "You made such stupid accusations that I didn't think you deserved an answer."

"About what?" Agnes asked, as bewildered as I was.

Carl said, "You must have realized by now that Lotty and I were lovers for some years in London. I thought it would be forever, but that's because I didn't know Lotty had married medicine."

"Unlike you and music," Lotty snapped.

"Right," I said, leaning over to serve myself scalloped potatoes and salmon from the tray the waiter had brought. "You both had strong senses of vocation. Neither of you would budge. Then what happened?"

"Then Lotty developed TB. Or so she said." Carl bit off the words.

He turned back to Lotty. "You never told me you were ill. You never said good-bye! I got your letter—letter? A notice in *The Times* would have told me more!—when I returned from Edinburgh, there it was, that cold, cryptic note. I ran across town. That imbecile landlady in your lodgings—I can still see her face, with the horrible mole on her nose and all the hairs sticking out of it—she told me. She was smirking. From *her* I learned you were in the country. From *her* I learned you'd instructed her to forward all your mail to Claire Tallmadge, the Ice Queen. Not from you. I loved you. I thought you loved me. But you couldn't even tell me good-bye."

He stopped, panting, then added bitterly, "To this day I do not understand why you let that Tallmadge woman run you around the way she did," he said to Lotty. "She was so—so supercilious. You were her little Jewish pet. Couldn't you ever see how she looked down on you? And the rest of that family. The vapid sister, Vanessa, and her insufferable husband, what was his name? Marmalade?"

"Marmaduke," Lotty said. "As you know quite well, Carl. Besides, you resented anyone I paid more attention to than you."

"My God, you two," Max said. "You should join Calia up in the nursery. Could we get to the point?"

"Besides," Lotty said, flushing again at Max's criticism, "when I returned to the Royal Free, Claire—Claire felt her friendship with me was inappropriate. She—I didn't even know she retired until I saw it in the Royal Free newsletter this spring."

"What did the Radbukas have to do with this?" Don asked.

"I went to see Queen Claire," Carl snarled. "She told me she was forwarding Lotty's mail to a receiving office in Axmouth in care of someone named Sofie Radbuka. But when I wrote, my mail was returned to me, with a note scribbled on the envelope that there was no one there by that name. I even took a train out from London one Monday and walked three miles through the countryside to this cottage. There were lights on inside, Lotty, but you wouldn't answer the door. I stayed there all afternoon, but you never came out.

"Six months went by, and suddenly Lotty was back in London. With no word to me. No response to my letters. No explanation. As if our life together had never taken place. Who was Sofie Radbuka, Lotty? Your lover? Did the two of you sit in there all afternoon laughing at me?"

Lotty was leaning back in an armchair, her eyes shut, the lines in her face sharply drawn. So might she look dead. The thought made me clutch at my stomach.

"Sofie Radbuka no longer existed, so I borrowed her name," she said in the thread of a voice, not opening her eyes. "It seems stupid now, but we all did unaccountable things in those days. The only mail I accepted was from the hospital—everything else I sent back unread, just as I did your letters. I had a mortal condition. I needed to be alone while I coped with it. I loved you, Carl. But no one could reach me in the alone place I was. Not you, not Max, no one. When I—recovered—I had no capacity for talking to you. It—the only thing I knew to do was draw a line. You—you never seemed inconsolable to me."

Max went to sit next to her, taking her hand, but Carl got up to pace furiously about the room. "Oh, yes, I had lovers," he spat over his shoulder. "Lovers aplenty that I wanted you to know about. But it was many years before I fell in love again and by then I was out of practice, I couldn't make it last. Three marriages in forty years and how many mistresses in between? I'm a byword among women in orchestras."

"Don't blame me for that," Lotty said coldly, sitting up. "You can choose how to act. I don't bear responsibility for that."

"Yes, you can choose to be remote as ever. Poor Loewenthal, he wants you to marry him and can't figure out why you won't. He doesn't realize you're made of scalpels and ligatures, not heart and muscle."

"Carl, I can manage my own business," Max said, half laughing, half exasperated. "But returning to the present, if I may, if the Radbukas are gone, how exactly did this man tonight get the name in the first place?"

"Yes," Lotty agreed. "That's why I was so startled to hear it."

"Do you have any sense of how to find that out, Victoria?" Max asked.

I yawned ferociously. "I don't know. I don't know how to get him to let me see these mystery documents. The other end of the investigation would be his past. I don't know what kind of immigration records might survive from '47 or '48, when he would have come into this country. If he really was even an immigrant."

"He is at least a speaker of German," Lotty said unexpectedly. "When he first arrived, I wondered if any of his story was true—you know, on the tape he claimed to have come here as a small child, speaking German. So I asked him in German if he was brought up on the myth of the Ulrichs as wolflike warriors. He clearly understood me."

I tried to remember the sequence of remarks in the hall but I couldn't quite get everything straight. "That's when he said he wouldn't speak the language of his slavery, isn't it?" Another yawn engulfed me. "No more tonight. Carl, Michael, the concert today was brilliant. I hope the rest of the tour goes as well—that this disturbance in the field doesn't affect your music. Are you going on with them?" I added to Agnes.

She shook her head. "The tour goes on for four more weeks. Calia and I will stay with Max another five days, then return directly to England. She should be in kindergarten right now, but we wanted her to have this time with her Opa."

"By which time I will also know the story of Ninshubur the faithful hound by heart." Max smiled, although his eyes remained grave.

Morrell took me by the hand. We stumbled out to his car together while Don trailed behind us, getting in a few lungfuls of nicotine. An Evanston patrol car was inspecting Morrell's car stickers: the town makes money by having capricious parking regulations. Morrell was outside his own parking zone, but we got into the car before the man actually wrote a ticket.

I slumped against the front seat. "I've never been around so much emotion for so many hours."

"Exhausting," Morrell agreed. "I don't think this man Paul is a fraud, do you?"

"Not in the sense that he's deliberately trying to con us," I murmured, my eyes shut. "He sincerely believes what he's saying, but he's alarming; he believes a new thing at the drop of a hat."

"It's a hell of a story, one way or another," Don said. "I wonder if I should go to England to check up on the Radbuka family."

"That gets you kind of far from your book with Rhea Wiell," I said. "And as Morrell advised me yesterday, is it really necessary to go sleuthing after Lotty's past?"

"Only insofar as it seems to have invaded the present," Don answered. "I thought she was lying, didn't you? About it being someone at the Royal Free, I mean."

"I thought she was making it clear it was her business, not ours," I said sharply, as Morrell pulled into the alley behind his building.

"That history between Lotty and Carl." I shivered as I followed Morrell down the hall to the bedroom. "Lotty's pain, Carl's, too, but Lotty feeling so alone she couldn't tell her lover she was dying. I can't bear it."

"Tomorrow's my last day here," Morrell complained. "I have to pack, and I have to spend the day again with State Department officials. Instead of with you, my darling, as I would prefer. I could have done with less trauma tonight and more sleep."

I flung my clothes onto a chair, but Morrell hung his suit tidily in the closet. He did at least leave his weekend bag to unpack in the morning.

"You're a little like Lotty, Vic." Morrell held me in the dark. "If something goes amiss with you, don't creep away to a cottage under a fake name to lick your wounds alone."

They were a comfort, those words, with his departure so close, with the turbulence of the last few hours still shaking me. They spread around me in the dark, those words, calming me into sleep.

Lotty Herschel's Story:

V-E Day

I took Hugo to Piccadilly Circus for the V-E Day celebrations. Masses of people, fireworks, a speech by the king broadcast over loudspeakers—the crowd was euphoric. I shared some of the feeling—although for me complete euphoria was impossible. It wasn't just because of the newsreels of Belsen and other camps that had sickened the English that spring: stories of death had been floating in from Europe with the immigrant community for some time. Even Minna had been furious over some of the MPs' callous response to the men who had escaped from Auschwitz when it was first being built.

I would get impatient with Hugo, because he couldn't remember Oma and Opa, or even Mama, very clearly. He hardly remembered any German, whereas I had to hang on to the language because that's what Cousin Minna spoke at home. In 1942 she had married Victor, a horrid old man who she was sure was going to inherit the glove factory. He had a stroke before the owner died and it went to someone else, so there she was, stuck with an elderly sick husband and no money. But he was from Hamburg, so of course they spoke German to each other. It took me

longer than Hugo to learn English, longer to fit in at
school, longer to feel at home in England.

For Hugo, coming to England at five, life began with
the Nussbaum family. They treated him like a son. In fact,
Mr. Nussbaum wanted to adopt Hugo, but that upset me
so much that the Nussbaums dropped the idea. I see
things differently now, see Hugo's turning to them,
trusting them, as the natural state of a five-year-old, not an
abandonment of my parents—and of me. Probably if I'd
lived with someone who cherished me, my reaction to the
idea would have been different—although Mr. Nussbaum
was always very kind to me and tried to include me in his
regular Sunday outings with my brother.

But I was especially angry with Hugo on V-E Day,
because he thought the end of the war meant he would
have to return to Austria. He didn't want to leave the
Nussbaums or his friends at school, and he was hoping I
would explain to Mama and Papa that he would only
come for the summers.

I realize now my anger was partly fueled by my own
anxieties. I longed for the loving family I'd lost, longed to
put Cousin Minna and her constant criticism behind me,
but I, too, had friends and a school that I didn't want to
leave. I was turning sixteen, with two years to work toward
my higher-school certificate. I could see that it would be as
hard to return to Austria as it had been to come to
England six years earlier—harder, since the ruin of war
might make it impossible for me to finish school there.

Miss Skeffing, the headmistress at the Camden High
School for Girls, was on the board at the Royal Free
Hospital. She had encouraged me to do the science course
that would prepare me for medical-school entrance. I
didn't want to leave her, or the chance to read medicine.
Although I saw very little of Claire these days, since she
was starting her junior houseman rotation, I didn't want to
leave her, either. After all, it was Claire's example that
made me stand up to Cousin Minna and insist on

applying to the Camden school. Minna was furious—she wanted me to leave school at fourteen to help make money in the glove factory. But I reminded her that since she wouldn't recommend my father for a job in 1939, she had a nerve expecting me to quit school to take one now.

She and Victor also tried to put a stop to my going to meet friends for Miss Herbst's music evenings. During the war years, those evenings were a lifesaver. Even for someone like me, with no musical ability, there was always something to do—we staged operas, held impromptu glees. Even during the Blitz, when you found your way around London by guess, I would slam out of Minna's house and move through the black streets to Miss Herbst's flat.

Sometimes I'd go by bus: that was an adventure, because the buses had to obey the blackout, so you wouldn't know one was coming until it was almost on top of you, and then you'd have to guess where to get off. Once on the way home, I guessed wrong and landed miles away from Minna's. A street warden found me and let me spend the night in their shelter. It was great fun, drinking watery cocoa with the wardens while they talked over football scores, but my little adventure left Minna more sour than ever.

Much as we were worried about our families, none of us—not just me or Hugo, but no one in that group at Miss Herbst's—wanted to resume life in German. We saw it as the language of humiliation. Germany or Austria or Czechoslovakia were the places where we'd seen our beloved grandparents forced to scrub the paving stones on their hands and knees while crowds stood around jeering and throwing things at them. We even changed the spelling of our names: I turned Lotte into Lotty; Carl used a C instead of the K he'd been born with.

On V-E night, after the king's speech, I put Hugo on the tube back to Golders Green, where the Nussbaums lived, and met up with Max and some of the others in

Covent Garden to wait for Carl, who'd gotten a job with
the Sadlers Wells orchestra, which was playing that night.
Thousands of people were in Covent Garden, the one
place in London you could get a drink in the middle of the
night.

Someone was passing bottles of champagne through
the crowd. Max and the rest of our group put our personal
worries to one side and became riotous with the other
revelers. No more bombs, no more blackouts, no more
minuscule bits of butter once a week—although of course
that was ignorant optimism; rationing went on for years.

Carl eventually found us sitting on an overturned
barrow in St. Martin's Lane. The owner, who sold fruit,
was a little drunk. He was carving apples carefully into
slices and feeding them to me and another girl in our
group, who later became utterly suburban, bred corgis,
and voted Conservative. At the time she was the most
sophisticated of our set, wearing lipstick, dating American
servicemen, and getting nylons for her pains, while I
darned my cotton stockings, feeling like a dowdy schoolgirl
next to her.

Carl bowed grandly to the barrow owner and took a
slice of apple out of the man's hand. "I will feed Miss
Herschel," he said, and held the piece of apple out to me.
I suddenly became aware of his fingers, as if they were
actually touching my body. I put my hand around his wrist
to guide the apple to my mouth.

XIX

Case Closed

The dreams woke me in the grey light of predawn. Nightmares of Lotty lost, my mother dying, faceless figures chasing me through tunnels, while Paul Radbuka watched, alternating between weeping and manic laughter. I lay sweating, my heart pounding. Next to me, Morrell slept, his breath coming out in soft little snorts, like a horse clearing its nose. I moved into the shelter of his arms. He clung to me in sleep for a few minutes, then rolled over without waking.

By and by my heart rate returned to normal, but despite yesterday's fatigues I couldn't get back to sleep. All of last night's tormented confessions churned in my head like clothes pounding in a washing machine. Paul Radbuka's emotions were so slippery, so intense, that I couldn't figure out how to respond to him; Lotty and Carl's history was just as overwhelming.

It didn't surprise me to hear that Max wanted to marry Lotty, although neither of them had ever mentioned it around me. I seized on the small problem instead of the large, wondering if Lotty was so used to her solitary life that she preferred to be on her own. Morrell and I had talked about living together, but even though we'd both been married in our younger days, we couldn't quite agree on giving up our privacy. For Lotty, who'd always lived on her own, it would be an even harder move.

It was clear that Lotty was hiding something about the Radbuka family, but I had no way of knowing what. It wasn't her mother's family—she'd been startled by that suggestion, almost affronted. Perhaps some poor immigrant family whose fate had mattered terribly to her? People have unexpected sources of shame and guilt, but I couldn't imagine something that would shock me so much it would make me turn against her . . . something she wouldn't even tell Max.

What if Sofie Radbuka had been a patient whose care she had bungled during her medical training? Sofie Radbuka had died, or was in a vegetative coma; Lotty blamed herself and pretended to have tuberculosis so she could go to the country to recuperate. She'd taken Radbuka's name in some kind of guilt storm that had her overidentifying with the patient. Aside from the fact that it contradicted everything I knew about Lotty, it still wouldn't turn me from her.

The notion that she'd pretended to have TB so she could go to the country and carry on an affair with a Sofie Radbuka—or anyone—was ludicrous. She could have had an affair in London without jeopardizing a training program that women in the forties entered only with great difficulty.

It unnerved me to see Lotty teetering on the edge of collapse. I tried to recite Morrell's good advice: that I should not sleuth after her; that if she didn't want to tell me her secrets, it was her demons, not my failure, that made her keep them to herself.

I should stick to my business, anyway, to exploring the kind of financial shenanigan that Isaiah Sommers had hired me to untangle. Not that I'd done much about that situation, either, other than get him to stir up Bull Durham to denounce me in public.

It was only five-forty. I could do one little thing for Isaiah Sommers. Which Morrell would holler about if he knew. I sat up. Morrell sighed but didn't move. Pulling on the jeans and sweatshirt out of my overnight bag, I tiptoed out of the room with my running shoes. Morrell had absconded with my cell phone and picklocks. I went back to the room for his backpack, which I took to his study with me—I didn't want the clanking of keys to wake him. I left a note on his laptop: *Gone to the city for an early appointment. See you tonight for supper? Love, V.*

Morrell's place was only six blocks from the Davis L stop. I walked across, in company with other early commuters, joggers, people out with their dogs. Amazing how many people were on the streets, and how many looked fresh and fit. The sight of my own red-stained eyes in the bathroom mirror had made me flinch—the Madwoman of Chaillot let loose upon the town.

The express trains for the morning rush were running; in twenty minutes I was at my own stop, Belmont, a few blocks from my apartment. My car was out front, but I needed to shower and change so that I looked less like the ghost of my own nightmares. I crept in quietly, hoping the dogs wouldn't recognize my step. Trouser suit, crepe-soled shoes. Peppy gave a sharp bark as I tiptoed back outside, but I didn't slow down.

I stopped at a coffee bar on my way to Lake Shore Drive for a large orange juice and an even larger cappuccino. It was almost seven now; the morning commute had begun in earnest, but I still made it to Hyde Park before seven-thirty.

I gave a perfunctory nod to the guard at the entrance to the Hyde Park Bank building. It wasn't the same man

Fepple had warned against me on Friday. This man gave me a cursory glance over his newspaper but didn't challenge me: I was professionally dressed, I knew where I was going. To the sixth floor, where I pulled on latex gloves to start work on Fepple's locks. I was so tense, listening for the elevator, that it took me a moment to realize the locks were already open.

I slipped into the office, snarling as I tripped once more on the torn corner of linoleum. Fepple was behind his desk. In the pale light coming through the window, I thought he'd fallen asleep in his chair. I hesitated at the door, then decided to put a bold face on it, wake him, force him to hand over the Sommers file. I switched on the overhead light. And saw that Fepple would never speak to anyone again. His mouth was missing. The side of his head, the carpet of freckled skin, nothing left of them but a smear of bone and brain and blood.

I sat abruptly on the floor. Head between my knees. Even with my nose muffled I thought I could smell blood. My gorge rose. I willed my mind to other matters: I couldn't add my vomit to the crime scene.

I don't know how long I sat like that, until voices in the hall made me realize how precarious my position was: in an office with a dead man, with picklocks in my pocket and latex gloves on my hands. I stood up, so fast that my head swam again, but I shook off the faintness and turned the dead bolt to lock myself in.

Trying to make it a clinical exercise, I edged around the desk to look at Fepple. A gun had fallen to the floor just below where his right arm dangled. I squinted at it: a twenty-two SIG Trailside. So he had shot himself? Because whatever he'd seen in the Sommers file had unbalanced his mind? His computer was still on, in a suspend state. Suppressing my nausea, I gingerly stretched an arm past his left side, using a picklock to bring up the screen so that I wouldn't disturb any evidence. A block of text came back to life.

> When my father died this was a flourishing agency but I am a failure as an agent. I have watched my sales and profits go in a downward spiral for five years. I thought I could cheat my way out of debt but now that the detective is watching me I'm afraid I would be a failure even at that. I've never married, I've never known how to attract women, I can't face myself any longer. I don't know how to pay my bills. If anyone cares, perhaps my mother, I'm sorry. Howard

I printed it out and stuffed the paper in my pocket. My hands inside their latex gloves were wet. Black spots swam around my eyes. I was very aware of Fepple's shattered head next to me, but I couldn't look at it. I wanted to leave the obscene mess, but I might not get another chance to find the Sommers file.

The cabinets were open, which surprised me: when I was here last week, Fepple had made quite a point of unlocking them when he wanted to put the papers away, then promptly locking them again. The third drawer, the one where he'd stuck the Sommers file, was labeled *Rick Hoffman's clients.*

The files were jammed into the drawer, some upside down, none in any kind of order. When I pulled out the first file, *Barney Williams*, I thought I was at the end of the alphabet, but it was followed by *Larry Jenks*. With an uneasy eye on the clock, I emptied the drawer and replaced the folders one at a time. The Sommers file wasn't there.

I flipped through the folders looking for anything that related to Sommers. There wasn't anything in them but copies of policies and payment schedules. About three-quarters of them were closed cases, where the policy was stamped *Paid* with the date or *Lapsed for nonpayment* with the date. I looked in the other drawers but found nothing. I took a half dozen of the paid policies: I could get Mary Louise to check on whether they'd been paid to the beneficiary.

I listened uneasily to voices coming from the hall, but I couldn't leave until I'd looked for the Sommers papers in the mess on the desk. The papers were flecked with bits of blood and brain. I didn't want to disturb them—an experienced tech could tell in a flash that someone had been searching—but I wanted that file.

Bracing myself, keeping my eyes shielded, willing myself to believe there was nothing in the chair, I leaned over the desk, pulling back the edges of the documents in front of Fepple. I worked my way outward from the middle in a circle. When I found nothing, I moved around to Fepple's side of the desk, trying not to step in anything, and looked in the desk drawers. Nothing but signs of his dismal life. Half-eaten bags of chips, an unopened box of condoms covered in cracker crumbs, diaries dating back to the 1980's when his father was booking appointments, books on how to improve your table-tennis game. Who would have thought he had enough stick-to-it-iveness to pursue a sport?

It was nine now. The longer I stayed, the more likely it was that someone would come in on me. I went to the door, standing to the left of the frame so I couldn't be seen through the glass, listening for sounds from the hall. A group of women was passing, laughing about something, wishing each other a good morning: how was the weekend, heavy workload this morning in Dr. Zabar's office, how was Melissa's birthday party. Silence, then the elevator bell and a pair of women with an infant. When they had gone, I slid the door open a crack. The hall was empty.

As I went out, I saw Fepple's briefcase in the corner

behind me. On an impulse, I picked it up. While I waited for the elevator, I stuffed the latex gloves into the case along with the files I was borrowing.

I hoped I didn't have anything on me to link me to the crime scene, but when I got off the elevator at the bottom, I saw my shoe had left a nasty brownish smear on the car floor. I somehow managed to walk out the door with my head up, but as soon as I was out of the guard's sight lines I skittered around the corner, barely making it to the alley before throwing up my orange juice and coffee.

XX

Hunter in the Middle

Back home, I scrubbed my shoes obsessively, but all the perfumes of Dow Chemical wouldn't wipe them clean. I couldn't afford to throw them out, but I didn't think I could bear to wear them again, either.

I took off the suit, inspecting every inch under a strong light. There didn't seem to be anything of Fepple on the fabric, but I bundled it up for the dry cleaner anyway.

I had stopped at a pay phone on Lake Shore Drive to call in the news of a dead body in the Hyde Park Bank building. By now the police machinery should be in motion. I walked restlessly to the kitchen door and back. I could call one of my old friends on the force for an inside report on the investigation, but then I'd have to reveal that I'd found the body. Which would mean I'd spend the day answering questions. I tried calling Morrell, hoping for comfort, but he'd already left for his meeting at the State Department.

I wondered what Fepple had done with my business

card. I hadn't seen it on his desk, but I wasn't looking for anything that small. The cops would come after me if they figured out I was the detective mentioned in Fepple's suicide note. If it was a suicide note.

Of course it was. The gun had fallen from his hand to the floor underneath, after he shot himself. He felt like a failure and couldn't face himself any longer, so he shot away the lower half of his face. I stopped at the kitchen window to stare at the dogs, which Mr. Contreras had let into the garden. I should take them for a run.

As if catching my gaze, Mitch looked up at me and grinned wolfishly. That nasty little smile of Fepple's when he'd read the Sommers file, when he said he was going to take over Rick Hoffman's client list. That was the smile of someone who thought he could capitalize on another person's weakness, not the smile of a man who hated himself so much he was going to commit suicide.

This morning he'd been in the same suit and tie he'd worn on Friday. Who had he dressed up for? A woman, as he had implied? Someone he tried to romance, but who told him horrible things about himself, so horrible that he came back to the office and committed suicide? Or had he dressed for the person who'd called him when he was talking to me? The person who told him how to ditch me: go to a pay phone, await further instructions. Fepple cut through the little shopping center, where his mystery caller picked him up. Fepple figured he could cash in on some secret he'd seen in the Sommers file.

He tried to blackmail his mystery caller, who told Fepple they needed to talk privately in his office—where he shot Fepple, staging it to look like suicide. Very Edgar Wallace. In either case, the mystery caller had taken the Sommers file. I moved restlessly back to the living room. More likely Fepple had left the file on his bedside table, along with old copies of *Table-Tennis Tips*.

I wished I knew what the police were doing, whether they were accepting the suicide, whether they were testing for gunpowder residue on Fepple's hands. Finally, for want of something better to do, I went down to the yard to collect the dogs. Mr. Contreras had his back door open; when I went up the half flight of stairs to tell him I was going to take the dogs with me for a run and then to my office, I could hear the radio.

Our top local story: the body of insurance agent Howard Fepple was found in his Hyde Park office this morning following an anonymous tip to police. The forty-three-year-old Fepple apparently killed himself because the Midway Insurance Agency, started by his grandfather in 1911, was on the brink of bankruptcy. His mother, Rhonda, with whom he lived, was stunned by the news. "Howie didn't even own a gun. How can the police go around saying he shot himself with a gun he didn't have? Hyde Park is real dangerous. I kept telling him to move the agency out here to Palos, where people actually want to buy insurance; I think someone broke in and murdered him and dressed it up to look like he killed himself."

Area Four police say they will not rule out the possibility of murder, but until the autopsy report is complete they are treating Fepple's death as a suicide. This is Mark Santoros, Global News, Chicago.

"Ain't that something, cookie." Mr. Contreras looked up from the *Sun-Times,* where he was circling racing results. "Guy shooting himself just because he come on hard times? No stamina, these young fellas."

I muttered a weak agreement—ultimately I would tell him that I'd found Fepple, but that would be a long conversation which I didn't feel up to holding today. I drove the dogs over to the lake, where we ran up to Montrose Harbor and back. Sleep deprivation made my sinuses ache, but the three-mile run loosened my tight muscles. I took the dogs with me down to the office, where they raced around, sniffing and barking as if they had never been inside the place before. Tessa yelled out at me from her studio to get them under control *at once* before she took a sculpting mallet to them.

When I had them corralled inside my own place, I sat at my desk for a long while without actually moving. When I was little, my granny Warshawski had a wooden toy she'd get out for me when we went to visit. A hunter was in the middle, with a bear on one side and a wolf on the other. When you pushed the button once, the hunter swung around to point his rifle at the wolf while the bear jumped up to threaten him. If you pushed it again, he turned to the bear while the wolf jumped up. Sommers. Lotty. Lotty. Sommers. It was as if I were the hunter in the middle, who kept swerving between the two images. I couldn't keep track of either one's problem long enough to focus on it before the other popped up again.

Finally, wearily, I switched on my computer. Sofie Radbuka. Paul had found her in a chat room on the Web. While I was searching, Rhea Wiell called.

"Ms. Warshawski, what did you do to Paul last night? He was waiting outside my office this morning when I got in, weeping, saying you had ridiculed him and kept him from his family."

"Maybe you could hypnotize him and get him to recover a memory of the truth," I said.

"If you imagine that is funny, you have such a perverse sense of humor I would believe anything of you." The vestal virgin had turned so icy her voice could have put out the sacred fire.

"Ms. Wiell, didn't we agree on as much privacy for Mr. Loewenthal as you demanded for Paul Radbuka? But Paul tracked Max Loewenthal down in his home. Did he think of that all by himself?"

She was human enough to be embarrassed and answered more quietly, "I didn't give him Max Loewenthal's name. Paul unfortunately saw it himself in my desk file. When I said you might know one of his relatives, he put two and two together: he's very quick. But that doesn't mean he should have been subjected to taunting," she added, trying to regain the upper hand.

"Paul barged in on a private party, and unnerved everyone by making up three different versions of his life story in as many minutes." I knew I shouldn't lose my temper, but I couldn't keep myself from snapping, "He's dangerously unstable; I've been wanting to ask why you found him a good candidate for hypnotherapy."

"You didn't tell me you had special clinical skills when we met on Friday," Wiell said in a honeyed voice even more irritating than her icy fury. "I didn't know you could evaluate whether someone was a good candidate for hypnosis. Do you think he was dangerously unstable because he threatened the peace of mind of people who are embarrassed to claim a relationship with him? This morning, Paul told me that they all know who Sofie Radbuka was, but that they refused to tell him, and that you goaded them on. To me this is heartless."

I took a deep breath, trying to tamp down my annoyance—I needed her help, which would never be forthcoming if I kept her pissed off at me. "Fifty years ago, Mr. Loewenthal looked for a Radbuka family who had lived in Vienna before the war. He didn't know the family personally: they were acquaintances of Dr. Herschel's. Mr. Loewenthal undertook to search for any trace of them when he went back to central Europe in 1947 or '48 to hunt for his own family."

Mitch gave a short bark and ran to the door. Mary Louise came in, calling out to me about Fepple. I waved to her but kept my attention on the phone.

"When Paul said he was born in Berlin, Mr. Loewenthal said that made it extremely unlikely that Paul was related to the Radbukas he'd looked for all those years back. So Paul instantly offered two alternative possibilities—that he'd been born in Vienna, or even in the Lodz ghetto, where the Viennese Radbukas had been sent in 1941. We all—Mr. Loewenthal, me, and a human-rights advocate named Morrell—thought that if we could see the documents Paul found in his father's—foster father's—papers after his death, we could work out whether there was any possibility of a relationship. We also suggested DNA testing. Paul rejected both suggestions with equal vehemence."

Wiell paused, then said, "Paul says you tried to keep him out of the house, then you brought in a group of children to taunt him by calling him names."

I tried not to screech into the mouthpiece. "Four little ones came pelting downstairs, caught sight of your patient, and began yelling that he was the big bad wolf. Believe me, every adult within a twenty-foot radius moved rapidly to break that up, but it upset Paul—it would unnerve anyone to have a group of strange kids mock him, but I gather it awoke unpleasant associations in Paul's mind to his father—foster father. . . . Ms. Wiell, could you persuade Paul to let me or Mr. Loewenthal look at these documents he found in his father's papers? How else can we trace the connection Paul is making between himself and Mr. Loewenthal?"

"I'll consider it," she said majestically, "but after last night's debacle I don't trust you to consider the best interests of my patient."

I made the rudest face I could muster but kept my voice light. "I wouldn't deliberately do anything that might harm Paul Radbuka. It would be a big help if Mr. Loewenthal could see these documents, since he's the person with the most knowledge of the history of his friends' families." When she hung up, with a tepid response to think about it, I let out a loud raspberry.

Mary Louise looked at me eagerly. "Was that Rhea Wiell? What's she like in person?"

I blinked, trying to remember back to Friday. "Warm. Intense. Very convinced of her own powers. She was human enough to be excited by Don's book proposal."

"Vic!" Mary Louise's face turned pink. "She is an outstanding therapist. Don't go attacking her. If she's a little aggressive in believing her own point of view—well, she's had to stand up to a lot of public abuse. Besides," she added shrewdly, "you're that way yourself. That's probably why you two rub each other the wrong way."

I curled my lip. "At least Paul Radbuka shares your view. Says she saved his life. Which makes me wonder what kind of shape he was in before she fixed him: I've never been around anyone that frighteningly wobbly." I gave her a thumbnail sketch of Radbuka's behavior at Max's last night, but I didn't feel like adding Lotty and Carl's part of the story.

Mary Louise frowned over my report but insisted Rhea would have had a good reason for hypnotizing him. "If he was so depressed that he couldn't leave his apartment, this at least is a step forward."

"Stalking Max Loewenthal and claiming to be his

cousin is a step forward? Toward what? A bed in a locked ward? Sorry," I added hastily as Mary Louise huffily turned her back on me. "She clearly has his best interests close at heart. We were all rather daunted by his showing up uninvited at Max's last night, that's all."

"All right." She hunched a shoulder but turned back to me with a determined smile, changing the subject to ask what I knew about Fepple's death.

I told her about finding the body. After wasting time lecturing me on breaking into the office, she agreed to call her old superior in the department to find out how the police were treating the case. Her criticism reminded me that I'd stuffed some of Rick Hoffman's other old files into Fepple's briefcase, which I'd dumped into the trunk and forgotten. Mary Louise said she supposed she could check up on the beneficiaries, to see whether they'd been properly paid by the company, as long as she didn't have to answer any questions about where she'd gotten their names.

"Mary Louise, you're not cut out for this work," I told her when I'd brought Fepple's canvas case in from my car. "You're used to the cops, where people are so nervous over your power to arrest that they answer your questions without you needing any finesse."

"I'd think you could find finesse without lying," she grumbled, taking the files from me. "Oh, gross, V I. Did you have to spill your breakfast on them?"

One of the folders had a smear of jelly on it, which was now on my hands as well. When I looked deeper into the bag, I saw the remains of a jelly donut mushed up with the papers and other detritus. It was gross. I washed my hands, put on latex gloves, and emptied the case onto a piece of newspaper. Mitch and Peppy were extremely interested, especially in the donut, so I lifted the newspaper onto a credenza.

Mary Louise's interest was caught; she put on her

own pair of gloves to help me sort through the rubble. It wasn't a very appetizing—or informative—haul. An athletic supporter, so grey and misshapen it was hard to recognize, jumbled in with company reports and Ping-Pong balls. The jelly donut. Another open box of crackers. Mouthwash.

"You know, it's interesting that there's no diary, either in here or on his desk," I said when we'd been through everything.

"Maybe he had so few appointments he didn't bother with a diary."

"Or maybe the guy he was seeing Friday night took the diary so no one would see Fepple had an appointment with him. He took that when he grabbed the Sommers file."

I wondered if wiping the jelly out of the interior of the case would destroy vital clues, but I couldn't bring myself to dump the contents back into the mess.

Mary Louise pretended to be excited when I went to the bathroom for a sponge. "Gosh, Vic, if you can clean out a briefcase, maybe you can learn to put papers into file jackets."

"Let's see: first you get a bucket of water, right?—oh, my, what's this?" The jelly had glued a thin piece of paper to one side of the case. I had almost pulped it running the sponge over the interior. Now I took the case over to a desk lamp so I could see what I was doing. I turned the case inside out and carefully peeled the page off the side.

It was a ledger sheet, with what looked like a list of names and numbers in a thin, archaic script—which had bloomed like little flowers in the places it was wet. Jelly mixed with water had made the top left part of the page unreadable, but what we could make out looked like this:

	29/6	6/7	13/7	20/7	27/7
* к, Ж			✓	✓	✓	✓
* ferg, Simon ++✓	✓	✓	✓	✓	✓
Brodsky, Gillal ++		✓	✓	✓	✓
Hurstein, I ++		✓	✓		✓
Sommers, H.	✓	✓	✓	✓	✓
Sommers, Aaron ++	✓	✓		✓	✓

"This is why it's such a mistake to be a housecleaning freak," I said severely. "We've lost part of the document."

"What is it?" Mary Louise leaned over the desk to see it. "That isn't Howard Fepple's handwriting, is it?"

"This script? It's so beautiful, it's like engraving—I don't see him doing it. Anyway, the paper looks old." It had gilt edging; around the lower right, which had escaped damage, the paper had turned brown with age. The ink itself was fading from black to green.

"I can't make out the names," Mary Louise said. "They are names, don't you think? Followed by a bunch of numbers. What are the numbers? They can't be dates—they're too weird. But it can't be money, either."

"They could be dates, if they were written European style—that's how my mother did it—day first, followed by month. If that's the case, this is a sequence of six weeks, from June 29 to August 3 in an unknown year. I wonder if we could read the names if we enlarged them. Let's lay this on the copier, where the heat will dry it faster."

While Mary Louise took care of that, I looked through every page of the company reports in Fepple's bag, hoping to find another sheet from the ledger, but this was the only one.

XXI

Stalker in the Park

Mary Louise started work on the files I'd pulled out of Rick Hoffman's drawer. I turned back to my computer. I'd forgotten the search I'd entered for Sofie or Sophie Radbuka, but the computer was patiently waiting with two hits: an invitation from an on-line vendor to buy books about Radbuka, and a bulletin board for messages at a family-search site.

Fifteen months earlier, someone using the label *Questing Scorpio* had posted a query: *I am looking for information about Sofie Radbuka, who lived in the United Kingdom in the 1940's.*

Underneath it was Paul Radbuka's answer, entered about two months ago and filling pages of screen. *Dear Questing Scorpio, words can hardly express the excitement I felt when I discovered your message. It was as if someone had turned on a light in a blacked-out cellar, telling me that I am here, I exist. I am not a fool, or a madman, but a person whose name and identity were kept from him for fifty years. At the end of the Second World War, I was brought from England to America by a man claiming to be my father, but in reality he was a committer of the most vile atrocities during the war. He hid my Jewish identity from me, and from the world, yet made use of it to smuggle himself past the American immigration authorities.*

He went on to describe the recovery of his memory with Rhea Wiell, going into great detail, including dreams in which he was speaking Yiddish, fragments of memories of his mother singing a lullaby to him before he was old enough to walk, details of his foster father's abuse of him.

I have been wondering why my foster father tracked me down in England, he concluded, *but it must be because of Sofie Radbuka. He might have been her torturer in the concentration camps. She is one of my relatives, perhaps even my mother, or a missing sister. Are you her child? We might be brother and sister. I am yearning for the family I have never known. Please, I implore you, write back to me, to PaulRadbuka@survivor.com. Tell me about Sofie. If she is my mother or my aunt, or possibly even a sister I never knew existed, I must know.*

No follow-up was posted, which wasn't too surprising: his hysteria came through so clearly in the document that I would have shied away from him myself. I did a search to see if Questing Scorpio had an e-mail address but came up short.

I went back to the chat room and carefully constructed a message: *Dear Questing Scorpio, if you have information or questions about the Radbuka family that you would be willing to discuss with a neutral party, you could send them to the law offices of Carter, Halsey, and Weinberg.* These were the offices of my own lawyer, Freeman Carter. I included both the street address and the URL for their Web site, then sent an e-mail to Freeman, letting him know what I'd done.

I looked at the screen for a bit, as if it might magically reveal some other information, but eventually I remembered that no one was paying me to find out anything about Sofie Radbuka and settled down to some of the on-line searches that make up the better part of my business these days. The Web has transformed investigative work, making it for the most part both easier and duller.

At noon, when Mary Louise left for class, she said all six policies I'd brought with me from Midway were in order: for the four where the purchaser was dead, the beneficiaries had duly received their benefits. For the two still living, no one had submitted a claim. Three of the policies had been on Ajax paper. Two other companies had issued the other three. So if the Sommers claim had been fraudulently submitted by the agency, it wasn't a regular occurrence.

Exhaustion made it hard for me to think—about that, or anything else. When Mary Louise had left, waves of fatigue swept over me. I moved on leaden legs to the cot in my supply room, where I fell into a feverish sleep. It was almost three when the phone pulled me awake again. I stumbled out to my desk and mumbled something unintelligible.

A woman asked for me, then told me to hold for Mr. Rossy. Mr. Rossy? Oh, yes, the head of Edelweiss's U.S. operations. I rubbed my forehead, trying to make blood flow into my brain, then, since I was still on hold, went to the little refrigerator in the hall, which I share with Tessa, for a bottle of water. Rossy was calling my name sharply when I picked up the phone again.

"*Buon giorno,*" I said, with a semblance of brightness. "*Come sta? Che cosa posso fare per Lei?*"

He exclaimed over my Italian. "Ralph told me you were fluent; you speak it beautifully—almost without an accent. Actually, that's why I called."

"To speak Italian to me?" I was incredulous.

"My wife—she gets homesick. When I told her I'd met an Italian speaker who shared her love of opera, she wondered if you'd do us the honor of coming to dinner.

She was especially fascinated, as I was sure she would be, by the idea of your office among the *indovine*—p-suchics," he added in English, correcting himself immediately to "sychics." "Do I have this correct now?"

"Perfect," I said absently. I looked at the Isabel Bishop painting on the wall by my desk, but the angular face staring at a sewing machine told me nothing. "It would be a pleasure to meet Mrs. Rossy," I finally said.

"Is it possible that you could join us tomorrow evening?"

I thought of Morrell, leaving for Rome on a ten A.M. flight, and the hollow I would feel when I saw him off. "As it happens, I'm free." I copied the address—an apartment building near Lotty's on Lake Shore Drive—into my Palm Pilot. We hung up on mutual protestations of goodwill, but I frowned at the painted seamstress a long moment, wondering what Rossy really wanted.

The page I'd found in Fepple's briefcase was dry now. I set the machine to enlarge the copy and came up with letters big enough to read. The original I tucked into a plastic sleeve.

Sumner, Simon ++✓

Brodsky, Hillal ++

Herstein, J ++

Sommers, H.

Sommers, Aaron ++

The script was still hard to make out, but I could read Hillel Brodsky, I or G Herstein, and Th. and Aaron

Sommers—although it looked like Pommers I knew it had to be my client's uncle. So this was a list of clients from the Midway Agency—that seemed like a reasonable assumption. What did the crosses mean? That they were dead? That their families had been defrauded? Or both? Perhaps Th. Sommers was still alive.

The dogs, restless from five hours inside, got up and wagged their tails at me. "You guys think we should get in motion? You're right. Let's go." I shut down my system, carefully slid the original of the fragment into my own case, and took Fepple's briefcase with me back to the car.

The clock was ticking and I had business-hours errands to run. I gave the dogs a chance to relieve themselves but didn't take the time to run them before driving out the O'Hare corridor to Cheviot Labs, a private forensics lab I often use. I showed the fragment of paper to the engineer who's helped me in the past.

"I know metal, not paper, but we've got someone on staff here who can do it," he said.

"I'm willing to pay for a priority job," I said.

He grunted. "I'll talk to her. Kathryn Chang. One of us'll call you tomorrow."

I was just ahead of the afternoon rush, so I kept the increasingly restless dogs in the car until we got to Hyde Park, where I threw sticks into the lake for them for half an hour. "Sorry, guys: bad timing to take you two today. Back in the car with you."

It was four, when a lot of duty rosters change; I drove over to the Hyde Park Bank building. Sure enough, the same man who'd been here Friday was on duty. He looked at me without interest when I stopped in front of his station.

"We kind of met on Friday afternoon," I said.

He looked at me more closely. "Oh, yeah. Fepple said you'd been harassing him. You harass him to death?"

He seemed to be joking, so I smiled. "Not me. It was on the news that he'd been shot, or shot himself."

"That's right. They say the business was going down the toilet, which doesn't surprise me. I've worked here nine years. Since the old man died I bet I could count the evenings the young one worked late. Must have been disappointed with the client he saw on Friday."

"He came back with someone after I left?"

"That's right. But must not have amounted to anything after all. I suppose that's why I didn't see him leave: he stayed up there and killed himself."

"The man who came in with him—when did he leave?"

"Not sure it was a man or a woman—Fepple came back along with a Lamaze class. I think he was talking to someone, but I can't say I was paying close attention. Cops think I'm derelict because I don't photograph every person that passes through here, but, hell, the building doesn't even have a sign-in policy. If Fepple's visitor left at the same time as the pregnant couples, I wouldn't have noticed them special."

I had to give up on it. I handed him Fepple's canvas bag, telling him I'd found it on the curb.

"I think it might belong to Fepple, judging by the stuff inside. Since the cops are being a pain, maybe you could just drop it in his office—their problem to sort out if they ever come back here again." I gave him my card, just in case something occurred to him, along with my most dazzling smile, and headed for the western suburbs.

Unlike my beloved old Trans Am, the Mustang didn't handle well at high speeds—which wasn't a problem this afternoon, because we weren't going anywhere very fast. As the evening rush built, I sat for long periods without moving at all.

The first leg of the trip was on the same expressway I'd taken when I went to see Isaiah Sommers on Friday.

The air thickened along the industrial corridor, turning the bright September sky to a dull yellowish grey. I took out my phone and tried Max, wondering how Lotty and he were faring after last night's upheavals. Agnes Loewenthal answered the phone.

"Oh, Vic—Max is still at the hospital. We're expecting him around six. But that horrid man who came to the house last night was around today."

I inched forward behind a waste hauler. "He came to the house?"

"No, it was worse in a way. He was in the park across the street. When I took Calia out for a walk this afternoon he came over to try to talk to us, saying he wanted Calia to know he wasn't really a big bad wolf, that he was her cousin."

"What did you do?"

"I said he was quite mistaken and to leave us alone. He tried to follow us, arguing with me, but when Calia got upset and began to cry he started to shout at us—imploring me to let him talk to Calia by himself. We ran back to the house. Max—I called Max; he called the Evanston police, who sent a squad car around. They moved him off, but—Vic, it's really frightening. I don't want to be alone in the house—Mrs. Squires didn't come in today because of the party yesterday."

The car behind me honked impatiently; I closed a six-foot gap while I asked if she really had to stay in Chicago until Saturday.

"If this horrid little man is going to be stalking us, I might see if we can get on an earlier flight. Although the gallery I went to last week wants me to come in on Thursday to meet with their backers; I'd hate to lose that opportunity."

I rubbed my face with my free hand. "There's a service I use when I need help bodyguarding or staking out places. Do you want me to see if they have someone who can stay in the house until you go home?"

Her relief rushed across the airwaves to me. "I'll have to talk to Max—but, yes. Yes, do that, Vic."

My shoulders sagged when she hung up. If Radbuka was turning into a stalker, he could become a real problem. I called the Streeter Brothers' voice mail to explain what I needed. They're a funny bunch of guys, the Streeter Brothers: they do surveillance, bodyguarding, and furniture moving, with Tom and Tim Streeter running a changing group of nine, including, these days, two well-muscled women.

By the time I finished my message, we had passed into the exurbs. The road widened, the sky brightened. When I left the tollway, it was suddenly a beautiful fall day again.

XXII

Grieving Mother

Howard Fepple had lived with his mother a few blocks west of Harlem Avenue. These weren't the suburbs of great wealth but of the working middle class, where ranch houses and colonials sit on modest plots and neighborhood children play in each other's yards.

When I pulled up in front of the Fepple home, only one car, a late-model navy Oldsmobile, sat in the drive. Neither news crews nor neighbors were paying their respects to Rhonda Fepple. The dogs strained to follow me from the car. When I locked them in, they barked their disapproval.

A flagstone path, whose stones were cracked and overgrown with weeds, curved away from the driveway to a side entrance. When I rang the bell, I saw that the paint on the front door had peeled loose in a number of places.

After a long wait, Rhonda Fepple came to the door. Her face, with the same carpet of freckles as her son's, held the blank, stunned look most people wear after a harsh blow. She was younger than I'd expected. Despite the grief that was collapsing her inside her clothes, she had only a few lines around her red-stained eyes, and her sandy hair was still thick.

"Mrs. Fepple? I'm sorry to bother you, but I'm a detective from Chicago with a few questions about your son."

She accepted my identity without even wanting a name, let alone some identification. "Did you find out who shot him?"

"No, ma'am. I understand you told the officers on the morning shift that Mr. Fepple didn't own a gun."

"I wanted him to, if he was going to stay in that creepy old building, but he just laughed and said there wasn't anything in the agency anyone would want to steal. I always hated that bank, those halls with all the little turnings off them, anyone could lie in wait for you there."

"The agency wasn't doing very well these days, I understand. Was it more prosperous when your husband was alive?"

"You're not trying to say what they told me this morning, are you? That Howie was so depressed he took his own life? Because he wasn't that kind of boy. Young man. You forget they grow up." She patted the corners of her eyes with a tissue.

It was comforting somehow to know that even a dreary specimen like Howard Fepple had someone who mourned his death. "Ma'am, I know this is a really hard time for you to try to talk about your son, with the loss so fresh, but I want to explore a third possibility—besides suicide or a random break-in. I'm wondering if there was anyone who might have specifically had a quarrel with your son. Had he talked to you about any conflicts with clients lately?"

She stared at me blankly: thinking new thoughts was hard in her grief-drained state. She stuffed the tissue back into the pocket of the old yellow shirt she was wearing. "I suppose you better come in."

I followed her into the living room, where she sat on the edge of a sofa whose cabbage roses had faded to a dull pink. When I took a matching armchair at right angles to her, dust bunnies bounced along the walls. The new piece in the room, a tan Naugahyde recliner parked in front of the thirty-four-inch television, had probably belonged to Howard.

"How long had your son been working at the agency, Mrs. Fepple?"

She twisted her wedding ring. "Howie wasn't much interested in insurance, but Mr. Fepple insisted he learn the business. You can always make a living in insurance, no matter how bad times are, he always said. That's how the agency survived the Depression, he was always telling Howie that, but Howie wanted to do something—well, more interesting, more like what the boys—men—he went to school with were doing. Computers, finance, that kind of thing. But he couldn't make a go of it, so when Mr. Fepple passed away and left the agency to him, Howie went ahead and tried to make it work. But that neighborhood has gone steep downhill since when we used to live there. Of course, we moved out here in '59, but all Mr. Fepple's clients were on the South Side; he didn't see how he could move the agency and look after them."

"So you lived in Hyde Park when you were growing up?" I asked, to keep the conversation going.

"South Shore, really, just south of Hyde Park. Then when I got out of high school I went off to work as a secretary to Mr. Fepple. He was quite a bit older, but, well, you know how these things go, and when we found Howie was on the way, well, we got married. He had never married before—Mr. Fepple, I mean—and I guess he was excited at the idea of a boy to carry on—his father started the agency—you know how men are about things like that. When the baby came, I stayed at home to look after him—back then we didn't have day care, you know, not like now. Mr. Fepple always said I spoiled him, but he was fifty by then, not much interested in children." Her voice trailed away.

"So Mr. Howard Fepple only started work at the agency when his father died?" I prompted. "How did he learn the business?"

"Oh, well, Howie used to work there weekends and summers, and he spent four years there after college. He went out to Governors State, got a degree in business. But like I said, insurance wasn't really his cup of tea."

The mention of tea galvanized her into thinking we should have something to drink. I followed her into the kitchen, where she pulled a Diet Coke out of the refrigerator for herself and handed me a glass of tap water.

I sat at the kitchen table, pushing aside a banana peel. "What about the agent who worked for your husband, what was his name? Rick Hoffman? Your son seemed to admire his work."

She made a face. "I never took to him. He was such a fussy man. Everything had to be just so. When I worked there he was always criticizing me because I didn't keep the file drawers the way he wanted them organized. It was Mr. Fepple's agency, I told him, and Mr. Fepple had a right to set up files the way he wanted them, but Mr. Hoffman insisted I get all his files arranged in this special way, like it was some big deal. He did these little sales, burial policies, that kind of thing, but the way he acted you'd think he was insuring the pope." She waved her arm in a vague gesture, making the dust bunnies bounce.

"Somehow he made a lot of money doing it, money Mr. Fepple sure never saw. Mr. Hoffman drove a big Mercedes, had a fancy apartment someplace on the North Side.

"When I saw him show up with that Mercedes, I told Mr. Fepple he must be embezzling, or part of the mob or something, but Mr. Fepple always went through the books very carefully, no money was ever missing or anything. When time went on, Mr. Hoffman got stranger and stranger, by what Mr. Fepple said. He drove the girl who came there later on—after Howie was born, after I quit to look after him—out of her mind. He was always fussing around his papers, she said, taking them in and out of files. I think he kind of went senile toward the end, but Mr. Fepple said he wasn't doing any harm, let him come into the office and shuffle his papers around."

"Hoffman had a son, right? Did his boy and yours hang out together?"

"Oh, goodness me, no—his boy started college the year Howie was born. I don't know if I ever even met him, it was just Mr. Hoffman always talking about him, how everything he did was for his boy—of course, I shouldn't poke fun, I felt the same way about Howie. But somehow it griped me, all the money he could come up with to spend on his son, while Mr. Fepple, who owned the agency, didn't have near as much. Mr. Hoffman sent his son off to some fancy eastern school to college, someplace that sounded like Harvard but wasn't. But I never heard his boy amounted to anything much, even with all that expensive education."

"Do you know what became of him? The son, I mean?"

She shook her head. "I heard he was like a hospital clerk or something, but after Mr. Hoffman passed away, we didn't hear anything about him. It wasn't like we knew anyone who knew him, in a social way, I mean."

"Did your son talk about Hoffman lately?" I asked. "Did he mention problems with any of Mr. Hoffman's old clients? I'm wondering in particular if any of them might have threatened him. Or maybe made him so depressed about the business that he didn't see how he could make it work."

She shook her head, sniffling again as she thought of her son's last days. "But that's why I don't think he killed himself. He was, oh, sort of excited, like he gets—got—when he had a new idea in mind. He said he finally understood how Hoffman made so much money out of his list. He figured he could get me a Mercedes of my own if I wanted. Pretty soon, he said. Now, well, I do clerical work up in Western Springs, and I guess I'll just keep on until I retire."

The bleakness of the prospect depressed me almost as much as it did her. I asked abruptly when she'd last seen her son.

Tears leaked from the corners of her eyes. "Friday morning. When I was leaving for work he was getting up. He said he had a dinner meeting with a client, so he'd be home late. Then, when he didn't come home, I got worried. I called the office off and on on Saturday, but he does sometimes—did sometimes—go to these table-tennis tournaments out of town. I thought maybe he forgot to tell me. Or maybe he had a date—I did kind of wonder, the way he dressed so carefully Friday morning. I try—tried—to remember he's not still a child, although it's hard, when he's living right here at home."

I tried to get a client name from her, wondering if Isaiah Sommers had come around threatening him. But much as she would have liked to blame Howie's death on some black person from the South Side, Rhonda Fepple couldn't remember his mentioning any names.

"The officers who talked to you this morning, they didn't bother to search your son's room, did they? No, I didn't think they would—they were too fixed on their suicide theory. Could I take a look?"

She still didn't ask me for identification but led me

down the hall to her son's room. She must have given him the master suite when her husband died—it was a large room, with a king-size bed and a small desk.

The room smelled of sour sweat and other things I didn't want to think about. Mrs. Fepple murmured something apologetic about laundry and tried to pick up some of the clothes from the floor. She stood looking from a polka-dotted shirt in her left hand to a pair of shorts in her right, as if trying to figure out what they were, then let them fall back to the floor. After that she just stood, watching me as if I were the television screen, a soothing but meaningless piece of motion in the room.

Rummaging through dresser and desk drawers, I found cell phones from two earlier generations of models, a collection of startling porn that Fepple had apparently printed off the Web, a half dozen broken calculators, and three table-tennis paddles, but no documents of any kind. I went through his closet and even looked between the mattress and box springs. All I found was another collection of porn, this time magazines that dated back several years—he must have forgotten about them when he learned how to cruise the Net.

The only insurance documents in the room were company pamphlets stacked on the desktop. Not the Sommers file nor even a datebook—which hadn't been in his briefcase or office—nor any more pages like the one I'd found in his briefcase this morning.

I pulled one of the photocopies of the page from my own case and showed it to her. "Do you know what this is? It was in your son's office."

She looked at it with the same apathy she'd given my search. "That? I couldn't tell you."

She started to hand it back to me, then said it might be Mr. Hoffman's handwriting. "He kept these leather books with his name stamped on the cover in gold. He'd take them around with him to his customers and check off when they paid, just like on here."

She tapped the check marks with her index finger. "One day I picked up his book when he was in the washroom, and when he came back you'd think I was a Russian spy going after the atom bomb, the way he carried on. Like I knew what any of it meant."

"Does this writing look like Hoffman's writing?"

She shrugged. "I haven't seen it in years. I just remember it was scrunched up like this, kind of hard to read, but real even, like it was engraving."

I looked around, discouraged. "What I hoped to find was some kind of diary. Your son didn't have one on his desk at the office, nor in his briefcase. Do you know how he kept track of his appointments?"

"He had one of those handheld gadgets, one of those electronic things. Yeah, like that," she added when I showed her my Palm Pilot. "If it wasn't on him, then whoever killed him must've stolen it."

Which either meant an appointment with his killer or—a random attack where the killer stole pawnable electronics. The computer had been left there—but it would have been hard to smuggle past the guard. I asked Mrs. Fepple if the cops had returned her son's possessions to her, but those were still part of crime-scene evidence; the technicians were keeping them until the autopsy gave them a definitive report of suicide.

"Was he renting month-by-month, or is there a lease?"

He'd gone to month-by-month. She agreed to lend me a spare office key that she'd kept, but the thought of having to get all those files packed up by the end of September, and of having to work with the various companies to shift active policyholders to a new agency, made her droop further into her yellow shirt.

"I don't know what I thought you'd be able to tell me, but it doesn't seem like you're going to be able to find who killed him. I gotta lie down. Somehow, all this, it has me worn out. You'd think all you'd do is cry, but it's like all I can do is sleep."

XXIII

Fencing in the Dark

My long trek north to Morrell's took me through the disturbing vistas of the western suburbs: no center, no landmarks, just endless sameness. Sometimes row on row of ranch houses, sometimes of more-elaborate, more-affluent tracts, but all punctuated with malls showing identical megastores. The third time I passed Bed Bath & Beyond and Barnes & Noble I thought I was driving in circles.

"Sometimes I feel like a motherless child, a long way from home," I sang, as I sat in a stationary lane at one of the everlasting tollbooths on the rim road around the city. I was motherless, after all, and forty miles from Morrell's home.

I flung my change into the box and scoffed at myself for melodramatic self-pity. Real grief lay in Rhonda Fepple's story: the childless mother. It's so out of the order of nature, and it exposes you as so fundamentally powerless, to have a child die before you: you never really recover from it.

Howie Fepple's mother didn't think her son had committed suicide. No mother would want to believe that of her child, but in Fepple's case it was because he was excited—he finally understood how Rick Hoffman had made enough money out of his book to drive a Mercedes—and he was going to get one for Rhonda.

I pulled out my phone to call Nick Vishnikov, the chief deputy medical examiner, but the traffic suddenly cleared; the SUV's around me quickly accelerated to eighty or ninety. The call could wait until it didn't put my life in danger to make it.

The dogs panted gently over my shoulder, reminding me that it had been some hours since their last run. When I finally reached the Dempster exit I pulled off at a forest preserve to let them out. It was dark now, the park officially closed, with a piece of chain blocking me from going farther than a few yards off the main road.

While Mitch and Peppy excitedly set off after rabbits I stood at the chain with my cell phone, calling first Morrell to tell him we were only eight miles away, then trying Lotty again. She had left the clinic, her receptionist, Mrs. Coltrain, told me.

"How did she seem?"

"Dr. Herschel is working too hard: she needs to take some time off for herself." Mrs. Coltrain has known me for years, but she won't gossip about Lotty with anyone, not even to agree with Max when he mocks her imperial manner.

I tapped the phone thoughtfully. If I was going to have a heart-to-heart with Lotty I should do it sitting down at home, but this was Morrell's last night in Chicago. The dogs were crashing around somewhere near me. I called to them, to remind them that I was here and in charge of the pack. When they'd run up, sniffed my hands, and torn off again, I reached Lotty at home.

She cut short my attempt to express concern at her collapse yesterday. "I'd rather not discuss it, Victoria. I'm embarrassed that I created such a disturbance in the middle of Max's party and don't want to be reminded of it."

"Maybe, oh physician, you should consult a doctor yourself. Make sure you're okay, that you didn't hurt yourself when you fainted."

Her voice took on a sharper edge. "I'm perfectly fine, thanks very much."

I stared into the dark underbrush, as if seeing it would enable me to penetrate Lotty's mind. "I know you weren't in the room with Radbuka last night when he was going on about his past, but did Max tell you Radbuka found a posting on a bulletin board from someone wanting information about Sofie Radbuka? I went on the Web today and found the site. Radbuka is convinced she must have been his mother or his sister; at least, he wrote a long message to that effect. Lotty, who was she?"

"You found Sofie Radbuka on the Web? That's impossible!"

"I found someone who wanted information about her, saying that she lived in England during the forties," I repeated patiently.

"Max didn't think fit to tell me that," she snapped. "Thank you very much."

She hung up, leaving me uncomfortably alone in the dark woods. A sense of being both forlorn and ridiculous made me call the dogs back to me again. I could hear them thrashing around, but they wouldn't come. I had kept them penned up all day—they weren't going to reward me by being good dogs now.

Before going to the car for a flashlight so I could track them, I made one last call—to Nick Vishnikov at the morgue. After all, the place never closes. When I dialed the number—which I know by heart—I got the one thin piece of luck the Fates were allowing me today: Vishnikov, who pretty much chooses his hours, was still there.

"Vic. How's Morrell? He in Kabul yet?"

"Tomorrow," I said. "Nick—there's a guy with a

head wound who came in this morning. The police are calling it suicide."

"But you murdered him and you want to confess." Autopsies make him ferociously cheerful.

"Howard Fepple. I want to be a hundred-fifty percent certain that he put that SIG Trailside to his head all by himself."

He hadn't done Fepple's case. While he put me on hold to check the files, I fiddled with the dogs' leashes, wishing I hadn't let them disappear into the dark—I couldn't hear them now.

"I handed it off to one of my juniors since it seemed straightforward, and he treated it as routine suicide, but I see he didn't check the hands for gunpowder—he relied on the fact that the victim ate the gun. We still have the body—I'll review it before I leave. Do you have evidence of murder?"

"People do the darnedest things, but I have a guy who told his mother he was on to something hot, and I have a mystery visitor to his office. I'd love it if the state's attorney pulled Fepple's phone logs."

"I'll let you know if there's anything to change the verdict. Later, Vic."

I wondered whether my client had gone around with a gun to threaten Fepple, but Isaiah Sommers didn't strike me as the kind of person who would set up an elaborate trap. If Fepple had been murdered by the person who called him when I was in the office on Friday, that was someone who was planning to kill and planning a way to avoid being seen. He had gone in and out of the building with big enough groups of people to avoid notice. He'd shown Fepple how to get away from me. It didn't sound like Isaiah Sommers.

Momentarily forgetting the dogs, I got the Sommers number from directory assistance. Margaret Sommers answered, her voice heavy with hostility, but after a moment's pause, in which she couldn't think of a reason not to, she brought her husband to the phone. I told him about Fepple's death.

"I searched both the office and his home and couldn't find a trace of your uncle's file," I said. "The police are labeling this a suicide, but I think someone killed him, and I'm sort of thinking they killed him to get that file."

"Who would do that?"

"It could be that whoever perpetrated the fraud to begin with left some kind of record behind that they don't want anyone else to find. It could be someone got pissed enough at the guy over something else to kill him."

When I paused, he exploded. "You accusing me of going in there to murder him? My wife was right. Alderman Durham was right. You never had the least—"

"Mr. Sommers, I've had a long day. I'm out of finesse. I don't think you killed the guy. On the other hand, you've clearly got a temper. Maybe your wife or the alderman pushed you to stop waiting for me to get results, to go see Fepple yourself. Maybe his smirking do-nothing attitude goaded you to act."

"Well, it didn't. He didn't. I agreed to wait for you and I am waiting for you. Even though the alderman thinks I'm making a big mistake."

"He does? What does he recommend?"

Peppy and Mitch bounded up to me. I smelled them before I saw them, darker shapes against the darkness of the clearing where I stood—they had rolled in something rank. My hand over the mouthpiece, I ordered them to sit. Peppy obeyed, but Mitch tried to jump on me. I pushed him away with my foot.

"That's just it. He doesn't have a plan I can follow. He wants me to initiate a suit against Ajax, but like I asked him, who's going to pay all those legal bills? Who has that kind of time? My wife's brother, he took on a big lawsuit, it dragged through the courts for thirteen years. I don't want to wait thirteen years to get my money back."

In the background I could hear Margaret Sommers demanding to know why he wanted to tell the whole world her private business. Mitch lunged at me again, knocking me off-balance. I sat down hard, the phone still clutched to my ear. I tried to push Mitch away without shouting into the mouthpiece. He barked in excitement, thinking we were having a wonderful game together. Peppy tried to shove him out of the way. By now I smelled just as bad as the two of them. I clipped their leashes on and stood up.

"Am I ever going to get any satisfaction out of this situation?" Sommers was demanding. "I'm sorry about the agent: that was a terrible way to die, but it's no joke to come up with all that cash for a funeral, Ms. Warashki."

"I'm going to talk to the company tomorrow, to see if they'll offer a settlement." I was going to pitch it to them as a way of building PR ammo against Durham, but I didn't think it would help relations with the client if I told him that. "If they offer you something on the dollar, would that be acceptable?"

"I—let me think about it."

"Very wise, Mr. Sommers," I said, tired of standing around in the dark with my smelly dogs. "Your wife should have a chance to tell you I'm trying to rob you. Call me tomorrow. Oh—do you own a gun yourself?"

"Do I—oh, I see, you want to know if I'm lying about killing that agent."

I rubbed a hand through my hair, realizing a second too late how much it stank of rotten rabbit. "I'm trying to assure myself that you couldn't have killed him."

He paused. I could hear him breathing heavily in my ear while he thought it over and then reluctantly revealed that he owned a nine-millimeter Browning Special.

"That's reassuring, Mr. Sommers. Fepple was killed with a Swiss model, different gauge. Call me tomorrow about whether you'll take a deal from the company. Good night."

As I yanked the dogs toward the car, a forest-preserve deputy pulled into the clearing behind my Mustang, shining his searchlight on us. He demanded over his bullhorn that I come over. When we got to the car, he seemed disappointed to find that we were a law-abiding trio, with both dogs hitched up: the deputies love to ticket people for disobeying the leash laws. Mitch, incurably friendly, lunged toward the man, who backed away in disgust from the stench. He seemed to be looking for some grounds for a ticket but finally said only that the park was closed and he was going to watch to see that we moved on.

"You are an evil animal," I said to Mitch when we were back on Dempster, the deputy ostentatiously tailing us. "You not only stink yourself, but you've gotten that gross smell all over me. It's not like I have clothes to burn, you know."

Mitch stuck his head over the backseat, grinning happily. I opened all the windows, but it was still a tough ride. I had intended to stop at Max's, to find out how they were doing and to see what Max could tell me about Lotty's history with the Radbuka family. Right now all I really wanted was to fling the dogs into a tub and dive in after them, but to be prudent, I swung past Max's house before going to Morrell's. Leaving Mitch in the car, I took Peppy and a flashlight and walked through the park across the street from Max's. We surprised several bundles of students tied up in love knots, who backed away from us in disgust, but Radbuka at least didn't seem to be hovering nearby.

At Morrell's, I chained the dogs to the back-porch railing. Don was out there with a cigarette. Inside, I could hear Morrell tinkering with a Schumann piano concerto, too loudly to hear my arrival.

"Warshawski—what've you been doing?" Don demanded. "Arm-wrestling skunks?"

"Don. This is great. You don't get enough exercise. You can help me wash these wonderful animals."

I went in through the kitchen, taking a garbage bag to wrap my clothes in when I stripped. I put on an old T-shirt and cutoffs to bathe the dogs. My suggestion that he help wash them had made Don scuttle. I laughed as I scrubbed Mitch and Peppy, then went into the shower myself. By the time the three of us were clean, Morrell was waiting in the kitchen for me with a glass of wine.

Pre-departure nerves had turned Morrell edgy. I told him about Fepple, and the depressing life he seemed to have led, and how the dogs had rolled in something so rotten that they'd scared off a sheriff's deputy. He expressed shock and amusement in the right places, but his mind wasn't with me. I kept the news of Radbuka's stalking the Loewenthals, and Lotty's disturbing behavior, to myself—Morrell didn't need worries about me to take with him into the Taliban's world.

Don was going to stay on at Morrell's while he worked on his project with Rhea Wiell, but Morrell said it wasn't cowardice over dog bathing that had driven him away but Morrell's own orders: he'd sent Don to a hotel so we could have this last evening alone together.

I made up little bruschette with pears and Gorgonzola, then put together a frittata, taking elaborate care, even caramelizing onions for it. I'd laid by a special bottle of Barolo. A meal of love, a meal of despair: remember me, remember that my meals make you happy and return to me.

As I should have expected, Morrell was completely prepared, with everything packed into a couple of lightweight bags. He'd stopped his paper, forwarded his mail to me, left me money to pay his bills. He was nervous and excited. Although we went to bed soon after eating, he talked until close to two in the morning: about himself, his parents—whom he almost never mentioned—his childhood in Cuba where they had come as emigrants from Hungary, his plans for his upcoming trip.

As we lay next to each other in the dark, he clung to me feverishly. "Victoria Iphigenia, I love you for your fierceness and your passionate attachment to truth. If anything should happen to me—not that I expect it to—you have my lawyer's name."

"Nothing will happen to you, Morrell." My cheeks were wet; we fell asleep like that, clutched in each other's arms.

When the alarm woke us a few hours later, I quickly took the dogs around the block while Morrell made coffee. He had talked himself out in the night; we were silent on the drive to the airport. In the backseat, the dogs, sensing our mood, whined nervously. Morrell and I share an aversion to long farewells: I dropped him at the terminal and quickly drove off, not even staying to see him go inside. If I didn't see him leave—perhaps he wouldn't be gone.

XXIV

Walrus Duty

At eight-thirty in the morning, traffic into the city was at a standstill. After last night, I couldn't face another horrible commute. Don wasn't coming back to Morrell's until later this afternoon—I could rest there for a bit. Avoiding the expressways altogether, I entered the alternative morning rush hour—kids going to school, people arriving for jobs at the little shops and delis that dot the area. They accentuated my sense of instability: Morrell gone, a hole in the middle of my life. Why didn't I live in one of those tidy white-sided houses, with children heading off for school while I went to some orderly job?

As I sat at the light at Golf Road I phoned in for my messages. Nick Vishnikov wanted me to call him. Tim Streeter had said he would be happy to provide some security for Calia and Agnes until they left on Saturday.

In my personal turmoil over Morrell's departure, I'd forgotten Radbuka's odd behavior. I stopped dawdling along with my maudlin thoughts and drove over to Max's as fast as I could. By this time of day, he's usually already in meetings, but when I reached his house, his LeSabre was still in the driveway. His face was heavy with worry when he answered the door.

"Victoria. Come in. Has Morrell left?" Before shutting the door he peered anxiously across the street, but only a lone jogger was visible, a silhouette moving along the lakeshore.

"I just dropped him at the airport. Did Agnes tell you I can arrange a little security for you?"

"That would be a help. If I had known what a chamber of horrors I'd open by participating in that Birnbaum conference, putting Calia at risk—"

"At risk?" I interrupted. "Has Radbuka been back? Did he make an overt threat against her?"

"No, nothing that concrete. But his obsession with being related to me—I can't understand it. This hovering around here—"

I interrupted to ask again if Radbuka had been back.

"I don't think so, but of course this house is so exposed, with a public park across the street— You think I'm blowing my worries out of proportion? Maybe so, maybe so, but I'm not young, and Calia is precious. Still, if you can arrange for someone reliable to be here—and of course I will pay the fee."

Max took me back to the kitchen to use the phone. Agnes was sitting there, drinking coffee, anxiously watching Calia, who was alternating spoonfuls of cornflakes with pleas to go to the zoo.

"No, darling. We're going to stay inside and paint pictures today," Agnes repeated.

I took a cup of coffee to the phone with me. Tom Streeter promised to have his brother Tim at Max's within the hour.

"With Tim on the case, you can be pretty secure going anywhere you want," I told Agnes.

"Is he the big bad wolf?" Calia demanded.

"No, he's a big good teddy bear," I said. "You'll see: you and your mama will both find him irresistible."

Max sat next to Calia, trying not to let his anxiety shine through as obviously as Agnes's. When I asked him what he could tell me about the Radbuka family he'd known in London, he got up again, taking me away from the eating alcove. He kept turning to look at Calia while he spoke.

"I didn't know them. Lotty has always claimed they were an acquaintance merely, and I have acquiesced in that."

Calia climbed down from the table, announcing she was through with breakfast, she was tired of the house, she was going outside *now*.

"When your grandpapa and I are through talking we'll go across to the park with the dogs," I said. "You hold tight for ten more minutes." I mouthed "television" at Agnes, who made a sour face but took Calia upstairs to the universal baby-sitter.

"You think the Radbukas were relations or close friends of Lotty's?" I said to Max.

"It's what I said Sunday night. Lotty always made it clear that one didn't discuss the Radbukas with her. I assume that's why she gave me the information about them in writing, to preclude any discussion. I don't know who they were."

He moved Calia's dishes to the sink and sat back down at the table. "Yesterday I went through such files as I have from that trip I made to central Europe after the war. I was looking for so many people that nothing stands out very clearly in my mind. Lotty had given me her grandparents' address on the Renngasse—that was where she lived before the Anschluss—a very tony address which had been taken over in '38 by people who wouldn't talk to me. I concentrated most of my energy in Vienna on my own family, and then I wanted to get to Budapest to look for Teresz's people. We weren't married then, of course, we were still very young."

His voice faded into memory. After a minute he shook his head with a sad little smile and continued. "Anyway, the notes I have about the Radbukas—well, let me get them."

While he went up to his study I helped myself to fruit and rolls from his refrigerator. He came back in a couple of minutes with a thick binder. He thumbed through it, opening it to a sheet of cheap grey paper encased in plastic. Even though the ink was fading to brown, Lotty's distinctive script—spiky and bold—was unmistakable.

Dear Max,

I admire your courage in taking this trip. Vienna for me represents a world I can't bear to return to, even if the Royal Free would grant me a leave of absence. So thank you for going, since I am as desperate for a conclusive answer as everyone else. I told you about my grandparents. If by a miracle they have survived and have been able to return to their home, it is Renngasse 7, third-floor front.

I want to ask you also to look for any record of another family from Vienna, named Radbuka. This is for someone at the Royal Free who sadly cannot recollect many details. For instance, the man's first name was Shlomo but the person doesn't know his wife's name, or even if they would have been registered with some kind of Germanized names. They had a son called Moishe, born around 1900, one daughter named Rachel, two other daughters whose names the person isn't sure of—one might be Eva—and a number of grandchildren of our generation. Also, the address isn't certain: it was on the Leopoldsgasse, near the Untere Augarten Strasse end: you turn right from U.A. onto L-gasse, then it's the second turning on your right, into the interior courtyard, and on the third floor at the back. I realize that's a hopeless way to describe what may now be a pile of rubble, but it's the best I can do. But please, I ask you to treat it as seriously as your search for our own families, please make every effort to see what trace you can find of them.

I am on duty tonight and tomorrow night both, so I won't be able to see you in person before you leave.

The remainder of the letter gave the names of some of Lotty's aunts and uncles and concluded with, *I'm enclosing a gold prewar five-Krone piece to help pay for your journey.*

I blinked: gold coins sound romantic, exotic, and wealthy. "I thought Lotty was a poor student, barely able to make her tuition and rooming payments."

"She was. She had a handful of gold coins that her grandfather had helped her smuggle out of Vienna: giving one of them to me meant wearing her coat and socks to bed in lieu of heat that winter. Maybe that contributed to her getting so sick the next year."

Abashed, I returned to the main question. "So you don't have any idea who in London asked Lotty for help?"

He shook his head. "It could have been anyone. Or it could have been Lotty herself, searching for relatives. I wondered if it might be one of her cousins' names: she and Hugo were sent to England; the Herschels had been quite well off before the Anschluss. They still had some resources, but Lotty once or twice mentioned very poor cousins who stayed behind. But I also thought it might be someone who was in England illegally, someone Lotty felt honor-bound to protect. I didn't have anything to go on, mind you. But one imagines something and that was the picture I painted to myself . . . or maybe it was Teresz's idea. I can't remember now. Of course Radbuka might have been a patient or colleague from the Royal Free for whom Lotty felt similarly protective."

"I suppose I could get in touch with the Royal Free, see if they have lists that date back to '47," I said doubtfully. "What did you find in Vienna? Did you go to—to—" I looked at Lotty's note and stumbled through the pronunciation of the German street names.

Max flipped through the binder to the back, where he pulled a cheap notebook from its own plastic cover. "I looked at my notes, but they don't tell me much. Bauernmarkt, where my own family lived, had been badly hit in the bombing. I know I did walk all through that area, through what they used to call the Matzoinsel, where the eastern European Jews gathered when they immigrated during the early years of the century. I'm sure I tried to find the place on the Leopoldsgasse. But the site of so much desolation was too depressing. My notes I kept for news from the different agencies I visited."

He opened the notebook carefully, so as not to tear the fragile paper. "Shlomo and Judit Radbuka: deported to Lodz 23 February 1941 with Edith—I think that's the name Lotty thought might be Eva—Rachel, Julie, and Mara. And a list of seven children, two to ten years old. Then I had a job tracking down what happened in the Lodz ghetto. Poland was a very difficult country then—it wasn't yet under communist control, but while some people were quite helpful, there were also ferocious pogroms against the remnants of the Jewish community. It was the same story of desolation and deprivation that existed all over Europe: Poland lost a fifth of its population to the war. I nearly turned tail a half dozen times, but finally I did get hold of some of the records of the ghetto authority. The Radbukas all were deported to a death camp in June of 1943. None of them survived.

"Of my own family, well, I found a cousin in one of

the DP camps. I tried to persuade him to come to England with me, but he was determined to return to Vienna. Where he did live out the rest of his life. At the time no one knew what would happen with the Russians and Austria, but in the end it worked out fine for my cousin. But he was always very reclusive after the war. I had looked up to him so as a child; he was eight years older than me, it was hard to see him so fearful, so withdrawn."

I stood silent, sickened by the images he was conjuring, before bursting out, "Then why did Lotty use the name Sofie Radbuka? I—that episode—the picture of Carl going to the country, looking for her cottage, Lotty staying behind the doors and using the name of a dead person—it's very unnerving. And it doesn't sound like Lotty."

Max rubbed his eyes. "Everyone has unaccountable moments in their lives. It may be that Lotty thought she was responsible for the loss or death of this Sofie Radbuka, whether it was a cousin or a patient. When Lotty thought she might be dying herself—well, we were all living difficult lives then, working hard, coping with the loss of our families. The deprivation in England after the war was still acute, too—we had our own bomb sites to clean up. There were coal shortages, bitter weather, no one had any money, food and clothes were still rationed. Lotty might have snapped under the strain, overidentified with this Radbuka woman.

"I do remember when Lotty came back from that illness. It was in winter, maybe February. She had lost a lot of weight. But she brought a dozen eggs and a half pound of butter back from the country with her and invited Teresz and me and the rest of our lot over for tea. She scrambled all the eggs up with the butter and we had a wonderful feast, and at one point she announced she would never again let her life be held hostage. She was so fierce we all rather backed away.

Carl refused to come, of course; it was years before he would speak to her again."

I told him about the bulletin board I'd found with Questing Scorpio's entry. "So there definitely was someone in England by that name in the forties, but my feeling is that Paul Radbuka's response was so intense that Scorpio didn't write back. I posted a message saying Scorpio could get in touch with Freeman Carter if there was something confidential to discuss."

Max shrugged helplessly. "I don't know. I don't know what any of it means. I just wish Lotty would either tell me what she's tormenting herself with—or stop carrying on in such a dramatic fashion."

"Have you spoken to her since Sunday night? I tried talking to her last night, but she bit my head off."

Max grunted. "This is one of those weeks where I wonder what keeps our friendship together. She's an important surgeon; she's sorry she was momentarily under the weather at my delightful party, but she's fine now, thanks very much, and she needs to make rounds."

The doorbell rang. Tim Streeter had arrived. He was a tall, rangy guy with a handlebar moustache and an engaging smile. Max called to Agnes, who quickly relaxed under Tim's calm air of confidence, while Calia, after a momentary suspicion, promptly announced he was a "lawrus" because of his giant moustache and offered to throw him dead fish. Tim made her squeal with laughter by blowing spluttery air through his moustache points. Max, much relieved, took off for the hospital.

Tim toured the premises, looking for vulnerable spots, then crossed the street to the park with Calia so she could play with the dogs. Calia brought Ninshubur with her, proudly showing Mitch and Peppy that her dog had tags just like theirs. "Ninshubur is Mitch's mummy," she announced.

After seeing the skillful way Tim kept between Calia and any passersby, seeming to make it part of a game instead of alarming the child, Agnes returned to the house to set up her paints. When the dogs had run the edge off their energy, I told Tim I needed to move on.

"There's not an imminent threat, as I understand it," he drawled.

"A hyper-emotional guy flailing around—not threatening directly, but making everyone uncomfortable," I agreed.

"Then I think I can do it on my own. I'll set up a camp bed in that sunroom: it's the one place with vulnerable windows. You've got the photos of the stalker, right?"

In the confusion of getting Morrell to O'Hare, I'd left my briefcase at his place. I had a set of photos in it, which I said I'd drop off in an hour or two on my way into the city. Calia pouted when I called the dogs to me, but Tim blew through his moustache and gave a walruslike bark. She turned her back on us and demanded that he bark again if he wanted another fish.

Lotty Herschel's Story:

Quarantine

I reached the cottage on a day so hot that not even the bees could bear it. A man who'd ridden the bus with me from Seaton Junction carried my suitcase up the road for me. When he finally left me, after asking for the eighth or ninth time if I was sure I could manage, I sat exhausted on the door-stone, letting the sun burn through my jumper. I'd darned it so many times that it was more mending thread than cotton at this point.

It had been hot in London, too, but a horrible city heat, where the yellow skies pushed down on you so hard your head began to buzz as if it were filled with cotton wool. At night I sweated so much that sheet and nightgown both were wet when I got up in the morning. I knew I needed to eat, but between the heat and the lethargy my physical condition induced it was hard to force food down.

When Claire examined me, she told me brusquely that I was starving myself to death. "Any infection on the wards could kill you in a week, the condition you're in right now. You need to eat. You need to rest."

Eat and rest. When I lay in bed at night, feverish nightmares consumed me. I kept seeing my mother, too weak from hunger and pregnancy to walk down the stairs with us when Hugo and I left Vienna. The baby died of malnutrition at two months. Nadia, they'd called her, meaning hope. They would not be hopeless. I knew the baby died because my father wrote to tell me. A Red Cross letter, with the prescribed twenty-five words, that reached me in March, 1940. The last letter from him.

I had hated the baby when my mother was pregnant because it took her from me: no more games, no more songs, only her eyes getting bigger in her head. Now this poor little sister whom I'd never seen haunted me, reproaching me for my nine-year-old jealousy. In the night as I sweated in the thick London air, I could hear her feeble cries growing faint with malnutrition.

Or I'd see my Oma, her thick silvery-blond hair, about which she was so vain that she refused to bob it. In her apartment on the Renngasse I would sit with her at night while the maid brushed it, the ends so long my grandmother could sit on them. But now, in my misery, I would see her, shaved as my father's mother had always been under her wig. Which image tormented me more? My Oma, shaved and helpless, or my father's mother, my Bobe, whom I refused to kiss good-bye? As I grew thinner and weaker in the London heat, that last morning in Vienna grew so loud in my head that I could hardly hear the world around me.

The cousins with whom I shared a bed, not coming to England, staying in bed, refusing to get up to walk to the station with us. Oma and Opa would pay for Lingerl's children, but not the daughters of my father's sisters, those dark girls with nut-shaped faces whom I so closely resembled. Oh, the money, Opa had no money anymore, except that little hoard of coins. The coins that bought me my medical training could have bought my cousins' lives. My Bobe stretching her arms out to me, her beloved Martin's daughter, and I with my Oma's jealous eyes on me giving her only a formal curtsy in farewell. I lay in bed weeping, begging my granny to forgive me.

I could hardly talk to Carl these days. Anyway, he wasn't much in London for me to talk to. In the spring the orchestra went to Holland to perform; he'd spent most of June and July in Bournemouth and Brighton, where his fledgling chamber group was engaged to play a series of promenade concerts. The few nights we'd had together this summer ended with my walking away, walking across London from his little flat to my bed-sitter, walking away from an energy and optimism that seemed incomprehensible to me.

Only on the wards did the images recede. When I changed the dressings on an old man's ulcerated wound or carefully cut open the newspapers in which some East End mother had stitched her sick baby, I could be present, in London, with people whose needs I could meet. When five of my classmates were on medical leave that winter I'd stepped up my work pace to pick up the slack. The teaching staff didn't like me: I was too serious, too intense. But they recognized my skill with patients, even in my second year.

I think that was why Claire had come looking for me. She'd shown up at the Royal Free for a conference— actually on the new drugs that were starting to come in for tuberculosis. Afterward, some professor probably suggested that a word from her might carry weight with me: get Miss Herschel to relax, take part in some of her year's sports or dramatics. It will make her a better-rounded person and ultimately a better doctor.

In the normal round of life our paths no longer crossed. Claire still lived with her mother, but since I'd left Cousin Minna's I never ran into her. Claire was doing her senior houseman's year at St. Anne's in Wembley, which meant long days covering casualty as well as the post-op and disease wards—women, even women like Claire Tallmadge, got the dregs of the housemen's jobs in those days. When I looked up and saw her across the room, I collapsed.

Carl often accused me of being in love with Claire. Oh, I was, but not in the way he imagined: not erotically, but with the infatuation a child has for an adulated adult. I suppose the flattery of my mimicry, even to the point of following her to the Royal Free, kept Claire paying a kind of attention to me. That was why it was so painful later, when she cut me off. But at that particular moment, it was more our different schedules, our different homes, that kept us apart.

Still, I was startled when she wrote me the following week, the week after I'd collapsed in front of her, to offer me the cottage. When I crossed London by train and bus to meet her for tea, she told me Ted Marmaduke and his brother Wallace had bought the cottage to use when they went sailing. After Wallace was killed at El Alamein, Ted didn't sail much. Vanessa hated boats; the country, real country, bored her. But Ted wouldn't sell the place; he even paid a local farm couple to keep the yard and premises in some kind of order. Claire said he imagined using it again when he and Vanessa had children—he pictured five or six children who would grow up to share his love of sports. Since they'd been married a decade now without even one robust blond child, I had a feeling that Vanessa's will would prevail here as in other matters, but it wasn't my business. I didn't care much about Ted and Vanessa's lives.

"Ted never liked me," I said, when Claire explained that her brother-in-law was offering me the place so that I could get the fresh air and food I needed. "Why would he let me have his country house? Isn't that the kind of encroachment he always warned you against?"

I used to hear Ted criticizing Claire for her involvement with me. Crouching behind the garden wall, I'd hear him say she should be careful, my kind would only take advantage, Claire replying that I was a funny little monkey without a mother, and what possible advantage could I take? Ted's brother Wallace, another tall blond man with a hearty laugh, putting in that she'd be surprised, people like me were always encroaching: You're young, Claire, inclined to think you know better than the rest of us. I assure you when you've seen the world a bit you'll think differently.

Should I be embarrassed at how much I heard from the other side of the garden wall? I suppose, I suppose—it was only my childish infatuation with Claire that made me creep down there when I saw them all in the garden on Sunday afternoons.

Now Claire flushed slightly. "War matured Ted. That, and losing Wallace. You haven't seen him, have you, since he got back? I expect he'll be quite a power in the city one of these days, but at home he's much gentler than he used to be. Anyway, when he and Vanessa were over for dinner on Sunday and I explained how ill you were, how you needed rest and fresh air, they both immediately thought of Axmouth.

"A local farmer named Jessup will probably sell you food cheaply; there's a decent doctor in Axmouth, you should be able to manage on your own. I'll come in December when my tour at St. Anne's ends, but if you feel desperate before that you can send me a telegram; I could probably get away for a day in an emergency."

Just as she'd got me to school, to the scholarships I'd needed, she now organized all the details of my life. She even validated my request for medical leave due to tuberculosis. And persuaded the registrar that I would recover faster in the country, with fresh food, than at a sanitorium. I felt powerless to resist her, powerless to say I'd rather take my chances in London.

When the time came to leave town, I didn't know what to say to Carl. He'd returned to London from Brighton a week earlier, a *succès fou,* in a state of such forceful energy that I could hardly bear to be around him. In ten days he and the other Cellini players were leaving for the second Edinburgh arts festival. His successes, his plans, his vision of chamber music, these were so consuming that he didn't even notice how ill I was. I finally wrote him a very awkward letter:

Dear Carl, I am taking medical leave from the Royal Free. I wish you great success in Edinburgh.

I tried to think of some sweet way to close, something that would evoke the evenings perched in the top balcony at the opera, our long walks along the Embankment, the pleasure we'd shared in his narrow bed at the hostel, before he started making enough money for a real flat. Those times all seemed dead to me now, as remote as my Oma and my Bobe. In the end I only added my name, putting the letter in the post outside Waterloo before boarding the train to Axmouth.

XXV

Paper Trail

As soon as I got to Morrell's I returned Nick Vishnikov's call. He came on the line with his usual abrupt staccato.

"Vic! Was that witchcraft? Or did you have some kind of evidence?"

"So it wasn't suicide." I stood at the kitchen counter, letting out a long breath.

"No gunpowder residue on the hand was the first pointer. And then a blow to the cranium, which must have stunned him long enough for the perp to shoot him—the junior who did the first autopsy didn't bother to check for other injuries. What did you notice?"

"Oh, the blow to the head," I said airily. "No, actually, I saw the details of his life, not those of his death."

"Well, whatever, congratulations—although Commander Purling at the Twenty-first District isn't happy. Since his team didn't spot the problem on site, he doesn't want it to be homicide. But as I told him, the SOC photos show the gun just below the vic's hand. If he'd killed himself, he would have lost the gun up around his head and it would have fallen away from his arm, not right under his hand. So Purling's assigned the case. Got to run."

Before he could hang up, I quickly asked if they were sure the SIG Trailside on the scene had killed Fepple.

"More witchcraft, Warshawski? I'll pass the question on to the lab. Later."

As I filled a bowl with water for the dogs, I wondered if I should call Commander Purling at the Twenty-first District to report what I knew. But it was so little—the mystery phone call on Friday night, the mystery visitor to Fepple's office—the cops would get all that from the bank guard and Fepple's phone logs. And anyway, if I called him, it would mean at best hours of explaining why I was involved. At worst—I could find myself in more trouble than I needed for having explored the scene of the crime on my own.

Besides, this wasn't my case, it wasn't my problem. My only problem was to try to get Ajax to pay the Sommers family what they were owed on Aaron Sommers's life insurance. Aaron Sommers, whose name appeared on an old ledger sheet in Howard Fepple's briefcase with two crosses next to it.

I called Cheviot Labs and asked for Kathryn Chang.

"Oh, yes: Barry gave me your sheet of paper. I took a preliminary look at it. From the watermark I'm saying it's of Swiss manufacture, the Baume Works outside Basel. It's a kind of cotton weave that they didn't make during the Second World War because of the shortage of raw material, so it dates from somewhere between 1925 and 1940. I can give you more precise dating than that when I've studied the ink—that will make it easier for me to date when the words were written. I can't make that a priority, though: it will be at least a week because of other jobs I have ahead of you."

"That's fine; this is enough for me for now," I said slowly, trying to turn the information over in my mind.

"Do you know—would this paper have been used primarily or exclusively in Switzerland?"

"Oh, no, by no means. The Baume Works aren't so important now, but well into the 1960's they were one of the biggest makers of fine paper and business paper in the world. This particular stock was widely used for things like address books, personal journals, that kind of thing. It is very unusual to see it treated like this, as accounting paper. The person who used it must have been very—oh, let me say, fond of himself. It would be helpful, of course, if I could see the book this was torn from."

"That would help me, too. But one thing I'd like to know in particular: can you tell when the different entries were written? Not the exact year—but, well, if some are more recent than others I'd like to know that."

"Right. We'll include that in your report, Ms. Warshawski."

It seemed to me it was time to visit Ralph again. His secretary remembered me from last week, but I couldn't see Ralph: his schedule was packed until six-thirty tonight. However, when I said I might be able to defuse Alderman Durham's protest, she put me on hold—as it turned out, long enough for me to read the entire sports section of the *Herald-Star*. When she came back, she said Ralph could squeeze me in for five minutes at noon if I got there on the dot.

"On the dot it is." I hung up and turned to the dogs. "That means we go back home, where you can lounge around the garden and I can put on panty hose. I know you will feel bereft, but ask yourselves—who really will be having more fun?"

It was ten-thirty now. I'd had a wistful hope of climbing into Morrell's bed for a nap, but I still had to drop photos of Radbuka off at Max's for Tim Streeter.

And I wanted to get back to my own place to change into something more appropriate than jeans for a Loop meeting. "Life's just a wheel and I'm caught in the spokes," I sang as I shepherded the dogs once more back to the car. All was still quiet at Max's when I stopped to drop off Radbuka's photographs. I zipped down the drive to Belmont, dumped the dogs with Mr. Contreras, and ran up the stairs to my own apartment.

Tonight was my dinner with the Rossys, my chance to chatter Italian to cheer up Bertrand's homesick wife. I put on a soft black trouser suit that could take me from meetings to dinner. A turtleneck that I could remove when I got to the Rossys' so that the rose silk camisole underneath dressed up the outfit. My mother's diamond-drop earrings I buttoned into a pocket. Pumps in my briefcase, the crepe-soled shoes I'd worn yesterday morning to step in Fepple's—I broke off the thought without completing it and ran back down the stairs. The pinball back in action.

I drove down to my office, then took the L into the Loop. At the Ajax building on Adams, a small band of protesters was still circling the sidewalk near the entrance. Without Alderman Durham there to lead the charge, the troops looked bedraggled. Every now and then they'd rouse themselves to chant something at the herd of people on their way from office to lunch, but for the most part they merely talked among themselves, posters drooping against their shoulders. These seemed to be the same signs they had carried on Friday—no reparations for slaveowners, no high-rises on the bones of slaves, and so on, but the flyer a dogged young man handed me on my way in had cut out the attacks on me. Literally cut out—the middle header asking me if I had no shame was gone, leaving a gap between the merciless Ajax and the compassionless Birnbaums. The text looked strange:

Ajax Insurance cashed her husband's life-insurance policy ten
years ago. When he died last week, they sent their tame detective
to accuse Sister Sommers of stealing it.

I guess this way they could just type my name back
in if I reverted to chief villain. I tucked the flyer into my
briefcase.

At noon on the dot, the executive-floor attendant
brought me to Ralph's antechamber. Ralph himself
was still in a meeting in his conference room, but
his secretary buzzed him and after the briefest wait
he emerged. This time I got a grim nod, not a grin and
a hug.

"Does trouble always follow you, Vic?" he said
when we were in his office with the door shut. "Or does
it just jump up to bite me anytime you're in the vi-
cinity?"

"If you really only have five minutes, don't spend it
blaming me for Alderman Durham's pickets." I sat on
one of the hard tubular chairs, while Ralph leaned
against the edge of his desk. "I came to suggest that you
make the Sommers family whole. Then you can issue a
big PR statement about how your respect for the
widow's grief—"

He cut me short. "We paid them ten thousand dollars in 1991. I won't double-pay a life-insurance
policy."

"The question is, who got that money back in 1991?
Personally, I don't think anyone in the Sommers family
ever saw it. That check started and stopped at the
agency door."

He folded his arms in an uncompromising line. "Do
you have proof of this?"

"You know, don't you, that Howard Fepple is dead?
There's no one—"

"He committed suicide because his agency was going

down the toilet. It was in our executive briefing this morning."

I shook my head. "Old news. He was murdered. The Sommers family file has disappeared. There's no one from the agency left to explain what really happened."

Ralph stared at me in angry disbelief. "What do you mean, he was murdered? The cops found his body, they found the suicide note. It was in the papers."

"Ralph, listen to me: barely an hour ago, the medical examiner called to tell me the autopsy proves murder. Don't you think it was funny that the Sommers family file disappeared at the same time Fepple was killed?"

"What are you trying to do to me? Am I supposed to believe this on your say-so?"

I shrugged. "Call the medical examiner. Call the watch commander at the Twenty-first District. I'm not trying to do anything but help my client—and give you a way of defusing the protest down there on Adams."

"All right: let's hear it." The scowl emphasized his incipient jowls.

"Make the Sommers family whole," I repeated steadily, trying not to let my own temper get the better of me. "It's only ten thousand dollars. That's one round-trip ticket to Zurich for a member of your executive committee, but it's the difference between penury and comfort for Gertrude Sommers and the nephew who fronted for the funeral. Make a big PR splash out of it. What can Durham do then? He may claim he forced you to take action, but he can't go around saying you stole the widow's mite."

"I'll think about it. But it isn't your best idea."

"Personally, I think it's a beauty. It shows how utterly reliable the company is, even in the most unreliable of situations. I could probably write the ad copy for you."

"Because it isn't your money."

I couldn't help smiling. "What, will Rossy storm in,

crying, 'Young man, every penny of this is coming out of your stock options'?"

"This isn't a joke, Vic."

"I know. The unfunny part is the connections nasty-minded people will make about the Sommers file vanishing. Did the company do something a decade back that they were eager to keep hidden?"

"We did not—categorically—" He cut off his own denial, remembering that we'd met over an Ajax claim fraud. "Is that what the cops think?"

"I don't know. I can put out some feelers, although if it's any comfort to you, what I'm hearing about the guy heading the investigation is that he doesn't want to break a sweat." I stood up, pulling a copy of the old ledger sheet from my briefcase. "This was the one document relating to Sommers that was left in Fepple's office. Does it mean anything to you?"

Ralph looked at it briefly, shaking his head impatiently. "What is this? Who are these people?"

"I was hoping you could tell me. When I was here last week, Connie Ingram, that young woman from your claims-records unit, left Sommers's company file up here. If it has copies of all the agency documents in it, maybe it's got a complete copy of this one. I don't know who these other people are, but the two crosses suggest they're dead. The original of this page is quite old. And here's a funny thing about it, Ralph: a forensics lab tells me the paper was made in Switzerland before the war. Second World War, I mean, not the Persian Gulf."

His face tightened. "You'd better not be trying to suggest—"

"Edelweiss? Good heavens, Ralph, the thought only drifted slightly through my mind. The lab says the paper was sold to narcissists all over the world—it was apparently quite expensive. But Swiss paper, a Swiss-made gun, both in an insurance agency that is attracting a lot of attention—the human mind isn't rational, Ralph, it just puts contiguous events together. And that's what mine is doing."

He looked at the paper now as if it were a cobra that had hypnotized him. The buzzer on his desk phone sounded, his secretary reminding him he was running late. He jerked his head away with a visible effort.

"You can leave this here—I'll have Denise check the file to see if there's anything else in this handwriting in it. Right now I need to run to another meeting. On reserves, on our potential exposure from Holocaust survivors, and other matters worth a whole lot more than ten thousand dollars. And than baseless accusations against Edelweiss."

On my way down, I stopped on the thirty-ninth floor, where claims processing took place. Unlike the executive floor, with an attendant behind a mahogany console to monitor traffic, there was no obvious person to ask the way to Connie Ingram's desk. There also weren't rosy Chinese rugs floating on oceans of parquet. Hard mustard matting took me through a labyrinth of cubicles, mostly empty because of the lunch hour.

Near the south end of the floor I found someone sitting at her desk, working the *Tribune* crossword while she ate bean sprouts out of a plastic container. She was a middle-aged woman with tight, dyed corkscrew curls, but when she looked up she gave me a warm smile and asked what I needed.

"Connie Ingram? She's on the other side. Come on, I'll take you over, it's too hard to figure out where anyone in the maze is if you're not one of the rats yourself."

She slid her feet back into her pumps and took me across to the other side of the floor. Connie Ingram was just returning to her desk with a group of other women. They were giving the usual return-to-work moans, along with a few quick plans for the afternoon coffee break. They welcomed me and my guide with friendly interest: much better to have someone to talk to than stare at computer screens and files.

"Ms. Ingram?" I gave my own forthright, girlfriends-together smile. "I'm V I Warshawski—we met last week in Ralph Devereux's office, looking at the Aaron Sommers file."

Her round face turned wary. "Does Mr. Rossy know you're here?"

I held out my security pass, turning my smile up a few watts. "I'm here at Ralph Devereux's invitation. Do you want to call up to his secretary to ask? Or do you want me to call Bertrand Rossy to tell him what I need?"

Her coworkers ranged themselves around her, protective, inquisitive. She muttered that she guessed that wasn't necessary, but what did I want, anyway?

"To look at the file. You know the agent who sold the policy is dead? His copy of the file is missing. I need to see the paperwork so I can try to figure out who filed the original death benefit claim. Mr. Devereux is considering the idea of paying the widow because of the confusion around the file, the agent's death, and so on."

She flushed. "I'm sorry, but Mr. Rossy told me definitely not to show the file to anyone outside the company. And anyway, it's still up on sixty-three."

"How about the microfiche? Didn't you say you printed the documents from the fiche? This is about an elderly woman who spent her life changing bedpans while her husband worked two shifts to make his premium payments. If the policy was paid out because of a bookkeeping error or because the agent committed a swindle, should this old woman have to suffer indignity on top of her bereavement?" Instead of writing copy for Ajax, I could be putting out stuff for Bull Durham.

"Honestly, it's company policy not to show our files

to outsiders: you can ask my supervisor when she gets back from lunch."

"I'm having dinner tonight with the Rossys. I'll mention it to him then."

At that, her face became even more troubled. She liked to please people: what if I and the all-powerful foreign boss were both angry with her? But she was an honest young woman, as well, and in the end, she stuck by the company's demands on her loyalty. I didn't like it—but I certainly respected her for it. I smiled my thanks for her time and left her with one of my cards in case she changed her mind.

XXVI

Hypnotic Suggestion

Outside, I turned the corner and went into the comparative quiet of the alley to check in with Tim Streeter. He was at the zoo with Calia. Radbuka had appeared in the park again as they were getting into Tim's car, but Tim had found him more annoying than alarming.

"Of course we both know that stalkers turn violent, but at least as far as today went, he seemed more bewildered than menacing: he kept saying he only wanted a chance to speak to Max, to find out about his true family. But Calia started shrieking, which brought Agnes to the scene. She yelled for the cops, who did eventually come, she says—I'd already taken off after him. I did tell Radbuka he would have to leave, that Max was swearing out a peace bond, which meant he could be arrested for hanging around the premises."

I blinked. "Is Max doing that?"

"I called the hospital and told him he really should. Anyway, everyone seems calm now. Agnes stayed at home to paint: I called my brother and told him to get up to look after the house. I wanted to get the kid out so that Agnes doesn't freak thinking her daughter's life is in imminent danger. Which it isn't. Guy is a nuisance, but he's physically no match for any of us."

I frowned, worried. "Could he have followed you to the zoo?"

"No. He was on a bike. My brother phoned from the house half an hour ago to say he did a thorough search of Max's garden and the park across the street and didn't see any sign of Radbuka."

"How's Calia now?"

"Fine. We're looking at real walruses—I'm supposed to be getting tips on how to beg for fish. Seeing me cool keeps her cool."

A delivery truck backed into the alley, its insistent beep making it impossible to hear anything else Tim was saying. I bellowed that I'd check at Max's later.

I skirted the edge of the truck, feeling unusually ineffectual. I hadn't made any progress on Radbuka's past. I hadn't done anything for the Sommers family. Lotty, whose state was alarming me, wouldn't talk to me. Rossy's apartment was near hers on Lake Shore Drive. I supposed I could try to drop in on her tonight on my way to dinner, but I couldn't think of a way to get her to confide in me.

I crossed Michigan Avenue to the statue garden by the Art Institute, where I called the office to see whether Mary Louise was making any progress showing Radbuka's photo to neighbors of the various Ulrich families listed around town. She'd been trying to dodge the assignment, but when I told her about Radbuka lurking around Max's she agreed we needed some kind of wedge. If she could find someone who knew Radbuka when he was still Ulrich, that might give us a starting point.

The easiest wedge would clearly come from getting Rhea Wiell to help out. Since I was in the Loop already, I decided to pay a surprise visit: maybe she'd be more responsive in person than on the phone. And if she wouldn't give me background material on her patient, maybe she'd at least help come up with a strategy for controlling him.

I walked the length of Michigan Avenue to Water Tower Place, stopping partway up for something the shop called a vegetarian sandwich. The mild day had drawn a throng of office workers outside for lunch. I sat on a marble slab between a guy buried in a paperback and a couple of women who were smoking while denouncing someone's horrible behavior in asking them to fill out a second set of time sheets.

The sandwich turned out to be a thick roll with a few slices of eggplant and peppers. I crumbled up part of the roll for the sparrows who were pecking hopefully at my feet. Out of nowhere a dozen pigeons appeared, trying to muscle the sparrows aside.

The guy with the paperback looked at me in disgust. "You're only encouraging pests, you know." He dog-eared his page and got up.

"I wonder if you're right." I stood as well. "I always thought my work was keeping them at bay, but you may be on to something."

His disgust changed to alarm and he turned hastily into the office building behind us. I crumbled the rest of the bread for the birds. It was almost one o'clock. Morrell would be over the Atlantic now, away from land, away from me. I felt a little hollow below my diaphragm and increased my pace, as if I could leave loneliness behind me.

At Rhea Wiell's office, a young woman was sitting in the waiting room, her hands nervously clutching a cup of herbal tea. I sat down and studied the fish in the aquarium while the woman darted suspicious looks at me.

"What time is your appointment?" I asked.

"One-fifteen. Are you—when is yours?"

If my watch was right, it wasn't quite ten after. "I'm

a drop-in. I'm hoping Ms. Wiell will have a break in her schedule this afternoon. How long have you been seeing her? Has she been helpful?"

"Very." She didn't say anything else for a minute, but as I continued to watch the fish and the silence built, she added, "Rhea's helped me become aware of parts of my life that were shut away from me before."

"I've never been hypnotized," I said. "What's it like?"

"Are you afraid? I was, too, before my first session, but it's not like they show it in the movies. It's like riding an elevator down into the middle of your own past. You can get off on these different floors and explore them, only with the safety of having Rhea right next to you, instead of—well, being alone, or being with the monsters who were there when you had to live through the time originally."

The door to the inner room opened. The woman immediately turned to watch for Rhea, who came out with Don Strzepek. The two were laughing in a kind of easy intimacy. Don looked wide awake, while Rhea, instead of her flowing jacket and trousers, had put on a red dress that fit snugly around the bodice. When she saw me she flushed and withdrew slightly from Don.

"Have you come to see me? I have another appointment right now." For the first time in our brief acquaintance her smile held genuine warmth. I didn't take it personally—I knew it was the overflow from Don—but it made my own response more natural.

"Something rather serious has come up. I can wait until you're free, but we ought to talk."

She turned to the waiting patient. "Isabel, I'm not going to start your session late, but I need one moment alone with this woman."

When I moved with her to the entrance to her inner room, Don trailed after me. "Paul Radbuka has started stalking Mr. Loewenthal's family. I'd like to talk to you about strategies for managing the situation."

"Stalking? That's a fairly extreme criticism. You may be misinterpreting his behavior, but even if you are, we definitely should discuss it." She went behind her desk to look at her calendar. "I can fit you in at two-thirty for fifteen minutes."

She nodded regally to me, but when she glanced at Don her expression softened again. When she walked us out to the waiting area, it was to him that she said, "I'll see you at two-thirty, then."

"Looks as though things are going well with your book," I said once we were out in the hall.

"Her work is fascinating," Don said. "I let her hypnotize me yesterday. It was wonderful, like floating in a warm ocean in a totally secure boat."

I watched him reflexively touch his breast pocket while we waited for an elevator. "Have you stopped smoking? Or remembered buried secrets about your mother?"

"Don't be sarcastic, Vic. She put me in a light trance so I could see what it was like, not a deeper one for memory recovery. Anyway, she never uses a deeper trance until she's worked with a patient long enough to make sure they trust each other. And to make sure the patient's strong enough to survive the process. Arnold Praeger and the Planted Memory guys will definitely be sorry they've tried to trash her reputation when this book comes out."

"She's put some kind of spell on you," I teased as we rode to the lobby. "I've never heard you abandon journalistic caution before."

He flushed. "There are legitimate grounds for concern with any therapeutic method. I'll make that clear in the text. This isn't an apology for Rhea but a chance for people to understand the validity of recovered-memory work. I'll give the Planted Memory camp their say. But they've never taken the time to understand Rhea's methods."

Don had first met Rhea Wiell when I did, four days ago, and he was already a true believer. I wondered why her spell didn't work on me. When we met on Friday, she'd realized I approached her with skepticism, not Don's admiration, but she hadn't tried to charm me out of it. I'd thought perhaps she didn't try as hard with women as with men, but the young patient in the waiting room was clearly also a votary. Was Mary Louise right? Did Rhea and I instinctively distrust each other because we both wanted to command the situation? Or was my gut telling me there was a problem with Rhea? I didn't think she was a charlatan, but I did wonder if a steady diet of adulation from people like Paul Radbuka had gone to her head.

"Earth to Vic—for the third time, do you want coffee while we wait?"

I realized with a jolt that we were standing outside the elevators on the ground floor. "Is that what hypnosis is like?" I asked. "You become so lost in your own space that you lose awareness of the outside world?"

Don steered me outside so he could light a cigarette. "You're asking a novice. But I think they consider losing yourself like that akin to a trance. It's called imaginative dissociation, something like that."

I stood upwind from him while he finished his cigarette, checking in again first with Tim Streeter, who said there was nothing new to report, and then with my answering service. By the time I'd returned a couple of client calls, Don was ready to move into the hotel for a cup of coffee. In the tree-filled terrace at the Ritz, I got him to give me a digest of the research he'd been doing the last four days.

He had a wealth of data about the way in which

hypnosis had been used to treat people with traumatic symptoms. One man who'd had terrible fantasies about having his neck wrenched off his shoulders turned out to have seen his mother hanging herself when he was three: his father was able to confirm all the details that the son produced under hypnosis. The father had never discussed them with his son, hoping that the boy had been too young to understand what he was watching. There were also plenty of documented cases of people hearing what was said around them under total anesthesia and being able to reconstruct whole operating-room conversations through hypnosis. Rhea herself had worked with a number of incest victims whose memories recovered under hypnosis had been validated by siblings or other adults.

"We're going to be using several pairs in one chapter—the holder of memory and the suppressor of memory. But of course the most interesting chapter will be about Radbuka. So neither Rhea nor I is at all happy to have you questioning the validity of what he's saying."

I rested my chin on my hands and looked at him squarely. "Don, I don't doubt the value of hypnosis, or the validity of recovered memories, under certain strict guidelines. I sit on the board of a women's shelter, and I've witnessed the phenomenon myself.

"But in Radbuka's case, it's a question of who he is—emotionally and, well, genealogically, for want of a better word. Max Loewenthal isn't lying when he says the Radbukas aren't related to him, but Paul Radbuka so desperately wants the relationship to exist that he can't pay attention to reality. I can understand it, understand how growing up with an abusing father would make him reach out to other relatives. If I could just have access to some background information about him, I might be able to track down where—if at all—his life intersects with any of Max's London circle."

"But he doesn't want you to have that information. He called Rhea at noon while I was with her to say you were doing everything you could to bar him from his family. He implored her not to give you any details about him."

"That explains why she's so cold to me. I'm sure it's to her credit that she's so protective of her patients. But you were at Max's on Sunday—you saw what Radbuka was like. Even assuming all the things he remembered in hypnosis are true—it doesn't mean he's related to Max just because he wants that to be so." I tried to lighten the conversation by adding, "That would bring Rhea's work to the level of Timothy Leary on acid, talking to his chromosomes to recover his previous incarnations."

"Vic!" Don protested. "You really mustn't reduce this kind of therapy to a Jay Leno routine. A week ago I might have made the same kind of cheap joke, but— if you'd seen this process up close, learned about the kinds of things people grapple with as they unblock the past—you'd be more respectful, I guarantee it. In the case of Radbuka, too, Rhea knows the guy has a lot of problems. She's genuinely worried about what you're trying to do to him."

I looked at my watch and signaled for the check. "Don, I know you've only met me a few times during this past year, but do you think your friend Morrell would be in love with me if I was the kind of monster who deliberately drove a wedge between a war orphan and his family?"

Don smiled ruefully. "Oh, hell, Vic. Of course not. But you're very close to Loewenthal and his friends. Your own judgment could be distorted by your desire to protect them."

I was tempted to believe Rhea Wiell had given Don some posthypnotic suggestion to eschew me and all my works. But the real spell came from a deeper, more fundamental source, I realized, watching his eyes light up when I said it was time to cross back over to the office building. As my father used to say, never try to stop a man with an ax, or a man in love.

By the time I finished my conversation with Rhea, I was ready to bonk her on the head and take my chances on a self-defense plea. I'd started with the premise that we all wanted what was best for the main players in our little drama and that this meant not just Paul but Calia and Agnes as well. Rhea gave one of those regal nods that made me want to revert to my street-fighting roots. I concentrated on a painting of a Japanese farmyard that hung above her couch and told her about Paul's two attempts to accost Calia.

"The family is starting to feel as though they're being stalked," I said. "Mr. Loewenthal's lawyer wants him to swear out a peace bond, but I thought if you and I talked, we might head off an extreme confrontation."

"I don't believe Paul would stalk anyone," Rhea said. "He's not only very gentle, but he's easily frightened. I'm not saying he wasn't at Max's house," she added as I started to object, "but I imagine him standing in the park like the little match girl in the fairy tale, longing to be part of the festivities he can see through the window, while none of the rich children will acknowledge his existence."

I smiled, still on my best behavior. "Unfortunately, Calia is a five-year-old—an age where frightened, needy grown-ups are terrifying. Her mother is understandably alarmed, because she thinks someone might be threatening her child. When Paul comes out of the bushes at the two of them, it scares them both. His longing for a family may be making it hard for him to see how his behavior could appear to other people."

Rhea bent her head, a swanlike gesture that seemed to have a hint of acquiescence in it. "But why won't Max Loewenthal acknowledge him?"

I wanted to scream, "Because there's nothing to acknowledge, you fatheaded flea-brain," but I leaned forward with an expression of great earnestness. "Mr. Loewenthal truly is not related to your client. This morning he showed me the file he kept from his search for missing families in postwar Europe. The file includes a letter from the person who asked him to hunt for the Radbukas. On Sunday, when Paul crashed his party, Mr. Loewenthal offered to go over these papers with him, but Paul didn't want to make an appointment for a more convenient time. I'm sure Mr. Loewenthal would still be glad for Paul to see the papers if he thought that would set his mind at rest."

"Have you seen these documents, Don?" Rhea turned to him with a touching display of female fragility. "If you could take a look at them, if you agree with—with Vic, I would feel better."

Don swelled slightly at her trust in him. I tried not to make a mocking grimace but said I felt sure that Max would want things done as quickly as possible.

"I have a dinner engagement this evening, but if Don's free, I can ask Max to meet with him," I added. "In the meantime, it would be shocking if Paul were arrested because of this unhappy misunderstanding. So could you suggest that he stay away from the house until he hears from Mr. Loewenthal? If we could have a phone number where Mr. Loewenthal could reach him?"

Rhea shook her head, a contemptuous little smile at the corners of her mouth. "You really don't give up, do you? I am not going to let you have my client's home number or address. He sees you as the person who's keeping him from his family. If you were to show up on his front step, it would be a major disintegrating event to his fragile sense of self."

I felt all the muscles in my neck clench with the effort not to lose my temper openly. "I'm not challenging the work you've done with him, Rhea. But if I could see the documents he found in his father's—foster father's— papers, I could use them to track down who in London might have been part of his family. The journey he thinks he made, from his unknown birthplace to Terezin, and then to London and Chicago, is so tortuous that we might never be able to follow it. But at least the documents that told him his birth name might give a skilled investigator a place to start."

"You say you're not challenging my work, but in the next sentence you refer to the journey Paul *thinks* he made. This is a journey he did make, even though the details were blocked from his conscious mind for fifty years. Like you, I am a skilled investigator, but one with greater experience than you in exploring the past."

The discreet temple bell chimed; she turned to look at a clock on her desktop. "I need to clear my mind of all this conflict before my next patient arrives. I'll be certain to tell Paul that he can only expect hostility if he keeps trying to see Max Loewenthal."

"That will be helpful to all of us," I said. "I have someone showing Radbuka's photograph to neighbors of families named Ulrich in the hopes of finding his childhood home. So if he reports back to you that someone is spying on him—it's true."

"Families named Ulrich? Why would you want—"

She broke off, her dark soft eyes widening, first in bewilderment, then amusement. "If that's your best investigative effort, Vic, then Paul Radbuka is definitely safe from you."

I studied her for a moment, chin on hand, trying to decipher what lay behind her amusement. "So Ulrich wasn't his father's name after all? I'll keep that in mind. Don, where should I leave a message for you about whether Max is free to talk to you tonight? At Morrell's?"

"I'll ride down with you, Vic, give Rhea a chance to center herself. I have a cell-phone number I can give you."

He got up with me but lingered inside her consulting room for a private leave-taking. As I left, I noticed another young woman in the waiting room looking eagerly toward the inner door. It was a pity Rhea and I had gotten off to such a bad start: I would have liked to experience her hypnotic techniques to see whether they gave me the same rush they did her patients.

Don caught up with me outside the elevators. When I asked if he knew what the inside joke was about the name Ulrich, he shifted uncomfortably. "Not exactly."

"Not exactly? You mean you know sort of?"

"Only that it wasn't his father's—foster father's— last name. Not what the name really was. And don't ask me to find out: Rhea won't tell me because she knows you'll try to wheedle it out of me."

"I guess I should feel flattered that she thinks I'd be able to. Give me your cell-phone number. I'll call Max and get back to you, but I have to run: like Rhea, I need to center myself before my next appointment."

In the L going back to my car, I called Mary Louise to tell her she didn't have to go door-to-door with Radbuka's picture after all. I couldn't recap the whole conversation over the noise of the train but told her that it apparently wasn't his childhood name. She had started south, working her way west and north, and had only reached her third address, so she was happy to call it a day.

As I picked up my car at the Western L stop, I wondered idly what would happen if Rhea Wiell hypnotized Lotty. Where would an elevator to the past take Lotty? From her behavior on Sunday, the monsters on those lower floors were pretty ferocious. It seemed to me, though, that Lotty's problem wasn't that she couldn't remember her monsters but that she couldn't forget them.

I stopped in the office to check on mail and messages and whether I had any appointments for tomorrow that I'd forgotten. A couple of new things had come up. I entered them into my computer and pulled out my Palm Pilot to download them to the handheld device. As I did so I suddenly thought of Fepple's mother telling me her gadget-happy son used a device like mine for a diary. If he'd kept his appointments up to date, they should still be sitting in that machine in his office. And I had a key: I could go in happy and legal, with the implicit consent of Rhonda Fepple.

I quickly returned a few phone calls, looked at my e-mail, pulled up the missing persons bulletin board to see that Questing Scorpio hadn't answered my message, and went south again, to Hyde Park.

Collins, the four-to-midnight guard, recognized me. "Got some other tenants here we could do without if you want a hit list," he said with heavy humor as I passed.

I smiled weakly and rode up to the sixth floor. I had a hard time getting myself to open the door, not because of the yellow crime-scene tape sealing it, but because I didn't want to face the remains of Fepple's life again. I took a breath and tried the handle. A woman in a nurse's uniform heading to the elevator stopped to watch me. The police or the building management had locked the office. I took out my key and unlocked the door, breaking the yellow tape as I pushed it open.

"I thought that meant you can't go in," the woman said.

"You thought right, but I'm a detective."

She walked over to peer around me into the room, then backed away, her face turning grey. "Oh, my God. Is that what happened in there? Oh, my God, if this is what can go on in this building, I'm getting a job at the hospital, hours or no hours. This is terrible."

I was just as appalled as she was, even though I more or less knew what to expect. Fepple's body was gone, but no one had bothered to clean up after him. Pieces of brain and bone had hardened on the chair and desk. Those weren't visible from the door, but what you could see was the mess of papers, and on top of it, grey fingerprint powder showing up nests of footprints on the floor. The powder had drifted like dirty snow onto the desk, the computer, the strewn papers. I thought briefly of poor Rhonda Fepple, trying to sort through the wreckage. I hoped she had the sense to hire help.

The police hadn't bothered to shut down the computer. Using a Kleenex to protect my fingers, I hit the ENTER key and brought the system back up. I couldn't bring myself to sit on Fepple's chair, or even touch it, so I leaned across the desk to operate the keyboard. Even in my awkward posture, it only took a few minutes to retrieve his computer datebook. On Friday, he'd had a dinner date with Connie Ingram. He'd even added a note: *says she wants to discuss Sommers, but she sounds hot for me.*

I printed out the entry and scuttled out of the office as fast as I could move. The foul scene, the fetid air, the horrible image of Connie Ingram sounding hot for Fepple, all made me feel like throwing up again. I found a women's bathroom, which was locked. I stuck Fepple's door key in, which didn't turn the lock but did get someone on the inside to open it for me. I swayed over one of the sinks, washing my face in cold water, rinsing my mouth, pushing the worst of the images out of my mind—away from my stomach.

Connie Ingram, the earnest round-faced claims clerk whose company loyalty wouldn't let me look at her files? Or who was so loyal that she would date a recalcitrant agent and set him up for a hit?

A sudden rage, the culmination of the week's frustrations, swept over me. Rhea Wiell, Fepple himself, my vacillating client, even Lotty—I was fed up with all of them. And most of all with Ralph and Ajax. Chewing me out for the Durham protest, stiffing me over my request to see the company copy of Aaron Sommers's file—and staging this charade. Which they'd botched by stealing the guy's handheld but not wiping the entry out of the computer.

I shoved open the bathroom door and stalked to the elevator, the blood roaring in my head. I zoomed to Lake Shore Drive, honking impatiently at any car daring to turn in front of me, swooping through lights as they turned red—behaving like a mad idiot. On the Drive I covered the five miles to the Grant Park traffic lights in five minutes. The evening rush hour had built in the park, stalling me. I earned the irate whistle of a traffic cop by cutting recklessly around the stack of cars onto one of the side roads, flooring the car up to the Inner Drive.

As I got to the corner of Michigan and Adams, I had to stand on the brakes: the street was a mass of honking, unmoving cars. Now what? I wasn't going to get near the Ajax building in my car with this kind of blockage. I made an illegal and highly dangerous U-turn and roared back to the Inner Drive. By now I'd had so many near-misses I was coming to my senses. I could hear my father lecturing me on the dangers of driving under the influence of rage. In fact, once when he'd caught me in the act, he'd made me come with him when he had to untangle a crumpled teenager from the steering wheel through his chest. The memory of that made me take the next few blocks sedately. I left the car in an underground garage and walked north to the Ajax building.

As I got to Adams Street, the congestion built. This wasn't the normal throng of homebound workers but a penned-up crowd. I threaded my way into it with difficulty, moving along the edges of the buildings. Through the jam of people I could hear the megaphones. The protestors had come back to life.

"No deals with slaveowners!" they were shouting, mixed with "No money to mass murderers!" "Economic justice for all" vied with "Boycott Ajax! No deals with thieves."

So Posner had arrived. In full throttle, by the sound of it. And Durham had apparently come to rally his own troops in person. No wonder the street was backed up. Sidling past the crowd, I climbed up the steps to the Adams L platform so that I could see what was going on.

It wasn't quite the mob that had created havoc outside the Hotel Pleiades last week, but besides Posner with his Maccabees and Durham with the EYE team, there were a couple of camera crews and a lot of unhappy people who wanted to get home. These last pushed against me on the L steps, snarling at both groups.

"I don't care what happened a hundred years ago: I want to get home today," one woman was saying to her companions.

"Yeah. Durham's got a point, but no one's going to pay attention to it if he makes you pay overtime to the day care because you can't get there on time."

"And that other guy, that one in the funny hat and the curls and all, what's his problem?"

"He's saying Ajax stole life insurance from the Jews, but it all happened a long time ago, so who cares?"

I had thought I'd call Ralph from the street, but there was no way I could carry on a phone conversation in this melee. I climbed down from the platform and made my way along Wabash, past the cops who were trying to keep traffic moving, past the entrances to Ajax where security guards were letting frustrated commuters out one at a time, around the corner on Jackson to the alley behind the building where the buildings had their loading bays. The one for Ajax was still open.

I hoisted myself up to the metal lip where trucks decanted cargo and went inside. An overweight man in Ajax's blue security uniform slid off a stool in front of a large console filled with TV screens showing the alley and the building.

"You lost?"

"I'm a fraud investigator. Ralph Devereux—the head of claims—wants to talk to me, but the mob out front is making it impossible to get near the front entrance."

He looked me over, decided I didn't look like a terrorist, and called up to Ralph's office with my name. He grunted a few times into the mouthpiece, then jerked his head to bring me over to the phone.

"Hello, Ralph. How glad I am you're still here. We need to have a little conversation about Connie Ingram."

"We do indeed. I wasn't going to call you until tomorrow, but since you're here we'll talk now. And don't imagine you can come up with any excuse that will make your behavior acceptable."

"I love you, too, Ralph: I'll be right up."

The guard tapped the screens on the console to show me my route: a door at the rear of the loading bay led to a corridor which would take me to the main lobby. Once inside, I paused on my way to the elevators to stare at the dueling demonstrators. Durham, this time in executive navy, had the larger crowd, but Posner was controlling the chanting. As his little band of Maccabees circled past the door, I stood transfixed. Standing at Posner's left elbow, his childlike face beaming underneath his thinning curls, was Paul Radbuka.

XXVIII

(Old) Lovers' Quarrel

The elevator whooshed me to sixty-three so fast my ears filled, but I barely noticed the discomfort. Paul Radbuka with Joseph Posner. But why should I be startled? In a way it was a natural fit. Two men obsessed with memories of the war, with their identity as Jews, what could be more likely than that they'd get together?

The executive-floor attendant had left for the day. I went to the windows behind her mahogany station where I could see past the Art Institute to the lake. At the far horizon the soft blue became lost in clouds, so you couldn't tell where water ended and sky began. It looked almost artificial, that horizon, as if some painter had started to stroke in a dirty-white sky and then lost interest in the project.

I was due at the Rossys' at eight; it was just on five now. I wondered if I could tail Radbuka home from here—although perhaps he'd be going back to Posner's house tonight. Maybe he'd found a family who would take him in, nurture him in the way he seemed to need. Maybe he'd start leaving Max alone.

"Vic! What are you doing out here? You called from the loading dock fifteen minutes ago."

Ralph's angry, anxious voice jolted me back to the present. He was in shirtsleeves, his tie loosened, his eyes worried underneath his angry facade. It was the worry that made me keep my own voice level when I answered him.

"Admiring the view: it would be wonderful to leave all this turmoil and follow the horizon, wouldn't it? I know why I'm peeved about Connie Ingram, but I don't have any idea what's got you so upset."

"What did you do with the microfiche?"

"Oo-lu-lah vishti banko."

His mouth set in a thin line. "What the hell is that supposed to mean?"

"Your question made just as little sense to me. I don't know any microfiche, personally or by reputation, so you'd better start at the beginning—" I broke off. "Don't tell me your microfiche for the Sommers file is damaged?"

"Very nice, Vic: surprised innocence. I'm almost convinced."

At that my calm disappeared. I pushed past him to the elevator and hit the call button.

"Where are you going?"

"Home." I bit off my words. "I wanted to ask you why Connie Ingram was the last person to see Howard Fepple alive, and why she made him think she'd be a hot date, and why after that really hot date, Fepple was dead and the agency copy of Sommers's file had vanished. But I don't need the garbage you're flinging at me. I can take my questions directly to the cops. Believe me, they'll talk to little Miss Company Loyalty in a way that will get her to respond."

The elevator dinged to a stop behind me. Before I could get on, Ralph grabbed my arm.

"Since you're already here, give me two more minutes. I want you to talk to someone in my office."

"If I lose my chance to tail a guy who's in your demonstration, I am going to be one very cross detective, Ralph, so make it succinct for me, okay? Which raises another question in my mind: why are you focusing on your wretched microfiche when the building is under siege?"

He ignored my question, moving fast along the rosy carpets to his office. His secretary, Denise, was still at her post. Connie Ingram and a strange black woman were sitting stiffly on the tubular chairs. They looked nervously at Ralph when we came in.

Ralph introduced the strange woman—Karen Bigelow, who was Connie's supervisor in claims. "Just tell Vic here what you told me, Karen."

She nodded, turning to face me. "I know about the whole Sommers situation. I was on vacation last week, but Connie explained how she'd had to leave the file up here with Mr. Rossy. And how this private detective might try to get her to reveal confidential company information. So when she—when you—came around asking to see the fiche, Connie came straight to me. Neither of us was too surprised. As you know, of course, Connie here stood her ground, but she got kind of worried and went to check the microfiche. The card that included the Sommers file has gone missing. Not checked out or anything. Disappeared. And I understand you were alone on the floor for some time, miss."

I smiled pleasantly. "I see. I have to confess I don't know where the fiche are stored, or you might have legitimate grounds for suspicion. To you, who knows that rabbit warren on thirty-nine, it's all familiar, but to a stranger it's impenetrable. But there's one easy thing to do: check for fingerprints. Mine are on file with the secretary of state, because I'm a licensed investigator as well as an officer of the court. Get the cops in, treat it like a real theft."

The room was silent for a minute, then Ralph said, "If you were in that cabinet, Vic, you'd have wiped it clean."

"All the more reason to dust it. If it's covered with prints—besides Connie's, which belong there since she just checked the drawer—or claims she did—you'll know I wasn't in there."

"What do you mean, *claims* she did, Miss Detective?" Karen Bigelow gave me a hard look.

"It's like this, Ms. Supervisor: I don't know what kind of game Ajax is playing with the Sommers family claim, but it's a game whose stakes are mighty high, now that a man's been killed. Fepple's mother gave me a key to the agency office. I went down there today to see if I could find any trace of his appointment calendar."

I paused to stare hard at Connie Ingram, but her round face didn't show any special anxiety. "Now, whoever killed Howard Fepple swiped the Sommers file. They swiped his handheld electronic diary. But they didn't think to wipe out the appointment from his computer. Or—they were even more squeamish than I was about getting near the machine since it had his brains and blood all over it."

Both Bigelow and Connie flinched at that, which only proved they didn't like the idea of brains and blood and computers all mixed together. "Well, guess who had an appointment with Howard Fepple last Friday night? Young Connie Ingram here."

Her mouth widened in a giant O of protest. "I never. I never made an appointment to see him. If he put that in his diary, he's lying!"

"Someone is," I agreed. "I was with him Friday afternoon, and some very sophisticated person gave him a simple but slick method for ditching me. This person came back in with him under cover of a group of Lamaze parents and left with them. Probably after killing him. Connie Ingram is the only appointment he showed for Friday. And next to it he'd written, *says she wants to discuss Sommers, but she sounds hot for me.*" I pulled the diary printout from my bag and waved it at her.

"He wrote that down about me? I only ever talked to him on the phone, to ask him to double-check about the payment. And that was last week right after you first came here. Mr. Rossy asked me to. I live at home. I live with my mother. I would never—I never made that kind of phone call." She buried her face in her hands, crimson with shame.

Ralph snatched the printout from me. He looked at it, then tossed it contemptuously aside. "I have a Palm. You can enter events after the date—anyone could have typed that in. Including you, Vic. To deflect criticism away from your helping yourself to our microfiche."

"Another thing for technicians to look at," I snapped. "You can back-enter dates, but you can't fool the machine: it will tell you what day those keystrokes were typed. It seems to me we've just about covered anything useful here: I need to get these technical problems to the cops before little Miss Innocence here goes down and wipes out the hard drive."

Tears were streaming down Connie's face. "Karen, Mr. Devereux, honest, I was never down in that agent's office. I never said I'd go out with him, even though he asked me to, why would I? He didn't sound like a nice person on the phone."

"He asked you out on a date?" I interrupted her wailing. "When was that?"

"When I called down there. After you were here last week I called him, like I said, like Mr. Rossy and Mr. Devereux asked me to. To find out what he had in his files, and he said, he talked in this kind of nasty way, he said, 'Lots of juicy stuff. Wouldn't you like to see it? We could share a bottle of wine and go over the file together.' And I said, 'No, sir, I just want you to send me copies of all your relevant documents so I can find out how this policy got a check issued on it when the policyholder was still alive.' And then he said more stuff, really, I can't repeat it, and he seemed to think it would be fun to have a date, but honestly, I know I still live with my mother and I'm thirty-three, but I'm not a desperate virgin like—anyway, I never said I would see him. If he put it in his calendar, he was a liar and I'm not sorry he's dead, so there!" She ran sobbing from the room.

"Does that satisfy you, Miss Detective?" Karen Bigelow said coldly. "Seems to me you could find something better to do than bully an honest, hardworking girl like Connie Ingram. Excuse me, Mr. Devereux, I'd better make sure she's all right."

She started to sail majestically from the room, but I moved to block her path. "Ms. Claims Supervisor, it's great that you support your staff, but you came up here to accuse me of theft. Before you go off to mop up Connie Ingram's tears, I want that accusation cleared up."

She breathed heavily at me. "I heard from the girl who took you over to Connie's workstation that you were wandering around the floor. You could have been in those files."

"Then we'll call the cops. I won't have this kind of accusation made lightly about me. Besides which, someone is trying to make sure no copies of that file remain. I may be advising my client to sue Ajax. In which case, if you can't find the documents you're going to look mighty stupid in court."

"If that's your goal, you'd have all the more motive for stealing the fiche," Ralph said.

Red lights of anger were starting to dance in front of me. "And I'll bring an action for slander."

I moved to his desk and started pressing keys on the phone. It had been a long time since I'd dialed the work number for my dad's oldest friend on the force, but I still knew it by heart. Bobby Mallory has made a reluctant adjustment to my career as a detective, but he still prefers that when we meet it be for family events.

"What do you think you're doing?" Ralph demanded, as an officer answered the phone.

"I'm doing what you should have done, calling the cops." I turned to the phone. "Officer Bostwick, it's V I Warshawski: is Captain Mallory in?"

Ralph's eyes glittered. "You have no authority to bring the cops into this building. I will speak to this officer and tell him so."

It was a sign of the change in Bobby's attitude toward me that although I'd never met Officer Bostwick he recognized my name. He told me that Bobby was unavailable; was there a message?

"A murder in the Twenty-first District, officer— there's evidence in the computer, which was left running and left in the vic's office." I gave him Fepple's address and date of death. "Commander Purling may not have realized the importance of the computer. But I'm at the Ajax Insurance company, where the vic did a lot of business, and there may be a question of checking the time when data was entered."

"Ajax?" Bostwick said. "They're having a lot of trouble these days—Durham and Posner are out front right now, aren't they?"

"Yes, indeed, the building is surrounded by demonstrators, but the claims vice president thinks this agent's death merits more of his attention than a few protesters."

"Doesn't sound like a few to me, miss, the way they

were asking for backup out there on Adams. But give me the details about this computer—I'll make sure a forensics unit gets down to it. Commander Purling, well, with the Robert Taylor Homes in his district, he doesn't have time to do a lot of finesse work."

A discreet way of saying the guy was a lazy jerk. I gave Bostwick the details about Fepple and the importance of the date, adding that I had seen the victim shortly before he left for an appointment on Friday evening. Bostwick repeated back what I said, double-checked the spelling of my name, and asked where Captain Mallory could reach me if he wanted to discuss the situation.

I hung up and glared at Ralph. "I'm respecting the privacy of your company and your authority over it, but you had damned well better make a call like that yourself if you want to find out who really was in your microfiche cabinet. Especially if you're going to keep accusing me of theft. We should know by the end of the day tomorrow, or Thursday at the latest, when that date with Connie Ingram was entered in Fepple's computer. If it was before I last saw him on Friday, then Ms. Ingram's going to be crying for a bigger audience than us. By the way, what happened to your paper file? The one Rossy hung on to last week?"

Ralph and Karen Bigelow exchanged startled glances. "I guess he still has it," the supervisor said. "It hasn't been checked back into our unit."

"Is his office up here? Let's go ask him about it—unless you think I wandered in and stole it after we spoke at noon, Ralph."

He flushed. "No, I don't imagine you did. But why did you go down to the thirty-ninth floor at noon without telling me? You'd been with me seconds earlier."

"It was an impulse; it only occurred to me when I got to the elevators. You had pretty much stiffed me on the file, and I was hoping Ms. Ingram would let me see it. Can we at least go see Rossy, get the paper file back from him?"

"The chairman went down to Springfield today. The Holocaust Recovery Act is coming up in front of the banking and insurance committee—he wanted to testify against it. Rossy went with him."

"Really." My brows went up. "He'd invited me to dinner tonight."

"What'd he do that for?" Ralph's flush deepened into resentment.

"When he called yesterday to invite me, he said it was because his wife was homesick and wanted someone she could speak Italian with."

"Are you making that up?"

"No, Ralph. I'm not making up anything I said this afternoon. But maybe he forgot about the invitation. When did he decide to go to Springfield?"

Resentment was still uppermost in Ralph's mind. "Hey, I just run the claims department. Apparently not too well if people make off with our files. No one talks to me about deep subjects like legislative hearings. Rossy's got an office on the other side of the floor. His secretary's probably here: you can ask her if he's coming back tonight. I'll walk you over to see if he's still got the file."

"I should find Connie, Mr. Devereux," Karen Bigelow said. "But what should I do about the microfiche? Should I report the theft to security?"

Ralph hesitated, then told her she should lock the cabinet and declare it off-limits. "Conduct a desk-by-desk search of your unit tomorrow. Someone may have inadvertently kept the fiche after looking up some other file. If you don't find it by the end of the day, let me know: I'll call security."

"Look, you two," I said, impatient with this futile proposal, "Connie's name in Fepple's calendar is serious. If she didn't set up the date, someone did it using her name. Which means it was someone who knows her as a claims handler. And that means a very limited universe, especially since it wasn't me."

Ralph knotted his tie and unrolled his cuffs. "According to you, anyway."

XXIX

Strange Bedfellows

We found Rossy's secretary in the chairman's conference room, watching the early-evening news with the chairman's secretary, the head of the marketing department—whom I'd met at Ajax's hundred-fiftieth-birthday celebration—and five other people who were never introduced.

"We are demanding a boycott of all Ajax insurance by America's Jewish community," Posner was proclaiming to the camera. "Preston Janoff insulted the whole Jewish community, he insulted the sacred memories of the dead, by his remarks in Springfield today."

Beth Blacksin's face replaced Posner's on the screen. "Preston Janoff is the chairman of the Ajax Insurance group. He testified today against adoption of a bill that would require life-insurance companies to scan their books to see if they have any outstanding obligations to families of Holocaust victims."

The camera switched to Janoff, standing in front of the legislative chamber in Springfield. He was tall, silver-haired, somber in a charcoal suit that suggested, but didn't emphasize, mourning.

"We understand the pain of those who lost loved

ones in the Holocaust, but we believe it would be an insult to the African-American, to the Native American, and to other communities who have suffered greatly in this country, to single out for special treatment people whose families were killed in Europe. And Ajax did not sell life insurance in Europe in the decades before the Second World War. For us to turn our files inside out on the off chance that one or two policies might come to light would place an extraordinary burden on our shareholders."

One of the legislators rose to ask if it wasn't true that Edelweiss Re of Switzerland was now the owner of Ajax. "Our committee wants to know about Edelweiss's life-insurance policies."

Janoff held up a copy of Amy Blount's history, "One Hundred Fifty Years of Life and Still Going Strong." "I believe this booklet will show the committee that Edelweiss was a small regional player in the life-insurance business in Switzerland during the war. The company has made copies available to all members of the legislature. Again, any involvement with consumers in Germany or eastern Europe would have been very small."

A babble erupted as various members sprang to their microphones, but the program returned us to the Global studio, where Murray Ryerson, who occasionally did political commentary for Global, was speaking. "Later this afternoon, the House Insurance Committee voted eleven-to-two to table the proposed bill, which effectively kills it. Joseph Posner has been leafletting, telephoning, and picketing in an effort to start a nation-wide boycott of all Ajax Insurance products in retaliation. It's too early to tell if he's succeeding, but we have heard that the Birnbaum family will continue to use Ajax for their workers' compensation coverage, business reputedly worth sixty-three million dollars in premiums to Ajax this year. Alderman Louis Durham hailed Janoff's speech and the vote with mixed reactions."

We were treated to a close-up of Durham outside the Ajax building in his beautifully cut jacket. "Ideally, we want to see compensation for victims of African slavery in this country. Or at the very least in this state. But we appreciate Chairman Janoff's sensitivity to the issue, to not letting Jews dominate a discussion of reparations in Illinois. We will take our fight for reparations for the victims of slavery directly to the legislature now, and we will fight until we win."

When the evening news anchor, sitting next to Murray in the studio, came on the screen saying, "In other news, the Cubs lost their thirteenth straight today at Wrigley," Janoff's secretary switched off the set.

"This is wonderful news—Mr. Janoff will be terrifically pleased," she said. "He hadn't heard the vote when he and Mr. Rossy left Springfield. Chick, can you go on-line and find out who voted with us? I'll call him in his car: he was going straight from Meigs to a dinner meeting."

A fresh-faced young man obediently left the room.

"Was Mr. Rossy going to dinner with him?" I asked.

The rest of the room turned to stare at me as if I had dropped in from Pluto. Rossy's secretary, an extremely glossy specimen with shiny black hair and a tailored navy dress, asked who I was and why I wanted to know. I introduced myself, explaining that Rossy had invited me to dinner in his home this evening. When Rossy's secretary took me back to her own desk to check her calendar, the room started buzzing behind us: if I'd been invited to the Rossy home, I must be powerful; they needed to know who I was.

Rossy's secretary tapped rapidly across the corridor on very high heels. Ralph and I trailed in her wake.

"Yes, Ms. Warshawski: I remember getting your number for Mr. Rossy yesterday morning, but he didn't tell me he'd invited you to dinner—it's not in my book. Shall I check with Mrs. Rossy for you? She is the decision-maker on his social calendar."

Her hand was already poised over the phone. She hit a speed-dial button, talked briefly with Mrs. Rossy, and assured me that they were expecting me.

"Suzanne," Ralph said as she started to pack up her desk. "Bertrand took a claims file away to study last week. We're anxious to get it back—there's an open investigation going on with it."

Suzanne tapped into Rossy's inner office and came back almost immediately with the Sommers file. "I'm so sorry, Mr. Devereux. He left a message in his dictation that I was to get this back to you, but he decided at the last minute to go to Springfield with Mr. Janoff; in the flurry of getting him down there, the file slipped my mind. Mr. Rossy wanted to make sure you knew how much he appreciated the work Connie Ingram did for him on this."

Ralph grunted unenthusiastically. He didn't want to admit doubts about his staff, but my finding Connie Ingram's name in Fepple's diary was clearly troubling him.

"I know Connie Ingram was helpful in tracking down the agent's copy of the paper trail on this file," I said. "Did Mr. Rossy ask her to call on Fepple—the agent—in person?"

Suzanne lifted her perfectly tweezed eyebrows, as if astonished that a peon would try to worm her boss's secrets out of her. "You'd have to ask Mr. Rossy that. Perhaps you'll have a chance to do so at dinner."

"Really, Vic," Ralph spluttered as we got back to his office. "What are you trying to suggest? That Connie Ingram was involved in killing an insurance agent? That Rossy somehow ordered her to do it? Get a grip on yourself."

I thought of Connie Ingram's round, earnest face and

had to admit she didn't seem likely either as a murderer or a murderer's tool. "But I want to know how her name got into Fepple's diary if she didn't make the appointment or if she didn't go down herself to his office and back-enter it," I added stubbornly.

Ralph bared his teeth in a snarl. "I wouldn't put it past you to do it. If you thought that would get you in the door."

"That brings us back to where we started. Why don't you let me thumb through the Sommers file so I can get out of here and leave you in peace."

"Somehow peace is not what you ever leave me in, V I."

There was just enough of a double edge to his tone that I hastily took the file from him and started thumbing through the contents. He stood over me while I carefully looked at each page. I couldn't see anything odd, either in the client payment reports or the claim-payment record. Aaron Sommers had started paying weekly installments on May 13, 1971, and had paid the policy in full in 1986. Then a death claim, signed by the widow, and notarized, had been filed in September 1991 and duly paid a few days later. There were two copies of the canceled check—the one Connie had originally printed from the fiche, and one which Fepple had faxed to her from his files. They looked identical.

A copy of Rick Hoffman's worksheet, where he'd typed up the figures for the weekly payments, was attached to a letter to Ajax alerting them to the sale. I had hoped the signature would be in the same ornate writing as the document I'd found in Fepple's briefcase, but it was a very ordinary, nondescript hand.

Ralph inspected each document as I finished with it. "I guess it's okay," he said when we got to the end.

"Guess? Is there something wrong?"

He shook his head, but he still looked puzzled. "Everything's here. Everything's in order. It's like ten thousand other claim folders I've inspected in the last twenty years. I don't know why something doesn't seem quite right. You run along: I'm going to stand over Denise while she copies every document, so that there are two witnesses to the contents."

It was after six now. In the event that Posner was still out front, I wanted to get downstairs to see if I could pick up Radbuka's trail. I was almost at the elevators when Ralph caught up with me.

"Vic—sorry. I was out of line earlier. But the coincidence of you being on the floor, the fiche missing, and knowing that you sometimes use, well, unorthodox methods—"

I made a wry face. "You're right, Ralph. But I really swear, scout's honor, that I was nowhere near your fiche."

"I wish I knew what in hell was so important about this one lousy life-insurance case." He slammed the flat of his hand against the elevator wall.

"The agent who sold it—Rick Hoffman—he's been dead for seven years now. Would the company still have a record of his home address, his family, anything about him? He had a son—guy who'd be, I don't know, close to sixty now—maybe he has papers that would shed some light on the situation." It was a straw, but we didn't have any more substantial building material right now.

Ralph pulled a small notebook from his breast pocket and scribbled a note. "I start the afternoon accusing you of theft and end it as your errand boy. I'll see what I can find out. I wish you hadn't called the cops, though. Now they'll be around wanting to interrogate Connie. Who I refuse to believe killed the guy. She might have shot him—if she had a gun—if she'd agreed to go see him—and if he'd stepped across the line. But can you picture her scheming to make a murder look like suicide?"

"I've always been way too impulsive, Ralph, but—you can't fling accusations at me without something more to go on than my unorthodox methods. Also, you need to face the fact that someone was in that drawer. Your and Ms. Bigelow's solution is a Band-Aid: the team investigating Fepple's murder should know that someone stole that microfiche. You should get them in here, regardless of the PR consequences. As for Connie Ingram, she should answer those questions, but you can show you're a good guy by alerting Ajax's legal team. Make sure senior counsel is with her when she's questioned. She seems to trust Ms. Bigelow; have Bigelow sit in on the interrogation. A lot will hinge on when her name was entered into Fepple's computer. And whether she has an alibi for last Friday night."

The elevator door pinged. As I got on, Ralph asked me casually where I'd been on Friday night.

"With friends who will vouch for me."

"Your friends would, Vic," Ralph said sourly.

"Cheer up." I put a hand in between the doors to keep them from closing. "Connie Ingram's mother will do the same for her. And Ralph? Trust your instinct on that Sommers file: if your sixth sense is telling you something isn't quite right, try to figure it out, will you?"

The street was quiet by the time I reached the lobby. The bulk of homebound commuters were gone, making it pointless for Posner and Durham to parade their troops. A few extra cops lingered at the intersection, but except for flyers scattered along the curb, there was no sign of the mob that had been here when I arrived. I'd missed a chance to tail Radbuka home. Radbuka, whose father's name hadn't been Ulrich.

On my way to the garage I stopped in a doorway to call Max, partly to tell him I didn't think Radbuka would be around tonight, partly to see if he'd be willing to show Don the papers about his search for the Radbuka family.

"This Streeter fellow is very good with the little one," Max said. "It's been a big help to have him here. I think we'll ask him to stay on tonight, even if you know that this man calling himself Radbuka won't be coming around."

"You should keep Tim, no question: I can't guarantee Radbuka won't bother you, just that he's attached himself to Joseph Posner for the moment. I saw him marching with Posner outside the Ajax building an hour ago—and I'm betting that's making him feel accepted enough to keep him away from you overnight—but he's a loose cannon; he could come shooting back."

I told him about my meeting with Rhea Wiell. "She's the one person who seems able to exercise some control over him, but for some reason she isn't willing to. If you let Don look at your notes from your difficult trip to Europe after the war, he might persuade her that you really aren't related to Paul Radbuka."

When Max agreed, I left a message on Don's cellphone voice mail, telling him he should call Max.

It was six-thirty—not enough time for me to go home or to my office before dinner. Maybe I would try to drop in on Lotty, after all, before going to the Rossys'.

Six-thirty here, one-thirty in the morning in Rome, where Morrell would be just about landing. He'd spend tomorrow in Rome with the Humane Medicine team, fly to Islamabad on Thursday, and travel by land into Afghanistan. For a moment I felt bowed down by desolation: my fatigue, Max's worries, Lotty's turmoil—and Morrell, half a world away. I was too alone in this big city.

A homeless man selling copies of *Streetwise* danced over to me, hawking his paper. What he saw in my face made him change his pitch.

"Honey, whatever's happening to you, it can't be

that bad. You got a roof over your head, right? You got three squares a day when you take the time to eat them? Even if your mama's dead you know she loved you—so cheer up."

"Ah, the kindness of strangers," I said, fishing a single out of my jacket pocket.

"That's right. Nothing kinder than strangers, nothing stranger than kindness. You heard it here first. You have a blessed evening, and keep that pretty smile coming."

I won't say he sent me on my way laughing with delight, but I did manage to whistle "Whenever I feel afraid" as I walked down the steps to the garage.

I took Lake Shore Drive north to Belmont, where I got off and started nosing around for a parking place. Lotty lived half a mile up the road, but street parking is at such a premium here that I grabbed the first space I saw. It turned out to be a lucky opening, only half a block from the Rossys' front door.

I had kept deferring phoning Lotty on my way north: I wouldn't do it from the street downtown because I didn't want background noise interfering. I wouldn't do it from the car because it's dangerous to drive and dial. Now—I'd do it as soon as I'd shut my eyes for five minutes, emptied my mind, gotten the illusion of rest so I could be strong enough for whatever emotional fastballs Lotty pitched at me.

I pulled the lever so that the front seat was stretched almost horizontal. As I leaned back, I saw a limo pull up in front of Rossy's building. I watched idly, wondering if it was Rossy, being dropped at home by Ajax's chairman, ecstatic over today's favorable vote in Springfield. Janoff and Rossy would take a limo back from Meigs Field, sharing a drink and a merry laugh in the backseat. When no one got out after several minutes, I lost interest—the car was waiting to pick up someone from the building.

Rossy must be pretty ecstatic himself over today's vote: Edelweiss Re had acquired Ajax to serve as their U.S. beachhead. They wouldn't have been pleased at all if Illinois had voted that they had to scour their records hunting out policies sold to people who were murdered in Europe—a search like that would have cost a tidy bundle. Ajax must have tossed a fair amount of cash at the legislature to get the vote to go their way—but I suppose they figured that was cheaper than opening up their life-insurance book to public scrutiny.

Of course, it wasn't likely that Ajax had sold many policies in central or eastern Europe in the 1930's, unless they had a subsidiary that had done a lot of business there, which I didn't think was the case. Insurance, like most business, had been regional before the Second World War. Still, Edelweiss itself might have had a Holocaust exposure. But as Ajax chairman Janoff had contended today, waving Amy Blount's history at the legislature, Edelweiss had only been a small regional player before the war.

I wondered idly how they'd turned into the international giant they were today. Maybe they'd made out like bandits during the war itself—there must have been a lot of money to be made, insuring all the chemicals and optics and crap the Swiss produced for the German war effort. Not that it was relevant to the bill that the state was considering, which only dealt with life insurance, but people vote emotions, not facts. If someone showed that Edelweiss had gotten rich on the Third Reich's war machine, the legislature would punish them by making them open their life-insurance files.

The limo driver opened his door and stood up. I blinked: it was a Chicago cop. Someone from the city on official business was up here. When the building door swung open, I sat up, looking to see if the mayor was coming out. The man who actually emerged made my jaw drop. I'd seen that bullet head and perfectly tailored navy jacket downtown only two hours ago. Alderman Louis "Bull" Durham. A lot of powerful people lived on this stretch of Lake Shore Drive, but I was betting it was Bertrand Rossy he'd been visiting.

While I was still staring at the front of Rossy's building, wondering who was paying off whom, I got a second jolt: a figure in a bowler hat, tassels visible under his open coat, rose like a jack-in-the-box from the bushes and marched into the lobby. I got out of my car and moved down the street so I could see into the front door. Joseph Posner was gesticulating at the doorman. What on earth was going on?

XXX

Party Time?

When I jogged, panting, into the Rossys' foyer an hour later, I'd temporarily forgotten Durham and Posner. My mind was mostly on Lotty, whom I'd once again left in distress—but I was also very aware that I was late, despite running the half mile down the street from her apartment. I'd stopped, breathless, at my car to trade my turtleneck and crepe-soled shoes for the rose silk camisole and pumps. I stood still while I carefully put on my mother's earrings, then combed my hair as I ran across the street. I tried to apply a little makeup in the elevator on my way to the eleventh floor. Even so, I felt disheveled when I got off—and worse when my hostess left her other guests to greet me.

Fillida Rossy was a woman in her early thirties, almost as tall as me. Her raw-silk palazzo pants, with a nubby sweater in the same dull gold hugging her chest, emphasized both her slenderness and her wealth. Her dark-blond curls were pulled back from her face with a couple of diamond clips, and another larger diamond nestled in the hollow above her breastbone.

She took my outstretched hand in both of hers and almost caressed it. "My husband has made me so interested in meeting you, signora," she said in Italian. "Your talk to him was so full of entertaining surprises: he told me how you read his palm."

She led me forward by the hand to greet the other guests, who included the Italian cultural attaché and his wife—a dark, vivacious woman around Fillida's age—a Swiss banking executive and his wife—both much older—and an American novelist who had lived for many years in Sorrento.

"This is the detective about whom Bertrand has been speaking, the one who conducts her business among the palm readers."

Fillida patted my own palm encouragingly, like a mother presenting a shy child to strangers. Uncomfortable, I withdrew my hand and asked where Signor Rossy was.

"*Mio marito si comparta scandalosamente,*" she announced with a vivid smile. "He has adopted American business habits and is on the telephone instead of greeting his guests, which is scandalous, but he will join us shortly."

I murmured "*piacere*" to the other guests and tried to switch my thinking from English, and my conversation with Lotty, to Italian and the rival merits of Swiss, French, and Italian ski slopes, which was apparently what they had been discussing when I arrived. The attaché's wife exclaimed enthusiastically over Utah and said that of course for Fillida, the more dangerous the slope the better she liked it.

"When you invited me to your grandfather's place in Switzerland our last year in school, I stayed in the lodge while you went down the most terrifying run I have ever seen—without even getting your hair out of place, as I remember it. Your grandfather puffed out through his moustache and pretended to be nonchalant, but he was incredibly proud. Is your little Marguerita growing up similarly fearless?"

Fillida threw up her hands, with their beautifully manicured nails, and said her reckless days were behind her. "Now I can hardly bear to let my babies out of my sight, so I stay with them on the beginner slopes. What I will do when they pine for the giant runs I don't know. I've learned to pity my own mother, who suffered agonies over my recklessness." Her gaze flickered to the marble mantelpiece, where photographs of her children were standing—so many of them that the frames were almost stacked on top of one another.

"Then you won't want to take them to Utah," the banker's wife said. "But there are good family slopes in New England."

Skiing wasn't a subject I knew enough about to participate—even if I spoke Italian often enough to plunge at once into the rapid talk. I began to wish I had called to cancel and stayed with Lotty, who had seemed even more distressed and anxious this evening than she'd been on Sunday.

After I'd seen Posner go into the Rossys' building, I'd walked up the street to Lotty's, not sure whether she would invite me up or not. After some hesitation, she had let the doorman admit me, but she was waiting in the hall when I got off the elevator on her floor. Before I could say anything, she demanded roughly what I wanted. I tried not to let her harshness hurt me but said I was worrying about her.

She scowled. "As I told you earlier on the phone, I'm sorry I spoiled Max's party, but I'm fine now. Did Max send you to check on me?"

I shook my head. "Max is occupied with Calia's safety. He's not thinking about you right now."

"Calia's safety?" Her thick black brows twitched together. "Max is a doting grandfather, but I don't think of him as a worrywart."

"No, he's not a worrywart," I agreed. "Radbuka has been stalking Calia and Agnes."

"Stalking them? Are you sure?"

"Hanging out across the street, accosting them when they leave, trying to make Agnes admit that Calia is related to him. Does that sound like stalking, or just a friendly visit?" I snapped, angry in spite of myself at her scornful tone.

She pressed her palms into her eyes. "That's ridiculous. How can he think she's related?"

I shrugged. "If any of us knew who he really was, or who the Radbukas really were, it might make that question easier to answer."

Her generous mouth set in a hard line. "I don't owe any explanation—to you, to Max, least of all to this absurd creature. If he wants to play at being a survivor of Theresienstadt, let him."

"Play at? Lotty, do you *know* he's playing at it?"

My voice had risen; the door at the opposite end of the hall opened a crack. Lotty flushed and took me into her own apartment.

"I don't, of course. But Max—Max didn't find any Radbukas when he went to Vienna. After the war, I mean. I don't believe—I'd like to know where this bizarre man came up with the name."

I leaned against the wall, my arms crossed. "I told you I went out on the Web and found the person looking for information about Sofie Radbuka. I left my own message, saying he or she should communicate with my lawyer if they wanted to initiate a confidential conversation."

Her eyes blazed. "Why did you take it on yourself to do that?"

"There are two impenetrable mysteries here: Sofie Radbuka of the 1940's in England, Paul Radbuka of Chicago today. You want information about Paul, he wants information about Sofie, but neither of you is willing to divulge anything. I have to start somewhere."

"Why? Why do you have to start anywhere? Why don't you leave it alone?"

I seized her hands. "Lotty. Stop. Look at yourself. Ever since this man came on the scene last week, you've been demented. You've been howling on the sidewalk and then insisting that the rest of us pay no attention because there isn't a problem. I can't believe this isn't spilling over into the operating room. You're a danger to yourself, your friends, your patients, carrying on like this."

She jerked her hands away and looked at me sternly. "I have never compromised the attention I give my patients. Ever. Even in the aftermath of the war. Certainly not now."

"That's just great, Lotty, but if you think you can go on like this indefinitely, you're wrong."

"That's my business. Not yours. Now, will you have the goodness to go back to this Web address and retract your message?"

I chose my words carefully. "Lotty, nothing can threaten the love I have for you: it's too deep a part of my life. Max told me he has always respected the zone of privacy you erected around the Radbuka family. I would do that, too, if it weren't for this heartbreaking torment you're suffering. That means—if you won't tell me yourself what is torturing you, I need to find it out."

Her expression turned so stormy I thought she was going to blow up again, but she mastered herself and spoke quietly. "Mrs. Radbuka represents a part of my past of which I am ashamed. I—turned my back on her. She died while I was ignoring her. I don't know that I could have saved her. I mean, probably I couldn't have saved her. But—I abandoned her. The circumstances don't matter; it's only my behavior that you need to know about."

I knit my brow. "I know she wasn't part of your

group in London, or Max would know her. Was she a patient?"

"My patients—I can treat them because our roles are so defined. It's when people are outside that box that I become less reliable. I've never stinted a patient, not ever, not even in London when I was ill, when it was bitterly cold, when other students whisked through consultations as fast as possible. It's a relief, a salvation, to be in the hospital, to be the doctor, not the friend or the wife or the daughter, or someone else utterly unreliable."

I took her hands again. "Lotty, you've never been unreliable. I've known you since I was eighteen. You've always been present, warm, compassionate, a true friend. You're beating yourself up for some sin that doesn't exist."

"It's true we've been friends this long time, but you aren't God; you don't know all my sins—any more than I know yours." She spoke dryly, not the dryness of irony but as if she were too worn out for feeling. "But if this man, this man who thinks he's one of the Radbukas, is threatening Calia—Calia is the mirror of Teresz. When I look at her—Teresz was the great beauty in our group. Not only that, she had great charm. Even at sixteen, when the rest of us were gauche. When I look at Calia, Teresz comes back so vividly. If I really thought harm might come to Calia—"

She wouldn't finish the sentence. If she really thought harm would come to Calia, she would finally tell me the truth? Or—what?

In the silence that hung between us, I caught sight of the time and blurted out that I had to be at dinner. I didn't like the tautness in Lotty's face as she escorted me back to the elevator. Running down Lake Shore Drive to the Rossys'; I felt it was I who was the unreliable friend.

Now, in a living room weighted down with bronze sculpture, nubbed-silk upholstery, enormous oil paintings, as I listened to the glittery chatter of skiing and whether a city like Chicago could possibly produce first-class opera, I felt utterly untethered from the world around me.

XXXI

Rich Tastes

I moved away from the chatter to the French windows. They stood open so that guests could pass through the heavy drapes to stand on a small balcony. Lake Michigan lay in front of me, a black hole in the fabric of the night, visible only as a blot between the winking lights of airplanes heading for O'Hare and headlights of cars on the road below. I shivered.

"Are you cold, Signora Warshawski? You shouldn't linger in the night air." Bertrand Rossy had come through the window behind me.

I turned. "I don't often have the chance to see the view this clearly."

"Since I've been remiss in attending to my guests, I can scarcely chide you for avoiding them, as well, but I hope you will join us now." He held the curtain for me, giving me no choice really except to return to the gathering.

"Irina," he called in English to a woman in a traditional maid's uniform, "Signora Warshawski needs a glass of wine."

"I gather you spent the day saving millions of dollars for your shareholders," I said, also switching to English.

"That must have been very gratifying, having the legislature support you so quickly."

He laughed, his dimples showing. "Oh, I was there only as an observer. I was most impressed with Preston Janoff, most impressed. He is quite cool under attack."

"An eleven-to-two vote in committee sounds like the attack of the tabby cats."

He laughed again. "Attack of the tabby cats! What an original way you have of expressing yourself."

"What is it, *caro*?" Fillida Rossy, who had come to me herself with a glass of wine, took her husband's arm. "What is making you laugh so gaily?"

Rossy repeated my remark; Fillida smiled sweetly and echoed it again in English. "I must remember that. An attack of the tabby cats. Who were they attacking?"

I felt remarkably foolish and gulped my wine as Rossy explained the legislature's vote.

"Ah, yes, you told me when you got in. How clever of you to know firsthand about these legislative matters, signora. I must wait for Bertrand's reports." She straightened his tie. "Darling, this lightning bolt is so bold, don't you think?"

"How did you know the vote so exactly?" Rossy asked. "By more divination?"

"I saw the news in Janoff's conference room. About other things I'm woefully ignorant."

"Such as?" He pressed his wife's fingers, an assurance that she was the real center of his attention.

"Such as why Louis Durham would need to meet with you at home after the vote. I didn't think he and Ajax's senior staff were on such cozy terms. Or why that mattered to Joseph Posner."

Fillida turned to me. "You are indeed an *indovina*, signora. I laughed when Bertrand said you had read his palm, but this is remarkable, that you know so much of our private business."

Her voice was soft, uncritical, but under her poised,

remote gaze I felt embarrassed. I had imagined this as a bold stroke; now it seemed merely crude.

Rossy spread his hands. "Life in Chicago is not so different after all from Bern and Zurich: here as there it seems that the personal touch with city governors is helpful in the smooth running of the company. As to Mr. Posner—one understands his disappointment after today's vote." He clasped my shoulder lightly, as Laura Bugatti, the attaché's wife, joined us. "*Allora*. Why do we discuss matters which no one else understands?"

Before I could respond, two children of about five and six came in under the watchful eye of a woman in a grey nurse's uniform. They were both very blond, the girl with a thick mane of hair down her back. They were dressed for bed in nightwear that had kept a team of embroiderers busy for a month. Fillida bent over to kiss them good night and to instruct them to say good night to Zia Laura and Zia Janet. Zia Laura was the attaché's wife, Zia Janet the American novelist. Both came to kiss the children while Fillida smoothed her daughter's long hair around her shoulders.

"Giulietta," she said to the nanny, "we must put a rosemary rinse in Marguerita's hair; it's too coarse after a day in these Chicago winds."

Bertrand scooped his daughter up to carry her off to bed. Fillida folded down the collar of her son's pajama top and handed him to the nurse. "I will be in later, my darlings, but I must feed our guests or they will soon faint from hunger. Irina," she added to the maid in the same soft voice, "I want to serve now."

She asked Signor Bugatti to escort me in, giving his wife to the Swiss banker. On our way across the hall to the paneled dining room I stopped to admire an old grandfather clock, whose face showed the solar system. It struck nine as I was watching, and the sun and planets began revolving around the earth.

"Enchanting, isn't it?" Signor Bugatti said. "Fillida has exquisite taste." .

If the paintings and little bits of sculpture lining the rooms were hers, she not only had exquisite taste but plenty of money to indulge it. She had a whimsical side, too: next to a child's painting of the ocean she had placed snapshots of her children at the beach.

Laura exclaimed over it. "Oh, look, here's your little Paolo at Samos last summer. He's adorable! Are you letting him swim in Lake Michigan?"

"Please," Fillida said, putting up a hand to adjust the photograph of her son. "He longs to go in. Don't suggest it—the pollution!"

"Anyone who can brave the Adriatic can tolerate Lake Michigan," the banker said, and everyone laughed. "Do you agree, Signora Warshawski?"

I smiled. "I often swim in the lake myself, but perhaps my system has built up a tolerance for our local pollution. At least we've never isolated cholera in our coastal waters here in Chicago."

"Oh, but Samos, that's not the same as Naples," said the American novelist, the "Aunt Janet" who had kissed an unwilling Paolo good night a few minutes ago. "It's so typical of an American to feel superior about life here without experiencing Europe. America has to be number one in everything, even clean coastal waters. In Europe, one cares much more for the well-rounded life."

"So when a German firm becomes America's largest publisher, or a Swiss company buys Chicago's biggest insurer, they're not really concerned with market domination?" I asked. "It's a by-product of the well-rounded life?"

The banker laughed while Rossy, who'd just rejoined us—in a different, more subdued tie—said, "Perhaps Janet should have said that Europeans mask an interest in medals or winning behind a cloak of civilization. It's bad manners to show off one's accomplishments—they should emerge casually, by chance, under cover of other conversation."

"Whereas Americans are confirmed braggarts," the novelist persisted. "We're rich, we're powerful, everyone must bend to our way of doing things."

Irina brought in mushroom soup, pale brown with cream drizzled in the shape of a mushroom cap. She was a silent, efficient woman whom I first assumed had come with the Rossys from Switzerland, until I realized that Fillida and Rossy always broke into English to talk to her.

The table conversation ran on in Italian for several caustic moments on the deficiencies of American power and American manners. I felt my hackles rise: it's one of those funny things, that no one likes the family to be criticized by outsiders, even when the family is a collection of lunatics or bullies.

"So today's vote in the Illinois legislature wasn't about withholding life-insurance benefits from beneficiaries of Holocaust victims—it was about keeping America from imposing its standards on Europe?" I said.

The cultural attaché leaned across the table toward me. "In a manner of speaking, yes, signora. This black counselor—what is his name? Dur'am?—he makes a valid point in my eyes. Americans are so eager to condemn at a distance—the atrocities of a war which were truly atrocious, no one denies it—but Americans are not willing to examine their own atrocities at home, in the matter of Indians or of African slaves."

The maid removed the soup dishes and brought in roast veal loin with an array of vegetables. The dinner plates were cream-colored porcelain, heavily encrusted in gold with a large *H* in the middle—perhaps for

Fillida Rossy's birth name, although offhand I couldn't think of Italian names beginning with *H*.

Laura Bugatti said that despite Mafia terrorism in Italy or Russia, most European readers preferred to be shocked by American violence than their homegrown brand.

"You're right." The banker's wife spoke for the first time. "My family won't discuss violence in Zurich, but they are always quizzing me about murders in Chicago. Are you finding this true now with this murder in your husband's firm, Fillida?"

Fillida ran her fingers over the ornate filigree on her knife. She ate very little, I noticed—not surprising that she had deep hollows around her breastbone. "*D'accordo*. This murder was reported in the Bologna paper, I suppose because they knew I was living here. My mother has been phoning every morning, demanding that I send Paolo and Marguerita back to Italy where they'll be safe. In vain I tell her the murder was twenty miles from my front door, in a part of town most unsavory—which you could find certainly in Milan. Perhaps even in Bologna, although I can hardly believe it."

"Not in your own hometown, eh, *cara*?" Bertrand said. "If it is your home it must be the best town, with nothing unsavory about it."

He was laughing, saluting his wife with his wineglass, but she frowned at him. He scowled and put his glass down, turning to the banker's wife. Fillida's soft voice apparently carried a lot of wallop—no Bologna jokes at this dinner table—change your tie when she criticizes it—change the subject when she's annoyed at this one.

Laura Bugatti, noticing Fillida's irritation, quickly exclaimed in a girlish breathless voice, "Murder in Bertrand's firm? How come I know nothing about this?

You are keeping important cultural information from me," she pouted at her husband.

"One of the agents selling insurance for Ajax was found dead in his office," the banker replied to her. "Now the police are saying he was murdered, not suicided as they first thought. You worked for him, didn't you, Signora Warshawski?"

"Against him," I corrected. "He held the key to a disputed—" I fumbled for words: my Italian had never been geared to financial discussions. Finally I turned to Rossy, who translated *life-insurance claim* for me.

"Yes, anyway, he held the key to such a disputed claim with Ajax, and I could never get him to reveal what he knew."

"So his death leaves you frustrated," the banker said.

"Frustrated. And greatly baffled. Because all the papers relating to the claim have vanished. Even today someone rifled a file cabinet at the company to remove documents."

Rossy set his wineglass down with a snap. "How do you know this? Why wasn't I told?"

I spread my hands. "You were in Springfield. I, alas, was informed because your Signor Devereux suspected I might have been responsible for the theft."

"From my office?" he demanded.

"From the claims department. The copy in your office was intact." I didn't tell him about Ralph's nagging sense that something was amiss in the paper file.

"So you never saw the agent's documents in this case?" Rossy ignored my suggestion. "Not even when you went in after the death?"

I laid my knife and fork carefully against the gold crust on my plate. "Now, how were you aware that I went into Fepple's office after he died?"

"I spoke with Devereux this afternoon from

Springfield. He told me that you had brought him some kind of document from the dead agent's office."

The maid replaced our dinner plates with more gold-rimmed dishes, this time containing raspberry mousse circled by fresh fruit.

"The dead man's mother gave me an office key and asked me to look for any evidence that the police were ignoring. When I went in, I found that one piece of paper, which appeared to be a very old handwritten document. The only reason I even associate it with the disputed claim is that the dead policyholder's name was on it, but whether it was about the claim or something else altogether, I couldn't say."

Laura Bugatti once more clapped her hands. "But this is exciting: a mysterious document. Can you tell who wrote it? Or when?"

I shook my head. The questions were making me uncomfortable; there was no need for her to know I'd had the paper analyzed.

"How disappointing." Rossy smiled at me. "I have boasted of your supernatural gifts. Surely like Sherlock Holmes you know fifty-seven different kinds of paper by their ash?"

"Alas," I said, "my powers are very erratic. They extend more to people and their motivations than to documents."

"Then why are you even concerned?" Fillida asked, her fingers once again wrapped around the heavy handle of her unused spoon.

There was a kind of power in the soft, remote voice; it made me want to respond aggressively. "This is a claim affecting a poor African-American family on Chicago's South Side. It would be a wonderful opportunity for Ajax to make good the rhetoric that Preston Janoff uttered today, to pay the grieving widow her ten thousand dollars."

The banker said, "So you are pursuing the matter merely out of nobility, not because you have evidence?" His tone didn't make the words sound like a compliment.

"And why try to tie it to Bertrand's firm at all?" the novelist added.

"I don't know who cashed the check which Ajax issued in 1991," I said, returning to English to make sure I expressed myself clearly. "But two things make me think it was either the agent or someone at the company: my study of the claimant's family. And the fact that the original file has disappeared. Not only from the agency, but from the company as well—perhaps whoever took them didn't realize that a paper copy was still in Mr. Rossy's office."

"*Ma il corpo,*" the banker's wife said. "Did you see the body? Isn't it true that his posture, the placement of the weapon, that all these made the police believe it was suicide?"

"Signora Bugatti is right," I said. "Europeans do long for the details of American violence. Unfortunately, it was only after the murder that Mrs. Fepple gave me a key to her son's office, so I can't fill in the details of his body in death."

Rossy frowned. "I'm sorry if we seem voyeuristic to you, but as you heard, the mothers in Europe worry greatly about their daughters and their grandchildren. Perhaps, though, we can discuss something less bloodthirsty."

Fillida nodded at him. "Yes, I think this is enough discussion of bloodshed at my dinner table. Why don't we return to the drawing room for coffee."

As the rest of the group settled themselves on the nubby straw-colored couches, I offered thanks and apologies to Fillida Rossy. "*Una serata squisita.* But I regret that an early appointment tomorrow means I must depart without coffee."

Neither Fillida nor Bertrand made any effort to keep me, although Fillida murmured something about sharing an evening at the opera. "Although I cannot believe *Tosca* can be sung anywhere outside of La Scala. It is heresy to me."

Bertrand himself escorted me to the door, assuring me heartily that I'd brought them much pleasure. He waited with the door open until the elevator arrived. Behind him, I heard the conversation turn to Venice, where Fillida, Laura, and Janet all attended the film festival.

XXXII

Client in the Slammer

My face in the elevator mirror looked wild and haggard, as though I'd spent years in a forest away from human contact. I ran a comb through my thick hair, hoping that my hollow eyes were merely a trick of the light.

I took a ten from my wallet and folded it into the palm of my hand. In the lobby I gave the doorman what was supposed to be a charming smile, with a comment on the weather.

"Mild for this time of year," he agreed. "Do you need a taxi, miss?"

I said I didn't have far to go. "I hope it isn't hard getting taxis later—the rest of the Rossys' company seemed to be prepared to stick it out all night."

"Oh, yes. Very cosmopolitan, their parties. People often stay until two or three in the morning."

"Mrs. Rossy is such a devoted mother, it must be hard for her to get up with her children in the morning," I said, thinking of the way she had held and stroked them at bedtime.

"The nanny takes them to school, but if you ask me, they'd be happier if she was less devoted. At least the little guy, he's always trying to get her to let go of him in public. I guess he's seen in American schools little boys don't let their mothers hold them and fuss with their clothes so much."

"She's such a soft-speaking lady, but she seems to run the show upstairs."

He opened the door for an older woman with a small dog, commenting on the nice night they had for their walk. The little dog bared its teeth under its mop of white hair.

"You going to work there?" he asked when the pair were outside.

"No. Oh, no—I'm a business associate of the husband."

"I was going to say—I wouldn't take a job up there on a bet. She has very European views on the place of the help, including me: I'm a piece of furniture who gets her cabs. It's her money, what I hear, that runs the show. Mister married the boss's daughter, still asks 'how high' when the family says 'jump.' That's what I hear, anyway."

I fanned the flame gently. "I'm sure she must be good to work for, or Irina wouldn't have come from Italy with her."

"Italy?" he held the door for a couple of teenage boys but didn't stop to chat with them. "Irina's from Poland. Probably illegal. Sends all her money to the family back home like all the other immigrants. Nah, the missus brought a girl from Italy with her to look after the kids so they won't forget their Italian living here. Stuck-up girl who doesn't give you the time of day," he added resentfully: gossip about the bosses keeps a dull job interesting.

"So both women live here? At least Irina can sleep in after a late night like tonight."

"Are you kidding? I'm telling you, for Mrs. Rossy, servants are servants. The mister, no matter how late the guests stay, he's up at eight ready for work, and you'd better believe it isn't the missus who gets up first thing to make sure that morning coffee is ready the way he likes it."

"I know they entertain a lot. I kind of expected to see Alderman Durham at dinner, since he'd been over here earlier. Or Joseph Posner." I casually left the ten on the marble console where he had television screens showing him the elevators and the street.

"Posner? Oh, you mean the Jewish guy." The doorman gracefully pocketed the ten without pausing for air. "Not likely the missus would let either of them at the dinner table. Around six-thirty she comes sailing in, talking on her cell phone. I figure it's to the mister, since it's in Italian, but she hangs up and turns to me, she never shouts, but she still gets the message across that she is PO'd big time: 'my husband has invited some business associate to do business here tonight. It will be a black man arriving, who is to wait in the lobby until my husband gets here. I am not able to entertain a strange man while I try to get ready for my guests.' By which she means her makeup and so forth."

"So Mr. Rossy was expecting Alderman Durham. Did he invite Posner, too?"

The doorman shook his head. "Posner showed up unexpected and got into quite a shouting match with me when I wouldn't let him go sailing up on his own. Mr. Rossy agreed to see him as soon as the alderman had left, but Posner only stayed up there fifteen minutes or so."

"So Posner must have been pretty angry at getting such a short audience, huh?"

"Oh, Mr. Rossy's a good guy, not like the missus—he's always good for a joke or a tip, at least when she isn't looking—you'd think if you had a bundle you could spare a buck now and then when a guy runs all the way down to Belmont for a cab—anyway, Mr.

Rossy managed to calm the Jewish guy down in fifteen minutes. I don't get the funny dress, though, do you? We have a lot of Jews in this building and they're just as normal as you or me. What's the point of the hat and the scarf and all that?"

A taxi pulling up in front saved me from having to think of a response. The doorman sprang into action as the taxi decanted a woman with several large suitcases. I figured I'd learned what I could, although it wasn't as much as I wanted to know; I went out with him and crossed the street to my car.

I drove home across Addison, trying to make sense of the situation. Rossy had invited Durham to see him. Before the demonstration? After he got back from Springfield? And somehow Posner knew about it, so he'd followed Durham up here. Where Rossy calmed his angry suspicions.

I didn't know anything specific about Alderman Durham's cupidity—although those expensive suits wouldn't leave much left over for groceries if he bought them on his alderman's pay—but most Chicago pols have a price, and it usually isn't very high. Presumably Rossy had invited Durham to his home to buy him off. But what could Rossy offer Posner that would get that fanatic off his back?

It was close to midnight when I finally found a parking space on one of the side streets near my home. I lived three miles west of the Rossys. When I moved into my little co-op, the neighborhood was a peaceful, mostly blue-collar place, but it's become so crowded now with trendy restaurants and boutiques that even this late at night the traffic made the drive tedious. An SUV swerving around me in front of Wrigley Field reminded me to stop thinking and concentrate on traffic.

Late as it was, my neighbor and the dogs were still awake. Mr. Contreras must have been sitting next to his front door waiting for me, because I was barely inside when he came out with Mitch and Peppy. The dogs dashed around the tiny foyer snapping at me, showing they were miffed at my long absence.

Mr. Contreras was feeling lonely and neglected, as was I. Even though I was exhausted, after giving the dogs a short run around the block, I joined the old man in his cluttered kitchen. He was drinking grappa; I opted for chamomile tea with a shot of brandy. The enamel on the kitchen table was chipped, the only picture was a calendar from the Humane Society showing a bundle of puppies, the brandy was young and raw, but I felt more at ease here than in the Rossys' ornate drawing room.

"Morrell take off today?" the old man asked. "I could kind of tell you was feeling blue. Everything okay?"

I grunted noncommittally, then found myself telling him in detail about coming on Fepple's body, about the Sommers family, the missing money, the missing documents, and tonight's dinner party. He was annoyed that I hadn't told him sooner about Fepple—"after all, doll, you was in the kitchen with me when his murder come on the news"—but he let me get on with my tale after only a perfunctory grumble.

"I'm tired. I'm not thinking clearly. But it seemed to me tonight's dinner was a carefully orchestrated event," I said. "At the time I got swept along on the conversational tide, but now I feel as though they were herding me, corralling me into talking about something very specific, but whether it was finding Fepple's body or what I'd seen in the Sommers file I don't know."

"Maybe both," my neighbor suggested. "You say this gal in the claims department, her name was in the agent's computer, but she's saying she never was near the place. Maybe she was. Maybe she was down there after he got shot and she's scared to admit it."

I slid Peppy's silky ears through my fingers. "That's possible. If that were the case I can see Ralph Devereux being protective of her—but I have to confess, I can't see that it would matter much to Rossy or his wife. Not enough for them to invite me to dinner to pump me. He said it was because his wife was lonely and wanted me to talk Italian to her, but she was surrounded by friends, or sycophants at any rate, and she didn't need me, except to get information from."

I frowned, thinking it over. "The news of Fepple's body must have come in, so Rossy could have called to see how much I know—but I can't see why. Unless the company is more worried about this Sommers claim than they're admitting—which means it's the tip of some ugly iceberg that I'm not seeing.

"It was such a last-minute invitation—I wonder whether tonight's cast of characters was already in place or if the Rossys pulled them together on the spot, knowing they'd play along. Especially Laura Bugatti— she's the wife of the Italian cultural attaché. Her job was to be the excited ingenue."

"What's that supposed to mean?"

"She was the breathless airhead who could ask crude questions without seeming to know what she was doing. Although that could be her real personality. The truth is, they all made me feel big and crude, even the American who was there, some very acidulated writer. I hope I've never spent money on any of her books. It's almost like I was invited to be the entertainment. There was a show going on which I was starring in, but I was the only one who hadn't seen the script."

"Whether money buys happiness or not I couldn't say, but one thing I've known for years, cookie, and that's that money sure don't buy character. Which you've got ten times more of than any set of got-rocks who want to invite you to dinner just so they can jerk you around."

I kissed his cheek and got up: I was too bleary-eyed to think, let alone talk. Moving almost as stiffly as the old man, I went upstairs to bed, taking Peppy with me: both of us needed extra petting tonight.

The message light on my home machine was flashing. I was so exhausted I thought I'd let it go, but then I wondered if Morrell had tried to reach me. The first message was indeed from him, missing me, loving me, bone-tired but too excited to sleep. "Me, too," I muttered, replaying his voice several times.

The second message was from my answering service. Amy Blount had called, twice: "She's angry and insisting that you get in touch with her at once but wouldn't give details." Amy Blount? Oh, yes, the young woman who'd written a hundred fifty years of Ajax history.

At once. Not now, though. Not at one in the morning on a day that had started twenty hours ago. I switched off my phone, shed my suit, and tumbled into bed without taking off the camisole or my mother's diamond drop earrings.

For the first time in over a week I slept through the night, finally staggering out of bed when Peppy nosed me awake a little after eight. My right ear hurt from where my mother's earring had pressed into it in my sleep; the left one was lost in the bedding. I fumbled around until I found it and got both of them back in my safe, next to my gun. Diamonds from my mother, handguns from my father. Perhaps Fillida Rossy's writer friend could turn that into a poem.

While I'd been sleeping, my answering service and Mary Louise had both left messages saying that Amy Blount had again demanded to speak to me. I groaned and went to the kitchen to make coffee.

I sat on the back porch nursing a double espresso while Peppy sniffed around the yard, until I felt awake enough to stretch out my stiff joints. Finally, after doing a full workout—including a fast four miles over to the lake and back, with the dogs protesting at the speed I made them go—I reconnected myself to the outside world.

I reached Christie Weddington at my answering service. "Vic, Mary Louise has been trying to reach you, along with a bunch of other people. Amy Blount called again, and someone named Margaret Sommers."

Margaret Sommers. My client's wife who thought I was out to rob or maim her husband. I took the details of my messages and told Christie she could switch urgent calls over to my cell phone. I wandered into the kitchen with my portable phone, prepared to make breakfast while talking to Margaret Sommers. I called her office, where they told me she'd gone home for a family emergency. I went back to the living room to get the home number from my Palm Pilot.

She answered on the first ring, shouting at me, "What did you say to the police about Isaiah?"

"Nothing." The unexpected attack took me off-guard. "What's happened to him?"

"You're lying, aren't you? They came and got him this morning, right out of the Docherty Works. In front of his buddies and everything, saying he had to talk to them about Howard Fepple. Now who but you would have turned them on to my husband?"

I wished I'd stayed in bed. "Mrs. Sommers. I have not discussed your husband with the police. And I know nothing about what happened this morning. If you want to talk to me about it, start at the beginning, without hurling accusations at me: is he under arrest? Or just brought into the station for questioning?"

She was angry and upset, but she did her best to choke back her invective. Isaiah had called her from work to say the cops were taking him in for Fepple's murder. She didn't know the station number but it was the one at Twenty-ninth and Prairie, because she'd rushed up there but they hadn't let her see Isaiah.

"Did you talk to any of the detectives who are questioning him? Can you give me their names?"

There were two, whose names she'd managed to get even though they were acting like God Almighty, not having to tell her anything.

I didn't recognize either of them. "Did they tell you anything? Like why they brought your husband in to begin with?"

"Oh, they were so mean, I could kill them myself and not think twice about it. Treating me like it was all a big joke. 'You want to stick around and yell at us, honey, we could lock you up right next to him. Listen to you two make up lies together.' Those were their very words."

I could easily imagine the exchange, as well as Margaret Sommers's impotent fury. "But they must have had some grounds for arresting him. Were you able to figure that out?"

"I told you. Because you talked to them."

"I know this has all been a horrible shock," I said gently. "I don't blame you for your anger. But try to think of a different reason, because truly, Ms. Sommers, I didn't say anything to the police about your husband. Indeed, I had nothing to say to them."

"What—you didn't tell them about him being in the office on Saturday?"

I felt a chill in my stomach. "He was? He went to Fepple's office? Why did he do that? When did he go there?"

We went back and forth a few times, but she finally seemed to accept that I hadn't known about it. Margaret Sommers had pushed Isaiah into going to see Fepple in person. That was what it boiled down to, although she tried to dress it up as my fault: they couldn't trust me, I wasn't doing anything but cozying up to the insurance company. She'd talked to the alderman—seeing Fepple was actually his suggestion. So when Isaiah wouldn't set up an appointment, she did it herself from the office on Friday afternoon.

"The alderman?" I asked. "Which alderman would this be?"

"Alderman Durham, of course. On account of Isaiah's cousin being part of the EYE movement and all, he's always been very helpful to us. Only Fepple said we couldn't come on Friday because he was completely booked. He tried to put us off, but I pointed out we worked all week, we couldn't meet some university professor's schedule, hopping in and out of our jobs. So he acted like I was trying to make him give me a million dollars, but he said if I was going to make such a big deal out of it, calling the alderman, like I threatened to do, we could see him on Saturday morning. So we drove up there together: I'm tired of Isaiah letting people push him around like he does. There wasn't any answer when we knocked, and I was furious, thinking he'd made the appointment without any intention of keeping it. But when we opened the door we saw him laying there dead. Not right away, mind you, because the office was dark. But pretty soon."

"Just a minute," I said. "When you called, you accused me of siccing the cops on your husband. What made you say that?"

She didn't think she was going to tell me, but then she blurted out that the cops had gotten a call. "They said it was from a man, a black man, but I figured that was just their talk, their way of trying to get under my skin. No brother I know of would accuse my husband of murder."

Maybe the detectives had been trying to ride her and Isaiah, but maybe it was a brother who'd phoned in the tip. I let it pass: in her current distress, Margaret Sommers needed to blame someone. It might as well be me.

I went back to their visit to Fepple's office on

Saturday. "When you were in there, did you look for Mr. Sommers's uncle's file? Did you take any papers away with you?"

"No! Once we got into the office and saw him lying there? With his—oh, I can't stand even to say it. We left as fast as we could."

But they'd touched enough. My client must have left his fingerprints somewhere in the room. And thanks to me, the police had stopped looking at Fepple's death as a suicide. So Margaret Sommers wasn't completely wrong: I had ensured her husband's arrest.

XXXIII

Turmoil

I drummed a series of jangly chords on the piano after Margaret hung up. Lotty often criticizes me for what she calls my ruthless search for truth, knocking over people in my path without thinking about their wants and needs. If I'd known being so clever about Fepple's death would get Isaiah Sommers arrested—but it was useless to beat myself up for pushing the cops to do a proper investigation. It had happened; now I had to deal with the aftermath.

Anyway, what if Isaiah Sommers really had shot Fepple? He'd told me on Monday he had an unlicensed Browning, but that didn't preclude his also having an unlicensed SIG—although they're pricey, not the gun of choice for your average homeowner.

I hit two adjacent keys so hard that Peppy backed away from me. Staging Fepple's death to look like suicide? Too subtle for my client. Maybe his wife had engineered it—she certainly had a temper. I could see her growing furious enough to shoot Fepple or me or any number of people if they stepped in front of her gun.

I shook my head. The shot that killed Fepple hadn't

been fired in rage: someone had gotten close enough to put a gun in Fepple's mouth. Stunning him first, or having an accomplice who stunned him first. Vishnikov told me the whole job had looked professional. That didn't fit Margaret Sommers's angry profile.

I had forgotten breakfast while I was talking to her. It was after ten; I was suddenly very hungry. I walked down the street to the Belmont Diner, the last vestige of the shops and eateries of Lakeview's old working-class neighborhood. While I waited for a Spanish omelette, I called my lawyer, Freeman Carter. Isaiah Sommers's most urgent need was for expert counsel, which I had promised Margaret Sommers before we hung up. She had bristled at my offer of help: they had a very good lawyer in their church who could take care of Isaiah.

"Which matters more to you? Saving your husband or saving your pride?" I'd asked; after a pregnant pause she muttered she guessed they'd take a look at my lawyer, but if they didn't trust him right off they wouldn't keep him.

Freeman quickly took in my sketch of the situation. "Right, Vic. I have an assistant who can go down to the Twenty-first District for the time being. You have an alternative theory of the murder?"

"Fepple's last known appointment was on Friday night with a woman from Ajax Insurance. Connie Ingram." I didn't like tossing her to the wolves, but I wasn't going to have the state's attorney railroad my client, either. I told Freeman about the situation with the Sommers policy documents. "Someone in the company doesn't want those papers around, but my client couldn't possibly be the one who stole the microfiche out of the Ajax claims-department file cabinets. Of course, the company may say I did it for him—but we can cross that bridge if the road goes that far."

"And did you, Vic?" Freeman was at his dryest.

"Scout's honor, no, Freeman. I'm as hot to see those

documents as every other person in this benighted town, but so far I've only looked at one sanitized version. I'll keep sniffing around for evidence about the murder, in case the worst happens and we have to go to trial."

Barbara, the waitress who's worked at the Belmont Diner longest, brought my omelette as Freeman hung up. "You know, you look like every other Yuppie in Lakeview with that thing stuck to your ear, Vic."

"Thanks, Barbara. I try to fit into my surroundings."

"Well, don't make a habit of it: we're thinking of banning them altogether. I'm sick of people shouting their business to an empty table."

"What can I say, Barbara? When you're right, you're right. You want to put my food under the heat lamp while I go outside for my next call?"

She snorted and moved to the next table: the place was filling with people on their morning coffee breaks—the mechanics and repairmen who keep the area Yuppies comfortable. I ate half the omelette quickly, taking the edge off my hunger, before phoning Amy Blount. A strange woman answered, checking my identity before passing me on to Ms. Blount.

Like Margaret Sommers, Amy Blount was angry, but she was more restrained about it: she wished I had gotten back to her sooner—she was under considerable stress and hated hanging about for my phone call. How soon could I get down to Hyde Park?

"I don't know. What's the problem?"

"Oh. I've told the story so many times I forgot you don't know it. I had a break-in at my apartment."

She had come home at ten last night from a lecture in Evanston to find her papers strewn about, her computer damaged, and her floppy disks missing. When she called the cops, they didn't take it seriously.

"But those are my dissertation notes. They're irreplaceable. I have the dissertation written up and bound, but the notes, I would use those for another book. The police don't understand, they say it's impossible to track down all the burglaries in the city, and since no valuables are missing—well, I don't have valuables, just my computer."

"How did the intruders get in?"

"Through the back door. Even though I have a gate across it, they broke through it without any of the neighbors paying the least attention. Hyde Park is supposed to be such a liberal neighborhood, but everyone scuttles away at the first sign that anyone around them is in trouble," she added bitterly.

"Where are you?" I asked.

"At a friend's. I couldn't stay in the middle of all that mess, and I didn't want to clean it up until someone saw it who would pay attention to the problem."

I took her friend's address and told her either I or Mary Louise would be there within the next two hours. She tried to argue me into coming sooner, but I explained that emergency detectives were like emergency plumbers: we had to fit the job in around all the other broken boilers.

I finished the omelette but skipped the steak fries— my usual weakness, but if I ate one I'd eat them all, and then I'd be too logy to think very fast. And the day was looking like one that would require Einstein-like thought. I didn't wait for my bill but put fifteen dollars on the table and trotted back up Racine to my car.

I had a couple of errands to run in the financial district before going in to my office. As I drove downtown, I called Mary Louise to make sure she was able to work some more hours this afternoon so that she could go see Amy Blount's apartment. She was pretty terse with me, but I told her she'd see me soon enough to off-load her complaints in person.

Since I was down by the City–County building anyway, I went inside to find Alderman Durham's office.

Naturally he had one on the South Side, in his own ward, but aldercreatures mostly hang out in the Loop, where the money and power are.

I scribbled a note on my card: *In re the widow's mite and Isaiah Sommers.* After a mere fifteen minutes' wait, the secretary scooted me ahead of other supplicants, who gave me dirty looks for jumping the queue.

The alderman had a young man with him wearing the navy blazer with the Empower Youth Energy insignia on it: a gold eye with *EYE on Youth* embroidered around it. The alderman himself was dressed in Harris tweed, his shirt having the palest green stripe in it to match the green in the tweed.

He shook my hand genially and waved me to a seat. "So you have something to say about the widow's mite, Ms. Warshawski?"

"Have you kept up with that story, alderman? You know Margaret Sommers took your advice and insisted on a meeting with the agent, Howard Fepple, only to walk in and find him dead?"

"I'm sorry to hear it: that must have been a shock for her."

"She got a worse one this morning. Her husband has been brought in for questioning—the cops got a tip. They think he murdered Fepple—out of outrage over the guy robbing his aunt of her mite, so to speak."

He nodded slowly. "I can understand their reasoning, but I'm sure Isaiah wouldn't have killed a man. I've known him for years, you see, for years, because his aunt, bless her, had a son who was one of my boys before he passed. Isaiah is a fine man, a churchgoing man. I don't see him as a murdering man."

"Do you see who might have phoned in an anonymous tip to the police, alderman? Their technicians say they're pretty sure it was an African-American male who made the call."

He gave a great mirthless smile. "And you thought

to yourself, Who do I know who's an African-American male? Louis Durham. We're all alike, after all, we black men: animals at heart, aren't we."

I looked at him steadily. "I thought to myself, Who has been having surreptitious meetings with the European chief of the insurance company that holds the paper on Aaron Sommers? I thought to myself, I don't see what enticements those two men could offer each other—kill the Holocaust Asset Recovery Act in exchange for shutting down the demonstrations outside the Ajax building? But what if Mr. Rossy wanted something more—what if he wanted Isaiah Sommers to take the fall for the murder so that he could close the claim file and get the mess out of his hair? What if in exchange for shutting off your demonstration *and* getting someone to finger Isaiah Sommers, Rossy said he'd fly to Springfield to kill the IHARA bill for you?"

"You have a reputation as an investigator, Warshawski. This isn't worthy of you." Durham stood and moved to the door; the young man in the EYE blazer followed him.

I perforce got up to leave, as well. "Yes, but remember, Durham, I'm shameless—you wrote that on your placards yourself."

I picked up my car from the West Loop garage where I'd parked, more puzzled than angered by the encounter. What had he hoped to learn from me that got me in to see him so readily? What were he and Rossy doing together? Had one of his people really made that phone call that led to Isaiah Sommers's arrest? I couldn't put the pieces together in any meaningful way.

I was negotiating the tricky intersection at Armitage, where three streets come together underneath the Kennedy Expressway, when Tim Streeter called. "Vic, not to alarm you, but there's a bit of a situation."

My heart skipped a beat. "Calia? What's happened?

Where are you? Oh, help, hang on." I laid down rubber under the Kennedy, forced a semi turning onto the expressway to stand on his brakes with a loud blaring of his horn, and pulled into a gas station on the other side.

"Vic, calm down. The kid's here with me; we're at the Children's Museum in Wilmette. Agnes is fine. It's at the hospital. This guy Posner, you know, the one who's been—"

"Yeah, yeah, I know who he is."

"Okay, he's shown up at the hospital with a group of pickets denouncing Mr. Loewenthal and Dr. Herschel for keeping Jewish families apart. The kid and I were supposed to drop in on Mr. Loewenthal for a brown-bag lunch—Mom's working on her presentation for the gallery—but when we got to the hospital, Posner and his gang were out in force."

"Oh, *damn* him and the horse he rode in on, too." So much adrenaline was running through me that I was ready to bounce up to Bryn Mawr Avenue and take Posner apart with my own hands. "Radbuka there?"

"Yeah. That's when we got a bit of a situation: I didn't realize what it was at first, thought it might be a labor dispute or right-to-lifers. Wasn't until we got close up that I made out the signs. And then Radbuka saw the kid and wanted to make a move on her. I hustled her out of there but the cameras were rolling; she may be on TV tonight. Hard to say. Called Mr. Loewenthal from the car and came on up here."

He interrupted himself briefly to talk to Calia, who was whining in the background that she needed to see her Opa *now*. "I'd better go, but I told Mr. Loewenthal if he needs extra support to call my brother. I'll stick with the little one."

When we'd hung up I sat with my head in my hands, trying to order my mind. I couldn't just fly north to the hospital without doing something for Isaiah Sommers.

I forced myself to continue to my office, where Mary Louise greeted me with a severe reprimand over once again making myself so inaccessible overnight: it was no way to run this kind of business. If I wanted to unplug myself from the world to sleep, I should let her know so she could cover for me.

"You're right. It won't happen again—put it down to sleep deprivation clouding my judgment. Here's what's going on, though." I sketched out the situations with Sommers, with Amy Blount, and now the demonstration outside Beth Israel. "I can understand why Radbuka wants to hook up with Posner, but what does Posner get out of attacking Max and Lotty? He went to see Rossy last night—I'm wondering if Rossy somehow set him on to Beth Israel."

"Who knows why someone like Posner does anything?" Mary Louise said impatiently. "Look, I only have two more hours to give you today. I don't think it's very helpful for you if I spend it going over conspiracy theories. And really, Vic—it makes sense for me to deal with Sommers's situation—I can call the Finch to get the details of the investigation and give Freeman's assistant some support. But why did you agree to go all the way down to the South Side for this Amy Blount? The cops are right, you know—this kind of B&E is a dime a dozen. We just file reports—they do, I mean— and keep a lookout for stolen goods. If she didn't lose anything valuable, why waste your time on it?"

I grinned. "Conspiracy theory, Mary Louise. She wrote a history for Ajax. Ralph Devereux and Rossy are all hot on who's stealing Ajax files, or leaking Ajax files to Durham—at least, they were worrying about that last week. Maybe Rossy's spiked Durham's guns for now. If Amy Blount's papers and floppies have been rifled, I want to know what's missing. Is it something the alderman wanted for his campaign on slave reparations? Or is there really some junkie out there who's so addled that he thinks he can sell history papers for enough money to buy a fix?"

She scowled. "It's your business. Just remember when you're writing the rent and insurance checks in two weeks why you don't have more cash flow this month."

"But you will go down to Hyde Park to look over Ms. Blount's place? After you've gotten Sommers's situation squared away with the Finch?"

"Like I said, Vic, it's your business, it's your money to waste. But quite frankly, I can't see what good I'll do you by going to Hyde Park, or what benefit you'll get from joining Joseph Posner up at the hospital."

"I'll have a chance to talk to Radbuka, which I've been desperate for. And maybe I'll find out what Rossy and Posner had to say to each other."

She sniffed and turned to the phone. While she called the Finch—Terry Finchley, her old commanding officer from her days in the Central District—I went to my own desk. I had a handful of messages, one from an important client, and a half dozen e-mails. I dealt with them as quickly as I could and took off.

XXXIV

Road Rage, Hospital Rage,
Any Old Rage

The hospital was on the city's northwest side, far enough from the trendy neighborhoods that nearby traffic usually flowed fast. Today, though, when I was about a mile away, the main road got so heavy I tried the side streets. Five blocks from Beth Israel, I came to a total halt. I looked around frantically for an alley so I could escape to an alternate route, but as I was about to make a U-turn, it dawned on me that if the jam came from gapers rubbernecking at Posner's demonstrators, traffic would be blocked on all sides of Beth Israel. I pulled over to an empty meter and sprinted the last half mile.

Sure enough, I found Posner and several dozen protesters in the middle of the kind of crowd he seemed to adore. Chicago cops were furiously directing traffic at the intersection; staff in green-and-gold hospital security blazers were trying to guide patients to side entrances; television crews were filming. The last had attracted a crowd of gawkers. It was just on one—anyone coming back from lunch had probably stopped to enjoy the show.

I was too far back to read the signs, but I could hear

a chant that chilled my heart: *Max and Lotty, have a heart! Don't smash survivors' lives apart!*

I ran around to the back, to the service entrance, where I opened my wallet and flashed my PI license in the face of a security guard so fast he couldn't tell whether it was an FBI badge or a credit card. By the time he'd figured that out, I had disappeared into the labyrinth of halls and stairwells that make security at any hospital a nightmare.

I tried to keep my bearings but still ended up in radiation oncology and file storage before finding the main lobby. I could hear shouting from the group outside, but I couldn't see anything: Beth Israel is an old brick building, without a plate-glass front or even any windows low enough to see outside. Hospital guards, who were completely unused to this kind of chaos, were doing an ineffectual job of keeping gawkers from blocking the main entrance. An older woman sobbed helplessly to one side that she'd just had outpatient surgery, that she needed a taxi to get home, while a second woman with a newborn looked around anxiously for her husband.

I stared at the scene for an appalled moment, then told the guards to keep people away from the door. "Tell them that anyone who obstructs the entryway is facing a fine. The back exit is free and clear—get these patients out through there. Send an SOS to the cab companies to use the rear."

I watched until the startled guard started giving orders through his walkie-talkie before I marched down the corridor to Max's office. Cynthia Dowling, Max's secretary, interrupted a heated telephone exchange when she saw me.

"Cynthia, why doesn't Max get the cops to arrest that group of yahoos?"

She shook her head. "The board's afraid of alienating major donors. Beth Israel is one of the big Jewish charities in town. Most of the calls we've been getting since Posner hit the news have agreed with you, but old Mrs. Felstein is one of Posner's supporters—she survived the war in hiding in Moldavia, you know, but when she came here she made a fortune in gum balls. Lately she's been active in lobbying Swiss banks to release Holocaust victims' assets. And she's pledged twenty million dollars for our new oncology wing."

"So if she sees Posner carried off to a paddy wagon she'll cancel? But if someone who's having a heart attack dies because they can't get here, you'd face a lawsuit that would more than offset any pledge she made."

"That's Max's decision. His and the board's, and of course they're aware of the pitfalls." Her phone console started to blink; she pressed a button. "Mr. Loewenthal's office . . . No, I know you have a one-thirty deadline. As soon as Mr. Loewenthal is available I'll let him have your message. . . . Yes, I wish we weren't in the business of saving lives here; it would make us better able to drop everything to respond to media deadlines. Mr. Loewenthal's office, please hold. . . . Mr. Loewenthal's office, please hold." She looked at me, distracted, with her hand over the phone. "This place is so inefficient. The stupid temp the clerical pool sent me went to lunch an hour ago. She's probably out front enjoying the show, and even though I'm the executive director's secretary, the clerical office won't send me another backup."

"Okay, okay, I'll leave you to it. I have some questions for Posner—tell Max if you see him that I won't implicate the hospital."

When I got to the main lobby, I elbowed my way through to the front of the crowd, which was once again pushing against the revolving doors. As soon as I got outside I saw the reason for their avidity: the demonstrators had stopped marching and were clumped together behind Joseph Posner, who was shouting at a small woman in a hospital coat, "You're the worst kind of anti-Semite, a traitor to your own people."

"And you, Mr. Posner, are the worst kind of abuser of human emotion, exploiting the horrors of Treblinka for your own aggrandizement."

I would have known that voice anywhere, anger making her clip off words like so many cigar ends. I pushed past two of Posner's Maccabees to reach her side. "Lotty, what are you doing here? This is a losing battle—attention is this guy's meat and drink."

Posner, his nostrils flaring with anger, his mouth distorted in defiance, looked like a picture captioned *The gladiator waiting for the lion* in my childhood *Illustrated History of Rome*.

Lotty, a small but ferocious lion, shook me off. "Mind your own business for once, Victoria. This man is defaming the dead for his own glory. And he's defaming me."

"Then we'll take it to a court of law," I said. "There are television cameras catching every word on tape."

"Go ahead, take me to court, if you dare." Posner turned as he spoke, to make sure both his supporters and the reporters heard him. "I don't care if I spend five years in jail, if that will make the world understand my people's cause."

"Your people?" I kept my voice light, scornful. "Are you Moses now?"

"Will it make you happier if I call them my 'followers,' or my 'team'? Whatever you call them, they understand that it may be necessary to suffer or make sacrifices to get where we want to be. They understand that some of that suffering can take the form of ridicule from ignorant secularists like yourself, or this doctor here."

"What about the suffering of patients?" I asked. "An

elderly woman can't get home after surgery because you've blocked the front door. If her family sues you for millions in damages, will 'your people' understand that?"

"Victoria, I don't need you to fight my battles for me," Lotty said, her voice tight with anger. "Or to draw this imbecile's fire."

I ignored her. "By the way, Mr. Posner, you know that 'your people' have to keep moving—they can be arrested if they stand around gawking."

"I hardly need a strange woman to instruct me in the law," Posner said, but he gestured to his followers to start circling again.

Paul Radbuka was hovering near Posner's elbow, his mobile clown's face registering first delight at Posner's rebuttal, derision as Lotty spoke—and anger as he suddenly recognized me. "Reb Joseph, this woman—she's a detective, she's my enemy, she's the person who's turning my family against me."

The television crews, which had been focusing their cameras on Lotty and Posner, suddenly switched to Radbuka and me. Beyond the lights I heard someone say, "Is that Warshawski, the detective? What's she doing here?" Beth Blacksin called excitedly, "Vic, has the hospital hired you to investigate Posner's claims? Are you working for Max Loewenthal?"

I cupped my hands around my eyes so I could see past the glare of the camera lights. "I have a private question for Mr. Posner, Beth. It's not anything to do with the hospital."

I tapped Posner on the arm, telling him I'd like him to come with me away from the cameras. Posner said sternly that he couldn't talk privately with a woman.

I smiled brightly. "Don't worry: if your impulses get the better of you I can break one of your arms. Maybe both. But if you prefer, I can ask my question out loud on camera."

"Everything I have to say about this Lotty Herschel and about you, too, can be on camera," Radbuka butted in. "You think you can come up here to keep me away from my family, just like you hired that bully to stay with my little cousin over at Max's, but you won't get away with it. Rhea and Don are going to help me take my story to the world."

Posner tried to get Radbuka to be quiet, telling him he'd take care of the detective. To me he added that he had nothing to hide.

"Bertrand Rossy," I said softly, then looked toward the cameras and raised my voice. "Beth, I'm asking Mr. Posner about his meeting—"

With a rough gesture Posner turned his back to the cameras. "I don't know what you think you know, but you'd be making a mistake to talk about him on television."

"What meeting, Mr. Posner?" one of the reporters asked. "Is this anything to do with the defeat of the Asset Recovery bill on Tuesday?"

"You know I'm going to ask you about him, about why you pulled your demonstration away from Ajax," I said softly to Posner. "It's up to you whether it's on- or off-mike. You like publicity, and they are using directional mikes, so if I raise my voice, they'll pick up our conversation even if they're not right on top of us."

Posner couldn't afford to look indecisive in front of his troops. "Just to keep you from defaming my movement on television, I will talk to you away from the hospital. But not alone."

He called to another man to join him, ordering the rest of the group to wait in the group's bus until he got back. The television crews watched in astonishment as the demonstrators drifted off toward the parking lot, then they plunged forward with a babble of excited questions for Posner and me: what had made him decide to cancel the demonstration?

"We achieved our goals this afternoon," Posner said grandly. "We have made the hospital realize that Jewish-backed institutions are just as liable as secular ones to become complacent and indifferent to Jewish needs. We will be back, however: Max Loewenthal and Charlotte Herschel can feel assured of that."

"What about you, Dr. Herschel? What do you think of their assertion that you're keeping Paul Radbuka from his family?"

She curled her lip. "I'm a surgeon with a full-time practice: I don't have time for comic books. In fact, this man has kept me from my patients for long enough."

She turned on her heel and went back into the hospital. The reporters surged forward, wanting to know what I'd said to Posner. Who was my client? Did I suspect fraud in Posner's group, or in the hospital? Who was financing the demonstrations?

I told Beth and the other reporters that as soon as I had interesting information I'd share it with them—but that for right now I didn't know about any fraud involving Posner or the hospital.

"But, Beth," I added, "what brought you up here?"

"We were tipped off, you know how that works, Warshawski." She gave me an urchin's grin. "Not by him, though—a woman called the station. Could have been anyone, though."

Posner, annoyed that I'd stolen the limelight, snarled at me to come with him if I wanted to talk to him: he didn't have all day to spend on foolish women with imaginary ideas. He moved rapidly down the drive with his chosen henchman; I lengthened my stride to catch up with him.

A couple of reporters kept up a halfhearted pursuit. Radbuka, who hadn't followed the other demonstrators to the bus, began declaiming that Max was his cousin but wouldn't admit it, and I was the beast of Babylon who was keeping Max from talking to him, but the reporters already had that story; they weren't interested in the rerun. If I wasn't going to give the cameras raw meat, there wasn't anything to keep them around Beth Israel any longer. The crews wrapped up their equipment and headed to their vans.

XXXV

Amateur Sleuth

The crowd, realizing the show was over because the cameras had disappeared, began drifting away. By the time Posner and I were at the corner of Catalpa, the driveway in front of the hospital was almost empty. I laughed to myself: I should send Max a bill for this.

I turned to see what Radbuka was doing. He stood alone at the bottom of the drive, his hurt feelings at being abandoned by both Posner and the cameras darkening his mobile face. He looked around uncertainly, then ran down the street after us.

I turned back to Posner, who was impatiently tapping his watch. "So, Mr. Posner. Let's talk about you and Bertrand Rossy."

"I have nothing to say about him." His chin jutted out at a lofty angle: the Gladiator is not afraid of Death.

"Nothing about your meeting with him last night? Nothing about how he persuaded you to abandon your protest outside Ajax for one here at Beth Israel?"

He stopped in the middle of the sidewalk. "Whoever told you I met with him is lying. I have private reasons for being here. They have nothing to do with Rossy."

"Let's not start our nice little chat with accusations about lying: I saw you at Rossy's place—I had dinner with him and his wife last night."

"I didn't see you!"

"Now, that disclaimer is pretty pure proof that you were there." I gave a supercilious smile: Posner was so used to being the daddy in the story that I figured the way to keep him rattled was to treat him as if I found him childish.

"Reb Joseph, I don't think you should talk any more to this woman," the sidekick said. "She's trying to trick you into saying something that will discredit us. Remember what Radbuka said, that she's been keeping him from his family."

"That's not true, either," I said. "I'm eager for Paul to rejoin his true family. But I'm curious about the situation between your Holocaust Asset Recovery group and Ajax Insurance. I know you know Preston Janoff was in Springfield yesterday, killing the Illinois Asset Recovery Act, so what made you abandon Ajax? I'd think today your wrath against them would be greater than ever. My bet is that Bertrand Rossy told you something last night, or offered you a nice little bribe, that made you withdraw from the Loop to come up here."

"You're right, Leon." Posner turned away from me. "This woman doesn't know anything—she's playing a guessing game to keep us from disturbing her rich friends at the hospital."

Even though I was getting tired of being "this woman" instead of having a name, I kept my voice genial. "I may not know anything, but I can make guesses that Beth Blacksin at Global will listen to. And believe me, I did see you at the Rossys' last night—if I tell her that, she'll be parked on your doorstep for a week."

Posner had turned to leave, but at that he looked back at me, darting a worried glance at Leon, then up the street to see if the cameras were there.

I smiled. "I know that you were furious when you got to Rossy's place, so I figure it was because you knew he was talking to Alderman Durham: you were afraid Ajax was going to offer Durham some special deal that would undercut your movement.

"Rossy refused at first to see you at all when you showed up in the lobby, but you threatened over the house phone to expose him for doing business with Durham. Even so, Rossy said he wouldn't see you if Durham learned you were there. You arrived at Rossy's place angry, but by the time you and he finished, you were all smiles again. So Rossy gave you something. Not money, perhaps. But information. He knows you're aggressive with Jewish-run institutions that you think are too secular, so maybe he told you something that combined both insurance and one of Chicago's leading Jewish charities, Beth Israel. You should bring your protest up here, he told you, force the media to shine a light on the hospital and Max Loewenthal."

Standing on the corner in front of the Cozy Cup Café, I gave Posner a chance to answer. He didn't say anything, but he was looking worried, nervously chewing his cheek.

"What could it have been? Did he say, Oh, the hospital has been denying medical benefits to Holocaust survivors? No, that would be too crude—the media would have been all over that one. Maybe he said, Oh, Max Loewenthal got some kind of big bond package for the hospital in exchange for helping kill the bill. It sounds crazy, of course, because it is crazy, and in your heart of hearts you know any suggestion Rossy made is crazy. If you didn't, you'd be blaring it to the world. But

Bertrand Rossy would be happy because it would distract public attention from Ajax's role in killing the Asset Recovery Act. How am I doing? Is this the story you want me to share with Beth Blacksin and the rest of Chicago? That you're Bertrand Rossy's dupe?"

While I was speaking, Radbuka kept trying to interrupt, to say they were here strictly on the issue of Max and his family, but I raised my voice and talked past him.

Posner kept chewing his cheek. "You can't prove any of this."

"Very lame, Mr. Posner. After all, you're making accusations against Beth Israel that you can't prove. I *can* prove that you spent fifteen minutes with Bertrand Rossy last night. I don't have to prove that your conversation followed my story line—I only have to start the story moving around Chicago. The wires and Internet services will take it from there, because Rossy means Edelweiss, which means not only local but also international news."

"Are you trying to imply that I'm selling out the IHARA Committee?" Posner demanded.

I shook my head. "I don't know if you are or not. But of course if your group finds out that you wasted precious resources on a wild-goose chase, I don't expect they'll be very supportive of your leadership."

"Whatever you may choose to believe, I take our mission with utter seriousness. Alderman Durham may be on the streets for votes. He may leave the streets for money, but neither of these—"

"You know that Rossy offered him money to shut down his protest?" I interrupted.

He pressed his lips together without answering.

"But you did follow Durham to Rossy's place last night. Do you follow him every night?"

"Reb Joseph isn't like you," Radbuka burst out. "He doesn't set out to spy on people, make their lives miserable, deny them their rights. Everything he does is aboveboard. Anyone could tell you that Rossy talked to Durham last night: we all saw Durham go over to Rossy's car when it was stuck in traffic on Adams."

"What? Did Durham get in with Rossy?"

"No, he leaned over to talk to him. We could all see Rossy's face when he opened the window, and Leon said, Hey, that's the guy who's really running Ajax these—"

"Shut up," Leon said. "You weren't asked to take part in this conversation. Go wait in the bus with the rest of the group until Reb Joseph has finished with this woman."

Radbuka stuck out his lower lip in a babyish pout. "You can't order me around. I sought out Reb Joseph because he's doing something for people like me whose lives were destroyed by the Holocaust. I didn't risk being arrested today so I could be bossed around by a loser like you."

"Look, Radbuka, you only came along to take advantage—"

"Leon, Paul," Posner chided them, "this is only grist for this woman's mill, to see us fighting each other. Save your energies for our common enemies."

Leon subsided, but Paul wasn't part of the movement; he didn't need to obey Posner any more than he did Leon. In one of his rapid mood shifts, he turned angrily on Posner. "I only came along on your march last night and this one today to get help in getting to my family. Now you're accusing my cousin Max of cutting secret deals with the Illinois legislature. Do you think I'm related to someone who would act like that?"

"No," I put in quickly, "I don't think your relatives would do anything so awful. What happened last night, after Durham talked to Rossy on the street? Did they drive off together? Or did the cops take Durham in a separate car?"

"I didn't know the police took him," Radbuka said, ignoring shushing gestures from Posner and Leon, responsive as usual to anyone paying him serious attention—even when it was an ostensible enemy like myself. "All I know is Durham went off and got in his own car: we walked down to the corner of Michigan and saw him. It was parked right there in a no-parking zone, but of course he had a policeman guarding it, sleazebag that he is. And Reb Joseph didn't trust Durham, so he decided to follow him."

"Very enterprising." I smiled patronizingly at Posner. "So you skulked around in the bushes outside Rossy's building until you saw Durham come out. And then Rossy, who's got a lot of charm, talked you into believing some stupid rumor about the hospital."

"It wasn't like that, not at all," Posner snapped. "When I saw him with Durham, I wanted to see—I'd been aware for some time that Durham was trying to sabotage our efforts to force European banks and insurers to provide redress for the outright theft which they engineered in the wake of—"

"You can assume I understand the underlying issue, Mr. Posner. But Durham didn't manufacture the grounds for his protest. There's a growing group of people who believe companies which benefited from African slavery should pay reparations in the same way that companies which benefited from Jewish or Polish slave labor should."

His beard jutted toward me at an aggressive angle. "That's a separate issue. We're concerned about actual money, in bank accounts and unpaid life-insurance policies, that European banks and insurers have stolen. You've been working for one black man in Chicago whose claim was denied after he paid up his policy. I'm trying to do the same for tens of thousands of people whose parents thought they were leaving their children a financial cushion. And I wanted to know why Louis

Durham showed up outside Ajax so conveniently—he never started campaigning for slave reparations until we started our campaign to force Ajax to pay off life-insurance policies."

I was startled. "So you thought Rossy was bribing him to march against you? To disrupt operations at his own company? You should take it to Oliver Stone! But I guess you took it to Rossy himself. Did he say, Yes, yes, I confess: if you'll only picket Beth Israel instead of Ajax I'll stop giving money to Louis Durham?"

"Are you being stupid on purpose?" Posner spat at me. "Naturally Rossy denied any collusion. But he also assured me he would do a thorough internal search for any policies at Ajax or Edelweiss that belonged to Holocaust victims."

"And you believed him?"

"I gave him a week. He convinced me he was serious enough to have one week."

"Then what are you doing here?" I asked. "Why not give the boys some time off?"

"He came to help me." Paul Radbuka, pink with excitement, turned on me as suddenly as he'd accepted me a moment earlier. "Just because you won't let me see my family, just because you hired that—that Brownshirt to keep me from talking to my little cousin, that doesn't mean they're not my family. Let Max Loewenthal see how it feels to be ostracized for a change."

"Paul, you really need to understand that he is not related to you. You are not only making them and yourself miserable by stalking Mr. Loewenthal's family, you are running a serious risk of being arrested. Believe me, life in prison is terrible."

Radbuka scowled. "Max is the one who belongs in prison, treating me with this kind of contempt."

I looked at him, baffled about how to penetrate his dense cloud of denial. "Paul, who was Ulrich, really?"

"That was my foster father. Are you going to try to make me confess he was my real father? I won't! He wasn't!"

"But Rhea says that Ulrich wasn't his name."

His face turned from pink to red. "Don't try to call Rhea a liar. You're the liar. Ulrich left behind documents in code. They prove that my name is really Radbuka. If you believed in Rhea you'd understand the code, but you don't, you're trying to destroy her, you want to destroy me, I won't let you, I won't, I won't, I won't!"

I watched in alarm as he began shaking, wondering if he was having a seizure of some kind. When I moved to try to help him, Posner barked at me to keep my distance: he was not going to allow a woman to touch one of his followers, even if Radbuka himself was not aware of the danger a woman's touch posed. He and Leon supported Radbuka over to a bench at the bus stop. I watched for a moment, but Radbuka seemed to be calming down. I left the men to it and walked slowly up the street back to the hospital, hoping for a word with Max before returning to my office.

"Posner made a certain kind of sense," I told Max, when his weary secretary got him to give me five minutes, "with his ideas about Ajax bribing Durham to start demonstrating, but really, he must be as crazy as Paul Radbuka to stage a demonstration here. How are things going with your donors?"

Max doesn't often look his age, but this afternoon his skin was drawn tight and grey across his cheekbones. "I don't understand any of this, Victoria. Morrell's friend Don Strzepek came over last night. In good faith I let him look at my old notes; I thought he believed them. Surely a friend of Morrell's wouldn't have been abusing my trust?"

"But those notes—they don't have enough detail about the Radbukas for anyone to know if this guy

Paul is a relative or not—unless there's something in your file I didn't see?"

He made a tired gesture. "Just that letter of Lotty's, which you read. Surely Don wouldn't have used that to encourage Paul to believe he was a relative, would he?"

"I don't think so, Max," I said, but not with total confidence: I was remembering the glow in Don's eyes when he looked at Rhea Wiell. "I can try to talk to him tonight, though, if you'd like."

"Yes, why don't you do that." He sat heavily at his desk, his face an effigy. "I never thought I would be happy to see the last of my family, but I will be glad when Calia and Agnes get on that plane."

XXXVI

Rigmarole: New Word for the Same Old Story

I slowly walked back to my car and drove down to my office, obeying every speed limit, every traffic sign. The morning's adrenaline-fueled fury was long gone. I stared at the stack of messages Mary Louise had left for me, then caught up with Morrell at his hotel in Rome, where it was nine at night. The conversation both cheered and further depressed me. He said the kinds of things one wants to hear from a lover, especially when the lover is about to go into the land of the Taliban for eight weeks. But when we hung up I felt more forlorn than ever.

I tried to take a nap on the cot in my back room, but my mind wouldn't shut down. I finally got up again and determinedly went through the messages, returning phone calls. Halfway through the pile was a note to call Ralph at Ajax: the company had decided to make the Sommers family whole. I got back to him at once.

"Mind you, Vic, this is a one-time-only event," Ralph Devereux warned when I called him. "Don't expect to make it a habit."

"Ralph, this is wonderful news—but whose idea was

it? Yours? Rossy's? Did Alderman Durham call and urge you on to do this?"

He ignored me. "And another thing: I would greatly appreciate it if you let me know the next time you sic the cops on my employees."

"You're right, Ralph. I got caught up in an emergency at a hospital, but I should have called you. Did they arrest Connie Ingram?"

Mary Louise had left a typed report about Sommers and about Amy Blount which I was trying to scan while I talked: between Mary Louise's police contacts and Freeman Carter's skill, the state had let Isaiah Sommers go home, but they'd made it clear he was their frontrunner. The trouble was not his prints on the door per se: the Finch said the 911 techs had confirmed what the Twenty-first District cops had told Margaret Sommers: they'd received an anonymous phone tip—probably from a black male—which was what made them print the room.

"No. But they came right here to the building to question her."

"Right to the sacred halls of Ajax itself?"

When he sputtered a request to can the sarcasm, that it disrupted everyone's workday to have cops in the building, I added, "Connie Ingram was lucky, lucky to be a white female. Maybe it's embarrassing to have the cops question you in your office, but they took my client away from his workstation in cuffs. They hauled him over to Twenty-ninth and Prairie for a chat in a windowless room with a bunch of guys watching through the one-way glass. He's only eating at home tonight because I hired him the best criminal lawyer in town."

Ralph brushed that aside. "Karen Bigelow—Connie's supervisor, remember?—Karen sat in on the interrogation along with one of our lawyers. Connie was extremely upset, but the police seemed to believe her, or at least they didn't arrest her. The trouble is, Vic, they pulled phone records for Fepple's office and found several calls from her extension, including one the day before he was killed. She says she did call him, several times, to get him to fax his copies of the Sommers documents to her. But Janoff is pissed at having cops in the place, Rossy is pissed, and frankly, Vic, I'm not very happy myself."

I put down the notes to give him my full attention. "Poor Connie: it's a hard reward for doing your duty, to be grilled by the cops. I hope the company doesn't abandon her.

"Ralph, what deal did Rossy do with Durham and Posner to get them to call off their protests?"

"What the hell are you talking about?" He suddenly was really angry, not just blustering.

"I mean that Rossy swung down Adams Street yesterday while I was upstairs with you. He called Durham over to his car, met with him an hour later at his home, and finished up by talking privately to Joseph Posner. Today Posner was picketing Beth Israel Hospital, while Durham's left the arena. I called City Hall just now—Durham was in his office listening to pleas for exceptions to zoning ordinances in Stewart Ridge."

Ralph blew frosty air across the line to me. "Is it so strange that the managing director tries for a one-on-one with the guys who want to shut down his company? He's stuck in traffic like every other stiff in the Loop last night and sees his chance. Don't try to spin that into a conspiracy for me."

"Ralph, remember when we met? Remember how you got that bullet in your shoulder?"

The memory still rankled, how his boss had betrayed both him and the company. "What could Rossy possibly be doing that would involve a worthless agent on Chicago's South Side? Edelweiss couldn't have anything to do with Howard Fepple. Use your head, Vic."

"I'm trying, but it isn't telling me anything very intelligible. Listen, Ralph, I know you have mixed feelings about me, but you're a savvy insurance guy. Put these things together for me: all the Sommers documents disappear, except for the paper file—about which you think there's something amiss, although you can't put your finger on it—and that file spent a week in Rossy's office.

"Throw this in: either Connie Ingram or someone pretending to be her set up a date with Fepple for last Friday night. Who besides Ajax personnel knew she'd been talking to him? Next, Fepple's dead, and his copy of the file disappears, and Rossy invites me to dinner, very much on the spur of the moment. Whereupon Fillida and her Italian friends pump me in concert about Fepple, his death, and his files. And finally, there's that odd document I found in Fepple's papers, the one I showed you with Sommers's name on it. What does all this add up to in your mind?"

"That we dropped the ball on Sommers, and on Fepple," Ralph said coldly. "Preston Janoff's been over this with the head of agency management, wanting to know why we kept a relationship with a guy who produced a policy a month for us in his good years. Janoff's agreed to make the Sommers family whole: we'll send out a check tomorrow. On a total exception basis, as I said. But other than that—Vic, the Rossys' guests know you're a detective, they're avid about American crime, it's natural they should pump you. And tell me this: what earthly reason could Bertrand Rossy have for getting involved with a loser like Fepple, whom he never even heard of before last week?"

He was right. That was the crux of the problem. I couldn't think of a reason.

"Ralph, I was hearing last night that it's Fillida's money that runs Edelweiss, that Bertrand married the boss's daughter."

"That's not news. Her mother's family founded the company in the 1890's. They were Swiss, and they're still the majority shareholders."

"She's a funny woman. Very chic, very soft-spoken, but definitely in charge of what's said and done in the Rossy home. I gather she keeps close watch on what happens on Adams Street as well."

"Rossy's a substantial guy. Just because he married up doesn't mean he doesn't do the job well. Anyway, I don't have time for gossip about my managing director's wife. I have work to do."

"Oh, kiss my mistletoe," I said, but the line was dead.

I dialed back into Ajax and asked for Rossy's office. His secretary, the cool, well-groomed Suzanne, put me on hold. Rossy came on in a surprisingly short time.

When I thanked him for last night's dinner, he said, "My wife so enjoyed meeting you last night. She says you are refreshing and original."

"I'll add that to my resumé," I said politely, which earned me one of his hearty laughs. "You must be pleased that Joseph Posner's stopped haunting the Ajax premises."

"Of course we are. Any day without a disturbance in a big company is a good one," he agreed.

"Yep. It may not surprise you to learn he's moved his protesters up to Beth Israel Hospital. He spun me some rigmarole, which he says you gave him, about you promising a private search of the Edelweiss and Ajax policies if he'd leave Ajax alone and haunt Beth Israel instead."

"I'm sorry? This word is new to me, rigmarole."

"Farrago—a bunch of nonsense. What could the hospital possibly have to do with missing Holocaust assets?"

"That I don't know, Ms. Warshawski, or Vic—I feel I can call you Vic after our friendly evening last night.

About the hospital and Holocaust assets you would have to talk to Max Loewenthal. Is that all? Did you discover any new or unusual information about that unusual piece of paper from Mr. Fepple's office?"

I sat up very straight: I could not afford to be inattentive. "The paper is at a lab, but they tell me it was made at a plant outside Basel sometime in the thirties. Does that ring a bell with you?"

"My mother was only just born in 1931, Ms. Warshawski, so paper from that era means very little to me. Does it mean anything to you?"

"Nothing yet, Mr. Rossy, but I'll keep your intense interest in it in mind. By the way, there's a rumor floating around the street. That Alderman Durham only started his campaign on slave reparations after Ajax got worried about the Holocaust Asset Recovery pressure. Have you heard that?"

His laugh bounced along the line again. "The bad thing about being a senior officer is that one becomes too isolated. I don't hear rumors, which is a pity as they are after all the oil that turns the industrial engine, are they not? That is an interesting rumor, certainly, definitely, but it is also news to me."

"I wonder if it's also news to Signora Rossy?"

This time he paused fractionally before continuing. "It will be when I tell her. As you gathered last night, no affair of Ajax is too small for her keen interest. And I will tell her we have another new English expression from you. Rigmarole. I left a meeting for this rigmarole. Good-bye."

What had that netted me? Just about nothing, but I dictated it to my word-processing center at once, so I could study it when I wasn't feeling so overwhelmed—I still had a bunch more calls to make.

I went back to Mary Louise's notes first, before calling my lawyer. Freeman, on the run as usual, said he was convinced personally of Isaiah Sommers's innocence, but the anonymous phone tip and the fingerprints weren't good signs.

"Then I guess we need to find the real killer," I said with dogged cheerfulness.

"I don't think the guy can afford your fee, Vic."

"He can't afford yours, either, Freeman, but I'm still asking you to look after him."

Freeman chuckled. "So this will get added to your unpaid balance?"

"I send you a big chunk of change every month," I protested.

"Yep. You've gotten the balance down to thirteen thousand—before Sommers's fees, of course. But you'll go find me some evidence? Excellent. I was sure we could count on you. In the meantime I keep reminding the state's attorney that Fepple had a date Friday night with someone using the name Connie Ingram. Whom he was anxious to keep you from seeing. I'm running, Vic—we'll talk tomorrow."

That outstanding balance at Freeman's was one of my biggest headaches. It had gotten out of hand last year when I'd had serious legal troubles, but even before that it had always hovered in the four-figure range. I've been putting a thousand on it every month, but it seems like every month I also generate some new need for his billable hours.

I called Isaiah Sommers. When I told him that someone had ratted him out to the cops, he was flabbergasted. "Who could have done that, Ms. Warshawski?"

"How do you know she didn't do it herself?" Margaret Sommers hissed on the extension.

"The cops had a tip. From a man, by the way, Ms. Sommers, who sounded African-American to them on the replay. My sources in the department say they're pretty sure the call really was anonymous. I will keep looking into the situation, but it would be helpful if you could tell me of anyone who hates you enough to turn you in for murder."

"You can't keep looking," he mumbled. "I can't afford to pay you."

"Don't worry about that part. The investigation is getting big enough that someone else will pay the bill." He didn't need to know the someone would be me. "By the way, not that it's much consolation when you're worrying about a murder charge, but Ajax is going to pay your aunt the value of the policy."

"Funny how that happened just as your bill was going to grow," Margaret snapped.

"Maggie, Maggie, please—she just said someone else would be taking care of her bill. Ms. Warshawski, this is wonderful news; Margaret, she's just worried. Like I am, too, of course, but Mr. Carter, he seems like a good lawyer. A real good lawyer. And he's sure you and he together can get this bad business straightened out."

It's good when the client is happy. Trouble was, he seemed to be alone in his good cheer. His wife was miserable. As was Amy Blount. And Paul Radbuka. Me. Max. And most especially Lotty.

She had left the hospital for her clinic after her confrontation with Posner, but when I phoned, Mrs. Coltrain said Dr. Herschel wouldn't interrupt her schedule to talk to me. I thought of her vehement outcry yesterday evening, that she'd never stinted a patient, that it was a relief to be in the hospital, to be the doctor, not the friend or the wife or the daughter.

"Oh, Lotty, who were the Radbukas?" I cried to the empty room. "Whom do you feel you betrayed?" Not a patient, she'd said that last night. Someone she'd turned her back on whose death consumed her with guilt. It had to have been someone in England—otherwise how had Questing Scorpio gotten the name? A relative was all I could imagine, perhaps a relative who appeared in England after the war that Lotty couldn't cope with. Someone she had loved in Vienna, but whom the horrors of war had so damaged that Lotty turned away from her. I could see it, could see doing it myself. So why couldn't she talk to me about it? Did she really think I would judge her?

I checked Questing Scorpio again, but there was still no response to my posting. What else could I do—besides go home to walk the dogs, make dinner, go to bed. Sometimes routine is soothing, but at other times it's a burden. I searched for Edelweiss on the Web to see if I could come up with any information about Fillida Rossy's family. I sent the query through both Lexis and ProQuest and went back to the phone, calling Don Strzepek.

He answered my greeting cautiously, remembering that we hadn't parted very cordially yesterday. "Any word from the intrepid journalist?"

"He's made it as far as Rome without a scratch. I guess they're off to Islamabad tomorrow."

"Don't worry about him, Vic: he's been in worse places than Kabul, hard as it is for me to think of any offhand. I mean, it's not a war zone these days—no one's going to shoot at him. He may get heckled, but he's more likely to be the object of curiosity, at least among the kids."

I felt a little better. "Don, on a different subject—what did you think after you saw Max's notebooks last night? Do you agree that he didn't know the Radbukas before he made that trip to Vienna after the war?"

"Yes, it was clearly Dr. Herschel's connection, more than Max's. Especially since it was she who fainted at the party on Sunday when she heard Sofie Radbuka's name. She seemed to have an awful lot of detail about exactly how to hunt down the apartment on the Leopoldsgasse," he added hesitantly. "I'm wondering if the Radbukas were her family."

"So Radbuka can start stalking her instead of Max? You know he was at Beth Israel today, with Posner and his Maccabees, screaming to the world that Lotty and Max were trying to keep Holocaust survivors from their birth families?"

"I know it must be painful for them, but Paul really is a tormented spirit, Vic. If he could just find someplace to anchor himself it would calm him down."

"Have you actually talked to the recovered-memory poster boy yourself?" I asked. "Is there any hope of getting him to show you those papers his father left behind? The ones that proved to him that his father was with the *Einsatzgruppen* and that he himself was a camp survivor named Radbuka?"

Don paused to make a hissing noise—presumably inhaling smoke. "I did meet him briefly this morning— I guess before he joined Posner at the hospital. He's pretty agitated these days. Rhea wouldn't let me ask him too many questions for fear of getting him more upset. He won't let me see the papers—he seems to think I might be a rival for Rhea's affection, so he's clamming up on me."

I couldn't suppress a snort of laughter. "I've got to hand it to Rhea for sticking with the guy. He'd have me in the locked ward at Elgin within a week if I tried to follow his gyrations around the dance floor. Although of course you are a rival, I can see his point of view. What does Rhea say?"

"She says she can't betray a patient confidence, which of course I respect her for. Although my old reporter's instincts make that hard to do." He gave a little laugh that managed to sound both rueful and admiring. "She encouraged his involvement with Posner because Posner's giving him a sense of real family. But of course we didn't know when we saw him they were going to go picket Max at the hospital. I'm seeing her for dinner tonight, so I'll talk to her about it then."

I made a little structure out of paper clips while I chose my words. "Don, I asked Radbuka today who Ulrich was, and he had kind of a fit on the street, saying it was his foster father's name and that I was accusing Rhea of being a liar. But you know, yesterday she made quite a point that Ulrich *wasn't* the guy's name. She even seemed to be laughing at me a little over that."

He sucked in another lungful of smoke. "I'd forgotten that. I can try to ask her again tonight, but—Vic, I'm not going to play man in the middle between you and Rhea."

"No, Don, I don't expect you to." All I wanted him to do was be on my side, pump her for information, and feed it to me. That wasn't really asking him to be in the middle. "But if you can persuade her that Max isn't related to the Radbuka family, maybe she in turn can persuade Paul to stop making a scene up at Beth Israel. Only, Don, for God's sake, please don't feed Lotty to Rhea as a substitute for Max. I don't know if the Radbukas were cousins or patients or enemy aliens in London whom Lotty was close to, but she won't survive the kind of harassment Paul's been giving Max."

I waited for his response, but he wouldn't promise me anything. I ended up slamming the phone down in disgust.

Before giving up detecting for the day, I also phoned Amy Blount. Mary Louise's report had said that the break-in at her place had been the work of a pro, not a random smash-and-grab. *The padlock on the gate was intact,* Mary Louise had written.

Someone had run a torch around it, taking the gate apart: the scorch marks on the kitchen door were obvious. Because you were interested in her connection to Ajax, I asked her specifically about any Ajax documents. She didn't have originals; she had scanned various 19th-century files to a floppy, which was missing. In fact, all her dissertation notes were missing. The perps damaged her computer as well. Nothing else was gone, not even her sound system. I talked Terry into sending down a proper forensics crew, but we're still not likely to find the perps.

I commiserated with Ms. Blount over her misery, then asked if her paper files had been tampered with.

"Oh, yes, those are gone, too, all my research notes. Who could want them? If I'd known I was sitting on such hot material I'd have published my dissertation by now; I'd have a real job, instead of hanging on in this rathole writing diddly corporate histories."

"Ms. Blount, what papers had you copied from the Ajax files?"

"I did not take classified internal documents. I did not hand confidential company information to Alderman Durham—"

"Ms. Blount, please, I know this has been a tough twenty-four hours, but don't jump on me. I'm asking for quite a different reason. I'm trying to figure out what is going on at Ajax Insurance these days."

I explained what had been happening since I'd visited her on Friday—primarily Fepple's death, Sommers's problems, Connie Ingram's name appearing on Fepple's appointment register. "The real oddity was the fragment of a document I found."

She listened carefully to everything I said, but my description of the handwritten document didn't sound like anything she'd seen. "I'll be glad to look at it—I could come by your office tomorrow sometime. Offhand it sounds like something out of an old ledger, but I can't interpret all those marks unless I see them. If it has your client's name on it, it would be recent, at least by my standards. The papers I copied dated from the 1850's, because my research is on the economics of slavery."

She was suddenly depressed again. "All that material is missing. I suppose I can go back to the archives and recopy it. It's the sense of violation that gets me down. And the pointlessness of it all."

XXXVII

My Kingdom for an Address

Melancholy gave me a restless night's sleep. I got up at six to run the dogs. I was in my office by eight-thirty, even though I stopped for breakfast again at the diner, even though I made a detour to Lotty's clinic on my way down. I didn't see her—she was still at the hospital making rounds.

As soon as Mary Louise came in, I sent her to the South Side to see if any of Sommers's friends could help figure out who had fingered him. I called Don Strzepek back, to see if he'd had any luck—or I'd had any luck—in getting Rhea to take Paul's harassment of Max seriously.

He gave an embarrassed cough. "She said she thought it was a sign of strength in him that he was making new friends, but she could see that he might need a greater sense of proportion."

"So she'll talk to him?" I couldn't keep the impatience out of my voice.

"She says she'll bring it up at his next regular appointment, but she can't take on the role of managing her patients' lives: they need to function in the real world, fall, pick themselves up, like everyone else. If they can't do that, then they need more help than she can give them. She's so amazing," he crooned, "I've never known anyone like her."

I cut him short halfway through his love song, asking him if that high-six-figure book advance was clouding his objectivity on Paul Radbuka. He hung up, hurt: I wasn't willing to discover Rhea's good points.

I was still snarling to myself over that conversation when Murray Ryerson called from the *Herald-Star*. Beth Blacksin had told him about my private conversation with Posner yesterday at the demonstration.

"For old times' sake, V I," he wheedled me. "Far off the record. What was that about?"

"Far off the record, Murray? May Horace Greeley rise from the dead and wither your testicles if you talk even to your mother about this, let alone Blacksin?"

"Scout's honor, Warshawski."

He had never betrayed such a confidence in the past. "Off the record, I don't know what it means, but Posner and Durham both had private audiences with Bertrand Rossy, the managing director of Edelweiss Re, who's in Chicago overseeing their takeover of Ajax. I was wondering if Rossy had offered Posner something to get him to stop protesting at Ajax and move on to Beth Israel, but I didn't get anywhere with asking Posner. He might talk to you—women scare him."

"Maybe it's just you, V I—you scare me and I'm twice Posner's size. Durham, though—no one's ever pinned anything on him, even though the mayor has the cops sticking to him like his underwear. Guy's one smooth operator. But if I learn something splendid about either of them I promise I'll share."

I felt a little better when I'd hung up: it was good to have some kind of ally. I took the L downtown to meet with clients who actually were paying me to do sophisticated work on their behalf and got back to my office a little before two. The phone was ringing as I unlocked the door. I got to it just as the answering service did. It was Tim Streeter; in the background I could hear Calia howling.

"Tim—what's going on?"

"We have a small situation here, Vic. I've been trying to call you for the last few hours, but you didn't have your phone on. Our pal was back this morning. I have to admit, my guard was down; I assumed he was concentrating on Posner these days. Anyway, you know he goes everywhere by bicycle? Calia and I were in the park on the swings, when he came roaring across the grass on his bike. He grabbed at Calia. Of course I had her in my arms before he touched her, but he got that Nibusher, you know, that little blue dog she takes everywhere."

Behind him I could hear Calia scream, "Not Nibusher, he's Ninshubur the faithful hound. He misses me, he needs me right now, I want him now, Tim!"

"Oh, hell," I said. "Max needs to get a restraining order on this guy—he's like a disintegrating Roman candle these days. And that damned therapist is zero help—not to mention Strzepek. I should have been following Paul, made sure I got his home address. Will you call your brother and tell him I want him ready to tail Radbuka home from Posner's office or Rhea Wiell's, or wherever he next pops up?"

"Will do. I couldn't follow him out of the park, of course, because I needed to stay with the kid. This is not a good situation."

"Max and Agnes know? Okay, let me talk to Calia for a minute."

At first Calia refused to talk to "Aunt Vicory." She was tired, she was scared, and she was reacting the way kids do, digging her heels in, but when Tim said I had a message about Nebbisher she reluctantly came to the phone.

"Tim is very naughty. He let the bad man take Ninshubur and now he says his name wrong."

"Tim feels bad that he didn't look after Ninshubur for you, sugar. But before you go to bed tonight, I'll try to have your doggy back to you. I'm leaving my office right now to start looking, okay?"

"Okay, Aunt Vicory," she said in a resigned voice.

When Tim came back on the line, he thanked me for drying up the tears—he'd been starting to feel desperate. He'd reached Agnes at her gallery appointment; she was on her way home, but he'd rather protect the Israeli prime minister in Syria than look after another five-year-old.

I drummed my fingers on the desktop. I called Rhea Wiell, who was fortunately between appointments. When I explained the situation and said it would be really helpful if we could get the dog back today, she said she would bring it up with Paul when she saw him Friday morning.

"Of course, Vic, all he wants it for is as a talisman of the family that he sees as denying his ties to them. In the early days of his treatment with me, he would take little things from my office, thinking I didn't see him doing it: cups from the waiting room, or one of my scarves. As he became stronger, he stopped doing that."

"You know him better than I do, Rhea, but poor Calia is only five. I think her needs come first here. Could you call him now and urge him to return it? Or let me have his phone number so I can call him?"

"I hope you're not making up this whole episode in an effort to try to get his home number from me, Vic. Under the circumstances, I doubt you, of all people, could persuade him to see you. He has an appointment with me in the morning; I'll talk to him about it then. I know Don is convinced that Max Loewenthal is not related to Paul, but Max certainly holds the key to

Paul's door to his European relatives. If you could get Max to agree to see him—"

"Max offered to see him when Paul crashed the party on Sunday. He doesn't want to see Max—he wants Max to embrace him as a family member. If you could get Paul to let us look at his family papers—"

"No," she said sharply. "I thought as soon as you called that you'd come up with some other way of trying to wheedle me into letting you see those, and I was right. I will not violate Paul's privacy. He endured too many violations as a child for me to do that to him."

She hung up on me. Why couldn't she see her prize exhibit belonged in the locked ward at Menard? Or on heavy doses of antipsychotics.

That irritated thought gave me an idea. I looked up the number for Posner's Holocaust Asset Recovery Committee on Touhy. When a man answered, I pushed my nose down to make my voice sound nasal.

"This is Casco Pharmacy in River Forest," I said. "I need to reach Mr. Paul Radbuka."

"He doesn't work here," the man said.

"Oh, dear. We're filling his prescription for Haldol, but we don't have his address. He left this phone number. You don't know where we can reach him, do you? We can't fill a prescription for this kind of drug without an address."

"Well, you can't use our address; he's not on staff here."

"Very good, sir, but if you do have some way for me to reach him? This is the only phone number he gave us."

The man put the receiver down with a bang. "Leon, did that guy Radbuka fill out a form when he came in on Tuesday? We're starting to get his phone calls, and I, for one, have no wish to act as his answering service."

I heard talk back and forth on the floor, most of it complaining about Radbuka and why did Reb Joseph want to burden them with such a difficult person. I heard Leon, the trusted henchman Posner brought with him to our talk outside the hospital yesterday, rebuke them for questioning Reb Joseph's judgment, before picking up the phone himself.

"Who is this?"

"Casco Pharmacy in River Forest. We have a prescription for Haldol we're trying to fill for Mr. Paul Radbuka and we need his home address. This is a powerful antipsychotic drug; we cannot dispense it without some way of reaching him." I spoke in a nasal singsong, as if I'd been trained to reel off the bureaucratic litany by heart.

"Yeah, well, can you make a note in your records not to use this number? This is a business office where he sometimes does volunteer work, but we can't take his messages. Here's his home address."

My heart was beating as hard as if I were hearing a message from my lover. I copied down a number on Roslyn Street, then read it back, forgetting in my excitement to use my nasal singsong. But what difference did that make now? I had what I wanted. And I hadn't needed to break Rhea Wiell's jaw to get it.

XXXVIII

Heartbreak House

Roslyn was a tiny street, barely a block long, that emptied onto Lincoln Park. Radbuka's house was on the south side, near the park end. It was an old greystone whose front, like most of the houses in this exclusive block, was set close to the street. I wanted to smash down the door, charge in, and forcibly confront Radbuka, but I made as discreet a survey as I could. This close to Lincoln Park, a lot of joggers, dogwalkers, and other athletes kept passing me, even though it was still a bit early in the afternoon for people to be home from work.

The front door was a massive piece of wood, with a peephole making it possible for Radbuka to study his visitors. Keeping myself out of its range, I rang the bell, vigorously, leaning on it for four or five minutes. When there wasn't an answer, I couldn't resist the idea of going inside to see if I could find the documents that proved to him that Radbuka was his name. I tried the front door—it would be ridiculous to risk being spotted breaking and entering if I could get in easily—but the brass knob didn't turn.

I didn't want to stand with my picklocks in full view

of so many joggers; I'd have to go in through the back. I'd had to park three blocks from Roslyn Street. I returned to my car and took a navy coverall from a box in the back. A patch on the left pocket proclaimed *People's Power Service*. That and a tool belt completed an easy piece of camouflage. I took them into the women's rest room in the conservatory and came out a minute later, my hair covered in a blue kerchief, looking like a piece of the service woodwork the Yuppies would overlook.

Back at Radbuka's house, I tried the bell again, then went up a narrow strip of flagstones along the house's east side leading to the back. It was bisected by a ten-foot-high gate with a lock set in the middle. The lock was a complex dead bolt. I crouched down with my picklocks, trying to ignore the passersby in the hopes they would do the same to me.

I was sweating freely by the time I got the tumblers pressed back. The lock had to be opened by a key no matter which side of the gate you were on; I wedged a piece of paper into the bolt hole to keep the tongue from reengaging.

The lots on Roslyn were narrow—barely wider than the houses themselves—but deep, without the service alleys and garages that run between most streets in the city. An eight-foot-high wooden fence, somewhat dilapidated, separated the garden from the street behind.

Paul's father must have made a fortune doing whatever he did for the son to afford this house on this street, but either depression or lack of money made Paul let it go. The garden was a tangle of overgrown bushes and knee-high weeds. As I waded through them to the kitchen entrance, several cats snarled at me and moved off. A shiver ran down my spine.

The lock here seemed identical to the gate, so I used the same combination of picks and had it open in less than a minute. Before going into the kitchen, I pulled on a pair of latex gloves. Just so I wouldn't forget to do it later, I grabbed a dish towel from above the sink and wiped the outside knob on the back door.

The kitchen cabinets and appliances hadn't been replaced in a good thirty years. The pilots on the old stove glowed blue in the dim light; the enamel was chipped down to metal along the edges of the oven door. The cabinets were the kind of thick brown pressed wood that had been popular in my childhood.

Paul had eaten breakfast here this morning: the milk hadn't begun to curdle in the cereal bowl he'd left on the table. The room was cluttered with old newspapers and mail; a 1993 calendar still hung near the pantry. But it wasn't filthy. Paul seemed to keep on top of his dishes, more or less, which was more than could be said for me much of the time.

I went down the hall, past a dining room with a substantial table that could have seated sixteen. A breakfront held a collection of china, a delicate pattern of blue flowers on a creamy background. It looked as though there was enough china to give sixteen people a five-course meal without stopping to wash any plates, but the dust on the dishes showed that nothing like that had been attempted recently.

All of the rooms on the ground floor were like this, filled with heavy, carved furniture, but covered in dust. Haphazard stacks of paper stood everywhere. In the living room, I found a copy of the *Süddeutsche Zeitung* dating back to 1989.

A photograph on the wall by the fireplace showed a boy and a man in front of a cottage, with a lake in the background. The boy was presumably Paul, around ten or eleven, the man presumably Ulrich, a barrel-chested, balding figure who stood next to his son, smiling but stern. Paul was looking anxiously up at his father, but Ulrich stared straight ahead at the camera. You wouldn't look at the picture and say, Oh, these two must be related—either physically or by love.

A sitting room next to the main living room had apparently served as Ulrich's study. Originally he'd probably decorated it to look like some period-film version of an English country library, with a double leather kneehole desk, a leather armchair, and shelves for books covered in tooled leather—a complete Shakespeare, a complete Dickens, Thackeray, Trollope in English, and Goethe and Schiller in German. The books had been flung about with a furious hand; pages were crumpled, spines broken—a wanton display of destruction.

The same violent hand had taken the desk apart: the drawers stood open, papers pulled from them and tossed on the floor. Had Paul done this, attacking his dead father by pounding on his possessions? Or had someone been searching the house ahead of me? And for what? Who besides me cared about the papers linking Ulrich to the *Einsatzgruppen*? Or had Ulrich had other secrets?

I couldn't take the time right now to sift through the books and papers, especially since I didn't know what I was looking for. I'd have to get Mary Louise and the Streeter brothers to sort them later, if we could get Paul out of the house long enough.

Radbuka's silver mountain bike stood in the formal tiled entryway. So he'd come back here after snatching Ninshubur. Perhaps the morning's emotional upheaval had exhausted him and he'd tucked himself in bed with the little blue dog.

I went up a carved wood staircase to the second floor and started with the rooms at the south end of the hall, where the stairway opened. The biggest, with its set of heavy silver brushes monogrammed with a curlicue *U* and what looked like either an *H* or a *K*, must have belonged to Ulrich. The bedstead and wardrobe were massive carved pieces that might have been three hundred years old. Had Ulrich brought all this heavy furniture with him from Germany, from some opulent wartime looting? Or was buying them his sign to himself of success in the New World?

The musty smell in the room made me doubt that Paul had changed the linens since his father's death those six or seven years ago. I poked through the wardrobe and dresser drawers, wondering if Ulrich had left anything in his pockets or tucked beneath his severe pajamas. I was beginning to get discouraged. An old house filled with stuff that hadn't been sorted out in thirty years—I doubted if seven maids with seven mops could get through it in under a year.

My spirits flagging, I went across the hall. Fortunately, that room and another further up the passage were both empty, not even holding bedsteads—no houseguests for the Ulrichs. Paul's own bedroom was the last one on the left. It was the only room in the house with new furniture. He had made an effort to spruce it up—perhaps to separate himself from his father—with the most extreme, angular examples of modern Danish design. I looked through it carefully but didn't see Ninshubur. So had he gone out again—to Rhea?—carrying the dog with him as a trophy?

A bathroom separated Paul's bedroom from a hexagonal room overlooking the rank back garden. Heavy drapes in a dull bronze shut out any outside light. I flipped on the overhead light to reveal an extraordinary sight.

A large map of Europe was attached to one wall. Red pins were stuck into it. When I got close enough to read the lettering, I saw they marked the concentration camps of the Nazi era, the big ones like Treblinka and Auschwitz, and others like Sobibor and Neuengamme that I'd never heard of. Another, smaller map next to it showed the paths of the *Einsatzgruppen* through eastern Europe, with *Einsatzgruppe B* circled and underlined in red.

Other walls had the photographs of horror we've all become used to: emaciated bodies in striped clothes lying on boards; faces of children, their eyes large with fear, crammed into railway cars; helmeted guards with Alsatians snarling at people behind barbed wire; the chilling smoke from crematorium chimneys.

So startled was I by this display that I noticed the most shocking sight almost as an afterthought. I think my brain first saw it as one more garish exhibit, but it was horribly real: crumpled face-forward beneath the bronze drapes lay Paul Radbuka, blood staining the floor around his out-flung right arm.

I stood frozen for an interminable second before darting around the papers littering the floor to kneel next to him. He was lying partly on his left side. He was breathing in rasping, shallow gasps, bloody bubbles popping out of his mouth. The left side of his shirt was soaked with blood that had formed a pool on the floor beneath him. I ran to the bedroom and grabbed the comforter and a sheet. My own knees were stained now with blood, my right hand as well from where I'd pushed against the floor while feeling for his pulse. I returned to Radbuka, draping the comforter over him, turning him gently within its warmth so I could see where the blood was coming from.

I ripped his shirt open. The dog Ninshubur, greeny-brown with blood, fell out. I tore a length of sheet and pressed it against Radbuka's chest. Blood continued to come from a wound on the left side, but it was oozing, not spurting: he wasn't bleeding from an artery. When I lifted the pad I could see an ugly gash near the breastbone, the telltale jagged tear of bullet into flesh.

I tore another piece of sheet and made a pad, which I pressed firmly against the hole, then tied it into place with a long strip. I wrapped him in the comforter, head to toe, leaving just enough of his face showing that he could get oxygen through the labored breaths he was taking. "Keep you warm, buddy, until the paramedics get here."

The only phone I remembered was in the living room. I ran back down the stairs, leaving a trail of bloodstains on the carpet, and called 911. "The front door will be open," I said. "This is an extreme emergency, gunshot wound to the chest, victim unconscious, breath shallow. Paramedics should come up the stairs to the north end of the floor."

I waited for a confirmation, then unlocked the front door and ran back upstairs to Radbuka. He was still breathing, wheezing as he exhaled, gasping as he sucked in air. I felt the pad; it seemed to be holding. As I adjusted the comforter, I felt a lump in his pocket that must be his wallet. I pulled it out, wondering if it would have some proof of identity that would let me know his birth name.

No driver's license. An ATM card for the Fort Dearborn Trust in the name of Paul Radbuka. A MasterCard, same bank, same name. A card saying that in an emergency one should call Rhea Wiell, at her office. No insurance card, nothing to show any other identity. I slipped the wallet gently back into his pocket.

It dawned on me that I didn't look my best, with my latex gloves now red with blood and my picklocks in my tool belt. If the cops came with the paramedics, I didn't want to have to answer awkward questions about how I got in. I ran into the bathroom, washed my gloved hands quickly but thoroughly, and opened one of the windows in Paul's bedroom. I tossed the picklocks at an overgrown shrub in the garden, disturbing a cat that took off with a heart-stopping yowl. It disappeared between two broken boards in the back fence.

Back in the room with Paul, I picked up Ninshubur.

"Did you save his life, you poor little bloodstained hound? How'd you do it?"

I inspected the damp plush figure. It was the dog tags I'd given Calia for him. One of them was bent and dimpled where the bullet had struck. They were too soft to stop or deflect a bullet, but maybe they'd helped slow it down.

"I know you're a piece of evidence, but—I doubt you'd tell a forensics team much. We'll get you cleaned up and back to your little girl, I think."

I couldn't think of a better way to secure Ninshubur than the one Paul had used: I wrapped him in the last piece of sheet, unbuttoned my coveralls, and tucked him inside my blouse. I listened to Paul's breath and checked my watch: four minutes since I'd called. One more minute and I'd call again.

I got up and looked at the rest of the shrine, wondering what the shooter had wanted so badly that he—or she, of course—had shot Paul to get it. Whoever had rifled Ulrich's study had looked in here with the same ferocious impatience. The books were hurled open in the same horrifying fashion. I didn't touch them, in case there were fingerprints, but they seemed to be a major collection of Holocaust writings: memoirs, histories ranging from Elie Wiesel to William Shirer, with everything in between. I saw Lucy Dawidowicz's *War Against the Jews* flung against Judith Isaacson's *Seed of Sarah*. If Paul had read this stuff day after day, he might have had a hard time distinguishing his memories from everyone else's.

I was starting down the stairs to use the phone again when I finally heard footsteps in the front hall and a loud shout. "Up here," I called, taking off the latex gloves and stuffing them in a pocket.

The paramedics trotted up with their stretcher. I directed them to the end of the hall, following so as not to get in their way.

"You his wife?" the medics asked.

"No, a family friend," I said. "I was supposed to collect something from him and walked in on this—this chaos. He isn't married, doesn't have any family that I know of."

"Can you come to the hospital to fill out the forms?"

"He's got independent means; he can pay the bill himself if necessary. I think his wallet has something in it about whom to notify in an emergency. What hospital will you take him to?"

"Compassionate Heart—they're the closest. Go to the reception desk in the ER to fill out the forms when you get there. Can you help take this blanket away? We're going to shift him to the stretcher."

When I picked up the comforter, a key fell out—something Paul had been holding that had dropped from his flaccid grasp. I squatted to pick it up while they slid him to the stretcher. Being moved jolted him briefly awake. His eyes flickered open, not quite focusing, and he saw me kneeling at face level.

"Hurts. Who . . . you?"

"I'm one of Rhea's friends, Paul, remember?" I said soothingly. "You're going to be okay. Do you know who shot you?"

"Ilse," he said on a rasping breath. "Ilse . . . Bullfin. Rhea. Tell . . . Rhea. SS know where . . ."

"Bullfin?" I repeated doubtfully.

"No," he said, correcting me in a weak, impatient voice. I still couldn't make out the last name clearly. The paramedics started down the hall: every second counted. I trotted along to the top of the stairs. As they started down, Paul thrashed on the stretcher, trying to focus on me with his cloudy eyes. "Rhea?"

"I'll make sure she knows," I said. "She'll look after you." It seemed a harmless enough comfort to offer him.

XXXIX

Paul Radbuka and the
Chamber of Secrets

Radbuka passed out again as soon as he'd taken in my reassurance. The medics told me to stay in the house until the police came, as the cops would want to question me. I smiled and said sure, no problem, and locked the front door behind them. The cops might come at once, in which case I'd be trapped here. But in case I had a few minutes' grace I ran back up to the hexagonal room.

I pulled the gloves back on, then looked helplessly at the mess on the floor, at the drawers with papers pulled partway out of file folders. In two minutes what could I possibly find?

I noticed a second, smaller map of Europe over the desk, with a route drawn on in thick black marker, starting in Prague, where Paul had written *Terezin* in a wobbly hand, moving to Auschwitz, then to the southeast coast of England, and finally a heavily drawn arrow pointing west toward America. Berlin, Vienna, and Lodz were all circled, with question marks near them—I guessed he had marked his putative birthplaces and his reconstructed route through wartime Europe to England and America. So? So?

Faster, girl, don't waste time. I looked at the key that had dropped out of the comforter when the medics moved him. It was an old-fashioned one with squared-off wards—it could be to any kind of old-fashioned lock. Not a file cabinet, but to one of the rooms, a closet, something in the basement or the third floor, where I hadn't looked? I wouldn't have time for that.

This room was his shrine. Something in here that the perpetrators hadn't found? Not a desk lock, too big for that. No closets anywhere I could see. But these old houses always had closets in the bedrooms. I pulled back the drapes, revealing windows in the three pieces of wall that made up a kind of fake turret here. The drapes hung beyond the windows, covering the whole side of the room. I walked behind them and came on the closet door. The key worked in it perfectly.

When I found a pull cord for an overhead light, I could hardly take in what I was looking at. It was a deep, narrow room, with the same ten-foot ceiling as the bedroom. The left-hand wall was covered in pictures, some in frames, some taped, going up well above my head.

A number were photographs of the man who'd been in the picture in the living room, the one I assumed was Ulrich. These had been terribly disfigured. Heavy red and black swastikas covered them, blocking out the eyes, the mouth. On some Paul had written words: *You can see nothing because your eyes are covered—how does it feel when someone does it to you? Cry all you want, Schwule, you'll never get out of here. How do you feel now you've been locked in here all alone? You want some food? Beg for it.*

The words were venomous but puerile, the work of a child feeling powerless against a horribly powerful adult. In that interview Paul had given on Global TV, he'd said his father used to beat him, used to lock him up. The slogans scrawled on his father's photographs, were these the words he'd heard when he'd been locked in here? No matter who Paul was, whether he was Ulrich's son or a Terezin survivor, if he'd been locked in here, heard that torment, small wonder he was so unstable.

It wasn't clear whether the room was to punish Ulrich or to serve as Paul's refuge. Interspersed with Ulrich's disfigured face were pictures of Rhea. Paul had cut them from magazines or newspapers and then apparently taken them to a studio to have prints made—several shots which had been cut out of newsprint were repeated in glossy, framed photographs. Around these he had draped the things he'd lifted from Rhea's office. Her scarf, one of her gloves, even some pale lavender tissues. The cup he'd taken from the waiting room stood underneath with a wilted rose in it.

He'd also added memorabilia about Max to the wall. It made my stomach ache, seeing the way he'd accumulated information on Max's family in one short week: there was a set of photographs of the Cellini Ensemble, with Michael Loewenthal's face circled. Programs from the Chicago concerts they'd given last week. Photocopies of newspaper articles about Beth Israel Hospital, with Max's quotes circled in red. Maybe Paul had been heading here to add Ninshubur to the shrine when his assailant shot him.

The whole idea of the place was so horrible I wanted to run away from it. I shuddered convulsively but forced myself to keep looking.

Among the pictures of Rhea was a woman I didn't recognize, a framed five-by-seven photograph in a silver frame. It showed a middle-aged woman in a dark dress, with large dark eyes and heavy brows over a mouth that was smiling in a kind of wistful resignation. A placard he'd attached to the frame said, *My savior in England, but she couldn't save me enough.*

Facing the wall of pictures stood a little fold-up bed,

shelves of canned food, a ten-gallon water jug, and a number of flashlights. And underneath the cot an accordion file tied up in a black ribbon. A disfigured photograph of Ulrich was glued to the outside, with the triumphant scrawl, *I've found you out, Einsatzgruppenführer Hoffman.*

Dimly, from the world outside the closet, I heard the insistent ring of the front doorbell. It jolted me awake, away from the horrific symbols of Paul's obsession. I pulled the picture of his English savior from the wall, stuffed it into the accordion folder, jamming the folder inside my shirt, behind the bloody little dog. I ran down the stairs two at a time, bolted down the hall, and flung myself out the kitchen door.

I lay down in the rank grass, thankful for the protection of the bloodstained coverall. The accordion file pushed unpleasantly into my breasts. I inched my way around the side of the house. I could see the tail end of a cop car, but no one was watching the side of the house: they were expecting to find me, the helpful family friend, within. Still lying in the grass, I looked around for the bush where I'd tossed my picklocks. When I'd retrieved them, I crawled stealthily to the back fence, where I shed the bloodstained boiler suit and my kerchief, stuffing the picklocks into the back pocket of my jeans. I found the boards where I'd watched the cat vanish earlier, pried them apart, and shoved my way through.

As I walked down Lake View Street to my car, I joined the crowd of gapers watching the cops force their way into Radbuka's house. I tsked to myself in disapproval: I could have shown them how to do it in a much neater way. Also, they should have had someone at the side gate, to watch for anyone trying to leave through the back. These were not the best of Chicago's finest.

My front felt damp; looking down I saw that

Ninshubur had bled through the sheet and onto my blouse. Having discarded my bloodstained coverall to avoid being conspicuous, I now looked as though I'd played the central role in open-heart surgery. I turned away, clasping my arms across my sodden front, feeling Ninshubur squishing against the accordion file.

Bending over as if in intense stomach pain, I jogged the three blocks to my car. I took my shoes off: they were covered in blood, which I didn't want to transfer to my car. In fact, they were the same crepe-soled shoes I'd worn when I'd stepped in Howard Fepple's remains on Monday. Maybe it was time to kiss them good-bye. I pulled a brown paper bag from a nearby garbage canister and stuck them into that. I didn't have an alternate pair in the trunk, but I could go home and change. I found an old towel in the trunk and a rather rank T-shirt left over from pickup softball this past summer. I pulled the shirt over my bloodstained blouse. Inside the car, I took out the faithful hound and wrapped him in the towel on the seat next to me. His brown glass eyes stared at me balefully.

"You are still a hero, but one badly in need of a bath. And I need to call Tim to tell him about Radbuka."

Morrell had only been gone two days, and I was already talking to stuffed animals. Not a good sign. Back at Racine Avenue I ran up the stairs in my stocking feet, Ninshubur clutched tightly in one hand.

"Peroxide for you, my friend." I found the bottle under the sink and poured it liberally onto Ninshubur's head. It foamed up around his brown eyes. I took a brush and scrubbed hard all over his head and chest, murmuring, "Can this little paw ever be sweet again?"

I left him to soak in a pan of cold water, while I went into the bathroom to turn on the taps in the bathtub. Like the faithful dog Ninshubur, I was smeared in blood. I'd take my blouse—a beloved soft cotton in my favorite dark gold—to the cleaners, but the bra—the rose-and-silver bra Morrell had liked—I bundled into a plastic bag for the garbage. I couldn't stand the thought of Paul's blood against my breasts, even if I could get those brown stains out of the silver lace.

While the tub filled I called Tim Streeter up at Max's to let him know I had the faithful dog and that Paul would definitely not be in a position to bother them before Calia and Agnes boarded the plane on Saturday.

"I've got the dog soaking in a basin of peroxide. I'll put him in the dryer before I leave the house again, and hope he'll look respectable enough that he won't freak out Calia when she gets him back."

Tim let out a sigh of relief. "But who shot Radbuka?"

"A woman. Paul called her Ilse—I didn't quite get the last name—it sounded something like Bullfin. I'm utterly baffled. By the way, the police don't know I was in there, and I'd like them to continue in blissful ignorance."

"I never heard anything about you knowing where the dude lived," Tim said. "Dropped the dog on the street, did he, bicycling away?"

I laughed. "Something like that. Anyway, I'm going to take a bath. I'll come up in a couple of hours. I want to show Max a picture and some other stuff. How's the kid doing?"

She'd fallen asleep in front of the television, watching *Arthur*. Agnes, who'd canceled her appointment at the gallery, was curled up on the couch next to her daughter. Tim was standing in the playroom doorway where he could see both of them.

"And Michael's on his way into town. Agnes called him after this latest incident; he wants to stay close until Agnes and Calia fly home on Saturday. He's already in the air, landing at O'Hare in an hour or so."

"Even so, I think you should hang on, although there probably isn't any other risk to Calia," I said. "Just in case that prize fanatic Posner decides to carry on for his fallen disciple."

He agreed, but added that baby-sitting was harder work than moving furniture. "I'd rather carry a grand piano up three flights of stairs. At least when you got there you'd know where the piano was, and you'd be done for the day."

I switched my house phone over to the answering service while I soaked, obsessively sponging my breasts as if blood had seeped through the pores of my skin. I shampooed my hair several times as well before I finally felt clean enough to leave the tub.

Wrapped in a terry cloth robe, I returned to the living room: I'd dropped the accordion file on the piano bench when I'd run into the apartment. For a long moment I stared down at Ulrich's disfigured face, which looked even worse for the blood that had seeped onto it.

I'd been wanting to see these papers since Paul showed up at Max's last Sunday. Now that they were within my reach I almost couldn't bear to read them. They were like the special present of my childhood birthdays—sometimes wonderful, like the year I got roller skates, sometimes a disappointment, like the year I longed for a bicycle and got a concert dress. I didn't think I could bear to open the file and find, well, another concert dress.

I finally undid the black ribbon. Two leather-bound books fell out. On the front of each was stamped in peeling gold letters *Ulrich Hoffman*. So that was why Rhea Wiell had smirked at me: Ulrich was his first name. I could have called every Ulrich who'd ever lived in Chicago and never found Paul's father.

A black ribbon hung from the middle of one of the books. I set the other down and opened this one to its marker. The paper, and the ornate script on it, looked much the same as the fragment I'd found in Howard

Fepple's office. A person who was fond of himself, that was what the woman at Cheviot Labs had said, using expensive paper for keeping accounting notes. A domestic bully, king only of the tiny empire of his son? Or an SS man in hiding?

The page I was looking at held a list of names, at least twenty, maybe thirty. Even in the difficult script, one name in particular halfway down the page caught my eye:

Radbuka, Ꙩ †✓ 1943? 65

Next to it, in a hand so heavy it cut through the paper, Paul had written in red, *Sofie Radbuka. My mother, weeping for me, dying for me, in heaven all these years praying for me.*

My skin crawled. I could hardly bear to look at the page. I had to treat it as a problem, a conundrum, like the time in the PD when I'd represented a man who had skinned his own daughter. His day in court where I did my best, my God, because I'd managed to dissociate myself and treat it as a problem.

All the entries followed the same format: a year with a question mark, and then a number. The only variation I saw was that some had a cross followed by a check mark, others just a cross.

Lzuffroo, Ꙇ †✓ 1942v.43?-72

Dossob, J † 1941?-45

Did this mean they had died in 1943, or '41? With 72 or 45 something.

I opened the second book. This one held similar information to the scrap I'd found in Fepple's office, columns of dates, all written European style, most filled in with check marks, while some were blank. What had

Howard Fepple been doing with a piece of Ulrich Hoffman's old Swiss paper?

I sat down hard on the piano bench. Ulrich Hoffman. Rick Hoffman. Was that Paul Radbuka's father? The old agent from Midway with his Mercedes, and the books he carried around with him to check off who paid him? Whose son had an expensive education, but never amounted to anything? But—had he sold insurance in Germany as well? The man who'd owned these books was an immigrant.

I dug Rhonda Fepple's number out of my briefcase. Her phone rang six times before the answering machine picked up, with Howard Fepple's voice eerily asking for me to leave a message. I reminded Rhonda that I was the detective who had been to her house on Monday. I asked her to call me as soon as possible, giving her my cell-phone number, then went back to stare at the books again. If Rick Hoffman and Ulrich were the same man, what did these books have to do with insurance? I tried to match the entries with what I knew of insurance policies, but couldn't make sense of them. The front of the first book was filled with a long list of names, with a lot of other data that I couldn't decipher.

Anpfütz, L. 30 Neubürg (2ff) OU-13426-ü-L; 54 ltv; 20/10

Gurstein, J. 29 Ofeni (30 l) OU-14139-ü-L; 48 ltv; 8/10

The list went on for pages. I shook my head over it. I squinted at the difficult ornate writing, trying to interpret it. What about it had made Paul decide Ulrich was with the *Einsatzgruppen*? What was it about the name Radbuka that had persuaded him it was his? The papers were in code, he'd screamed at me outside the hospital yesterday—if I believed in Rhea I'd understand it. What had she seen when he'd shown these pages to her?

And finally, who was the Ilse Bullfin who had shot him? Was she a figment of his imagination? Had it been a garden-variety housebreaker whom he thought was the SS? Or was it someone who wanted these journals? Or was there something else in the house that the person had taken as she—he—whoever—tossed all those papers around.

Even laying out these questions on a legal pad at my dining room table didn't help, although it did make me able to look at the material more calmly. I finally put the journals to one side to see if there was anything else in the file. An envelope held Ulrich's INS documents, starting with his landing permit on June 17, 1947, in Baltimore, with son Paul Hoffman, born March 29, 1941, Vienna. Paul had X'd this out, saying, Paul Radbuka, whom he stole from England. The documents included the name of the Dutch ship they had arrived on, a certification that Ulrich was not a Nazi, Ulrich's resident-alien permits, renewed at regular intervals, his citizenship papers, granted in 1971. On these, Paul had smeared, Nazi War Criminal: revoke and deport for crimes against humanity. Paul had said on television that Ulrich wanted a Jewish child to help him get into the States, but there wasn't any reference to Paul's religion, or to Ulrich's, in the landing documents.

My brain would work better if I got some rest. It had been a long day, what with finding Paul's body and his unnerving refuge. I thought of him again as a small child, locked in the closet, terrified, his revenge now as puny as when he'd been a child.

XL

Confession

I slept heavily, but unpleasantly, tormented by dreams of being locked in that little closet with swastikaed faces leering down at me, with Paul dancing dementedly outside the door like Rumpelstiltskin, crying, "You'll never know my name." It was a relief when my answering service brought me back to life at five: a woman named Amy Blount had called. She said she had offered to look at a document for me and could stop by my office in half an hour or so if that was convenient.

I really wanted to get up to Max's. On the other hand, Mary Louise would have left a report on her day's interviews with Isaiah Sommers's friends and neighbors. Come to think of it, Ulrich Hoffman's books might mean something to Amy Blount: after all, she was a historian. She understood odd documents.

I put Ninshubur in the dryer and called Ms. Blount to say I was on my way to my office. When I got there, I made copies of some of the pages in Ulrich's books, including the one with Paul's heavy marginalia.

While I waited for Ms. Blount, I looked over Mary Louise's neatly typed report. She had drawn a succession of blanks on the South Side. None of Isaiah

Sommers's friends or coworkers could think of anyone with a big enough grudge against him to finger him to the cops.

His wife is an angry woman, but at the bottom I believe she is on his side—I don't think she set him up. Terry Finchley tells me the police right now have two competing theories:

1. Connie Ingram did it because Fepple tried to assault her. They don't like this because they believe what she says about not going to his office. They do like it because her only alibi is her mother, who sits in front of the tube most nights. They also can't get around the forensic evidence showing that Fepple (or someone) entered his "hot" date in his computer on Thursday, when everyone agrees Fepple was still alive.

2. Isaiah Sommers did it because he thought Fepple was robbing his family of ten thousand dollars they all could use. They like this better, because they can actually put Sommers at the scene. They can't prove he ever owned a 22-caliber SIG, but they can't trace the gun anyway. Terry says they'd risk going to court if they could completely discount Connie as a suspect; he also says they know that with Freeman Carter and you acting for Sommers, they need to have cast-iron evidence. They know Mr. Carter would demolish them in court since they can't put the SIG in Sommers's hands any more than anyone else's.

The only odd thing here is Sommers's cousin Colby—this is his other uncle's son, the one he told you might have stolen the policy to begin with; he hangs on the fringe of Durham's Empower Youth Energy. He's been flashing cash lately, and everyone is surprised, because he never has any.

This can't be the original life-insurance money, I scribbled on the page, *because that was cashed in almost a decade ago. I don't know if it's significant or not, but poke at it tomorrow morning, see if you can find anyone who knows where he got it.*

As I dropped the report back on Mary Louise's desk, Amy Blount came to the door. She had on her professional wardrobe, the prim tweed suit with a severe blue shirt. Her dreadlocks were once again tied back from her face. With the formal attire her manner had become more guarded again, but she took Ulrich's two journals and looked at them carefully, comparing them with the photocopy of the fragment I'd found in Fepple's office.

She looked up with a rueful smile that made her seem more approachable. "I hoped I was going to perform some kind of hocus-pocus on this, impress you beyond expression—but I can't. If you hadn't told me you'd found it in a German man's home, I'd have guessed some Jewish organization—the names all look Jewish to me, at least the ones on the document you found in the Midway Insurance office. Someone was keeping track of these people, marking off when they died; only Th. Sommers is still alive."

"You think Sommers is a Jewish name?" I was startled: I only associated it with my client.

"In this context, yes—it's there with Brodsky and Herstein, after all."

I looked at the paper again myself. Could this be a different Aaron Sommers altogether? Was that why the policy had been paid out? Because Fepple's father, or the other agent, had confused my client's uncle with someone else with the same name? But if it was just a case of simple confusion—why had someone cared enough to steal all the papers relating to the Sommers family?

"I'm sorry," I said, realizing I'd missed what else she'd been saying. "The dates?"

"What are they? Attendance records? Payment records? It doesn't take Sherlock Holmes to say they were written by a European person. And you know the man was German. Other than that, I can't help you. I didn't find anything like this in the files I looked at, but of course Ajax has company files, not client records."

She didn't seem quite ready to leave, so I asked her if she had heard any further accusations from Bertrand Rossy about feeding Ajax material to Alderman Durham. She played with a large turquoise ring on her index finger, twisting it and looking at it under the light.

"That was a strange event," she said. "I suppose that's really why I wanted to come by. To ask your opinion—or to trade professional opinions. I hoped I could tell you something about your document so that you could give me your opinion about a conversation."

I was intrigued. "You did your best, I'll do mine."

"This—is not an easy thing for me to tell you, and you would oblige me by promising to keep it confidential. That is, not to act on it."

I frowned. "Without knowing in advance—I can't promise that if it makes me party to a crime, or if the information would help clear my client of a potential murder charge."

"Oh! Your Mr. Sommers, you mean, your non-Jewish Mr. Sommers. It's not that kind of information. It's—it's political. It could be damaging politically, and embarrassing. For me to be known as someone who gave out the information."

"Then I can safely promise you that I will hold what you say in confidence," I said gravely.

"It concerns Mr. Durham," she said, her eyes on her ring. "As a matter of fact, he did ask me to give him documents from the Ajax files. He knew I was working on their history—everybody did. Mr. Janoff—you know, the chairman of Ajax—was quite gracious about introducing me to people at the gala they held for their hundred-fiftieth anniversary, even if he was a bit patronizing—you know how they do it, 'Here's the little gal who wrote up our history.' If I'd been white, or a man, would he have introduced me as 'the little guy'? But at any event, I met the mayor, I even met the governor, and some of the aldermen, including Mr. Durham. The day after the gala he—Mr. Durham, that is—called. He wanted me to give him anything I had found in the archives which would support his claim. I told him it wasn't mine to give, and that even if it were, I didn't believe in the politics of victimhood."

She looked up briefly. "He didn't take offense. Instead—well, I don't know if you've met him in person, but he can have a great deal of charm, and he exercised it on me. I also was—relieved—that he didn't start haranguing me as a race traitor, or something of that ilk, as people do sometimes when you don't go in lockstep with them. He said he would leave the door open for further discussions."

"And has he?" I prodded, when she stopped.

"He called me this morning and said he would take it as a favor if I would overlook his having asked me for the material. He said it had been out of line for him, and he was embarrassed to think that I might have thought of him as a man who would behave with such little attention to ethics."

She turned her head away. "Now that I'm here, this seems—you know someone stole all my research notes."

"And you're worrying whether he might have engineered the theft? And that he's called to ask you to lay off because he already has what he needs?"

She nodded, miserable, still unable to look at me. "When he called this morning, I was only annoyed. I thought, How gullible do you believe I really am, although I didn't say it."

"You want my professional opinion? Just with that bit of information—I'd agree with you. You see an empty cream jug and a cat licking its whiskers—you don't need to be Marie Curie to add two and two together. But there's another little wrinkle on this."

I told her about Rossy and Durham talking in the middle of Tuesday afternoon's demonstration and Durham going up to Rossy's apartment an hour later. "I've wondered if Ajax was trying to buy off Durham. Now—your news makes me wonder if Durham was trying to blackmail Rossy. Was there anything in the data that Edelweiss would pay blackmail to keep quiet?"

"I didn't see anything that struck me as that kind of secret. Nothing on Holocaust files, for instance, or even a serious slavery exposure. But there were hundreds of pages of archives, things I copied that I thought I might look at later for a different project, for instance. I'd have to be able to see them. And of course I can't." She turned her head so I wouldn't see the tears of frustration.

Durham and Rossy. What had brought them together? Posner had said it was only after he had started demonstrating outside Ajax that Durham began his campaign—but that didn't prove anything except Durham's flair for the limelight.

I leaned forward. "You're a trained thinker. I told you yesterday what's been going on around here. Now Durham's demonstration has completely stopped. He was a big presence at the Ajax building last week and up to Tuesday afternoon, when Rossy spoke to him. I called his office: they say they're pleased that Ajax blocked the Holocaust Asset Recovery Act since it didn't include an African slave reparations section. So they're putting their demonstrations on hold."

She flung up her hands. "It could be that simple. I suppose it could have nothing to do with my papers at all. I see it's a complicated problem. I'm sorry to say that I have another appointment—I'm teaching a seminar at the Newbery Library at seven—but if you can give me one of the photocopies I'll study it later. If something occurs to me, I'll call you."

I walked out with her, locking everything carefully. I brought the photocopies I'd made along with the two books themselves. I wanted Max to look at the material to see if he understood the German. The original might be easier for him to decipher than a photocopy.

I stopped at home to collect Ninshubur from the dryer. The little dog was still slightly damp, and he was a paler blue than he used to be, but the stains around his head and left side were almost gone: a week of being dragged around by a child would soon mix enough dirt into his fur to make the faint line of blood unnoticeable. Before I left, I tried Rhonda Fepple again, but she was either still out, or not up to answering the phone. I left my name and cell-phone number a second time.

I was getting into my car when I decided to go upstairs to my safe for my Smith & Wesson. Someone was shooting guns awfully close to me. If they started firing right at me, I wanted to be able to shoot back.

XLI

Family Party

As I drove north, I turned on the local news. Police were anxious to speak to the woman who had admitted paramedics to the home of a Lincoln Park shooting victim.

She told paramedics she was a family friend but didn't give a name. By the time police arrived to investigate the crime scene, she had fled, shedding the navy service coverall she was wearing. It's possible she belonged to a cleaning service and surprised a robbery in progress, since no obvious valuables were missing. The police are not releasing the name of the victim, who is in critical condition following surgery to remove a bullet from his heart.

Dang. Why hadn't I thought to say I was with a cleaning service? My navy coverall had been perfect for it. Hopefully the paramedics thought I was an illegal immigrant who had fled to avoid revealing my papers to the cops. Hopefully I hadn't left my prints on anything. Hopefully the person who had shot Paul hadn't been hanging around the house when I walked up to it.

To my surprise, when I got to Max's, not only was Michael Loewenthal there but also Carl Tisov—and Lotty. The strain was still evident in the lines around Lotty's mouth and forehead, but she and Carl actually seemed to be laughing together.

Agnes Loewenthal greeted me exuberantly. "I know I shouldn't be *so* pleased that someone's lying in hospital, but I'm ecstatic—Christmas and my birthday tied up in one gorgeous package. And Michael here to enjoy it with us."

Carl bowed to me with an extravagant flourish and handed me a glass of champagne. They were all drinking, except Lotty, who seldom touches alcohol.

"You came with Michael?" I asked.

He nodded. "Max is after all my oldest friend on the planet. If anything happened—well, a child is more important than one concert more or less. And Lotty even decided the same thing about one operation more or less. Then we got here and found we could relax, that that delusional menace won't be around again, at least not while the little one is here."

Before I could respond, Calia hurled herself into the living room, yelling, "Give me my Ninshubur!" Agnes promptly went to her, urging her to display a few manners.

I pulled the dog from my briefcase. "Your little puppy had a big adventure today. He saved a man's life, and he had to have a bath: he's still a bit damp."

She grabbed the dog from me. "I know, I know, he jumped into the river and carried the princess to safety. He's wet because 'Ninshubur, the faithful hound, leapt from rock to rock, heedless of any danger.' Did that bad man take his collar? Where are his tags like Mitch? Now Mitch won't know him."

"I took off his collar to give him his bath. I'll get it back to you tomorrow."

"You're bad, Aunt Vicory, you stoled Ninshubur's collar." She butted my leg.

"Aunt Vicory is good," Agnes remonstrated. "She went to a lot of trouble to get your little dog back. I want to hear you say thank you."

Calia ignored her, running around the room like a demented bumblebee, bouncing off furniture, off Michael, off me, and off Tim, who had appeared with a tray of sandwiches. Excitement over the sudden arrival of her father, whom she hadn't expected to see for some time, and excitement over the day's events had sent her completely over the top. At any rate, she didn't need my explanation of why her dog was damp and stained—it fit perfectly with the story of the faithful hound.

Michael and Agnes tolerated her antics for about three minutes before marching upstairs with her to the nursery suite. When they had gone, Max asked for a detailed capitulation of the events around Paul's shooting. I told him everything, including the frightening display devoted to himself and his family in Paul's closet.

"So you don't know who could have shot Paul?" Max said, when I'd finished.

I shook my head. "And I don't even know if it was someone who was after the books I found in that dreadful closet. Maybe the fact that he was telling everyone he had papers proving his father was with the *Einsatzgruppen* made some real Nazi conspirators seek him out. They didn't know he was a lunatic—they thought he was on to them. So they shot him. The evil temptress, of course, Ilse Bullfin, seduced Paul in order to get him to open the front door."

"Who?" Max demanded sharply.

"Didn't I tell you? I asked him who shot him, and he said a woman named Ilse. I know I didn't get the last name quite right. It sounded kind of like Bullfin."

"Could it have been Wölfin?" Max asked, saying the name in a fast, low voice.

I strained to hear the difference between what he said and what Paul had said. "*Vull,* you're saying, not *Bull*? Yes, I suppose it could be—the two sounds are very close. Is she German? Do you know her?"

"Ilse Wölfin—Ilse Koch, known as the She-Wolf. A most monstrous concentration-camp guard. If that's who this poor devil thinks shot him—umph. I'd like to lay all this in front of a psychologist—this shrine, his obsession with the Holocaust. I don't suppose he'd let anyone besides this Rhea Wiell actually talk to him, but I don't know if you could even count on it being a woman who shot him. I don't know enough about delusions—he might confuse an assailant with an SS guard, but would he still know the difference between a man and a woman? What do you think, Lotty?"

Lotty shook her head, the lines of strain deeper in her face. "That kind of pathology is beyond me. We only know he's been deluding himself for a week about his relations with you—but confusing you with his brother hasn't made him think you were his mother, after all."

Max shifted uneasily. "What hospital did you say he was going to? Compassionate Heart? I could send someone over there—he's so eager to be listened to he might talk to another doctor."

"But that doctor could not tell you any revelations this man Paul might make," Lotty protested. "You have no standing to get someone to reveal patient confidences to you."

Max looked absurdly guilty: he had clearly been planning to send a friend from Beth Israel who might, as a favor to Max, violate the standards of confidentiality.

"But what's in these books that made him keep them secret?" Carl said. "Do they show some reason to believe that's why he was shot?"

I pulled the accordion file out of my briefcase. I'd forgotten the picture of the woman I'd taken along. I laid it on the coffee table in front of the three.

"His *savior in England*, you can see he's labeled it," I said. "I couldn't help wondering—well, do you know her?"

Carl frowned at the dark, wistful face. "London," he said slowly. "I don't remember who, except that it's a long time ago, during the war years maybe, or right after."

"He had this on this wall, in the middle of his shrine to the therapist he worships?" Lotty said in a high queer voice.

"You know who she is?" I asked.

Lotty looked grim. "I know who she is—I can even show you the book where he found this picture, if Max has it on his shelves. But why—"

She interrupted herself to dart from the room. We heard her running up the stairs, her tread as always light, that of a young woman.

Max looked at the picture. "I don't recognize the face. This isn't the doctor in London Lotty worshiped as a child, is it?"

Carl shook his head. "Claire Tallmadge was very fair—the perfect English rose. I always thought that was part of Lotty's infatuation with her. It used to make my blood boil, how Lotty would let that family call her 'the little monkey.' Victoria, let's see these books you brought with you."

I handed over the accordion file. Max and Carl recoiled from the disfigured face on the front of it.

"Who is this?" Carl demanded.

"Paul's father," I said. "Paul had a ton of photographs of him in that secret room, all marked up like this. Not the blood—that got there when I took it away with me."

Lotty returned with a book, which she held open at a page of photographs. "Anna Freud."

We all stared from Paul's picture to the identical shot on the page, dumbfounded, until Carl said, "Of course. You took me to hear her speak, but she looked different—this is such an intimate picture."

"She was a refugee from Vienna, like us," Lotty explained. "I admired her to an extraordinary degree. I even volunteered at the nursery she ran in Hampstead during the war, you know, washing dishes, the kind of thing an unskilled teenager could do. Minna used to lash out at me—well, never mind that. For a time I imagined I would follow Anna Freud and become an analyst myself, but—well, never mind that, either. Why is this man claiming her as his savior? Does he imagine he was in the Hampstead nursery?"

The rest of us could only shake our heads, bewildered.

"What about these?" I handed over the ledgers.

"Ulrich," Max breathed, looking at the peeling gold leaf stamped on the front. "How stupid of me to forget it is more often a first name than a last. No wonder you couldn't find him. What are these?"

"I think they must have something to do with insurance," I said, "but you can see that Paul had put them in here with the label *Einsatzgruppenführer Ulrich Hoffman*. Since they were locked in his secret room, I'm assuming these documents convinced him his name was Radbuka, but I frankly don't get it. I showed them to a young historian who's been working in the Ajax archives; she said it looked like a Jewish organization's ledgers. Would that be possible?"

Max picked up the second volume and squinted at it. "It's been a long time since I tried reading this kind of old-fashioned German handwriting. These are addresses, I think. It could be some kind of Jewish welfare association, I suppose, a list of names and addresses—perhaps the group all bought insurance together. I don't understand the other numbers, though. Unless your historian friend is right: maybe S. Radbuka brought sixty-five people with her and K. Omschutz brought fifty-four." He shook his head, unsatisfied with that explanation, and looked back at the books. "*Schrei*. What city has a street called—oh, Johann Nestroy. The Austrian fairy-tale writer. Is this Vienna, Lotty? I don't remember either Nestroy or Schreigassen."

Lotty's skin looked waxen. She took the book from Max, her arms jerky, as if she were a marionette. She looked at the page where he was pointing, her finger moving slowly along the lines, reading the names under her breath.

"Vienna? Yes, it should be Vienna. Leopoldsgasse, Untere Augarten Strasse. You don't remember those streets? Where was your family driven after the Anschluss?" Her voice was a harsh squawk.

"We lived on Bauernmarkt," Max said. "We weren't relocated, although we had three other families, all strangers, pushed into our flat. I can't say I've wanted to keep these street names in my head all these years. I'm surprised you remember them."

His voice was pregnant with meaning. Lotty looked at him grimly. I hastily intervened before they could start fighting.

"This looks like the same paper stock and the same handwriting I found on a sheet of paper in the bag of a dead insurance agent on the South Side, which is why I'm assuming these are insurance documents. The old agent was named Rick Hoffman, and I'm betting he's Paul's father—stepfather or whatever. Would Rick be a nickname for Ulrich?"

"It could be." Max smiled wryly. "If he wanted to fit into America, he would have picked a name everyone could pronounce instead of something alien like Ulrich."

"If he sold insurance, he would have felt a special incentive to fit in," I said.

"Ah, yes, I do believe this is an insurance journal." Carl turned to a page that was filled with names and dates with check marks, like the fragment in Fepple's office. "Didn't your family buy insurance like this, Loewenthal? The agent came into the ghetto every Friday on his bicycle; my father and all the other men would pay their twenty or thirty korunas and the agent marked them off in his book. You don't remember such a thing? Oh, well, you and Lotty came from the haute bourgeoisie. These weekly payments, they were for people on small incomes. My father found the whole process humiliating, that he couldn't afford to go to an office, pay his money up front, like an important man—he used to send me down with the coins tightly wrapped in a twist of newspaper." He started looking through the pages of tiny ornate writing.

"My father bought his policy through an Italian company. In 1959 it occurred to me that I should claim that life insurance. Not that it was so much money, but why should the company get to keep it? I went through a long rigmarole. But they were adamant that without the death certificate, and without the policy number, they would do nothing for me." His mouth twisted bitterly. "I hired someone—I was in a position to hire someone—who went back through the company's records and found the policy number for me, but even so, they never would pay it because I couldn't present the death certificate. They are incredible thieves, in their glass skyscrapers with their black ties and tails. I make it an absolute policy that the Cellini accepts no money from any insurance companies. The management is livid over it, but I think: it could be my father's coins wrapped in a scrap of newspaper that they're using to buy their way onto artistic boards. They won't sit on mine."

Max nodded in sympathy; Lotty murmured, "All money has someone's blood on it, I suppose."

"Do you think these numbers are insurance sales, then?" I asked, after a respectful pause. "And the crosses, that means the person died? He put a check against those he could confirm, perhaps." In my bag on the floor my cell phone started to ring. It was Rhonda Fepple, speaking in the drugged, half-dead voice of the newly bereaved. Had there been an arrest? The police didn't tell her anything.

I took the phone out to the kitchen with me and told her the progress of the investigation, if such it could be called, before asking her if Rick Hoffman had been German.

"German?" she repeated, as if I had asked if he were from Pluto. "I don't remember. I guess he was foreign, now that you mention it—I remember Mr. Fepple swearing out some legal forms for him when Mr. Hoffman wanted to become a citizen."

"And his son, was his name Paul?"

"Paul? I think so. That could be right, Paul Hoffman. Yes, that's right. What? Did Paul come around and kill my boy? Was he jealous because Howie inherited the agency?"

Could Paul Hoffman-Radbuka be a murderer? He was such a confused person, but—murderer? Still, maybe he had thought Howard Fepple was part of some *Einsatzgruppen* conspiracy—if he knew Fepple had one of Ulrich's old ledger books, he might be crazy enough to think he had to destroy Fepple. It seemed absurd, but everything involving Paul Radbuka-Hoffman defied reason.

"Wouldn't your son have mentioned it, if he'd seen Paul Hoffman recently?"

"He might not have, if he had some secret plan in mind," Rhonda said listlessly. "He liked to keep secrets to himself; they made him feel important."

That seemed too sad an epitaph. More to brace myself than her, I asked if she had anyone to talk to, to help her through this time—a sister or a minister, perhaps.

"Everything seems so unreal since Howie died, I can't make myself feel anything. Even getting the house broken into didn't upset me like you'd think it would."

"When did that happen?" Her tone was as apathetic as if she were reciting a grocery list, but the information jolted me.

"I think it was the day after—after they found him. Yes, because it wasn't yesterday. What day would that be?"

"Tuesday. Did they take anything?"

"There's nothing here to take, really, but they stole my boy's computer. I guess gangs from the city come out here looking for things to steal to sell for drugs. The police didn't do anything. Not that I care, really. None of it matters now—I wasn't ever going to use a home computer, that's for sure."

XLII

Lotty's Perfect Storm

I stared out the kitchen window at the dark garden. The same person who shot Paul must have broken into Rhonda Fepple's house. They—she? Ilse Wölfin?—had killed Fepple. Not because of the Sommers file, but for some altogether different reason—to get the fragment from Ulrich Hoffman's ledgers I'd found in Fepple's bag. And then they'd careened around Chicago, looking for the rest of the books.

Howard Fepple, excited over the next big thing that was going to make him rich, had put the bite on a lethal hand. I shook my head. Fepple didn't know about Hoffman's journals: he'd gotten roused by something he saw in the Sommers policy file. He'd been excited, he'd told his mother she'd be driving a Mercedes of her own, he'd found out how Rick Hoffman made money from his lousy client list. Not because of the ledgers.

Behind me I heard raised voices, the front door slam, a car start.

Could it be simpler than that? Could Paul Hoffman-Radbuka have murdered Fepple? Maybe he was deluded enough to imagine that Fepple was part of his father's *Einsatzgruppe*. But then—who had shot Paul? I couldn't make sense of any of it. Gerbil on treadmill, going round and round. What had Fepple noticed that I wasn't getting? Or what paper had he seen that his murderer had taken away? These secret papers of Paul's which I thought would explain everything had only left me more confused.

I went back to an earlier issue. There had been an Aaron Sommers on the fragment of Ulrich's journals I'd found in Fepple's bag. Was that my client's uncle? Or had there been two Aaron Sommerses—one Jewish, one black?

Connie Ingram had talked to Fepple. That was a point of certainty—even if she'd never gone to see him, she had spoken to him. He had entered her name in his appointment software. Maybe she really had gone to Fepple's office—under Ralph's orders? I recoiled from the thought. Under Rossy's orders? If I showed Connie Ingram a copy of Ulrich's journals, would she tell me whether she'd seen something like this in Fepple's copy of the Sommers file?

I went back to the living room. Lotty had left.

"She gets more bizarre every time I see her," Carl complained. "She looked at that page where your lunatic had written in red that Sofie Radbuka was his mother in heaven, made a melodramatic speech, and took off."

"To do what?"

"She decided to go visit the therapist, Rhea Wiell," Max said. "Frankly, I think it's high time someone talked to the woman. That is, I know you've tried to do so, Victoria, but Lotty—she's in a professional position to confront her."

"Is Lotty going to try to see Rhea tonight?" I asked. "It's a little late to pay an office visit, I'd think. Her home address is unlisted."

"Dr. Herschel was going to go to her own clinic," Tim said from the corner where he'd been silently watching the rest of us. "She said she had some kind of directory in her office that ought to provide Ms. Wiell's home address."

"I guess she knows what she's doing." I ignored Carl's derisive comment. "I must say, I'd like to watch that confrontation: the Princess of Austria versus the Little Flower. My money's on Rhea—she has that myopia which constitutes a perfect armor. . . . Max, I'll let you have some privacy. I know it's been a long, tough week, even though Paul's misfortune has brought you some breathing room. But I wanted to ask you about the abbreviations in these books. Where are they? I wanted you to see—" I was shuffling through the papers on the coffee table as I spoke.

"Lotty took them with her," Carl said.

"She didn't. She couldn't have. They're crucial, those ledgers."

"Talk to her, then." Carl shrugged with supreme indifference and poured himself another glass of champagne.

"Oh, hell!" I started to get up, intent on running after Lotty, then thought again of a pinball in motion and sat back down. I still had the copies I'd made of the journal pages. Although I'd wanted Max to study the originals, he might figure something out from copies.

He took the pages, Carl leaning over his shoulder. Max shook his head. "Victoria, you have to remember, we haven't spoken or read German at all regularly since we were ten years old. These cryptic entries could mean anything."

"What about the numbers, then? If my young historian's speculation is correct, that this was some kind of Jewish association, would the numbers refer to anything special?"

Max hunched his shoulders. "They're too big to be members of a family. Too small to be financial numbers. And anyway, the values jump around quite a bit.

They can't be bank-account numbers, either—maybe they're the numbers for safe-deposit boxes."

"Oh, it's all a big if." I slapped the papers against the table in frustration. "Did Lotty say anything else? I mean besides going to her office—did she say whether these entries meant anything special to her? After all, the Radbuka name, that's the one she knows."

Carl made a sour face. "Oh, she had one of her typical histrionic fits. She doesn't seem to be any more mature than little Calia, screeching around the living room."

I frowned. "Do you really, truly not know who Sofie Radbuka was, Carl?"

He looked at me coldly. "I said everything I know about it last weekend. I don't need to expose myself further."

"Even if Lotty did have a lover with that name, which I don't believe—at least, not someone she left school to be with in the country—why would seeing the name make Lotty so jumpy and tormented all these years later?"

"The inside of her mind is as opaque to me as—as Calia's toy dog. When I was a young man, I thought I did understand her, but she walked away from me without one word of explanation or farewell, and we had been lovers for three years."

I turned helplessly to Max. "Did she say anything when she saw the name in the book, or did she just leave?"

Max stared in front of him, not looking at me. "She wanted to know if someone thought she needed to be punished, and if so, didn't they realize that self-torture was the most exquisite punishment yet devised, because victim and tormentor were never separated."

The silence that followed was so complete we could hear the waves breaking on Lake Michigan from the far side of the park. I gathered my papers together carefully, as though they were eggs which would crack at a false touch, and stood up to go.

Max followed me out to my car. "Victoria, Lotty is behaving in a way that I can't fathom. I've never seen her like this, except maybe right after the war, but then we were all—well, the losses we experienced—for her, as for me, for Carl, for my beloved Teresz, we were all devastated, so I didn't notice Lotty as particularly so. For all of us, those losses are a wound that always hurts in bad weather, so to speak."

"I can imagine that," I said.

"Yes, but that's not what I'm trying to tell you. In Lotty's case, in all these years she has never discussed them. She's always kept herself energetically focused on the task at hand. Not just nowadays, when all our lives keep us busy with the present and a more recent past. But never."

He smacked my car roof, bewildered, astonished at her reticence. The flat, hard sound contrasted unpleasantly with his low voice.

"Right after the war, there was a sort of shock, and even for some people a sense of shame about those many, many dead. People—at least, Jewish people—didn't talk about it in a public way: we weren't going to be victims, hanging around the table for crumbs of pity. Among the survivors of the dead, oh, we mourned in private. But not Lotty. She was frozen; I think it's what made her so ill that year that she left Carl. When she came back from the country the next winter, she had this patina of briskness that has never left her. Until now. Until this person Paul whoever he is appeared.

"Victoria, after I lost Teresz I never thought I would be in love again. And I never imagined with Lotty. She and Carl had been a couple, a passionate couple; also, my own mind was in the past—I kept thinking of her as Carl's girl, despite their long estrangement. But we did come together in that way, as I know you've seen. Our love of music, her passion, my calm—we seemed to balance each other. But now—" He couldn't figure out how to end the sentence. Finally he said, "If she doesn't return soon—return emotionally, I mean—we'll lose each other forever. I can't cope right now with more losses from the friends of my youth."

He didn't wait for me to say anything but turned on his heel and went back into the house. I drove soberly back to the city.

Sofie Radbuka. "Probably I couldn't have saved her life," Lotty had said to me. Was this a cousin who had died in the gas chambers, a cousin whose place on the train to London Lotty had taken? I could imagine the guilt that would torment you if that had happened: I survived at her expense. Her parting remark to Max and Carl, about self-torture.

I was following the winding road past Calvary Cemetery, whose mausoleums separate Evanston from Chicago, when Don Strzepek called. "Vic—where are you?"

"Among the dead," I said bleakly. "What's up?"

"Vic, you need to get down here. Your friend Dr. Herschel is carrying on in a really outrageous way."

"Where's here?"

"What do you mean, where's—oh, I'm calling from Rhea's house. She just left to go to the hospital."

"Did Dr. Herschel beat her up?" I tried not to sound too eager.

"Christ, Vic, this is really serious, don't joke around, pay attention. Did you know that Paul Radbuka was shot today? Rhea got the word partway through the afternoon. She's been terribly upset. For Dr.—"

"Was he killed?" I put in.

"He was fucking lucky. Home invaders shot him in the heart, but what the surgeon told Rhea was they used a low-enough-caliber gun that the bullet lodged in the heart without killing him. I don't understand it myself, but apparently it does happen. Amazingly enough, he should make a complete recovery. Anyway, Dr. Herschel somehow got hold of some papers of Paul's—" He stopped, as the connection hit him. "Do you know about these?"

"His father's ledgers? Yes. I was just looking at them, up at Max Loewenthal's. I knew Dr. Herschel took them with her."

"How did Loewenthal get them?"

I pulled into a bus stop on Sheridan Road so I could concentrate on the conversation. "Maybe Paul brought them up to him so that Max would understand why they were related."

I heard him light a cigarette, the quick sucking in of smoke. "According to Rhea, Paul kept them under lock and key. Not that she's been to his house, mind you, but he described his safe place to her. He brought his books in to show her but he wouldn't let Rhea, whom he totally trusts, keep them overnight. I doubt he would have lent them to Loewenthal."

A Sheridan Road bus pulled up next to me; an exiting passenger angrily pounded the hood of my car. "Why don't you give me the details if you have them. Where did this happen? Did some Beth Israel patient get fed up at the Posner demonstrations and open fire?"

"No, it was in his home. He's pretty muzzy now with anesthetic, but what he's said to the cops and to Rhea is that a woman came to the door wanting to talk to him about his father. Foster father."

I interrupted him. "Don, does he know who shot him? Can he describe her? Is he sure it's a woman?"

He paused uncomfortably. "As a matter of fact, he— uh, well, he's a little confused on that point. The anesthetic is making him a little hallucinatory and he says it was someone named Ilse Wölfin. The She-Wolf of the SS. That's immaterial. What matters is that Dr. Herschel called Rhea and told her they needed to talk, that Paul was dangerously unstable if he believed these papers proved he was Radbuka, and where did he get the idea that Sofie Radbuka was his mother. Of course, Rhea refused to see her. So Dr. Herschel announced she was going to Compassionate Heart of Mary to talk to Paul in person.

"Can you believe it?" His voice went up half an octave in outrage. "Guy is lucky to be alive, just out of surgery. Hell, she's a surgeon, she should know better. Rhea's gone over there to stop her, but you're an old friend, she'll listen to you. Go stop her, Warshawski."

"I find this request pretty ironic, Don: I've been begging Rhea for a week to use her influence with Paul Hoffman, as I guess his name really is, and she's been stiffing me as if I were a plague carrier. Why should I help her now?"

"Be your age, Vic. This isn't a playground. If you don't want to keep Dr. Herschel from looking like a fool, you should stop her from seriously hurting Paul."

A cop flashed his spotlight on me. I put the Mustang in gear and turned the corner past a Giordano's pizza parlor where a bunch of teenagers were smoking and drinking beer. A woman with short-cropped dark hair walked past with a Yorkie, who lunged fiercely at the beer-drinkers. I watched them cross Sheridan Road before I spoke again.

"I'll meet you at the hospital. What I say to Lotty depends on what she's doing when we get there. But you're going to love Ulrich Hoffman's journals. They really are in code, and if Rhea broke it, she's wasted on the world of therapy—she ought to be in the CIA."

XLIII

Bedside Manners

Compassionate Heart of Mary was perched on the fringe of Lincoln Park, where parking spaces are so scarce I've seen people get into fistfights over them. For the privilege of sitting in on Lotty and Rhea's encounter I had to pay the hospital garage fifteen dollars.

I got to the lobby at the same time as Don Strzepek. He was still miffed at me over my parting crack. At the reception desk, they said it was past visiting hours, but when I identified myself as Paul's sister—just arrived from Kansas City—they told me I could go up to the fifth floor, to the postop ward. Don glared at me, bit back a hot denial, and said he was my husband.

"Very good," I applauded as we got on the elevator. "She believed it because we're clearly having a little marital tiff."

He gave a reluctant smile. "How Morrell puts up with you—tell me about Hoffman's journals."

I pulled one of the photocopies from my case. He peered at it while we walked down the hall to Paul's room. The door was shut; a nurse in the hallway said a doctor had just gone in to look at him, but as I was his sister, she guessed it was all right if we joined them.

When we pushed open the door, we heard Rhea. "Paul, you don't need to talk to Dr. Herschel if you don't feel like it. You need to stay calm and work on healing yourself. There will be plenty of time to talk later."

She had placed herself protectively between his bed and the door, but Lotty had gone around to his right side, threading her way through all the different plastic bags hanging over him. Despite his greying curls, Paul looked like a child, his small frame barely showing under the covers. His rosy cheeks were pale, but he was smiling faintly, pleased to see Rhea. When Don went to stand next to her, his smile faded. Don noticed it, too, and moved slightly apart.

"Paul, I'm Dr. Herschel," Lotty said, her fingers on his pulse. "I knew the Radbuka family many years ago, in Vienna and in London. I trained as a doctor in London, and I worked for a time for Anna Freud, whose work you so greatly admire."

He turned his hazel eyes from Rhea to Lotty, a tinge of color coming into his face.

Whatever agitation she'd displayed to Carl and Max, Lotty was perfectly calm now. "I don't want you to get excited in any way. So if your pulse starts to go too fast, we're going to stop talking at once. Do you understand that?"

"You should stop talking right now," Rhea said, not able to keep anger from disturbing her vestal tranquillity. Don, seeing Paul's attention on Lotty, took Rhea's hand in a reassuring clasp.

"No," Paul whispered. "She knows my English savior. She knows my true family. She'll make my cousin Max remember me. I promise you, I won't get agitated."

"I have Ulrich's journals," Lotty said. "I will keep them safe for you, until you are able to look after them again. But I'm wondering if you can answer a question for me about them. You wrote a note in them, next to S. Radbuka's name, that Sofie Radbuka was your mother. I'm wondering how you know that."

"I remembered it," he said.

I moved next to Lotty and matched my tone to hers. "When you took Ulrich's journals to Rhea, she helped you remember that Radbuka was your real name, didn't she, Paul? There was a long list of names— Czestvo, Vostok, Radbuka, and many others. When she hypnotized you, you remembered that Radbuka was your real name. That must have been a very wonderful but very frightening moment."

Across the bed from us, Don gasped and moved involuntarily away from Rhea, who said to him, "It wasn't like that. This is why this conversation must stop now."

Paul, intent on my question, didn't hear her. "Yes, yes, it was. I could see—all the dead. All the people *Einsatzgruppenführer* Hoffman had murdered, falling into the lime pit, screaming—"

Lotty interrupted him. "You have to stay calm, Paul. Don't dwell on those painful memories right now. You remembered that past, and then out of all that list of names, you chose—you remembered—Radbuka."

Across the bed, Rhea looked murderous. She tried again to halt the interview, but Paul's attention was focused on Lotty, not her.

"I knew, because I'd been in England as a small boy. It had to be."

"Had to be?" Lotty asked.

He was very sensitive to people's emotions; when he heard the unexpected harshness in her voice he flinched and looked away. Before he could get too upset I changed the subject.

"What led you to know Ulrich was an *Einsatzgruppenführer*?"

"He listed the dead in each family or shtetl that

he was responsible for murdering," he whispered. "Ulrich . . . always bragged about the dead. The way he bragged about torturing me. I survived all that killing. My mother threw me into the woods when she saw them starting to push people with their bayonets into the lime pit. Some person took me to Terezin, but of course . . . I didn't know then . . . that was where we were going. Ulrich must have known . . . one person got away from him. He . . . found me in England . . . brought me here . . . to torture me over and over . . . for the crime of surviving."

"You were very brave," I said. "You stood up to him, you survived. He's dead. Did you know about those books of his before he died?"

"They were . . . locked up . . . in his desk. Living room. He . . . beat me . . . when I looked . . . in those drawers . . . when I was small. . . . When he died . . . I took . . . and kept . . . in my special place."

"And someone came today to get those books?"

"Ilse." He said, "Ilse Wölfin. I knew. She . . . came . . . to the door. First she was friendly. Learned from Mengele. Friends first . . . then torture. She said . . . she was from Vienna. Said Ulrich took these books to America . . . shouldn't have . . . after the war. I didn't understand at first . . . then . . . I tried to get . . . to my secret place . . . hide from her . . . pulled out her gun first."

"What did she look like?" I asked, ignoring an impatient aside from Lotty to stop.

"Fierce. Big hat. Sunglasses. Horrible smile."

"When he was selling insurance, here in Chicago, did Ulrich talk to you about these books?" I asked, trying to figure out a way to ask if he'd been at the Midway Agency lately, wondering if he'd been stalking Howard Fepple.

"The dead give us life, Ulrich used to say. Remember that . . . you will be rich. He wanted me . . . be . . .

doctor . . . wanted me . . . make money from the dead.
. . . I didn't want . . . to live among . . . dead. I didn't
want to stay in . . . closet. . . . Tortured me . . . called
me sissy, queer, always in German, always . . . in language of . . . slavery." Tears started to seep down his
face; his breath began coming in labored spurts.

Lotty said, "You need to rest, you need to sleep. We
want you to recover. I'm going to leave you now, but
before I go, who did you talk to in England? What
helped you remember your name was Radbuka?"

His eyes were shut, his face drawn and grey. "His
tally of the dead he'd killed himself . . . bragged in his
books . . . listed their names. Searched each name . . .
on the Internet. . . . Found one . . . in England . . .
Sofie . . . Radbuka . . . how I knew . . . which name
mine . . . and that I was sent to Anna Freud in England
. . . after the war. . . . Had to be."

Lotty kept her hand on his pulse while he fell asleep.
The rest of us watched dumbly while Lotty checked the
IV drips coming into his arms. When she left the room,
Rhea and I followed. Hot spots of color burned in
Rhea's face; she tried to confront Lotty in the hall, but
Lotty swept past her to the nurse's station, where she
asked for the charge nurse. She began an interrogation
about the drugs Paul was getting.

Don had come out of Paul's room more slowly than
the rest of us. He started a low-voiced conversation
with Rhea, his face troubled. Lotty finished with the
charge nurse and sailed on down the hall to the elevator. I ran after her, but she looked at me sternly.

"You should have saved your questions, Victoria.
There were specific things I was trying to learn, but
your questions sidetracked him and finally got him too
upset. I wanted to know how he latched on to Anna
Freud as his savior, for instance."

I got in the elevator with her. "Lotty, enough of this
crap. Isn't pushing Carl into the void enough? Do you

want to drive Max and me away from you, as well? You got angry the first time Paul mentioned England; I was trying to keep you from losing him. And also—we know what those journals meant to Paul Hoffman. I'd like to know what they meant to Ulrich. Where are they, by the way? I need them."

"For right now, you'll have to do without them."

"Lotty, I can't do without them. I need to find out what they mean to people who don't see the dead in them. Someone shot Paul for them. It may be that this fierce woman in sunglasses killed an insurance agent named Howard Fepple for them. His mother's house was broken into on Tuesday. Someone searched it, probably for these notebooks."

Amy Blount, I suddenly thought. Her place had been burgled on Tuesday, also. Surely it was too big a coincidence to think it wasn't connected to these Hoffman journals. She had seen the Ajax archives. What if the fierce woman in sunglasses thought Ulrich Hoffman's books had landed in the archives and thought perhaps Amy Blount hadn't been able to resist them? Which meant—it was someone who knew Amy Blount had been in those archives. It all came back to the folks at Ajax. Ralph. Rossy. And Durham on the sideline.

"Anyway," I added aloud, as the elevator doors opened onto the lobby, "if they mean that much to someone, you're risking a lot by holding on to them."

"That is definitely my lookout, not yours, Victoria. I'll return them to you in a day or so. There's something I need to look for in them first." She turned on her heel and stalked away from me, following a hallway sign-posted to the doctors' parking area.

Don and Rhea appeared from another elevator, Don saying, "Don't you see, sweetheart, this lays you open to the kind of criticism people like Praeger make, that you lead people to these memories."

"He knew he had been in England after the war," she

said. "That isn't something I thought of or led him to. And those memories of the lime pits—Don, if you'd been there—I've listened to many bone-chilling memories from my patients, but I've never wept before. I'd always kept my professional detachment. But to see your own mother thrown alive into a pit she'd been forced at gunpoint to fill with lime, to hear those screams—and then to know that the man responsible for your own mother's death had such power over you, locking you into a small closet, beating you, taunting you—it was utterly shattering."

"I can see that," I said, breaking into this private conversation. "But there are so many curious leaps in his story. Even if Ulrich somehow knew this one small boy escaped the lime pit, how did he keep track of him all through the vicissitudes of war, first in Terezin and then to England? If Ulrich really was an *Einsatzgruppenführer,* he'd have had plenty of chances to kill the kid during the war. But on Ulrich's landing papers, it says they docked in Baltimore from a Dutch merchant ship which sailed from Antwerp."

"That doesn't mean he didn't start from England," Rhea said. "As for your other point, a man with a guilty conscience might do anything. Ulrich is dead; we can't ask him why he was so obsessed by this small boy. But we know he thought having a Jewish child would help him get past immigration problems in America. So if he knew where Paul was, it was natural for him to take him, pretending to be his father."

"Ulrich had an official denazification certificate," I objected. "Nor was there any mention of Paul's Jewishness in the landing documents."

"Ulrich probably destroyed those once he was here and felt safe from prosecution," Rhea said.

I sighed. "You have a pat answer for everything, but Paul has a shrine to the Holocaust; it's filled with books and articles on survivor experiences. If he's immersed himself in these, he could be confusing other people's histories with his own past. After all, he says he was only twelve months old when he was sent to Terezin. Would he really know what he'd been seeing, if in fact he had witnessed his mother and the rest of his town being murdered in the way he describes?"

"You know nothing about psychology, or about survivors of torture," Rhea said. "Why don't you stick to the things you know about, whatever those might be."

"I do understand Vic's point, Rhea," Don said. "We need to talk seriously about your book. Unless there's something specific in these journals of Ulrich's, saying *This boy I brought with me is not my son, he's someone named Radbuka*—well, I need to examine them in detail."

"Don, I thought you were on my side," Rhea said, her myopic eyes filling with tears.

"I am, Rhea. That's why I don't want you to expose yourself by publishing a book that has holes someone like Arnold Praeger and the Planted Memory folks can find so easily. Vic, I know you're guarding the originals like the national vault, but would you let me examine them? I could do so in your office, under your eye."

I made a face. "Lotty's walked off with them, which makes me angry, but also worried—if Paul was shot by someone looking for them, they're about as safe to lug around as naked plutonium. She's promised to return them by the weekend. I did copy about a dozen pages and you can look at those, but—I understand the problem."

"Well, that's just dandy," Don said, exasperated. "How did you get hold of all this material to begin with? How do you know about Paul's shrine? You were in his house, weren't you?"

I nodded reluctantly—the situation was past the point where I could keep my presence on the scene a secret. "I found him right after he'd been shot and got the ambulance to him. The place had been ransacked, but he had a closet hidden behind the drapes in his Holocaust shrine. His assailant didn't think to look there. It was a truly dreadful place."

I described it again, the wall of photographs, the tell-tale balloon comments coming out of Ulrich's mouth. "Those things you say he took from your office, Rhea, they were there, draped around pictures of you."

"I'd like to see it," Don said. "Maybe there's some other crucial piece of evidence you overlooked."

"You could go in, and welcome," I said. "Once is enough for me."

"Neither of you has a right to violate Paul's privacy by going into his house," Rhea said coldly. "All patients idealize their therapists to some extent. Ulrich was such a monstrous father that Paul juxtaposes me against him as an idealized form of the mother he never knew. As for your going into the house, Vic—you called me this morning wanting his address. Why do that if you knew where he lived? If he'd been shot, how did you get inside? Are you sure you weren't the woman down there shooting him, because of your rage over his wanting to prove a close relationship with your friends?"

"I didn't shoot the little goober, even though he was acting like a great pain in the neck," I said softly, my eyes hot. "But I do have a sample of his blood now, on my clothes. I can send it out for a DNA profile. That will prove once and for all whether he's related to Max—or Carl or Lotty."

She stared at me in dismay. I pushed brusquely past her before she or Don could speak.

XLIV

The Lady Vanishes

I wondered if Paul was safe in his hospital room. If Ilse the She-Wolf learned he had survived her shot, would she come back to finish the job? I couldn't ask for a police posting without explaining about Ulrich's journals. And my mind boggled at the task of trying to make the cops understand that story, especially when I didn't fully understand it myself. I finally compromised by going back to the fifth floor to tell the charge nurse that my brother was scared of his attacker coming back to kill him.

"We worry about Paul," I said. "I don't know if you've noticed, but he lives in a world of his own. He thinks the Nazis are after him. Did Dr. Herschel tell you when she was talking to you that it would be best if no one goes in to see him unless I, or his doctor, or the therapist Rhea Wiell is here, as well? He'll get so agitated that he could get into serious respiratory difficulties right now."

She told me to write up something for the nursing station. She let me use her computer in the back room, then taped my message up at the station and said she

would make sure the central switchboard routed any
calls or visitors to them.

Before going home, I went to my own office to send
Morrell an e-mail, recounting the events of the day. *So
far no one has beaten me up and left me to die on the
Kennedy,* I wrote, *but I've been having a strenuous
time.* I finished with an account of the conversation in
Paul's hospital room. *You've done so much work with
torture victims—could this be a dissociative protection,
identifying with victims of the Holocaust? The whole
situation is really spooky.*

I ended with the messages of love and longing one
sends to distant lovers. What had sustained Lotty over
the years against such feelings? Had her sense of torment made her think she deserved loneliness and longing? When I got home, I sat on the back porch with Mr.
Contreras and the dogs for a long time, not talking
much, just drawing comfort from their presence.

In the morning, I decided it was time to visit Ajax
Insurance again. I phoned Ralph from my own office
and talked to his secretary, Denise. As usual, his calendar was full; once again I pleaded my case forcefully
but with charm and goodwill; once again, Denise
arranged to fit me in, twenty minutes from now if I
could get to Ajax by nine-thirty. I grabbed my briefcase
with the photocopies from Ulrich's journals and ran
down to the corner of North for a cab.

When I reached Ralph's office, Denise told me he
would be back from the chairman's office in two minutes. She settled me in his conference room with a cup
of coffee, but Ralph came in almost immediately, pressing his fingers along the corners of his eyes. He looked
too tired for this early in the day.

"Hi, Vic. We have a big exposure in the Carolina
flood zone. I can give you five minutes, and then I have
to move on."

I laid my photocopies on his conference table. "These are from the journals of Ulrich—Rick— Hoffman, the agent who sold Aaron Sommers his life-insurance policy all those years ago. Ulrich kept what seems to be a list of names and addresses, followed by a set of cryptic initials and check marks. Do they mean anything to you?"

Ralph bent over the papers. "This handwriting is just about impossible to read. Is there any way to get it clearer?"

"Blowing up the image seems to help. Unfortunately I don't have the originals to work with right now, but I can read some of this—I've been looking at it a couple of days."

"Denise," he shouted to his secretary. "Can you come here a minute?"

Denise obediently trotted in, not showing any annoyance at the peremptory summons, and took a couple of sheets to her copier. She came back with various sizes of blowups. Ralph looked at them and shook his head.

"Guy was really cryptic. I've seen a lot of agency files and—Denise!" he shouted again. "Call that gal in claims handling, Connie Ingram. Get her up here, will you?"

In his normal tone he added to me, "I just remembered what was odd about that file, that disputed-claim file. Connie'll know the answer." He turned to the page showing the names and addresses. "Omschutz, Gerstein—are these names? What's Notvoy?"

"Nestroy, not Notvoy. A woman I know says it's a street in Vienna."

"Austria, you mean? We had an agent on the South Side selling insurance in Vienna, Austria?"

"It's possible he started his insurance career there before the war. I don't know. I was hoping you'd look at these and be able to tell whether they were insurance-related or not. A definite no would be almost as helpful as a definite yes."

Ralph shook his head, rubbing his forehead again. "I can't tell you. If it is insurance, these numbers, the 20/w and the 8/w, they could refer to a weekly payment—although, hell, I don't know the German for week. Maybe it doesn't start with *w*. Also, what was the currency? Do these amounts make sense for payment figures? And these others, if this is insurance, they could be policy numbers, although they don't look like ones that I'm familiar with."

He held it out to me. "Can you read them? What's the initial letter, this thing that looks like a bee attacking a flower? And then a string of numbers, and then—is that a *q* or an *o*? And then there's an *L*. Hell, Vic—I don't have time for this kind of puzzle. It might be insurance, but I can't tell. I guess I could ask Rossy—he might know if it's a European system, but if it dates to before the war—well, they've changed all their systems since the war. He's a young guy, wasn't even born until 1958—he probably wouldn't know."

"I know it seems like it's just a puzzle," I responded. "But I think that insurance agent Fepple was killed because of it. Yesterday someone who was probably looking for these papers shot Rick Hoffman's son."

Denise came to the conference room door to let Ralph know Connie Ingram had arrived.

"Connie. Come on in. You doing okay? No more interviews with the police, I hope. Look, Connie, that claim file that's been causing everyone such a headache—Aaron Sommers. There weren't any personal notes from the agent in it. Something about it bugged me when I picked it up from Mr. Rossy, and looking at these, I remembered that's what was missing."

He turned to me to explain. "See, Vic, the agent

would work up a sheet, numbers, whatever, he'd have a letter or some notes or something that would end up in the file—we rely on their private assessment, especially in life insurance. Guy can have a doctor in his hip pocket to clear him on a physical, but the agent sees him, sees he lives like me, on French fries and coffee, and tells the company the prospect either isn't a good risk or needs to be rated higher, or whatever. Anyway, there wasn't anything in the Sommers file. So, Connie, what's the story—did you ever see any agent report in that file when you looked at it? He might have had handwriting like this."

Ralph handed one of the sheets to Connie. Her eyes widened and she put a hand over her mouth.

"What is it, Connie?" I asked.

"Nothing," she said quickly. "This writing is so queer I don't know how anyone could read it."

Ralph said, "But did you ever see any notes from the agent—what was his name? Ulrich Hoffman?—either written or typed? You didn't? You're sure? What happens when we pay a claim—do we deep-six all the background paper? I find that hard to believe—insurance thrives on paper."

Denise stuck her head through the doorway. "Your London call, Mr. Devereux."

"I'll take it in my office." Over his shoulder, as he left the conference room, he said, "Lloyds, about these flood losses. Leave the copies there—I'll show 'em to Rossy. Connie, think carefully about what you saw in the file."

I collected my set of copies and handed Denise the blowups she'd made. Connie scuttled out the door while I was thanking Denise for her help. I didn't see Connie when I got to the elevator: either she'd found a car waiting for her or she was hiding in the women's bathroom. In case it was the latter, I moved away from the elevators to admire the view of the lake. The executive-floor attendant asked if she could help me; I said I was just collecting my thoughts.

After another five minutes, Connie Ingram appeared, looking around like a scared rabbit. I was tempted to jump out and yell *boo,* but I waited near the window until the elevator light dinged, then trotted over to get into the car with her as the doors closed.

She looked at me resentfully as she pushed the button for thirty-nine. "I don't have to talk to you. The lawyer said so. He said to call him if you came around."

My ears filled as the elevator fell. "You can do it as soon as you get off. Did he also tell you not to talk to Mr. Devereux? Are you going to figure out an answer about whether you saw any agency notes in the file? In case he forgets that he asked—I know he's got a lot on his mind—I'll be calling regularly to remind him."

The door opened at thirty-nine; she shot out without responding to my genial farewell. I took the L back to my office, where I found an e-mail from Morrell.

I realized that even I, who thought I was a sophisticated traveler, had my expectations of the setting shaped by Rudyard Kipling. I wasn't prepared for the starkness, the grandeur—or most especially the way one feels obliterated by the mountains. You find yourself wanting to make defiant gestures: I'm here, I'm alive, acknowledge me.

As far as your question about Paul Hoffman or Radbuka, of course I am not an expert, but I do think someone who has been tortured, as he apparently was tortured by his father, could become very fragile emotionally. It would be painful to think your own father tortured you—you would imagine there must be something terribly wrong with you that provoked such behavior—children inevitably blame themselves in difficult situations. But if you could believe you were persecuted because of your historic identity—you were a Jew, you were from eastern Europe, you survived the death camps—then it would both glamorize your torture, give it a deeper meaning, and protect you from the pain of believing you were a terrible child whose father was justified in assaulting you. That's how I see it, at any rate.

My beloved Pepperpot, I already miss you more than I can say. It's horribly unsettling to have half the population missing from the landscape. I miss not just your face—I miss seeing women's faces.

I printed out the section that dealt with Paul and faxed it to Don Strzepek at Morrell's home machine with a scrawl, *For what it's worth.* I wondered how Don had left things with Rhea last night. Would he go ahead with his book on recovered memories with her? Or would he wait to see if Max and Lotty wanted to do a DNA match?

That was a mighty thin thread Paul Hoffman had hung his identity on, searching the Web for the names in those insurance records of Ulrich's until he found a query about one of them. He'd used that thread to attach himself to England immediately after the war.

Thinking about it reminded me of the picture of Anna Freud that Paul had hung in his closet. His savior in England. I called up Max's house and spoke with Michael Loewenthal—Agnes had been able to reschedule her appointment at the gallery, so he was minding Calia. He went to the living room for me and came back with the name of the biography Lotty had brought down from Max's study last night.

"We're coming into Chicago for a last look at the walruses in the zoo; I'll drop it off at your office. No, with pleasure, Vic—we owe you a lot for your care of our petite monster. But I confess to an ulterior motive:

Calia is being a brat about the dog's collar. We could pick it up."

I groaned—I'd left the wretched thing in my kitchen. I told Michael if I didn't get up to Evanston with it tonight I'd mail it to Calia in London.

"Sorry, Vic—no need for that much trouble. I'll stop by in about an hour with the book. By the way, have you spoken to Lotty? Mrs. Coltrain called from the clinic, concerned because Lotty had canceled all her appointments for today."

I told him our parting last night had been rocky enough that I hadn't felt like calling her. But when Michael hung up, I dialed Lotty's home number. It rang through to her crisp voice on the machine, giving various numbers to use if this was a medical emergency, and urging friends to leave their messages after the tone. I thought uneasily of a lunatic going around town shooting people to get at Hoffman's journals. But surely the doorman wouldn't let anyone in who didn't belong there.

I called Mrs. Coltrain, who was at first relieved to hear from me but became agitated when she found out I didn't know anything about Lotty's situation. "When she's really ill, she does cancel her appointments, of course, but she *always* talks to me about it."

"Did someone else call you?" Worry made my voice sharp.

"No, it's just—she left a message on the office answering machine. I couldn't believe it when I got in, so I took it on myself to call her at home and then to ask Mr. Loewenthal if she'd said anything to anyone at the hospital. No one there has heard anything, not even Dr. Barber—you know they cover for each other in emergencies. One of Dr. Herschel's teaching fellows is coming in at noon to look after any acute problems that come up in here, but—if she isn't ill, where is she?"

If Max didn't know, nobody did. I told Mrs.

Coltrain I'd check in at Lotty's apartment—neither of us saying it, both of us picturing Lotty lying unconscious on the floor. I found Lotty's building management in the phone book and got through to the doorman, who hadn't seen Dr. Herschel today.

"Does someone in the building have keys? Could I get in to see if she's all right?"

He consulted a list. Lotty had left Max and my names as people to call in any emergency; he guessed the super could let me in if I didn't have keys. When was I coming? In twenty minutes? He'd get Gerry up from the basement, where he was supervising a boiler-repair crew.

Mary Louise called as I was leaving. She was on the South Side with Gertrude Sommers—yes, the client's aunt—who wanted to tell me something in person. I'd forgotten about sending Mary Louise down to check on the client's dubious cousin—I'd left the note for her yesterday afternoon, but so much was going on it seemed like a month ago.

I tried not to sigh audibly. I was tired, and tired of running from one end of Chicago to the other. I told Mary Louise that unless some crisis developed at Lotty's place, I'd be at Gertrude Sommers's apartment in about ninety minutes.

XLV

Heard on the Street

The doorman at Lotty's building had seen me a number of times, but he and Gerry, the building super, still insisted on proof of my identity before Gerry took me up to the eighteenth floor. The precaution, which would normally have made me impatient, gave me some reassurance about Lotty's safety.

When we got to her apartment, Gerry rang the bell several times before undoing her locks. He went with me through the rooms, but there was no sign of Lotty, and no sign that any violent struggle had taken place.

While Gerry watched in mounting disapproval, I looked through the drawers in the side room that Lotty uses as a home office, and then in Lotty's bedroom, for Ulrich's journals. Gerry followed me from room to room while I imagined the places that people conceal things—behind clothes, under rugs and mattresses, inside kitchen cabinets, behind pictures on the wall, slipped in among the books on her own shelves.

"You don't have a right to be doing that, miss," he said when I was poking through Lotty's underwear drawer.

"You married, Gerry? Kids? You know if your wife or one of your daughters was having a dangerous pregnancy who everyone would tell you she should see? Dr. Herschel. Who takes her duties so seriously she never even calls in sick unless she's running a fever that she thinks would affect her judgment. Now she's suddenly vanished. I'm hoping for any sign that would tell me whether she left voluntarily or not, whether she packed a bag, anything."

He wasn't sure he believed me, but he didn't make further efforts to stop me. Of Ulrich's journals there wasn't a sign, so she must have taken them with her. She had left under her own steam. She must have.

"Is her car in the garage?" I asked.

He called down to the doorman on his walkie-talkie; Jason said he'd go out to look. That's how an intruder could infiltrate: wait until the doorman goes to the garage, then follow another tenant inside.

When we got downstairs, Jason was back at his station. Dr. Herschel's car was here—he once again abandoned his station to take me out to look. It was locked, and I didn't want to show off my parlor tricks by opening it in front of him, so I peered through the tinted windshield. Unlike me, Lotty doesn't leave her car strewn with papers, old towels, and stinking T-shirts. There wasn't anything on the seats.

I gave each of them my card and asked Jason to question people as they came home about whether anyone had seen her leave. "That way we can keep it casual," I said when he started to object. "Otherwise I'll have to bring the police in, which I'm very reluctant to do."

The two men exchanged glances: the building management would be annoyed if the cops came around to question the tenants. They pocketed their tens with suitable dignity and agreed not to let anyone up to Dr. Herschel's apartment unless Max or I was here.

"And you do keep an eye on the lobby, even when you're running another errand?" I persisted.

"We don't leave the lobby unattended, ma'am." Jason was annoyed. "I can always see it on the TV monitor in the garage. And when I go on break, Gerry stays here to cover for me."

I knew it wasn't a foolproof system, but I'd lose their cooperation if I criticized it any further. I sat in the Mustang for a bit, massaging the back of my neck. What had happened to her? That Lotty had a life of which I knew nothing had become abundantly clear in the last ten days. Just because she'd hugged her secrets to herself, did that mean I had to respect this secrecy? But conversely, did my friendship, my love, my concern, any of those give me the right to invade a privacy she'd gone to such lengths to protect? I thought it over. Probably not. As long as those damned books of Ulrich's weren't going to put her at risk. But they might. If only I could find someone who could interpret them for me. Maybe they would mean something to Bertrand Rossy.

I slowly put the car into gear and made the difficult drive to the South Side. Every week it gets harder to cross the heart of Chicago. Too many people like me, sitting one to a car. At the entrance to the expressway at North Avenue, I stopped for gas. Price was still going up. I know we pay less than half what they do in Europe, but when you're used to cheap fuel a thirty-dollar fill-up is a jolt. I crawled down the Ryan to Eighty-seventh, the exit nearest Gertrude Sommers's.

At her building, nothing seemed to have changed from two weeks ago, from the derelict Chevy out front to the despairing wail of the baby within. Mrs. Sommers herself was still rigidly erect in a dark, heavily ironed dress, her expression as forbidding as before.

"I told that other girl she might as well go," she said when I asked if Mary Louise was still there. "I don't like to talk to the police about my family. Even though she says she's private, not with the police anymore, she looks and talks like police."

She gave the word a heavy first-syllable stress. I made an effort to put Lotty out of my mind, to concentrate on what Gertrude Sommers had decided to tell me.

She waved me to a chair at the pressed-wood table along the far wall, then seated herself, with the sighing sound of stiff fabric against stocking. Her back was rigidly upright, her hands folded in her lap, her expression so forbidding that it was hard for me to meet her gaze.

"At Bible study on Wednesday night the reverend spoke to me. About my nephew. Not my nephew Isaiah, the other one. Colby. Do you think if his father had named him for a prophet, like Mr. Sommers's other brother named Isaiah, Colby would be an upright man, as well? Or would other temptations have always proved too strong for him?"

Whether this was a rhetorical question or not, I knew better than to try to answer. She was going to need time to come to the point. I would have to let her get there on her own. I slipped a hand into my pocket to turn off my cell phone: I didn't want its ringing to interrupt her.

"I've been worried about Isaiah since Mr. Sommers passed. He found money for the funeral out of his own pocket. He took it on himself to hire you, with money out of his own pocket, to find out what happened to Mr. Sommers's life-insurance money. Now, for acting like that good Samaritan, the police are hounding him, with that wife of his gnawing on him from behind. That's a good job he has at the engineering works, a fine job. She's lucky to have a man who's a hardworking churchgoer, like Mr. Sommers was before him. But she's like a baby, wanting what she can't have."

She looked at me sternly. "In my heart I've been

blaming you for Isaiah's troubles. Even though Isaiah kept saying you were trying to end them, not foment them. So when the reverend spoke to me about my nephew Colby, I didn't want to hear, but the reverend reminded me, 'Ears they have and hear not, eyes they have and see not.' So I knew the time had come for me to listen. Um-hmm."

She nodded, as if she were lecturing herself in that little grunt. "So I listened to the reverend telling me that Colby was flashing money around the neighborhood, and I thought, What are you trying to tell me—that Colby has my husband's insurance money? But the reverend said, nothing like that. Colby got paid for helping do a job.

"'A job,' I said. 'If my nephew Colby is getting money for working, then I'm on my knees to praise Jesus.' But the reverend told me, not that kind of job. The reverend said, 'He's been hanging out with some of those Empower Youth men.' And I said, 'The alderman does a lot of good in this neighborhood, I won't believe any ill of him.' And the reverend said, 'I hear you, Sister Sommers, and I don't believe ill of him, either. I know what he did for your son when he was a boy, what he did for you and Mr. Sommers when your boy was afflicted with the scourge of muscular dystrophy. But a man doesn't always know what the left hand of his left hand is doing. And some of the alderman's left hands are finding their way into people's pocketbooks and cash registers.'"

She gave another little grunt, "un-hnnh," her lips folded over in bitterness at having to repeat ill of her family to me, a stranger, a white woman. "So the reverend says, 'I've been hearing that your nephew Colby got paid good money to make a telephone call to the police. To tell them his cousin Isaiah had been in the office of that insurance agent who defrauded you of your husband's money and then got murdered. And if ever Cain hated Abel for being righteous in the eyes of the Lord, your nephew Colby has always hated his cousin Isaiah with that same hatred. I hear,' the reverend said, 'I hear he gladly made that phone call. And I hear that when these same left hands of the alderman's left hand wanted a gun, that Colby knew where to find it. And when they went breaking into an apartment in Hyde Park with a blowtorch, Colby was glad to stand lookout for them.'

"'I won't go to the police against my own family,' I told the reverend. 'But it's not right for Isaiah to lie in jail, as he will if the worst comes about from these police questions, because of the hatred of his cousin.' So when the other girl came around this morning, wanting to ask me about Colby—because someone had been telling her stories about him as well—I remembered you. And I saw the time had come to talk to you."

The news was so startling that I hardly knew what to say. Alderman Durham's EYE team deployed to kill Howard Fepple? That hardly seemed possible. In fact, I didn't think it could be possible, because the guard at the Hyde Park Bank would have noticed them—you wouldn't mistake Durham's EYE troops for expectant parents going up to a Lamaze class. But it must have been some EYE hangers-on who broke into Amy Blount's apartment.

I pressed my palms against my eyes, as if that would bring any clarity to my vision. Finally I decided to tell Gertrude Sommers a good deal of the events of the last week and a half, including the old journals that Ulrich Hoffman entered his payments in.

"I don't understand any of this," I finished. "But I will have to talk to Alderman Durham. And then—I may have to talk to the police, as well. One man is dead, another critically wounded. I don't understand what possible connection there is here between these old books of Hoffman's and the alderman—"

I halted. Except that Rossy had singled out Durham on the street on Tuesday. He was just back from Springfield, where they'd killed the Holocaust Asset Recovery Act, where Ajax had thrown its weight behind Durham's slave-reparations rider. And the demonstrations had stopped.

Rossy was from a European insurance company. Carl had thought Ulrich's records looked similar to the ones a European insurance agent had kept on his father many years ago. Was that what connected Rossy to the Midway Insurance Agency?

I picked up my briefcase and pulled out the photocopies of Ulrich's journal. Mrs. Sommers watched me, affronted at first by my inattention, then interested in the papers.

"What is that? It looks like Mr. Hoffman's handwriting. Is this his record of Mr. Sommers's insurance?"

"No. But I'm wondering if it's a record of someone else's insurance that he sold in Europe sixty-five years ago. Look at this."

Anspütz, L 30 Nestrong (2ff) N-13426-ü-L; 54 lw; 20/vo

Gurstein, J, 29 Afrui (30 l) N-14139-ü-L; 48 lw; 8/vo

"But it isn't an *E*, it's an *N*. So it can't be an Edelweiss policy number. Or it is, but they have their own company code."

"I suppose you know what you're talking about, young lady. But it doesn't mean a thing to me. Not one thing."

I shook my head. "These numbers don't mean anything to me. But other things are starting to make a horrible kind of sense."

Except for what her husband's insurance policy had

to do with all this. I would give a month's pay, and put icing on it, if I could see what Howard Fepple had found when he looked at Aaron Sommers's file. But if Ulrich had sold insurance for Edelweiss before the war, if he'd been one of those men coming into the ghetto on his bicycle on Friday afternoons, as Carl had been describing last night—but Edelweiss had been a small regional carrier before the war. So they said. So they said in "One Hundred Fifty Years of Life."

I got up abruptly. "I will get your nephew Isaiah cleared of all charges against him, one way or another, although exactly how I'll do that I have to say I honestly don't know right this minute. As for your nephew Colby—I'm not a fan of housebreaking, or people supplying others with guns for crimes. However, I have a feeling that Colby's in more danger from his accomplices than he is from the law. I have to go now. If my suspicions are correct, the heart of this mystery is downtown, or maybe in Zurich, not here."

XLVI

Ancient History

In my car, I turned my phone back on and called Amy Blount. "I have a different question for you today. The section of your Ajax history where you talked about Edelweiss—where did you get that material?"

"The company gave it to me."

I made a U-turn, one hand on the wheel, one on the phone. I braked to avoid a cat that suddenly streaked across the road. A little girl followed, screaming its name. The car fishtailed. I dropped the phone and pulled over to the curb, my heart pounding. I had been lucky not to hit the girl.

"Sorry—I'm demented right now, trying to do too many things at once, and driving stupidly," I said when I'd recovered enough to reestablish the connection. "Were these archival records? Financials, anything like that?"

"A summary of financials. All they wanted on Edelweiss was that little bit at the end. The book is really about Ajax, so I didn't see the need to look at Edelweiss archives." She was defensive.

"What was in the summary?"

"High-level numbers. Assets and reserves, principal

offices. Year-by-year, though. I don't remember the details. I suppose I could ask the Ajax librarian."

A couple of men came out of a derelict courtyard. They looked at the Mustang and then at me and gave a thumbs-up gesture for both of us. I smiled and waved.

"I need a way to find out if they had an office in Vienna before the war." Edelweiss's numbers didn't matter, come to think of it: maybe they really had been a small regional player in the thirties. But they could still have been selling insurance to people who were obliterated in the war's blistering furnaces.

"The Illinois Insurance Institute has a library which might have something that would help you," Amy Blount suggested. "I used it when I was doing research for the Ajax book. They have a strange hodgepodge of old insurance documents. They're in the Insurance Exchange building, you know, on West Jackson."

I thanked her and hung up. My phone rang as I was negotiating the merge onto the Ryan at Eighty-seventh, but nearly hitting that child a few minutes ago made me keep my attention on the road. Although I couldn't stop speculating about Edelweiss. They bought Ajax, a coup, acquiring America's fourth-largest property-casualty insurer at fire-sale prices. And then found themselves facing legislation demanding recovery of Holocaust-era assets, including life-insurance policies. Their investment could have turned from gold mine to bankruptcy court if they had a huge arrears of unpaid life-insurance claims all coming due at once.

Swiss banks were fighting tooth and claw to keep heirs of Holocaust victims from claiming assets deposited in the frantic years before the war. European insurers were stonewalling just as hard. It must be relatively rare for children to know their parents had insurance. Even if others, like Carl, had been sent downstairs with money to pay the agent, I was betting he was unusual in knowing what company held his father's policy. When my father died, it was only on going through his papers that I found his life insurance.

When not only your family, but your house, maybe even your entire town, has been obliterated—you'd have no records to turn to. And if you did, the company would treat you the way it had Carl: denying the claim because you couldn't present a death certificate. They really were a prize group of bastards, those banks and insurers.

My phone rang again, but I picked it up only to switch it off. If those books of Hoffman's contained a list of life-insurance policies bought by people like Carl's father or Max's, people who died in Treblinka or Auschwitz, it wasn't such a large list that Edelweiss would lose much from paying the claims. All it would do is give several hundred people the knowledge that their parents or grandparents had bought policies and give them the policy numbers. It wasn't as if there'd be a stampede on Edelweiss assets.

Unless, of course, states began passing Holocaust Asset Recovery Acts, such as the one Ajax torpedoed last week. The company would have had to make an audited search of its policy files—of all the hundred or so companies that made up the Ajax group, now including Edelweiss—and prove that it wasn't sitting on policies belonging to the dead of the war in Europe. That might have cost them a bundle.

Would Fepple have grasped this possibility? Could he have found enough information in Aaron Sommers's file to use it in an attempt at blackmail? He'd been excited at a way to make money. If this was it, was it a big enough reason for someone at Ajax to kill him? And who would have been the triggerman? Ralph? The jolly Bertrand? His soft-as-steel wife?

I accelerated around a couple of triple-trailer semis, impatient to start gathering any kind of information. Right now I was building a house from cards; I needed facts, good hard mortar and cement. Turning onto Jackson Boulevard, heading east into the Loop, I drummed my fingers on the steering wheel in an agony of impatience at every stoplight. Just west of the river, under the shadow of Union Station and its disreputable surrounding bars, I found an empty meter. I jammed in a fistful of quarters and ran the four blocks east to the Insurance Exchange.

The exchange is a tired old building near the southwest corner of the Loop, and the Illinois Insurance Institute proved to be one of the tireder offices in it. Old-fashioned hanging lights held a couple of malfunctioning fluorescent bulbs, which blinked in an irritating way on the woman who sat inside the entrance. She squinted up at me from a mailing she was assembling, like an owl who isn't used to seeing strangers in its neck of the forest. When I explained that I was trying to find out how big Edelweiss Insurance had been in the 1930's and whether they'd had an office in Vienna, she sighed and put down the sheaf of papers she was folding.

"I don't know that kind of thing. You can look in the library if you want, but I'm afraid I can't take time to help you."

She pushed back her chair and opened the door to a murky room in the back. It was stuffed beyond the firecode limit with shelves of books and papers.

"Things are kind of in chronological order," she said, waving an arm vaguely toward the left corner. "The further back you go in time the more likely they are to be in order—most people only come here to consult current documents, and it's hard for me to find the time to keep them organized. It would be a real help if you'd leave everything in the same shape you find it. If you want copies of anything, you can use my machine, but it's a dime a page."

The ringing phone sent her scurrying back to the front room. I went to the corner she'd waved at. For such a small space, it held a depressing amount of material—shelves of *National Underwriter* and *Insurance Blue Books;* speeches to the American Insurance Institute; addresses to international insurance congresses; hearings before the U.S. Congress to see whether ships sunk in the Spanish–American War had to be covered under marine policies.

I moved along as fast as I could, using a set of rolling stairs to climb up and down, until I found the section with documents dating to the 1920's and '30's. I flipped through them. More speeches, more congressional hearings, this time on insurance benefits for World War I veterans. My hands were black with dust when I suddenly found it: a squat fat book, whose blue cover had faded to grey. *Le Registre des Bureaux des Compagnies d'Assurance Européennes,* printed in Genève in 1936.

I don't read French well—unlike Spanish, it's not close enough to Italian for me to follow a novel—but a list of European insurance-company offices didn't demand a linguist. I was almost holding my breath when I took it underneath the dim lamp in the middle of the room, where I squinted painfully at the tiny print. The book's organization was difficult to figure out in bad light, in a language I didn't know, but I finally saw they had grouped offices by country and then by asset size.

In Switzerland the biggest company in 1935 had been Nesthorn, followed by Swiss Re, Zurich Life, Winterer, and a bunch of others. Edelweiss was far down on the list, but it had a footnote, which was in even smaller type than the body of the report. Even tilting the page to see it under different light, holding it so close to my nose I sneezed a half dozen times, I couldn't make out the tiny print. I looked toward the front room. The overworked factotum was apparently still stuffing letters into envelopes; it would be a shame to disturb her by asking to borrow the book. I tucked it into my briefcase, thanked her for her help, and told her I'd probably be back in the morning.

"What time do you open up?"

"Usually not until ten, but Mr. Irvine, he's the executive director, he sometimes comes in in the mornings. . . .Oh, my, look at your lovely jacket. I'm sorry, everything in there is so filthy, but it's just me; I don't have time to dust all those old books."

"That's okay," I said heartily. "It will clean." I hoped: my lovely silk–wool herringbone now looked as though it had been dyed grey by an inexpert hand.

I ran all the way back to my car and could hardly bear the traffic that slowed me on my way back to my office. At my desk, I used a magnifying glass to pick my way through the French footnote as best I could: the acquisition recent of Edelweiss A.G. by Nesthorn A.G., the most big company in Switzerland, would appear in the year following, when the Edelweiss numbers would not be something—seen? available? It didn't matter. Until that time, something something company reportage would be independent.

A merger between Nesthorn and Edelweiss, and now the company was called Edelweiss. I didn't understand that part, but I went on to the listing of offices. Edelweiss had three, one each in Basel, Zurich, and Bern. Nesthorn had twenty-seven. Two in Vienna. One in Prague, one in Bratislava, three in Berlin. They had an office in Paris, which had done a brisk business. The Viennese office, on Porzellangasse, had led the pack of twenty-seven in sales, with a 1935 volume almost thirty percent greater than any of its closest competitors. Had that been Ulrich Hoffman's territory, riding around on his bicycle, entering names in his ornate script? Doing a land-office business among families worried that the anti-Jewish laws in Germany would soon affect them, as well?

Those numbers in Ulrich's books that started with *N*

could be Nesthorn life-insurance policies. And after the merger with Edelweiss—I turned to my computer and logged on to Lexis-Nexis.

The results for my previous search on Edelweiss were there, but these were only contemporary documents. I scanned them anyway. They told me about the acquisition of Ajax, Edelweiss's decision to participate in a forum on European insurance companies and dormant Holocaust life-insurance policies. There were reports on third-quarter earnings, reports on their acquisition of a London merchant bank. The Hirs family was still the majority shareholder with eleven percent of the outstanding shares. So the *H* on Fillida Rossy's china was her grandfather's name. The grandfather with whom she used to ski those difficult slopes in Switzerland. A reckless risk-taker behind her soft voice and fussing over rosemary rinses for her daughter's golden mane.

I saved this set of results and started a new search, looking for old background on Nesthorn *and* Edelweiss. The database didn't go back far enough for articles about the merger. I let the phone ring through to my answering service as I struggled with a vocabulary and grammar too complex for my primitive ability.

La revue de l'histoire financière et commerciale for July 1979 had an article that seemed to be about German companies trying to establish markets in the countries they had occupied during the war. *Le nouveau géant économique* was making its neighbors nervous. In one paragraph, the article commented that, *on voudrait savoir,* the biggest company of insurance Swiss had changed its name from Nesthorn to Edelweiss, because there are too many persons who remember them from their *histoire peu agréable.*

Their less-agreeable history, would that be? Surely that didn't refer to selling life insurance whose claims they wouldn't pay. It must have to do with something else. I wondered if the other articles explained what. I attached them to an e-mail to Morrell, who reads French.

Do either of these articles explain what Nesthorn Insurance did in the forties that made them less agreeable to their European neighbors? How are you coming with getting a permit to travel to the northwest frontier? I hit the SEND key, thinking how strange it was that Morrell, thirteen thousand miles away, could see my words at virtually the same time I sent them.

I leaned back in my chair, eyes closed, seeing Fillida Rossy at dinner, stroking the heavy flatware with the *H* engraved on the handle. What she owned she touched, clutched—or what she touched, she owned. That restless smoothing of her daughter's hair, her son's pajama collar—she had stroked my own hand in the same disquieting way when she brought me forward to meet her guests on Tuesday night.

Could she feel so possessive of the Edelweiss company that she would kill to safeguard it from claimants? Paul Hoffman-Radbuka had been so certain it was a woman who had shot him. Fierce, sunglasses, big hat. Could that have been Fillida Rossy? She was certainly commanding enough behind her languid exterior. I remembered Bertrand Rossy changing his tie after her soft comment that it was rather bold. Her friends, too, had hurried to make sure nothing in the conversation annoyed her.

On the other hand, Alderman Durham kept swimming around the submerged rocks of the story. My client's cousin Colby, who had done lookout duty for the break-in at Amy Blount's place and who had fingered my client to the police, was on the fringes of Durham's EYE team. The meeting between Durham and Rossy on Tuesday—had Rossy agreed to kill the Holocaust Asset Recovery Act in exchange for Durham giving him a hit woman who could shoot Paul Hoffman-Radbuka? Durham was such a wily political creature, it was hard to believe he'd do something that would so lay him open to blackmail. Nor could I see a sophisticated man like Rossy getting himself tangled up in a hired-murder rap. It was hard to understand why either of them would involve the other in something as crude as the break-in at Amy Blount's.

I called Durham's office. The alderman's secretary asked who I was, what I wanted.

"I'm an investigator," I said. "Mr. Durham and I met briefly last week. I'm sorry to say that some of the people on the fringe of his extremely wonderful Empower Youth Energy project have shown up as part of a murder investigation I'm working on. Before I give their names to the police, I wanted to do the alderman the courtesy of letting him hear about them from me first."

The secretary put me on hold. As I waited, I thought again about the Rossys. Maybe I could take a quick run up there to see if the maid, Irina, would talk to me. If she could give the Rossys an alibi for last Friday night, well, it would at least eliminate them from consideration as Fepple's murderers.

Durham's secretary came back to the phone. The alderman was in committee meetings until six; he'd meet me at his South Side office at six-thirty before going to a community church meeting. I didn't want to be alone on Durham's home turf the way things were shaping up; I told the secretary I'd be at the Golden Glow at six-fifteen. Durham could see me on my ground.

XLVII

Bourbon, with a Twist

I skimmed through my messages, both in my in-box and on-screen. Michael Loewenthal had dropped off the biography of Anna Freud. The day had been so long I'd completely forgotten that conversation. I had also completely forgotten the little dog tags for Ninshubur.

The biography was too fat for me to read clear through in a quest for Paul Hoffman or Radbuka. I looked at the photographs, at Anna Freud sitting next to her father in a café, at the Hampstead nursery where Lotty had washed dishes during the war. I tried to imagine Lotty as a teenager. She would have been idealistic, ardent, but without the patina of irony and briskness which kept the world at arm's length from her now.

I flipped to the back to look up *Radbuka* in the index. The name wasn't there. I checked *concentration camps*. The second reference was to a paper Freud had written on a group of six children who came to England from Terezin after the war. Six children aged three and four who had lived together as a little unit, looking after one another, forming a bond so tight that the adult authorities didn't think they could survive apart. No names were mentioned, no other history. It sounded like the group Hoffman-Radbuka had described in his television interview last week, the group where Ulrich had found him, wrenching him away from his little friend Miriam. Could Paul really have been part of it? Or had he appropriated their story to his own?

I went back on-line to see if I could find a copy of the paper Freud had written about the children, "An Experiment in Group Upbringing." A central research library in London would fax it to me at the cost of a dime a page. Cheap at the price. I entered a credit-card number and sent the order, then looked at my phone messages. The most urgent seemed to be from Ralph, who had called twice—to my cell phone, when I was heading onto the Ryan three hours ago, and just now, when I'd been trying to decipher the less agreeable part of Nesthorn's past.

He was in a meeting, naturally, but Denise, his secretary, said he badly wanted to see the originals of the material I had shown him this morning.

"I don't have them," I said. "I saw them very briefly yesterday, when I made the copies I gave him, but someone else took them for safekeeping. They're quite valuable documents, I gather. Is it Bertrand Rossy who'd like to look at them, or Ralph himself?"

"I believe Mr. Devereux showed the blowups I made to Mr. Rossy at a meeting this morning, but Mr. Devereux did not indicate whether Mr. Rossy was interested in them."

"Will you take this message down exactly as I give it to you? Tell Ralph that it is really, honestly true that I don't have them. Someone else took them. I have no idea where the person who took them is, nor where that person stowed them. Tell him this is not a joke, it is not a way of stalling him. I want those books as badly as he does, but I don't know where they are."

I made Denise read the message back to me. I hoped it would convince Rossy, if it was Rossy pushing on

Ralph for them, that I truly didn't have Ulrich's books. I hoped I hadn't fingered Lotty in the process. That thought unnerved me. If I had—I couldn't take time to sit and fret: if I hustled, I could get to the Rossys' before my appointment with Durham.

I drove the two miles back to my apartment and took one of my mother's diamond drops from the safe. Her photograph on the dresser seemed to watch me sternly: my dad had given her those earrings on their twentieth anniversary. I'd gone with him to the Tucker Company on Wabash when he picked them out and put down a deposit, and I'd gone back with him when he made the final payment.

"I won't lose it," I told her photograph. I hurried out of the room, away from her eyes. As I passed the bathroom I caught sight of my own face in the mirrored door. I had forgotten the dust that I'd collected at the Insurance Institute. If I was going to be presentable at the Rossy building, I needed a clean jacket. I took a rose wool–rayon weave that hung loosely, concealing the bulge of my shoulder holster. The herringbone I tossed into the hall closet with my bloodstained gold blouse, then I remembered my idea of profiling Paul's DNA. In case I wanted to pursue that, I wrapped the gold blouse in a clean plastic bag and put it in my bedroom safe.

An apple from the kitchen would have to do for a late lunch: I was too nervous today to sit still for a proper meal. I saw Ninshubur's collar on the sink and stuck it in my pocket—I'd try to find time to get up to Evanston with that tonight if I could.

I clattered down the stairs, sketched a wave at Mr. Contreras, who stuck his head out the door when he heard me, and drove across Addison, past Wrigley Field, where the vendors were setting up their carts for one of the Cubs'—mercifully—final games of the season.

From a marginally legal parking space outside their

building, I called to the Rossy apartment. Fillida Rossy answered the phone. I hung up and leaned back in the front seat to wait. I could give the project until six, when I'd need to leave for my meeting with the alderman.

At four-thirty, Fillida Rossy came through the front door with her children and their nanny, who was carrying a large gym bag. As she had on Tuesday evening, Fillida was fussing endlessly with their clothes, retying the girl's sash, smoothing the collar outside the boy's monogrammed sweater. When he jerked away, she started wrapping the girl's long hair around her hands, all the time talking to the nanny. She herself was dressed in jeans with a crinkly warm-up jacket.

Someone drove a black Lincoln Navigator to the entrance. While the driver put the gym bag into the back, Fillida held both children tightly, apparently giving some last instructions to the nanny. She climbed into the front seat, without acknowledging the man who held the door and put her bag into the car for her. I waited while the children disappeared up the street with the nanny before crossing over to go into the building.

It was a different doorman on duty this afternoon than the one I'd met on Tuesday. "You just missed Mrs. Rossy; no one's up there but the maid. She speaks English, but not too great," he said. When I said that I'd lost one of my earrings at dinner and was hoping Mrs. Rossy had found it, he added, "You can see if she'll understand you."

I tried to explain over the house phone who I was and what I wanted. My father's mother spoke Polish, but my dad didn't, so the language hadn't been part of my childhood. Still, a few halting phrases got me upstairs, where I showed Irina the earring. She shook her head, starting to give me a long discourse in Polish. I had to apologize and tell her I didn't understand.

"I all clean on next day, and don't see nothing. But at party, I hear you speak Italy, I ask why, if your name Warshawska." She gave it the Polish pronunciation, with the appropriate ending for a woman.

"My mother was Italian," I explained. "My father was Polish."

She nodded. "I understand. Children talk like mother talk. In my family, same. In Mrs. Fillida's family, same. Mr. Rossy, he speak Italy, English, Germania, France, but children, only Italy, English."

I clucked sympathetically over the fact that no one in the household could communicate with Irina. "Mrs. Rossy is a good mother, is she, always talking to her children?"

Irina threw up her hands. "When she see children, she always holding, always—like—like cat or dog." She mimed petting. "Clothes, oh, my God, they has beautiful clothes, much much money. I buy all for my children what she pay on one dress for Marguerita. Children much money but not happy. No has friend. Mister, he very good man, happy, always polite. She, no, she cold."

"But she doesn't like to leave the children alone, does she?" I doggedly tried to keep the conversation on track. "I mean, they entertain here, but does she go out and leave the children behind?"

Irina looked at me in surprise. Of course Mrs. Rossy left the children. She was rich, she went to the gym, to go shopping, to see friends. It was only when she was home . . .

"Last Friday I thought I saw her at a dance at the Hilton Hotel. You know, for charity." I had to repeat the sentence a couple of different ways before Irina understood me.

She shrugged. "Is possible. Was not here, I not know where she and mister going. I in bed early. Not like today when many people coming for dinner."

My hint to leave. I tried offering her a tip for her

help, but she flung up her hands in disgust. She was sorry about my earring: she would keep looking for it.

As I drove up the street, I passed the children returning from their walk. They were punching at each other from either side of the nanny—happy families, as Tolstoy said.

So the Rossys hadn't been home on Friday night. That didn't mean they'd been in Hyde Park shooting Howard Fepple. Still, I could see Fillida phoning him, saying her name was Connie Ingram, persuading him she was hot for him. I could see her coming in with him and all the Lamaze parents—perhaps her husband melting into the group as well—twining herself around Fepple in his chair. Bertrand slips into the office, whacks the back of his head, she puts the SIG's barrel into his mouth. At the spray of blood and bone, she jumps off, places the gun under his chair. She's cool, but not cool enough to remember to get his hand on the gun so that the morgue will find gunpowder residue on it.

Then she and Bertrand search the office, find the Sommers file, and take off. Yesterday, Fillida went to Hoffman's house. How had she found the address when I hadn't been able to? Oh, of course, through Ulrich. They knew his name: they were looking for him, looking for those records of Edelweiss–Nesthorn sales. It must have made Rossy's eyes jump out of their sockets when Connie Ingram brought the Sommers file up to Ralph's office last week. The agent he was looking for, Ulrich Hoffman, right under his nose in Chicago. Maybe it took them a while to figure it out, but eventually they realized if he was dead they could still get his address a bunch of different ways. Old phone books, for instance.

I could see all of this happening. But how could I prove any of it? If I had world enough and time, I could probably find they'd gone to Ameritech for old phone books. The cops hadn't been able to trace the SIG that killed Fepple. Perhaps Fillida's friend in the Italian consulate had brought it in with her under diplomatic cover. "Laura, darling, I want to bring my guns with me. The Americans are so bizarre about guns—they all carry them the way we do pocketbooks, but they will make my life a misery of forms if I try to carry my own through customs with me."

As I cruised down Lake Shore Drive for my meeting with Durham, I thought uneasily about Paul Hoffman in his hospital bed. Where had Fillida Rossy been going on a Friday afternoon with her gym bag? Did she work out this late in the day, or did the bag hold a gun for finishing the job on Paul?

At the lights on Chicago Avenue, I called the hospital: there was a block on his room, so they wouldn't connect me. That was good. Could they give me a status report? His condition had been upgraded to serious.

When I'd found a meter a few blocks south of the Glow, I called Tim Streeter up at Max's. Max hadn't come home from work yet—Posner had been back at the hospital today. The demonstrations had been more subdued, but the board was meeting late to discuss the problem.

Tim was bored; they really didn't need him any longer. If I could get Calia Ninshubur's collar they would all be happy.

"Oh, that wretched collar." I told Tim if I couldn't get up to Evanston tonight, Calia would have to accept receiving it in the mail when she returned home. More important was my dilemma about Paul's safety, which I explained to him.

Tim said he'd talk to his brother to see if one of the women on their team would look after Paul for a few days. He himself needed a break from bodyguarding: four days of Calia had turned him prematurely white.

When we finished, I leaned my head wearily against the steering wheel. Too much was going on that I didn't understand and couldn't control. Where had Lotty gone? She'd stalked angrily off into the night last night, driven home—and disappeared. I dialed her apartment, where her clipped voice came on again from the machine. "Lotty, please call me if you are picking up your messages. I'm seriously worried." I called back up to Evanston, intending to leave a message for Max, but he'd just walked in the door.

"Victoria, have you had any word from Lotty? No? Mrs. Coltrain called, wanting to know if you had been able to get into her apartment."

"Oh, nuts—calling Mrs. Coltrain back went out of my head—I'm spinning in too many directions right now." I told Max about my tour through the apartment this morning and asked if he could tell Mrs. Coltrain about it himself.

"If Lotty disappeared of her own free will, how could she leave without letting us know?" I added. "Surely she must know how much this would upset all her friends, not to say Mrs. Coltrain and her clinic staff."

"She's seriously disturbed," Max said. "Something has knocked her off-balance, so that she's thinking only of some small world, not the bigger one with her friends in it. Her whole behavior is—it's frightening me, Victoria. I'm tempted to call it some kind of long-delayed post-traumatic breakdown, as if she held so much in for so many decades that it's hitting her with the force of a tidal wave. If you get any kind of word from her, no matter the hour, let me know at once. As I will you."

It helped that Max was as troubled as I. Post-traumatic stress—it's a diagnosis bandied about so glibly these days that one forgets how real and terrifying a condition it is. If Max was right, it could explain

Lotty's unbearable edginess lately, as well as her sudden evaporation. I wished I hadn't gotten myself bogged down in the trailing tentacles of the investigation: I wanted to find her now. I wanted to console her if that lay within my power. I wanted to bring her back to life. But I was frighteningly aware that I had few powers. I wasn't an *indovina*. I was barely making progress slogging through quicksand as an investigator.

I climbed stiffly out of the car. It was six-thirty; I was late for my meeting with the alderman. I walked up the street to the Golden Glow. It's the closest thing I have to a private club, not that it's private, but I've been a regular for so many years that they let me run a tab that I pay once a month.

Sal Barthele, who owns the place, flashed me a smile but didn't have time to come around to say hello—the horseshoe mahogany bar, which her brothers and I had helped her retrieve from a Gold Coast mansion when it went under the wrecking ball ten years ago, was three-deep with weary traders. The half dozen little tables with their signature Tiffany lamps were also crowded. I scanned the room but didn't spot the alderman.

Durham came in just as Jacqueline, who was working the floor, whizzed past me with a full tray. She handed me a glass of Black Label without breaking stride and went on to a table where she served eight drinks without checking the order. I took a deep swallow of scotch, steadying myself from my worries about Lotty, bracing myself to talk to the alderman.

Jacqueline saw me edge my way to the door to greet Durham: she flashed an arm at me, pointing to a table in the corner. Sure enough, just as Durham had given me an easy greeting, the five women clustered at the table hopped up to leave. By the time the alderman and I were sitting down, half the bar had emptied as people ran to catch seven-o'clock trains. I'd wondered if he would come with an escort; now that the room had cleared I could see two youths in their EYE blazers standing just inside the door.

"So, Investigator Warshawski. You are still on your quest to link African-American men with any crime that floats by your nose." It was a statement, not a question.

"I don't have to go on a quest," I said with a gentle smile. "The news gets hand-delivered to me. Colby Sommers has not only been flashing a roll but telling everyone and their dog Rover what he did to—well, I hate to say earn, that demeans the hard work that most people do for a living. Let's call it scoring."

"Call it what you want, Ms. Warshawski. Call it what you want, it doesn't change the ugly truth behind the insinuations." When Jacqueline hovered briefly in front of us, he ordered Maker's Mark and a twist; I shook my head—one whisky is my limit when I'm in a tricky conversation.

"People say you're smart, alderman; people say you're the one man who can give the mayor a run for his money in the next election cycle. I don't see it myself. I know Colby Sommers was a lookout when a couple of EYE youths broke into Amy Blount's apartment earlier this week. When you and I talked on Wednesday, I was wondering about an anonymous tip the cops got, one to frame Isaiah Sommers. Now I know Colby Sommers made that phone call. I know that Isaiah and Margaret Sommers went to Fepple's agency the Saturday morning his body was lying there, brains and blood all over everything, on your advice. I guess what I don't know is what Bertrand Rossy could possibly offer you to make you get up to your neck in his problems."

Durham smiled, a genial smile that didn't reach his eyes. "You don't know much, Ms. Warshawski, because there's no way you can know folks in my ward. It's no secret that Colby Sommers hates his cousin: everyone along Eighty-seventh Street knows that. If he tried to frame Isaiah for murder and if he got involved in the fringes of hard-core crime, it doesn't shock me the way it might you: I understand all the indignities, all the centuries of injustice, that make black men turn on themselves, or turn on their own community. I doubt you could ever understand such things. But if Colby has tried to harm his cousin, I'll make a call to the local police commander, see if I can't help sort that out so that Isaiah doesn't suffer needlessly."

"I hear things, too, alderman." I twirled the last small mouthful of whisky in my glass. "One of the most interesting is about you and reparations for descendants of slaves. An important issue. A good one to put the mayor in a bind over—he can't afford to alienate the international business community by pushing it; he can't afford to look bad to his constituents by ignoring it, especially since he backed the City Council's condemnation of slavery."

"So you understand local politics, detective. Maybe that means you'll vote for me, if I ever run for an office that covers whatever chardonnay district you live in."

He was deliberately trying to goad me; I gave him a quizzical smile to show I understood the effort even if I didn't get the reason. "Oh, yes, I understand local politics. I understand it might not look so good if people found out that you only started on your campaign when Bertrand Rossy came to town. When he—persuaded—you to take the spotlight off Joseph Posner and the Holocaust asset issue by banging the drum over reparations for slavery."

"Those are mighty ugly words, detective, and as you know, I am not a patient man when it comes to people like you slandering me."

"Slander. Now, that assumes a baseless accusation. If I wanted to take the trouble, or ask, say, Murray Ryerson at the *Herald-Star* to take the trouble, I'm betting we could find some substantial chunk of change moving from Rossy to you. Either something from him personally, or something on an Ajax corporate check. I'm betting from him personally. And maybe he was even savvy enough to give you cash. But someone will know about it. It's just a question of digging deep enough."

He didn't flinch. "Bertrand Rossy is an important businessman around town, even if he is from Switzerland. And like you say, one of these days I might want to run for mayor of Chicago. It can't hurt me to have support in the business community. But most important to me is my own community. Where I grew up. And where I know most people by their first names. They're the Chicagoans who need me, they're the ones I work for, so I'd best be getting to a meeting with them."

He drained his glass and signaled for a check, but I waved a hand to Jacqueline, meaning Sal should add it to my bar tab. I didn't want to be indebted to Alderman Durham for anything, not even one mouthful of scotch whisky.

XLVIII

Bodies Building

At the end of the trading day, the South Loop empties fast. The streets take on the forlorn and tawdry look that human spaces acquire when they've been abandoned: every piece of garbage, every abandoned can and bottle, stood out on the empty streets. The L screeching overhead sounded as remote and wild as a coyote on the prairie.

I walked the three blocks to my car very fast, looking around every few steps into doorways and alleys, zigging back and forth across the street. Who would come for me first—Fillida Rossy, or Durham's EYE gang?

Durham had not only brushed me off, he'd done so with a studied offensiveness that was designed to make me angry. As if he hoped that focusing on racial injustice would keep me from thinking about the specifics of the crimes Colby Sommers was involved in.

So what wasn't I supposed to think about? It seemed to me I was getting a tolerably clear picture of why Ulrich's journals mattered. And of how Howard Fepple had been killed. I was also starting to see the connection between Durham and Rossy. They had a beautifully dovetailed set of needs: Rossy handed Durham an attention-getting campaign issue, gave him the cash to fund it, and manipulated the legislature into linking the Holocaust with slave reparations, making it too big an issue for them to touch. Durham in exchange took the spotlight away from Ajax, Edelweiss, and Holocaust asset recovery. It was lovely, in a perverted way.

What I didn't understand was what Howard Fepple had seen in the Sommers file that made him think he had a big payday coming. I supposed it could have been something to do with Ulrich's European life-insurance book—that Fepple, like me, like anyone in insurance, knew Edelweiss couldn't afford an exposure on Holocaust life-insurance policies.

But that didn't explain how Ulrich had made his money. Thirty years ago he wouldn't have been blackmailing his Swiss employers, because thirty years ago Holocaust bank accounts and Holocaust life-insurance policies didn't matter to state legislatures or the U.S. Congress. Ulrich must have been doing something more local. He didn't seem like a criminal mastermind, just an ugly guy who horribly abused his son and found a quiet way to turn a plug nickel into a silver dollar.

A man lurched out of the shadows in front of me. I didn't know I could get my hand inside my shoulder holster so fast. When the man asked for the price of a meal, old Ezra filling the air around him, sweat trickled down the back of my neck. I stuck the gun in my jacket pocket and fished in my bag for a dollar, but he'd seen the gun and ran down a side street on unsteady legs.

I drove back to my office, keeping an uneasy eye on the rearview mirror, checking for tails. When I got to Tessa's and my warehouse, I parked away from the building. I had my gun in my hand when I let myself in. Before settling at my desk, I searched Tessa's studio, the hall, the bathroom, and all the subdivisions of my office—it's hard to break in to our building but not impossible.

I put in a call to Terry Finchley at the police department. He'd been Mary Louise's commanding officer her last three years on the force and was the person she still turned to for inside information on police investigations. I knew he wasn't involved in the Sommers murder directly, but he knew about the investigation because he'd been getting information about it to Mary Louise. He wasn't in, either. I hesitated, then left a message for him with the desk sergeant: *Colby Sommers is a hanger-on with the EYE team. He knows something about Howard Fepple's murder; he also was involved in the break-in in Hyde Park where you sent the forensics unit on Wednesday.* The sergeant promised to pass it on.

When I switched on my computer, I felt unreasonably let down that Morrell hadn't responded to my e-mail. Of course, it was the middle of the night in Kabul. And who knew where he was—if he'd gone into the backcountry already, he wouldn't be anywhere near a phone hookup. Lotty off in some desolate place that I couldn't penetrate, Morrell at the ends of the earth. I felt horribly alone and sorry for myself.

The fax of Anna Freud's article on the six toddlers from Terezin had come in. I turned to it resolutely, determined not to wallow in self-pity.

The article was long, but I read it through with total attention. Despite the clinical tone of the piece, the heartbreaking destruction of the children came through clearly—deprived of everything, from parental love to language, fending for themselves as toddlers in a concentration camp, somehow coming together to support one another.

After the war, when the British admitted a number of children from the camps to help them learn to live in a terror-free world, Freud took over the care of these six:

they were far too young for any of the other programs. And they were such a tight little group that the social workers were afraid of separating them, afraid of the added trauma that separation would create in their young lives. They were all close, but two had formed a special bond with each other: Paul and Miriam.

Paul and Miriam. Anna Freud, whom Paul Hoffman called his savior in England, cutting her photograph from her biography to hang in his chamber of secrets. Freud's Paul, born in Berlin in 1942, sent to Terezin at twelve months, just as Paul Hoffman had claimed for himself in the interview on television. The only one of the six about whose family nothing was known. So if your name was Paul, and your father was a German who brutalized you, locked you in a closet, beat you for any signs of feminine character, maybe you would start to think, This is my story, the children in the camps.

But Paul and Miriam weren't Anna Freud's children's real names. In a study of real people, Freud had used code names to protect their privacy. Paul Hoffman hadn't understood that. He'd read the article, absorbed the story, imagined his little playmate Miriam for whom he cried so piteously on television last week.

The hairs stood up on the back of my neck. I felt an overwhelming desire for my own home and bed, for privacy away from other people's soul-sickening traumas. I wasn't up to driving north to Evanston. I put Ninshubur's little collar in a padded mailer, addressed it to Michael Loewenthal's London home with a note for customs, *used goods, no declared value,* and dropped it in a mailbox with some airmail postage. I kept an eye out on the street all the way home, but neither Fillida nor the EYE team seemed to be stalking me.

I was happy when Mr. Contreras waylaid me as I came into the lobby. When he learned I hadn't eaten all day, except for my apple, he exclaimed, "No wonder you're discouraged, doll. I got spaghetti on the stove. It ain't homemade, like you're used to, but it's plenty good enough for an empty stomach."

It was, indeed—I ate two bowls of it. We drove the dogs to a park and let them romp in the dark.

I fell early to sleep. In the night, I had my most dreaded nightmare, the one where I was trying to find my mother and only came on her as she was lowered into her grave, wrapped in so many bandages, with tubes coming from every arm, that she couldn't see me. I knew she was alive, I knew she could hear me, but she gave no sign. I woke from it weeping, saying Lotty's name aloud to myself. I lay awake for an hour, listening to sounds from the world outside, wondering what the Rossys were doing, before falling back at last into a fitful sleep.

At seven, I got up to run to the lake with the dogs while Mr. Contreras followed us in my Mustang. The idea that I might be in danger worried him powerfully; I could see he was going to stick close at hand until the Edelweiss business was resolved.

The lake was still warm, even though the September days were drawing short; I went into the water with the dogs. While Mr. Contreras threw sticks for them I swam to the next rock outcropping and back. When I rejoined the three of them I was tired but refreshed, the misery of the previous night eased from my mind.

As we drove home I turned on the radio to catch the news at the top of the hour. *Presidential election blah-blah, violence on the West Bank and Gaza blah-blah.*

In our top local story, police have released the iden-tity of a woman whose body was found early this morning in the Sundown Meadow Forest Preserve. A Countryside couple came on the body when they were running their dogs in the woods a little before six this morning. Countryside police now tell us that her name was Connie Ingram, thirty-three, of LaGrange. She lived with her mother, who became worried when her daughter did not return from work last night.

"She doesn't have a boyfriend," Mrs. Ingram said. "She often stayed late on Fridays to go for a drink with her girlfriends at work, but she always caught the 7:03."

When her daughter failed to come home by the last train, Mrs. Ingram called local police, who told her they didn't take a missing person's report until someone had been gone for seventy-two hours. Still, by the time Mrs. Ingram talked to LaGrange police, her daughter was already dead: the Cook County Medical Examiner estimates that she was strangled around eight P.M.

Ingram had worked at Ajax Insurance in the Loop since graduating from high school. Coworkers say she had recently been troubled by accusations from Chicago police that she was involved in the murder of longtime Ajax insurance agent Howard Fepple earlier this week. Countryside and LaGrange authorities are cooperating fully with the Chicago police in the investigation.

In other local news, a South Side man was shot and killed in an apparent drive-by shooting as he was walking home from the L last night. Colby Sommers had been involved in Alderman Louis Durham's Empower Youth Energy program as a boy; the alderman said he is sending condolences to the family.

Is the end of summer getting you down? Turn to—

I turned off the radio and pulled over to the curb. Mr. Contreras looked at me in alarm. "What's up, doll? She a friend of yours? You're white as my hair right now."

"Not a friend—the young woman in the claims department I've been telling you about. Yesterday morning when I went down to Ajax, Ralph Devereux taxed her with knowing something about these wretched old journals that Lotty's wandered off with."

Connie Ingram disappeared for a few minutes on her way to the elevator. I thought she was hiding from me, but maybe she was in Bertrand Rossy's office, seeking advice.

Fepple must have sent a sample of his goods to the company: how else had they known he really could blackmail them? He'd sent them to poor little Connie Ingram, because she was in touch with him. She went directly to Bertrand Rossy because Rossy was taking a personal interest in the work she was doing on the Sommers file. It must have been almost unbearably exciting for a claims handler to be pulled out of the pit by the glamorous young executive from the new owners in Zurich. He swore her to secrecy; he knew she wouldn't betray his interest in the case to Ralph, to her boss Karen Bigelow, to anyone, because he could gauge her excitement pretty clearly.

But she was a company woman; she was worried when she left Ralph's office. She wanted to be loyal to the claims department, but she needed to consult Rossy first. So what did Rossy do? Arranged a secret meeting with her at the end of the day. ("We can't talk now, my schedule is full; I'll pick you up at the bar across the street after work. But don't tell anyone. We don't know who in this company we can trust.") Something like that. Taken her to the forest preserve, where she might have imagined sex with the boss, and strangled her when she turned to smile at him.

The scenario made me shudder in disgust. If I was right. Peppy leaned her head across the backseat and nuzzled me, whimpering. My neighbor wrapped a towel around me.

"You get into the passenger seat, doll, I'm driving you home. Tea, honey, milk, you need that and a hot bath right now."

I didn't fight him, even though I knew I couldn't afford to sit around for very long. While he boiled water for tea and fussed around with bread and eggs I went upstairs to shower.

Standing under the hot water, drifting, my mind turned up what Ralph had said yesterday to Connie. Something like, *I didn't think we ever deep-sixed papers in an insurance company*. If Fepple had sent her samples of his wares, so to speak, she'd have kept them.

I turned off the water abruptly and dried myself quickly. Say Rossy took care of the claims master file, cleaning out anything in Ulrich's handwriting. He'd found the microfiche copy—nothing simpler than for him to roam the floors of the building after hours: just checking on local operations. Hunt for the right drawer, abstract the fiche, and destroy it.

But I'd guess Connie had a desk file—the documents she needed to consult every day on a case while she was actively working on it. It probably hadn't occurred to Rossy—he'd never done a day's clerical work in his life. And I bet Fepple's stuff was in it.

I scrambled into my clothes: jeans, running shoes, and the softly cut blazer to conceal my gun. I ran down the stairs to Mr. Contreras's place, where I took the time to drink the hot, sweet tea he'd made and eat scrambled eggs. I was impatient to be going—but I owed him the courtesy to sit at the table for fifteen minutes.

While I ate I explained what I wanted to do, muting his protest at my taking off again. The clinching argument in his eyes was that the sooner I got going on Rossy and Ajax, the sooner I'd be able to start looking for Lotty.

XLIX

Clerical Work

I ran back up to my apartment to collect my bag—and to call Ralph, so I'd know where he was instead of bouncing around town hunting for him. My phone was ringing when I got upstairs. It stopped before I got my door opened but started again as I rummaged in my briefcase for my Palm Pilot.

"Vic!" It was Don Strzepek. "Don't you ever check your messages? I've left four in the last hour."

"Don, knock it off. Two people connected with my investigation were murdered last night, which is way bigger in my mind than returning your phone calls."

"Well, Rhea was lucky she wasn't murdered last night. A masked gunman broke into her place, looking for those damned books of Ulrich Hoffman's. So if you can clean the snot off your nose and be responsive, go get them back from Dr. Herschel before someone else is hurt."

"Broke into her home?" I was horrified. "How do you know they were after Ulrich's books?"

"The attacker demanded them. Rhea was terrified: the bastard tied her up, held a gun on her, started tossing stuff out of her bookshelves, going through her personal things. She had to say that Lotty had them."

I felt the air drain from me, as if I'd been kicked in the solar plexus. "Yes, I can see that."

My voice was as dry as the dust under my dresser, but Don was full of his own alarms and didn't notice. At four this morning, Rhea woke to find someone standing over her with a gun. The person was completely covered in a ski mask, gloves, a bulky jacket. Rhea couldn't tell if it was a man or a woman, a black person or a white, but the attacker's size and ferocity made her think it was a man. He pulled a gun on her, forced her downstairs, taped her hands and feet to a dining-room chair.

The intruder had said, "You know what we want. Tell us where you've hidden them." She protested that she didn't know, so the man had growled out: the books of her patient Paul Hoffman.

Don's voice shook. "Prick said he'd already searched her office. She says it was the worst part, in a way, that she had to keep asking him to repeat what he was saying—he apparently spoke in a kind of growl that was hard to understand. Something deep in the throat; that's why she couldn't even tell the sex of the speaker. Also, well, you know how it is when you're terrified, especially if you're not used to physical attacks—your brain doesn't process stuff normally. And this—people look so horrible in ski masks and everything. It's paralyzing to see someone in that getup. They don't look human."

It flitted through my mind that Rhea could test her own theories by getting herself hypnotized, to see what she could recall of her assailant, but the episode had been too traumatic for me to make sport of her. "So she said, Don't shoot me, Dr. Herschel took the books?"

"The assailant was tossing her china on the floor. She watched him smash a teapot that her grandmother's great-grandmother brought from England in 1809." Don's voice took on a sharp edge. "He said he—she—whoever—knew Rhea was the person closest to Paul Hoffman—he knew his name and everything—and she was the only person Hoffman would have given the books to. So Rhea said someone else had taken the books from the hospital last night. When the bastard threatened her, she gave them Dr. Herschel's name. Not everyone has your physical stamina, Vic," he added when I didn't say anything.

"It may be okay," I said slowly. "Lotty's disappeared and taken the books with her. If they're still looking for Ulrich's journals, it confirms that Lotty disappeared on her own, that she wasn't coerced. The police have been around, I presume? Did she tell them about the connection to Paul Hoffman?"

"Oh, yeah." I could hear him sucking in a mouthful of smoke, then Rhea, plaintive in the background, reminding him that she hated cigarette smoke, and his "Sorry, sweet," into the mouthpiece, although not addressed to me.

Was that where Fillida Rossy had been going so fast with her gym bag yesterday afternoon? Down to Water Tower Place to search Rhea Wiell's office? No Ulrich journals in the office, so the Rossys waited until the middle of the night, after the end of their dinner party. Rossy returned from murdering Connie, the two of them entertained, Bertrand sparkling with wit, and then went off to terrorize Rhea Wiell in her home.

"What did Rhea say to the cops?" I asked.

"She told them you'd been in Paul's house Thursday, so you may get a visit from the investigating team."

"She's a never-ending ray of sunshine." Then I remembered my carefully worded message to Ralph yesterday afternoon—that I didn't have Ulrich's books, that someone else had taken them away. I'd been trying to protect Lotty, but all I'd done was expose Rhea Wiell. Naturally the Rossys—or whoever was after the books—had looked first for the person Hoffman was closest to. I could hardly complain if she'd sicced them onto me in turn.

"Hell, Don, I'm sorry." I cut short his expostulation. "Look, whoever is after these books is lethal. I'm totally, utterly thankful that they didn't shoot Rhea. But—if they go to Lotty's and don't find the notebooks there, they may think Rhea was lying. They may come after her again and be more ferocious this time. Or they may think she gave them to you. Can you go away for the weekend? Go to New York, go to London, go somewhere where you can feel reasonably safe?"

He was shaken. We talked about the possibilities for several minutes, but before he hung up I said, "Look, Don. I've got more bad news for you on your recovered memory project. I know seeing those books of Ulrich's already raised some doubts in your mind, but this story of Paul's, that he was a kid in Terezin who was taken to England, where Hoffman scooped him up, I'm afraid he may have adapted that from someone else's history."

I told him about Anna Freud's article. "If you can find out what happened to the real 'Paul' and 'Miriam' in that article—well, I'd hate for you to take your Paul's history public. A lot of readers would recognize Freud's article and know he had appropriated the story of those kids."

"Maybe the evidence will prove he's right." Don spoke without much conviction. "The children couldn't have stayed with Anna Freud's staff forever; they have to have grown up somewhere. One of them could well have come to America with Ulrich, who might have called him Paul, thinking that was his real name." He was trying hard to hang on to the shreds of his belief in his book—and in Rhea.

"Maybe," I said doubtfully. "I'll send you a copy of the article. The children were placed in adoptive homes through a foster parents' organization under Freud's supervision. I have a feeling they would have made sure

Paul went to a stable two-parent home, not into the custody of a widowed immigrant, even if he wasn't an *Einsatzgruppenführer*."

"You're trying to ruin my book just because you don't like Rhea," he grumbled.

I kept my temper with an effort. "You're a well-respected writer. I'm trying to keep you from making a fool out of yourself with a book that would be poked full of holes the minute it hit the street."

"It seems to me that's my lookout, mine and Rhea's."

"Oh, boil your head, Don," I said, my sympathy gone. "I have two murders to attend to: I don't have time for this kind of crap."

I hung up and found Ralph Devereux's home number. He'd moved away from the Gold Coast apartment where he'd lived when I used to know him, but he was still in the city, in the trendy new neighborhood on South Dearborn. I got his voice mail. On a Saturday he might be out running errands, or playing golf, but someone on his staff had been murdered. I bet he was in the office.

Sure enough, when I called over to Ajax, Ralph's secretary answered the phone. "Denise, V I Warshawski. I was very sorry to hear about Connie Ingram. Is Ralph in? I'm going to be there in about twenty minutes to talk to him about the situation."

She tried to protest: he was down the hall meeting with Mr. Rossy and the chairman; he'd called all his claims supervisors to come in and they were waiting in his conference room; the police were there right now interrogating the staff—there was no way he could fit me in. I told her I was on my way.

When I got to Ajax I had a bit of luck. Detective Finchley was in the lobby, talking to one of his juniors. The Finch, a slender black man in his late thirties, is always perfectly turned out; even on a Saturday morning his shirt was ironed to knife creases along the collar. He called me over as soon as he saw me.

"Vic, I didn't get your message about Colby Sommers until this morning. Idiot on duty last night didn't think it was important enough to page me at home, and now the dirtbag is dead. Drive-by, they're calling it. What do you know about him?"

I repeated what Gertrude Sommers had told me. "It was all based on word from the reverend at her church. Trouble is, I talked to Louis Durham about it last night."

"You're not saying Durham's responsible for this, are you?" He was indignant.

"Ms. Sommers's reverend says the left hand of Durham's left hand isn't always as well washed as it should be. If Durham talked it over with someone on his EYE team, maybe they felt the heat was getting too close. I'd check with Ms. Sommers, find out who this reverend is—he seems pretty well plugged into the neighborhood."

"Anytime you're within five miles of a case it gets totally screwed up," Terry complained. "Why are you here this morning? Don't tell me you think Alderman Durham shot Connie Ingram!"

"I'm here to see the head of the claims department— he values my opinion more than you do." That was a lie—but Terry'd gone out of his way to hurt my feelings: I wasn't going to expose myself to more insults by telling him my theories about Fepple, Ulrich, and the Swiss.

The insult was worth it, though: when I moved past him to the elevators, the security staff didn't challenge me—they figured I was one of Terry's detectives.

I rode up to the sixty-third floor, where the executive-floor attendant was at her station even though it was a Saturday morning. Poor Connie

Ingram: in life she'd been a minor cog in the large corporate engine. In death she caused senior executives to devote their weekends to her care.

"Detective Warshawski," I said to the attendant. "Mr. Devereux is expecting me."

"The police? I thought you were finished up here."

"That was Detective Finchley's team, but I'm overseeing the whole case, including the agency murder. You don't need to call—I know my way to Devereux's office."

She didn't try to stop me. When an employee has been murdered and the police are in, even executive-floor staff lose their poise. Ralph's secretary looked at me with a worried frown, but she also didn't try to send me away.

"He's still with Mr. Rossy and the chairman. You can wait out here if you want."

"Is Karen Bigelow in the conference room? I can talk to her in the meantime."

Denise's frown deepened, but she got up from her desk to escort me to the conference room. When I went in, the seven people at the long oval table were talking in a jerky, desultory way. They looked up eagerly but sank back in their seats when they saw it was me, not Ralph. Karen Bigelow, Connie's supervisor, recognized me after a moment and pinched her lips together in a scowl.

"Karen, you remember Ms. Warshawski? She'd like a word."

When the boss's secretary says that, it's tantamount to a command. Bigelow didn't like it, but she pushed away from the table and came with me to the outer office. I made the conventional overtures—I was very sorry to hear of the death, I knew it must be quite a shock—but she wasn't going to unbend for me.

My own lips tightened. "All right, let's do this the hard painful way. We all know Connie was in touch with Howard Fepple before he died and that he sent her copies of documents from his agency file. I want to see her desk file. I want to see what he sent her."

"So you can go to the police and blame this poor dead girl some more? Thank you, no."

I smiled grimly. "So there is a desk file—I wasn't sure. If we could go see it, we'll find in it the reason for Howard Fepple's death, and for her own. Not because she had—"

"I don't have to listen to this." Bigelow turned on her heel.

I shouted over her own raised voice. "Not because she had anything to do with his death. But because the documents were dangerous in a way that she didn't understand."

Ralph walked into his office at that unfortunate moment. "Vic!" he snarled in fury. "What the hell are you doing here? No, don't bother answering. Karen, what's Warshawski trying to persuade you to do?"

The other six supervisors had come to the conference-room door at my shout. The expression on Ralph's face made them scuttle back to their seats before he had time to order them to move.

"She wants to see poor little Connie's desk file on the Sommers case, Ralph," Karen Bigelow said.

Ralph turned a ferocious glare onto me: someone must have been chewing him out down in the chairman's office. "Don't you ever dare—*dare*—come into this building and try to suborn my staff behind my back again!"

"You have a right to be angry, Ralph," I said quietly. "But two people are dead and a third is in critical condition because of whatever scam the Midway Agency was working around the Aaron Sommers claim. I'm trying to find out what it was before anyone else is shot."

"The Chicago cops are working on it." His mouth was tight with anger. "Just leave them to it."

"I would if they were getting anywhere close, but I know things they don't, or at least I'm putting together things that they aren't."

"Then tell them about it."

"I would if I had any real evidence. That's why I want to see Connie's desk file."

He stared at me bleakly, then said, "Karen, go back to the conference room—tell the rest of the team I'll be with you in two minutes. Denise, do we have coffee, rolls, whatever? Could you get on that, please?"

Anger was still making a pulse throb in his temple, but he was trying hard not to take it out on his staff. He motioned me to his inner office with a jerk of his head—I didn't need nice treatment.

"All right. Two minutes to sell me and then I'm meeting with my staff." He shut the door and stared pointedly at his watch.

"The agent who originally sold Aaron Sommers his policy in 1971 was involved in something illegal," I said. "Howard Fepple apparently didn't know about it until he looked up Aaron Sommers's file. I was in the office with him when he did: it was clear it held something—documents, notes, I don't know what—that grabbed his attention. When he faxed his agency material to Connie, I'm presuming he included something that he thought gave him a way to blackmail the company.

"No one knows what the original agent, Ulrich Hoffman, was up to. All the copies of the original Sommers policy documents have disappeared. The only thing left is the sanitized version. You yourself said yesterday that there should be handwritten notes from the agent in it, but those have all disappeared. If Connie kept a desk copy, it's gold. And it's dynamite."

"So?" His arms were crossed in an uncompromising attitude.

I took a deep breath. "I believe Connie was reporting directly, privately, to Bertrand Ros—"

"Goddamn you, no!" he bellowed. "What the hell are you up to?"

"Ralph, please. I know this must seem like déjà vu all over again, me coming in, accusing your boss. But listen for just one minute. Ulrich Hoffman used to be an agent for Edelweiss in Vienna during the thirties, back when it was called Nesthorn. He sold burial policies to poor Jews. Came the war, who knows what he did for eight years, but in 1947 Ulrich landed in Baltimore, somehow moved on to Chicago, and started doing the only work he knew, selling burial policies to poor people, in this case African-Americans on Chicago's South Side."

"I'm sure all this history is fascinating," Ralph interrupted me with heavy sarcasm, "but my staff is waiting for me."

"Old Ulrich kept a list of his Viennese clients. The life-insurance policies that Edelweiss claims they never sold," I hissed. "Their line has been they were a small regional company, they weren't involved with people who died in the Holocaust. Edelweiss *was* a small company back then, but Nesthorn was the biggest player in Europe. If Ulrich's books come to light, then this charade Rossy and Janoff played in Springfield on Tuesday—getting the legislature to kill the Holocaust Asset Recovery Act—is going to cause a backlash the size of a tidal wave."

"Damn you, Vic, you can't prove any of this!" Ralph smacked his aluminum desktop so hard he winced in pain.

"No, because those wretched journals of Ulrich's keep disappearing. But believe me, Rossy is hot on their trail. The head office in Zurich can't afford for this to come to light. Edelweiss can't afford for anyone to see those books of Ulrich's. I'm betting Rossy and his wife engineered Howard Fepple's death. I'm betting he killed poor little Connie. I'm betting he told her she was on a top-secret project, working just for him, that she couldn't tell anyone, not Karen, not you, not her mother. He was handsome, rich, powerful; she was a plain little Cinderella toiling in the ranks. He probably was her Prince Charming fantasy come to life. She was loyal to Ajax, and he was Ajax—no conflict for her there, but a lot of excitement."

Ralph was very white. He unconsciously massaged his right shoulder, where he'd taken a bullet from his old boss ten years ago.

"I presume the police are connecting Connie's murder to Ajax, or you all wouldn't be gathered here on a Saturday," I said.

"The girls—women—she usually had a drink with on Friday nights say she canceled because she had to work late," Ralph said leadenly. "She certainly left the building when everyone else did, according to her coworkers. When one of them teased her about having a date that she didn't want to tell them about, she became very embarrassed, said it wasn't like that, but she'd been asked to keep it confidential. The cops are looking at the company."

"So will you let me take a look at Connie's desk file?"

"No." His voice was barely above a whisper now. "I want you to leave the building. And in case you're imagining stopping on thirty-nine to hunt for it yourself, don't: I'm sending Karen down to Connie's desk right now to collect all her papers and bring them up here. I'm not going to have you riding through my department like a cowgirl herding mavericks."

"Will you promise me one thing? Two things, actually. Will you look through Connie's papers without telling Bertrand Rossy about it? And will you let me know what you find?"

"I'm not promising you anything, Warshawski. But you can rest assured that I'm not jeopardizing what's left of my career by taking this story to Rossy."

L

Jumped for Joy

Before I left Ralph's office, I gave Denise another copy of my card. "He's going to want to get in touch with me," I said with more confidence than I felt. "Make sure he knows he can reach me on my cell phone anytime this weekend."

I almost couldn't bear not seeing Connie Ingram's desk file myself, but Karen Bigelow rode with me as far as the thirty-ninth floor, assuring me that she would summon building security if I followed her to Connie's workstation.

When I left the building, I turned into a whirlwind of useless activity. Don Strzepek had decided not to take my advice on leaving town; I got him to persuade Rhea to let me visit her in her town house on Clarendon, hoping a firsthand description of her attacker would tell me one way or another if it had been one of the Rossys.

That was my first wasted hour. Don let me into the house, past a waterfall with lotus flowers floating in it, to a solarium, where Rhea sat in a large armchair. Her luminous eyes peered at me from a cocoon of shawls. While she sipped herbal tea and Don held her hand, she stepped me through the events of the night before. When I tried to press her on anything—the height, the build, the accent, the strength, of her assailant, she leaned back in the chair, a hand over her forehead.

"Vic, I know you mean well, but I have been over this ground, not just with Donald and the police, but with myself. I put myself in a light trance and spoke the whole incident into a tape recorder, which you may listen to—if any detail had stuck out I would have recalled it then."

I listened to the tape, but she refused to reinduce a trance so that I could question her myself. I suggested that she might have noticed the color of the eyes glittering through the ski mask, the color of the mask or of the bulky jacket the person wore—her trance recital didn't cover any of those points. At that she became wearily belligerent: if she had thought such questions would produce useful answers, she would have asked them herself.

"Don, could you help Vic find her way out. I'm exhausted."

I didn't have time to waste on anger or arguments. I went back past the lotus petals, only venting my feelings by pinging a penny against the Buddha at the top of the waterfall.

I next drove down to the South Side, to Colby Sommers's mother, to try to gather any information about Isaiah's cousin's last evening on the planet. Various relations were comforting her, including Gertrude Sommers, who talked with me softly in one corner. Colby had been a weak boy and a weak man; he had liked to feel important by hanging out with dangerous people, and now, sadly, he'd paid the price. But Isaiah, Isaiah was a different story: she wanted to make sure I knew that I could not let Isaiah share Colby's fate.

I nodded bleakly and turned to Colby's mother. She

hadn't seen her son for a week or two, she didn't know what he'd been up to. She did give me the names of some of Colby's friends.

When I tracked them to a local pool hall, they put their cues aside, watching me with a glittering hostility. Even when I broke through the haze of reefer and bitterness that enveloped them, they didn't tell me much. Yes, Colby had hung with some brothers who did sometimes run errands for Durham's EYE team. Yes, he'd been flashing a roll for a few days, Colby was like that. When he was in the money, everyone got a share. When he was flat, everyone else was expected to ante up. Last night he'd said he was going to be doing something with the EYE brothers, but names? No, they knew no names. Neither bribes nor threats could shake them.

I left, frustrated. Terry didn't want to suspect Alderman Durham, and the guys on the South Side were too intimidated by the EYE team to rat them out. I could go see Durham again myself, but that would be wasted energy when I didn't have a viable lever. And anyway, right now my worries about Lotty, and Ulrich's journals, made it more important that I try to figure out a way to get to the Rossys.

I was wondering if there was some way I could start checking their alibis for last night without showing myself too obviously when my cell phone rang. I was northbound on the Ryan, in that stretch where sixteen lanes cross each other again and again in something like a maypole dance—not the place to distract myself. I pulled off at the nearest exit to answer.

I'd hoped for Ralph, but it was my answering service. Mrs. Coltrain had called me from Lotty's clinic. It was urgent, I should get back to her at once.

"She's at the clinic?" I looked at the dashboard clock—Lotty's Saturday hours were nine-thirty to one; it was past two now.

I don't know the weekend operators at my service; this man read me the number Mrs. Coltrain had given him and hung up. It was the clinic, all right—perhaps she'd stayed on to do some paperwork.

Mrs. Coltrain is usually calm, even majestic—in all the years she's managed the flow of people at Lotty's storefront, I've only seen her flustered once, and that was when the clinic was invaded by an angry mob. When I called back today, she sounded as agitated as she had that day six years ago.

"Oh, Ms. Warshawski, thank you for calling. I—something strange has come up—I didn't know what to do—I hope you—it would be good if you—I don't want to impose. Are you busy?"

"What's wrong, Mrs. Coltrain? Has someone broken in?"

"It's—it's something from Dr. Herschel. She—she—uh—sent a packet of dictation."

"From where?" I demanded sharply.

"It doesn't say on the packet. It came Federal Express. I've been—trying to listen to it. Something strange has happened. But I don't want to bother you."

"I'll be there as fast as I can. Half an hour at the outside." I made a U on Pershing and accelerated back onto the Ryan, calculating route, calculating time. I was ten miles south of the clinic here, but the expressway curved sharply west before it reached the Irving Park Road exit. Better to get off on Damen and drive straight north. Eight miles to Damen, eight minutes unless the traffic glued. Then three miles on city streets to Irving, another fifteen minutes.

My knuckles were white on the steering wheel, I was clutching it so hard. What was wrong? What was in the tape? Lotty was dead? Lotty was a hostage somewhere and Mrs. Coltrain couldn't bear to tell me on the phone?

The light at Damen was interminable. Steady, Old

Paint, I admonished myself. No need to shoot out the tires on the Beemer that crowded around me to prove I had a right to the intersection. When I finally got to the clinic, I parked at a reckless angle and jumped out.

Mrs. Coltrain's silver Eldorado was the only car in the tiny parking strip Lotty had installed on the clinic's north edge. The whole street had a Saturday afternoon sleepiness to it: a woman with three small children and a large trolley of laundry was the only person I saw.

I ran to the front and tried the door, but it was locked. I pushed the after-hours bell. After a long pause, Mrs. Coltrain asked in a quavering, tinny voice who it was. When I identified myself, there was another long pause before she buzzed me in.

The lights were turned off in the waiting room, I suppose to deter would-be patients from thinking anyone was here. In the greenish light that filtered in through the glass fire blocks, I felt as though I were under water. Mrs. Coltrain wasn't at her station behind the counter. The whole building appeared deserted—absurd, since she had just buzzed me in.

Sharply calling her name, I pushed open the door that led to the examining rooms. "Mrs. Coltrain!" I called again.

"I'm back here, dear." Her voice came to me faintly from Lotty's office.

She never called me "dear": even after knowing me for fifteen years I'm always "Ms. Warshawski." I pulled out my Smith & Wesson and ran down the hall. She was behind Lotty's desk, her cheeks white underneath her powder and rouge. I couldn't take in the scene at first; it took me a second to notice Ralph. He was wedged into a back corner of the room on one of Lotty's patient chairs, his arms tied to the chair arms, a piece of surgical tape over his mouth, his grey eyes black in his very white face. I was trying to take this in when his face contorted; he jerked his head toward the door.

I turned, bringing up my gun, but Bertrand Rossy was close behind me. He grabbed my gun arm, and my shot went wide. He was using both hands on my right wrist. I kicked him hard on his shin. His hold slackened. I kicked again, harder, and wrenched my gun hand away.

"Up against the wall," I panted.

"*Fermatevi.*" Fillida Rossy spoke sharply behind me. "Stop or I will shoot this woman."

She had appeared from some hiding place to stand behind Mrs. Coltrain's chair. She held a gun against Mrs. Coltrain's neck. Fillida looked strange; I realized after a moment that she had covered her blond hair in a black wig.

Mrs. Coltrain was shaking, her mouth moving wordlessly. My lips tight with fury, I let Rossy take the Smith & Wesson. He pinned my arms behind me, wrapping them with surgical tape.

"In English, Fillida. Your newest victims can't understand you. She just said I should stop or she would shoot Mrs. Coltrain," I added to Ralph. "So I've stopped. Is that another SIG, Fillida? Do your friends at the consulate smuggle them in from Switzerland for you? The cops can't trace the one you used on Howard Fepple."

Rossy hit me on the mouth. His smiling charm had sure disappeared. "We have nothing to say to you in any language, whereas you have much to say to us. Where are Herr Hoffman's notebooks?"

"You have a lot to say to me," I objected. "For instance, why is Ralph here?"

Rossy made an impatient gesture. "It seemed easiest to bring him."

"But why? Oh—oh, Ralph, you found Connie's desk

file and you took it to Rossy. I begged you not to do that."

Ralph shut his eyes tightly, unwilling to look at me, but Rossy said impatiently, "Yes, he showed me that silly girl's notes. Silly, conscientious little creature, keeping all her desk records. It never occurred to me—she never said a word to me."

"Of course not," I agreed. "She took her clerical procedures for granted; you know nothing of the details of work at that level."

They had killed so many people, these two, I couldn't think of a way to talk them out of killing three more. String them out, string them out while it comes to you. Above all, keep your voice calm, conversational: don't let them see you're terrified.

"So was Fepple threatening to reveal that Edelweiss really had a huge Holocaust policy exposure? Would Connie Ingram even have understood the implications of that?"

"Of course not," Rossy said, impatient. "In the sixties and seventies, Herr Hoffman began to submit death certificates to Edelweiss for his European clients—the ones he had sold life insurance to in Vienna before the war."

"Can you believe such a thing?" Fillida was incensed over Hoffman's effrontery. "He collected the life insurance for many Viennese Jews. He didn't even know that they were dead, he had no proper procedures, he made up the death certificates. It is a total outrage, the way he stole money from me and my family."

"But Aaron Sommers wasn't a Viennese Jew," I objected, sidetracked for a moment by the lesser problem.

Bertrand Rossy snapped impatiently, "Oh, this Hoffman, he must have become crazy. Either that or forgetful. He had insured an Austrian Jew named

Aaron Sommers in 1935 and a black American of the same name in 1971. So he submitted a death claim for the black man instead of the Jew. It was all so foolish, so unnecessary—and yet, for us, so fortunate. He was the one agent we hadn't been able to find with a large book of prewar Jewish policies. And then it turned out he was right here in Chicago. That day in Devereux's office, when I looked in the Sommers papers and saw Ulrich Hoffman's signature on his agency work sheet, I could hardly believe my fortune. The man we had been seeking for five years was right here in Chicago. I'm still astounded that you and Devereux didn't notice my excitement."

He paused to congratulate himself on his public performance. "But Fepple, he was a total idiot. He found one of Hoffman's old registers in the Sommers file, together with some blank signed death certificates. He thought he could blackmail us over the false death certificates. He didn't even understand that the Holocaust claims were more important. Much more important."

"Bertrand, enough of this history," Fillida said in Italian. "Get her to tell you where the doctor is."

"Fillida, you must speak English," I said in English. "You're in America now, and these two unfortunates can't understand you."

"Then understand this," Rossy said. "Unless you tell us where those books are at once, we will kill both these friends of yours, not fast with a bullet, but slowly with great pain."

"That woman last night, the therapist of Hoffman's son, she said this Jewish doctor has them. These are my books. They belong to my family, to my company. They must come back to me," Fillida said, her accent strong, her English not as smooth as her husband's. "But this clerk opened the safe and nothing is in it. Everybody knows you are the friend of this Jewish doctor, the best friend. So you tell us where she is."

"She's disappeared," I said. "I thought you guys had her. It's a relief to know she's safe."

"Please don't make the mistake of assuming we are stupid," Rossy said. "This office clerk is totally expendable now that she's opened the doctor's safe."

"Is that why poor Connie Ingram had to die?" I asked. "Because she couldn't tell you where Ulrich Hoffman's notebooks were? Or because she would have told Ralph or the cops about fraudulent death certificates—your own obsession with Hoffman and Howard Fepple?"

"She was a very loyal employee of the company. I feel regret over her death."

"You took her out for a lovely dinner, treated her with the kind of charm that persuaded Grandpapa Hirs's little girl to marry you, and then took her to the forest preserve to kill her. Did you let her think you were attracted to her? Does it cheer you up, the thought that a naive young woman responds to you the same way the rich boss's daughter does?"

Fillida curled her lip scornfully. "*Che maniere borghesi.* Why should I bother my head if my husband gratifies the fantasies of some poor little creature?"

"She's complaining that I have bourgeois manners," I explained to Ralph and to Mrs. Coltrain, who was staring straight ahead, glassy with shock. "In her world, if your husband sleeps with the staff it's just a throwback to those old medieval customs. The queen of the castle doesn't bother her head over it because she's still queen. What is it, Fillida? Because you're the queen you shoot anyone who doesn't bow to you? Because you're queen of Edelweiss, no one is allowed to get money from the company—you'll shoot them if they submit a claim? You need to hold Edelweiss the way you hold your silverware and your daughter's hair, don't you?"

"You are ignorant. It is my family's company, the Edelweiss. My mother's grandfather, he started this company, only then of course it was called the Nesthorn. The Jews forced us to change the name after the Second World War, but they cannot force us to let go of our company. I am protecting the future of my children, of Paolo and Marguerita, that is all."

She was angry, but she kept her gun pointed at Mrs. Coltrain. "That that cretin Howard Fepple could think he could drain money from us, it is unbelievable. And the Jews, only wanting money all the time, believing they could come to demand more money from us, that is an affront, an outrage. Speak quickly now, tell me where are these books of Signor Hoffman."

I felt very tired, very aware of how weak and ineffectual I was with my arms pinned behind me. "Oh, those Jews, paying their few pennies a week to Nesthorn so that you could ski at Mont Blanc and shop on Monte Napoleane. And now their grandchildren, their own little Paolos and Margueritas, want the company to pay what you owe them. That is a terribly bourgeois attitude: don't they understand the aristocratic outlook—that you get to collect the premium and never have to pay on the policies? It's a pity the Chicago police have such a limited worldview. When they've matched fibers from Bertie's clothes to Connie Ingram's body, well, that will make a big impact on a bourgeois jury, believe me."

"The police require a reason to think about Bertrand at all." Fillida shrugged elegant shoulders. "I myself do not see such a thing happening."

"Paul Hoffman could identify you, Fillida. Your hand slipped badly on the trigger there, didn't it?"

"That lunatic! He couldn't identify me in a thousand

years. He thinks I am a concentration-camp guard. Who would even suggest me as being in his house!"

"Max Loewenthal. He knows what's happening here. Carl Tisov. Dr. Herschel herself. You and Bertie are like a couple of elephants going musth through the jungle. You can't keep killing everyone in Chicago without getting caught out yourselves."

Rossy looked at his watch. "We need to be going soon, if Alderman Durham will only get here. Fillida, he advised against bullet wounds, so break the clerk's arm. Persuade this detective that we are serious in our quest."

Fillida turned her gun over and slammed the stock against Mrs. Coltrain's arm. Mrs. Coltrain screamed, the pain ripping her out of her shocked frozenness. The horrible noise turned everyone toward her.

In that brief window of distraction, I launched myself at Rossy. I whirled, kicking him hard in the stomach, turning again as he lashed out at me to kick him on the kneecap. He was punching at me, but he wasn't a street fighter. I was. I ducked underneath his flailing arms and butted him square in the solar plexus. He gagged and backed away.

Out of the corner of my eye I saw Fillida taking aim. I hit the floor. I was demented now. Unable to use my hands, I lay on my back kicking at Rossy over and over. I was screaming in rage, in impotent fury, as Fillida came around to the front of the desk to point her gun at me. I didn't want to die like this, helpless on the floor.

Behind me I heard Ralph give an enraged grunt. He got to his feet, dragging the chair with him, and flung himself at Fillida just before she fired. His blow knocked her off balance. Her gun went off but she fell, with Ralph in his chair falling on top of her. She screamed as he crashed onto her abdomen.

Mrs. Coltrain stood up behind the desk. "I have

called the police, Mr. Rossy, as I believe your name is. They will be here at any moment."

Her voice wobbled a bit, but she was back in command of her clinic. Hearing that majestic tone, the same one she used to keep small children from fighting in the waiting room, I lay on the floor and laughed.

LI

Wily Coyote

I sat on the edge of Ralph's bed, holding his right hand between both of my own. It was late on Saturday night, but the charge nurse told me he wouldn't sleep until he'd talked to me.

"I don't have much luck with my corporate loyalties," he said. "Why couldn't I listen to you the second time around if I wouldn't the first? So many people dead. Poor Connie. And me with another bullet in the shoulder. I guess I just can't stand for you to be right, can I?"

"At least they got your left shoulder this time," I said. "Now you're symmetrical. Ralph, you're a good guy and a team player. You wanted your team to be as good as you were, and I was telling you they weren't. You're too honest yourself to believe the worst of the people around you. And anyway, you saved my life. I can't possibly feel anything but overflowing gratitude." I brought his right hand to my lips.

"That's generous." His eyes flickered shut for a moment. "Connie. Why did she?"

"I don't think she was being disloyal to you or to the company, but I imagine Rossy turned her head. There was the big boss in from the new owners in Switzerland, telling her to report directly to him, that she shouldn't tell anyone what he said to her because someone in the company was embezzling, and it might be anyone, you, her immediate supervisor Karen. I imagine that was how he worked it. Anyone who had spent fourteen years toiling as a claims clerk would have been thrilled, but she had that extra quality of loyalty and reliability. He said not to talk, she kept quiet. And then, he was sophisticated, he was glamorous."

"It's a warning to me to cut out cheeseburgers," Ralph said with a gleam of humor. "Guy's only two years younger than me. I need to look more glamorous to my young claims handlers. So he romanced her and strangled her. What a horrible ending for her. Can they make it stick?"

"Terry Finchley, the detective in charge, he got a search warrant. They're looking at Rossy's clothes, fingerprints—they may get a match with the marks on her neck. He and Fillida were so single-mindedly arrogant, they probably didn't try too hard to conceal evidence.

"Fillida, that's another story. She could face a lot of charges—Fepple's murder, attacking Paul Hoffman, attacking Rhea Wiell, but she's attractive, rich. They're searching for her prints or clothes fibers or anything at Paul's house, but she's going to be hard for the state's attorney to nail down. At least those cheeseburgers of yours did some good: when you came down on her you cracked her pelvis. She won't ski anywhere anytime soon."

He smiled briefly, the twisted smile that reminded me of the old Ralph, and shut his eyes. I thought he had drifted off to sleep, but as I started to get up he looked up at me again.

"What was Alderman Durham doing at the clinic? I saw him as they were carrying me off on a stretcher."

"Oh, Fillida and Bertrand had gone berserk," I said.

"They thought they'd get a bomb, blow the three of us up, make it look as though anti-abortion terrorists had been responsible. They told Durham to get one for them—they assumed that they'd bought him, that he was just another one of their servants who'd do what they wanted.

"See, Rossy had been doing favors for Durham in exchange for some muscle: Rossy got the legislature to block the Holocaust Asset Recovery Act unless it included slavery reparations, he gave Durham money so Durham could build a war chest to run for mayor— along with this high-profile issue, slavery reparations, to build a citywide platform on. In return for all this help, Durham directed Rossy to some South Side muscle when Rossy wanted to break in to Amy Blount's apartment to see if she had the Hoffman notebooks. But he's a wily coyote, the alderman—he never put anything in writing. He never directly told Rossy he could find muscle for him.

"Rossy thought he'd bought Durham. But the alderman wants to be mayor more than he wants to be Al Capone. He called the cops, told them the Rossys were trying to get a bomb at the clinic. So the cops were on their way, even though they got there kind of late."

The alderman now looked like Mr. Virtue. He'd given me a bit of a smirk in passing, the smirk of the man who'd gotten clean away with having Colby Sommers killed and who had a nice stash to launch his citywide campaign besides. He'd confessed to Terry Finchley, more in sorrow than in outrage, that some of the young men on his EYE team weren't as rehabilitated as he would have wished. And the Finch, normally one of the city's straightest, levelest cops, had read me a lecture on my prejudice in flinging accusations at the alderman. If I had to win every match in order to be happy, I'd be a mighty sad detective—

but this was one round where the loss stuck in my craw.

The charge nurse came into the room. "He's recovering from trauma. You've had your five minutes twice over, out you go, now."

Ralph was asleep. I bent to kiss his forehead where the shock of greying hair still flopped over.

Down in the Beth Israel parking lot, I dug my fingers into my shoulders before climbing into my car. They were still sore from being tied behind my back. I'd gone home to rest when I finally finished talking to the cops, but I was still beat.

At home I'd felt honor bound to tell Mr. Contreras what had happened, before stumbling up to bed. I slept a few hours, but I woke up still tired clear to the bone. All that death, all the energy I'd spent trying to figure it out, had turned on such sordidness. Fillida Rossy, protecting her great-grandfather's company. Protecting her wealth and position. Not that she was the Lady Macbeth behind Bertrand—he didn't need his wife to screw his courage to the sticking point. He'd had his own arrogance, his own sense of entitlement.

When I got up, before driving to the hospital to see Ralph, I'd gone to my office to e-mail Morrell: *How I wish you were here. How I need your arms around me tonight.*

He wrote back at once with love, commiseration—and a précis of the articles on Edelweiss I'd sent him yesterday. Not that it mattered now, just another little part of Fillida's family's wealth, Nesthorn had insured a lot of Nazi bigwigs during the war and had even forced people in occupied Holland and France to buy life insurance from them. In the sixties, they thought it would be prudent to change their name to Edelweiss because local resentment against the Nesthorn name still ran high in western Europe.

Standing in the parking lot, I gave a bark of mirthless laughter and shook my shoulders out again. A giant figure loomed out of the shadows and moved toward me.

"Murray!" I gasped, my gun in my hand before I knew I'd drawn it. "Don't freak me after a day like this one."

He put an arm around me. "You're getting too old for these tall buildings, Warshawski."

"You're right about that," I agreed, putting my gun away. "Without Ralph and Mrs. Coltrain, I'd be on a slab about now."

"Not to mention Durham," he said.

"Durham?" I snapped. "I know he's painting himself as Mr. Clean, but that lying piece of politician knows he got away with murder!"

"Maybe. Maybe. But I had a few words with the aldercreature this afternoon. Off the record, unfortunately. But he said that last night he looked at you, looked at Rossy, figured he'd better bet on the local talent. Said he'd read some of your file, saw that you often got your butt whipped good but usually landed on top. Who knows, Warshawski—he gets to be mayor, maybe you'll be police superintendent."

"And you can run his press office," I said dryly. "Guy did a lot of mean nasty stuff. Including cheerfully helping frame Isaiah Sommers for Howard Fepple's murder."

"He didn't know it was Isaiah Sommers, not from what my gofers in the police department tell me. I mean, he didn't know Isaiah was a relative of the Sommers family who he'd helped out back in the '90's." Murray kept his arm around my shoulders. "When he found that out he forced Rossy to settle Gertrude Sommers's claim. And he tried to get the cops to keep an open mind on the murder investigation. It's why they didn't charge Isaiah Sommers. Now it's your turn. I want to see these mystery journals or ledgers or whatever that the Rossys were stampeding through town trying to find."

"I want them, too." I pulled away from his arm and turned to face him. "Lotty's vanished with them."

When I told Murray about Lotty's disappearance after the fracas with Rhea at Paul Hoffman-Radbuka's bedside, he looked at me somberly. "You're going to find her, right? Why did she take the books away?"

I shook my head. "I don't know. They told her . . . something that they didn't tell anyone else."

I leaned into my car for my briefcase and found a set of the photocopies I'd made of the journal pages. "You can have this. You can run it if you want."

He squinted at the sheet in the dim light. "But what does it mean?"

I leaned wearily against my car and pointed at the line that read "Omschutz, K 30 Nestroy (2h.f) N–13426–Ö–L." "As I understand it, we're looking at a record for K. Omschutz, who lived at 30 Nestroy Street in Vienna. The 2h.f means he was in apartment 2f at the rear of the building. The numbers are the policy numbers, with a tag meaning it was an Austrian life-insurance policy—Ö for Österreich—the Austrian for Austria. Okay?"

After a minute's squinting scrutiny he nodded.

"This other sheet just gives the face value of the policy in thousands of Austrian schillings, and the weekly payment schedule. It wasn't a code. It meant something quite clear to Ulrich Hoffman: he knew he'd sold K. Omschutz a policy with a face value of fifty-four thousand schillings and a weekly payment of twenty schillings a week. As soon as Ralph Devereux at Ajax realized that it applied to prewar life-insurance claims, he put it together with the material that he found on his dead claims handler's desk. That was what made him blow caution to the winds and storm into Bertrand Rossy's office this morning."

Ralph had gone over this with me when I got to the hospital tonight, his mouth twisted in bitter mockery over his recklessness. I was utterly weary of the entire business, but Murray was so excited at getting even a few pages of the Hoffman journals as a scoop that he could hardly contain himself.

"Thanks for letting me scoop the town, Warshawski: I knew you couldn't stay mad at me forever. What about Rhea Wiell and Paul Hoffman or Radbuka? Beth Blacksin was feeling mighty peeved after she got to the clinic this afternoon and found out that whole business could turn out to be a fraud."

Blacksin had been hovering behind the cops with the ubiquitous camera crews at the clinic. I'd answered as many questions then as I could so I wouldn't have to face them later. I told them about the Rossys, about the Holocaust claims and Ulrich's notebooks.

I didn't know what Don was planning to do with his book, but I didn't feel any special desire to protect him. I told the cameras about Paul Hoffman, about the Anna Freud material, about Paul's chamber of secrets. When Beth's eyes lit up at the thought of getting that scene on tape, I remembered Lotty's fury at the way in which books and movies titillate us over the horrors of the past. Don, wanting to put it all in a book for Envision Press. Beth, knowing her contract was coming due, seeing her show's ratings zoom if she filmed Paul's private horrors. I told Murray I'd walked out on them mid-sentence.

"I don't blame you. Getting the news doesn't mean we have to carry on like jackals at suppertime."

He opened the car door for me—an unusual act of gallantry. "Let's go downtown to the Glow, V I. You and I have a lot of catching up to do—on life, not just life insurance."

I shook my head. "I need to go up to Evanston to see Max Loewenthal. I'll take a rain check, though."

Murray leaned down and kissed me full on the lips, then quickly closed my car door. In my rearview mirror I watched him standing there, watching me, until my car had turned down the exit ramp.

LII

The Face in the Picture

Beth Israel was near enough to the expressway that I took it up to Evanston. It was past ten now, but Max had wanted to talk things over. He was feeling deeply lonely tonight, since Calia and Agnes had left for London and Michael and Carl had flown west to rejoin the Cellini in San Francisco.

Max fed me cold roast chicken and a glass of St. Emilion, something warm and red for comfort. I told him what I knew, what I was guessing, what I thought the fallout would be. He was more philosophical than I about Alderman Durham, but he was disappointed that Posner hadn't been implicated in any of the scandal.

"You're sure he wasn't playing a role somehow? Something that you could expose that would force him away from the hospital?"

"He's just a fanatic," I said, accepting another glass of wine. "Although they're actually more dangerous than people like Durham, who are playing the game—well, as a game—for power or position or money. But if we catch up with Lotty and find those books of Ulrich's, then we can publicize those life-insurance policies that Edelweiss or Nesthorn sold during the thirties.

We can force the Illinois legislature to revisit the Holocaust Asset Recovery Act. And Posner and his Maccabees will go back downtown to Ajax or the State of Illinois building, which will get him out of your hair."

"Lotty and the notebooks," Max repeated, turning his wineglass round and round in his hands. "Victoria, while Calia was here and I was concerned about her safety, I wasn't worrying so intensely about Lotty. Also, I see now, now that he's gone back to the tour, I was protecting myself from Carl's scorn. Lotty's high flair for drama, he keeps calling her recent behavior. The way she disappeared on Thursday—Carl says it's the same thing she did all those years ago in London. Turning her back, walking away without a word. It's what she did to him, you know, and he says I am a fool if I think that isn't what she's doing to me. She leaves, she says nothing for weeks or months, and then perhaps she returns, or perhaps not, but there's never an explanation."

"And you think?" I prodded, when he was quiet.

"I think she's disappeared now for the same reason she disappeared then, whatever that was," he burst out. "If I was twenty, as Carl was then, I might be as hurt in my own sense of self and less worried about her: one's passions run higher at twenty. But I am very worried about her. I want to know where she is. I called her brother Hugo in Montreal, but they've never been close; he hasn't heard from her in months and has no idea what's going through her head, or where she might have run to. Victoria, I know you are worn, I see it in the fine lines around your mouth and eyes. But can you do anything to find her?"

I massaged my sore shoulders again. "I'm going to the clinic in the morning. Lotty actually did FedEx a packet of dictation to Mrs. Coltrain—she was transcribing it when Fillida Rossy jumped her. Mrs.

Coltrain says there's nothing to indicate where Lotty is—it's a short tape, leaving instructions about her surgical schedule. But Mrs. Coltrain is going to let me into the clinic in the morning so I can listen to it myself and inspect the wrapping. She hopes it will mean something to me. Also, she says Lotty left papers on her desktop; maybe they'll tell me something. Beyond that—I can try to ask the Finch or Captain Mallory to pull Lotty's phone records—they would show who she called the night she disappeared. Airline lists. There are other things I could do, but they won't happen fast. We'll hope for something in her own papers."

Max insisted that I stay the night. "You're asleep on your feet, Victoria. You shouldn't be out driving. Unless you're desperate to go to your own home, you can sleep in my daughter's old room. There's even some kind of nightshirt in there that's clean."

It was his own fear and loneliness that made him want me there, as much as his concern for my well-being, but both were important reasons to me. I called Mr. Contreras to reassure him of my safety and was glad, actually, to climb one flight of stairs to a bed instead of spending another half hour in my car to reach one.

In the morning, we drove down together to the clinic. Mrs. Coltrain met us at nine, looking as sedately groomed as if Rossys and attempted murder were no more harrowing than sick women and screaming children. Fillida hadn't broken her arm when she smashed it with the gun stock, but she had given Mrs. Coltrain a deep bruise; her forearm was resting in a sling to protect the damaged area.

She wasn't quite as calm as she appeared: when she'd settled us at her workstation with the tape player, she confided, "You know, Miss Warshawski, I think I am going to get someone in on Monday to take the doors off those closets in the examining rooms. I don't think

I can go in there without being afraid someone is hiding behind the door."

That was what Fillida had done: hidden in an examining-room closet until she thought the clinic was empty, and then jumped Mrs. Coltrain at her workstation. When Fillida realized that the notebooks weren't on the premises, she'd forced Mrs. Coltrain to bring me to the clinic.

Now Mrs. Coltrain played the tape for Max and me, but although we listened to it clear to the end, through half an hour of staticky silence on the second side, neither of us got anything out of it except that Dr. Barber was to take Lotty's two urgent surgical cases on Tuesday and Mrs. Coltrain was to work with the chief of surgery to reschedule the others.

Mrs. Coltrain took us back to Lotty's office so I could inspect the papers Lotty had left on her desk. My stomach muscles clenched as we walked down the hall. I expected to find the chaos we'd left behind last night: broken chairs, blood, overturned lamps, and the police mess on top of it. But the broken furniture was gone, the floor and desk were scoured clean, the papers neatly laid on top.

When I exclaimed over the tidiness, Mrs. Coltrain said she had come in early to make things right. "If Dr. Herschel showed up, she would be so distressed to find all that wreckage. And anyway, I knew I couldn't face it for thirty seconds, so full of all that violence. Lucy Choi, the clinic nurse, she came in at eight. We gave it a good going-over together. But I kept out all the papers that were on Dr. Herschel's desk yesterday. You sit down here, Ms. Warshawski, and look them over."

It felt strange to sit behind Lotty's desk, in the chair where she had so often greeted me, sometimes brusquely, more often with empathy, but always with a high energy. I turned over the papers. A letter from the archivist at the National Holocaust Museum in

Washington, dated six years back, telling Dr. Herschel that they regretted not being able to find any records of the people whom she was trying to trace, Shlomo and Martin Radbuka, although they could confirm the deaths of Rudolph and Anna Herschel in 1943. They referred her to several data banks that traced Holocaust victims which might be more helpful. Her correspondence with those other data banks showed that no one had had any useful information for her.

Lotty had also left out a stack of newsletters from the Royal Free Hospital in London, where she'd done her medical training. I turned over the pages. Stuck between two of the sheets was a photograph. It was an old picture, the edges creased from much handling, which showed a very young woman, fair, whose eyes, even in the faded paper, sparkled with life. Her hair was bobbed and curled in the style of the 1920's. She was smiling with the provocative self-confidence of someone who knows herself beloved, whose desires were seldom denied. It was inscribed on the back, but in German in a heavy European script which I couldn't decipher.

I handed it to Max, who frowned over it. "I'm not good with this old German, but it's written to someone named Martin, a love message from—I think it says *Lingerl*—inscribed in 1928. Then she's rewritten it to Lotty: *Think of me, dearest little Charlotte Anna, and know that I am always thinking of you.*"

"Who is this? Dr. Herschel's mother, do you think?" Mrs. Coltrain picked up the picture respectfully by the edges. "What a beautiful girl she was when this was taken. Dr. Herschel should keep it in a frame on her desk."

"Perhaps it's too painful for her to see that face every day," Max said heavily.

I turned to the newsletters. They were like all such documents, filled with tidbits of information about graduates, amazing achievements of the faculty, status of the hospital, especially under the severe retrenchments forced by the shrinking National Health budgets. Claire Tallmadge's name jumped out at me from the third one I looked at:

Claire Tallmadge, MRCP, has given up her practice and moved to a flat in Highgate, where she welcomes visits from former students and colleagues. Dr. Tallmadge's unbending standards earned her the respect of generations of colleagues and students at the Royal Free. We will all sadly miss the sight of her erect presence in her tweed suits moving through the wards, but the Fellowship being established in her honor will keep her name bright among us. Dr. Tallmadge promises to keep busy with writing a history of women's medical careers in the twentieth century.

Lotty Herschel's Story:
The Long Road Back

When I reached the rise overlooking the place, I couldn't go on. I couldn't move at all. My legs suddenly weakened at the knees and I sat abruptly to keep from falling. After that I remained where I landed, looking over the grey and blowing ground, hugging my knees to my chest.

When I realized I'd left my mother's photograph behind, I'd become frantic. I searched my suitcase at least a dozen times, and then I called the various hotels where I'd stayed. Many times. "No, Dr. Herschel, we haven't found it. Yes, we understand the importance." Even then I couldn't resign myself to its loss. I wanted her with me. I wanted her to protect me on my journey east as she hadn't protected me on my journey west, and when I couldn't find her picture, I almost turned around at Wien-Schwechat Airport. Except at that point I couldn't imagine where I'd go back to.

I walked the city for two days, trying to see behind its bright modern face the streets of my childhood. The flat on the Renngasse was the one place I recognized, but when I rang the bell, the woman who now lived in it greeted me with contemptuous hostility. She refused to let me inside: anyone could pretend they had been a child in an apartment; she knew better than to fall for confidence tricksters. It must have been the nightmare of this family of squatters, someone like me coming back from the dead to reclaim my home from them.

I made myself go to the Leopoldsgasse, but many of those crumbling old buildings had disappeared, and even though I knew the right intersection to look for, nothing looked familiar to me. My Zeyde, my Orthodox grandfather, had threaded his way through this warren with me one morning to a vendor who sold ham. My Zeyde traded his overcoat for a greased paper full of thin-sliced fatty meat. He wouldn't touch it himself, but his grandchildren needed protein; we could not starve to death to uphold the laws of *kashruth*. My cousins and I ate the pink slices with guilty pleasure. His overcoat fed us for three days.

I tried to re-create that route, but I only ended up at the canal, staring into the filthy water so long that a policeman came to make sure I wasn't planning to jump.

I rented a car and drove into the mountains, up to the old farmhouse at Kleinsee. Even that I couldn't recognize. The whole area is a resort now. That place where we went every summer, the days filled with walks, horseback rides, botany lessons with my grandmother, the nights with singing and dancing, my Herschel cousins and I sitting on the stairs peeping into the drawing room where my mother was always the golden butterfly at the center of attention—the meadows were now filled with expensive villas, shops, a ski lift. I couldn't even find my grandfather's house—I don't know if it was torn down or turned into one of the heavily guarded villas I couldn't see from the road.

And so finally I drove east. If I couldn't find a trace of my mother or my grandmothers in life, then I would have to visit their graves. Slowly, so slowly other drivers spewed epithets at me—rich Austrian they took me to be from my rental license plates. Even at my slow pace I couldn't help finally reaching the town. I left the car. Continued on foot, following the signposts in their different languages.

I know people passed me, I felt their shapes go by, some stopping above me, talking at me. Words flew by me, words in many languages, but I couldn't understand any of them. I was staring at the buildings at the bottom of the hill, the crumbling remnants of my mother's last home. I was beyond words, beyond feeling, beyond awareness. So I don't know when she arrived and sat cross-legged next to me. When she touched my hand I thought it was my mother, finally come to claim me, and when I turned, eager to embrace her, my disappointment was beyond recounting.

You! I choked out a word, not bothering to hide my bitterness.

"Yes," she agreed, "not who you wanted, but here anyway." Refusing to leave until I was ready to leave, taking a jacket and wrapping it around my shoulders.

I tried for irony. You are the perfect sleuth, tracking me down against my will. But she said nothing, so I had to prod, to ask what clues had led her to me.

"The newsletters from the Royal Free—you left them on your office desk. I recognized Dr. Tallmadge's name, and remembered you and Carl arguing over her that night at Max's. I—I flew to London and visited her in Highgate."

Ah, yes. Claire. Who saved me from the glove factory. She saved me and saved me and saved me, and then she dropped me as if I were a discarded glove myself. All those years, all those years that I thought it was out of disapproval, and now I see it was—I couldn't think of a word for what it was. Lies, perhaps.

Carl used to get so angry. I brought him to the Tallmadges' for tea several times, but he despised them so much that he finally refused to return. I was so proud of them all, of Claire and Vanessa and Mrs. Tallmadge and their Crown Derby tea service in the garden, and he saw them as patronizing me, the little Jewish monkey they could feed bits of apple to when it danced for them.

I was proud of Carl, too. His music was something so special that I was sure it would make them all, but especially Claire, realize I was special—a gifted musician was in love with me. But they patronized that, as well.

"As if I was the monkey's organ-grinder," Carl told me furiously, after they'd asked him to bring his clarinet along one day. He started playing, Debussy for the clarinet, and they talked among themselves and applauded when they realized he'd finished. I insisted it was only Ted and Wallace Marmaduke, Vanessa's husband and brother-in-law. They were Philistines, I agreed, but I wouldn't agree that Claire had been just as rude.

That quarrel took place the year after V-E Day. I was still in high school but working for a family in North London in exchange for room and board. Claire, meanwhile, was still living at home. She was applying for her first houseman's job, so our paths seldom crossed unless she went out of her way to invite me to tea, as she did that day.

But then, two years later, after she'd finished saving me that last time, she wouldn't see me or answer my letters when I returned to London. She didn't return the phone message I left with her mother, although perhaps Mrs. Tallmadge never delivered it—what she said to me when I called was, "Don't you think, dear, that it's time you and Claire led your own lives?"

My last private conversation with Claire was when she urged me to apply for an obstetrics fellowship in the States, to make a fresh start. She even saw that I got the right recommendations when I was applying. After that, the only times I saw her were at professional meetings.

I looked briefly at Victoria, sitting on the ground beside me in her jeans, watching me with a frowning intensity that made me want to lash out: I would not have pity.

If you've been to see Claire, then you must know who Sofie Radbuka was.

She was cautious, knowing I might bite her, and said hesitantly she thought it was me.

So you're not the perfect detective. It wasn't me, it was my mother.

That flustered her, and I took a bitter pleasure in her embarrassment. Always so forthright, making connections, tracking people down, tracking me down. Let her be embarrassed now.

My need to talk was too great, though; after a minute I said, It was me. It was my mother. It was me. It was my mother's name. I wanted her. Not only then, but every day, every night I wanted her, only then most especially. I think I thought I could become her. Or if I took her name she would be with me. I don't know now what I was thinking.

When I was born, my parents weren't married. My mother, Sofie, the darling of my grandparents, dancing through life as if it were one brightly lit ballroom; she was a light and airy creature from the day of her birth. They named her Sofie but they called her the Butterfly. *Schmetterling* in German, which quickly became Lingerl or Ling-Ling. Even Minna, who hated her, called her Madame Butterfly, not Sofie.

Then the butterfly became a teenager and went dancing off with Vienna's other bright young things to go slumming in the Matzoinsel. Like a modern-day teenager going to the ghetto, picking up black lovers, she picked up Moishe Radbuka out of the Belarus immigrant world. Martin, she called him, giving him a western name. He was a café violinist, almost a Gypsy, except he was a Jew.

She was seventeen when she became pregnant with me. He would have married her, I learned from the family whispers, but she wouldn't—not a Gypsy from the Matzoinsel. So then everyone in the family thought she should go to a sanatorium, have the child, give it up discreetly. Everyone except my Oma and Opa, who adored her and said to bring the baby to them.

Sofie loved Martin in her way, and he adored her the way everyone in my world did, or at least the way I imagine they did. Don't tell me otherwise, don't feed me the words of Cousin Minna: slut, harlot, lazy bitch in heat, all those words I heard for eight years of my London life.

Four years after me came Hugo. And four years after him came the Nazis. And we all moved into the Insel. I suppose you saw it, if you've been tracking me, the remains of those cramped apartments on the Leopoldsgasse?

My mother became thin and lost her sparkle. Who could keep it at such a time, anyway? But to me as a child—I thought at first living with her all the time would mean she would pay attention to me. I couldn't understand why it was so different, why she wouldn't sing or dance anymore. She stopped being Ling-Ling and became Sofie.

Then she was pregnant again, pregnant, sick when I left for England, too sick to get out of bed. But she decided to marry my father. All those years she loved being Lingerl Herschel, coming to stay with her parents when she wanted her old life on the Renngasse, going to the Insel to live with Martin when she wanted him. But when the iron fist of the National Socialists grabbed all of them, Herschels and Radbukas, and squeezed them into a ball together in the ghetto, she married Martin. Perhaps she did it for his mother, since we were living with her. So my mother for a brief time became Sofie Radbuka.

In my child years on the Renngasse, even though I wanted my mother to stay with me, I was a well-loved child. My grandparents didn't mind that I was small and dark like Martin instead of blond and beautiful like their daughter. They were proud of my brains, that I was always number one or two in my class in my few years in school. They even had a kind of patronizing affection for Martin.

But they thought his parents were an embarrassment. When they had to give up their ten-room flat on the

Renngasse and move in with the Radbukas, my Oma—she acted as though she had been asked to live in a cow byre. She held herself aloof, she addressed Martin's mother formally, as "Sie," never as "Du." And me, I wanted my Oma Herschel to keep loving me best, I needed that love, there were so many of us all cramped together, I needed someone to care about me—Sofie was caught up in her own misery, pregnant, sick, not used to any kind of hardship, getting spite from the Radbuka cousins and aunts who felt she'd mistreated their own darling Martin—Moishe—all those years.

But don't you see, it made me treat my other grandmother rudely. If I showed my Bobe, my Granny Radbuka, the affection she craved from me, then my Oma would push me away. On the morning Hugo and I left for England, my Bobe, my Granny Radbuka, longed for me to kiss her, and I would only curtsy to her.

I choked down the sobs that started to rise up in me. Victoria handed me a bottle of water without saying anything. If she had touched me I would have hit her, but I took her water and drank it.

So ten years later, when I found myself pregnant, found myself carrying Carl's child that hot summer, it all grew dark in my head. My mother. My Oma—my Grandmother Herschel. My Bobe—my Grandmother Radbuka. I thought I could make amends to my Bobe. I thought she would forgive me if I used her name. Only I didn't know her first name. I didn't know my own granny's name. Night after night I could see her thin arms held out to hold me, to kiss me good-bye. Night after night I could see my embarrassed curtsy, knowing my Oma was watching me. No matter how many nights I recalled this scene, I could not remember my Bobe's first name. So I used my mother's.

I wouldn't have an abortion. That was Claire's first suggestion. By 1944, when I was tagging around after Claire trying to learn enough science so that I could be like

her, be a doctor, all my family was already dead. Right here
in front of us they shaved my Oma's silver hair. I can see it
falling on the floor around her like a waterfall, she was so
proud of it, she never cut it. My Bobe. She was already
bald under her Orthodox wig. The cousins I shared a bed
with, whom I resented because I didn't have my own
canopied bed anymore, they were dead by then. I had
been saved, for no reason except the love of my Opa, who
found the money to buy a passage to freedom for Hugo
and me.

All of them, my mother, too, who sang and danced
with me on Sunday afternoons, they were here, here in
this ground, burned to the ashes that are blowing in your
eyes. Maybe their ashes are gone, as well, maybe strangers
took them away, bathing their eyes, washing my mother
down the sink.

I couldn't have an abortion. I couldn't add one more
death to all those dead. But I had no feelings left with
which to raise a child. It was only the thought that my
mother would come back that kept me going during the
war when I lived with Minna. We're so proud of you,
Lottchen, she and my Oma would say, you didn't cry, you
were a good girl, you did your lessons, you stayed first in
your class even in a foreign language, you tolerated the
hatefulness of that prize bitch Minna—I would imagine the
war ending and them embracing me with those words.

It's true that by 1944 we were already hearing reports in
the immigrant world about what was happening—here in
this place and in all the other places like it. But how many
were dying, nobody knew, and so each of us kept hoping
that our own people would be spared. But in the wave of
a hand, they were gone. Max looked for them. He went to
Europe, but I couldn't, I couldn't bear it, I haven't been to
central Europe since I left in 1939—until now—but he
looked, and he said, They are dead.

So I felt horribly trapped: I wouldn't abort the
pregnancy, but I could not keep the baby. I would not

raise one more hostage to fortune that could be snatched
from me at a moment's notice.

I couldn't tell Carl. Carl—if he'd said, let's get married,
let's raise the child, he would never have understood why I
wouldn't. It wasn't because of my career, which would
have been destroyed if I'd had a baby. Now—now girls do
it all the time. It isn't easy, to be a medical student and a
mother, but no one says, That's it, your career is over.
Believe me, in 1949, a baby meant your medical training
was finished forever.

If I'd told Carl, told him I couldn't keep the child, he
would have always blamed me for putting my career first.
He would never have understood my real reasons. I
couldn't tell him—anything. No more families for me. I
know it was cruel of me to leave without a word, but I
couldn't tell him the truth, and I couldn't lie. So I left
without speaking.

Later I turned myself into the saver of women with
difficult pregnancies. I think I imagine every time I leave
the operating room that I have saved not myself but some
small piece of my mother, who didn't live long after the
birth of that last little sister.

So my life went on. I wasn't unhappy. I didn't dwell on
this past. I lived in the present, in the future. I had my
work, which rewarded me richly. I loved music. Max and
I—I never thought to be a lover again, but to my surprise
and my happiness, as well, that happened between us. I
had other friends, and—you, Victoria. You became a
beloved friend before I noticed it happening. I let you
draw close to me, I let you be another hostage to
fortune—and over and over you cause me agony by your
reckless disregard for your own life.

She muttered something, some kind of apology. I still
wouldn't look at her.

And then this strange creature appeared in Chicago.
This disturbed, ungainly man, claiming to be a Radbuka,
when I knew not one of them survived. Except for my own

son. When you first told me about this man, Paul, my
heart stopped: I thought perhaps it was my child, raised as
he claimed by an *Einsatzgruppenführer*. Then I saw him at
Max's and realized he was too old to be my child.

But then I had a worse fear: the idea that my son might
somehow have grown up with a desire to torment me. I
think—I wasn't thinking, I don't know what I thought, but
I imagined my son somehow rising up to conspire with
this Paul whoever he is to torture me. So I flew to Claire to
demand that she send me to my child.

When Claire came to my rescue that summer, she said
she would place my child privately. But she didn't tell me
she gave him to Ted Marmaduke. To her sister and her
brother-in law who wanted children they couldn't have.
Want, have, want, have. It's the story of people like them.
Whatever they want, that they must get. And they got my
child.

Claire cut me out of her life so that I should never see
my son being raised by her sister and her husband. She
pretended it was disapproval of my thinking so little of my
medical training that I would get pregnant, but it was
really so I would never see my child.

It was so strange to me, seeing her last week. She—she
was always my model—of how you behave, of doing
things the right way, whether at tea or in surgery. She
couldn't bear for me to see she was less than that. All
those years of her coldness, her estrangement, were only
due to that English sin, embarrassment. Oh, we laughed
and cried together last week, the way old women can, but
you don't overcome a gap of fifty years with one day's
tears and embraces.

Wallace, Ted and Vanessa called my baby. Wallace
Marmaduke, for Ted's brother who died at El Alamein.
They never told him he was adopted. They certainly never
told him he had Jewish ancestry—instead, he grew up
hearing all the lazy contempt I used to hear when I
crouched on the far side of Mrs. Tallmadge's garden wall.

Claire showed me a photograph album she'd kept of his life: she'd had some notion she'd leave it for me if she died before me. My son was a small dark child, like me, but then, so had Claire and Vanessa's father been a small dark man. Perhaps Vanessa would have told him the truth, but she died when he was seventeen. Claire sent me a note at the time, a note so strange I should have realized she was trying to tell me something that she couldn't put into words. But I was too proud to look behind the surface back then.

Imagine Wallace's shock when Ted died last fall: he went through Ted's papers and found his own birth certificate. Mother, Sofie Radbuka instead of Vanessa Tallmadge Marmaduke. Father, unknown, when it should have been Edward Marmaduke.

What a shock, what a family uproar. He, Wallace Marmaduke, was a Jew? He was a churchwarden, a regular canvasser for the Tories, how could he be a Jew, how could his parents have done this to him? He went to Claire, convinced there was some mistake, but she decided she couldn't extend the lie that far. No mistake, she told him.

He was going to burn the birth certificate, he was going to destroy the idea of his birth identity forever, except that his daughter—you met his daughter, Pamela? She's nineteen. It seemed to her romantic, the unknown birth mother, the dark secret. She took her father's birth certificate away with her, she posted that notice on the Internet, that Questing Scorpio you found. When she heard I had shown up, she came at once to my hotel, bold like all those Tallmadges, with the self-assurance of knowing your place in the universe is secure, can never be taken from you.

"She's very beautiful," Victoria ventured. "Dr. Tallmadge brought her to my hotel so I could meet her. She wants to see you again; she wants to learn to know you."

She looks like Sofie, I whispered. Like Sofie at seventeen when she was pregnant with me. Only I lost her picture. I wanted her with me. But I lost her.

I wouldn't look at Victoria, at that concern, that pity, I would not let her or anyone see me so helpless. I bit my lip so hard it bled salt into my mouth. When she touched my hand I dashed her own away. But when I looked down, my mother's photograph lay on the ground next to me.

"You left it on your desk among the Royal Free newsletters," she said. "I thought you might want it. Anyway, no one is truly lost when you carry them with you. Your mother, your Oma, your Bobe, don't you think that whatever became of them, you were their joy? You had been saved. They knew that, they could carry that comfort with them."

I was digging my fingers into the ground, clutching at the roots of the dead weeds I was sitting on. She was always leaving me. My mother would come back and leave, come back and leave, and then she left me for good. I know that I'm the one who left, they sent me away, they saved me, but it felt to me as though once again she had left, and this time she never came back.

And then—I did the same thing. If someone loved me, as Carl once did, I left. I left my son. Even now, I left Max, I left you, I left Chicago. Everyone around me should experience the same abandonment I did. I don't mind that my son can't endure the sight of me, leaving him the way I did. I don't mind Carl's bitterness, I earned it, I sought it. What he will say now, when I tell him the truth, that he did have a son all those years ago, whatever ugly words he showers on me, I will deserve them.

"No one deserves that pain," Victoria said. "You least of all. How can I feel angry with you? All I have is anguish for your grief. As does Max. I don't know about Carl, but Max and I—we're in no position to be your judges, only your friends. Little nine-year-old Lotty, setting off alone on your journey, your Bobe surely forgave you. Can't you now forgive yourself?"

The fall sky was dark when the awkward young policeman shone his flashlight on us; he did not like to intrude, he said in halting English, but we should be leaving; it was cold, the lighting was bad on this hillside.

I let Victoria help me to my feet. I let her lead me along the dark path back.

About the Author

SARA PARETSKY is the author of eleven other books, including the bestselling *Hard Time, Tunnel Vision, Guardian Angel,* and *Burn Marks*. She lives with her husband in Chicago.